Praise for THE ARNIFOUR AFFAIR

"Colin has Holmes' arrogance but is dimpled and charming,
while Ethan is a darker Watson . . . the relationship between
the leads is discreetly intriguing."

—*Kirkus Reviews*

"Pendragon matches Sherlock Holmes in his arrogance . . .
he is redeemed, in part, by his brains and his
gentle treatment of Pruitt."

—*Publishers Weekly*

"The mystery is extremely well done, the characters carefully
drawn, and the story moves quickly to a satisfying conclusion."

—*Washington Independent Review of Books*

Books by Gregory Harris

THE ARNIFOUR AFFAIR

THE BELLINGHAM BLOODBATH

THE CONNICLE CURSE

Published by Kensington Publishing Corporation

THE
CONNICLE
CURSE

A Colin Pendragon Mystery

GREGORY HARRIS

KENSINGTON BOOKS
www.kensingtonbooks.com

KENSINGTON BOOKS are published by

Kensington Publishing Corp.
119 West 40th Street
New York, NY 10018

All Kensington titles, imprints, and distributed lines are available at special quantity discounts for bulk purchases for sales promotion, premiums, fund-raising, educational, or institutional use.

Special book excerpts or customized printings can also be created to fit specific needs. For details, write or phone the office of the Kensington Special Sales Manager: Kensington Publishing Corp., 119 West 40th Street, New York, NY 10018. Attn. Special Sales Department. Phone: 1-800-221-2647.

Kensington and the K logo Reg. U.S. Pat. & TM Off.

eISBN-13: 978-0-7582-9272-8
eISBN-10: 0-7582-9272-4
First Kensington Electronic Edition: March 2015

ISBN-13: 978-0-7582-9271-1
ISBN-10: 0-7582-9271-6
First Kensington Trade Paperback Printing: March 2015

10 9 8 7 6 5 4 3 2 1

Printed in the United States of America

For Liz and Gary
And
April and Chris
With much love

CHAPTER 1

Annabelle Connicle was right; the blood was everywhere.

We had accompanied her back to her home in West Hampton, Colin as eager to see the scene of what sounded like a ghastly attack as I was to make certain she reached her home safely. The poor woman had already fainted once in our study and remained as pallid as milk glass, her lips tinged blue and her eyes so drawn and red that she looked not to have slept in days.

Several Scotland Yard carriages were on-site by the time we arrived at the Connicle estate. Mrs. Connicle had sent for them even as she herself had rushed to our Kensington flat to implore Colin's help. While it was the right thing to do, it was bound to prove problematic for Colin given that the Yard's senior inspector, Emmett Varcoe, was eternally envious of Colin's flawless record for solving the crimes we were brought in on. The one thing I was happy to note, however, was that the coroner's wagon was nowhere to be found. A positive sign that not only was there no body to collect but also that the reprehensible coroner, Denton Ross, would not be here. That suited me just fine.

Mrs. Connicle had insisted we come inside despite the fact that I had caught Colin staring with noticeable longing at the gardener's shed in the side yard, which a gaggle of bobbies were indifferently circling. The house was a hush of shadows and un-ease as we entered, the shades drawn, presumably to block any view of the work being done by the Yard. It took a moment for my eyes to adjust before I noticed the black-suited, heavyset man with a thinning pate sitting in the drawing room and the girl in maid's attire pacing the floor behind him. The instant the door swung back with a resounding *click,* the girl twirled about and bolted toward us.

"Oh, Mrs. Connicle," she gasped. "Thank heavens you're back."

"That's enough now, Letty," Mrs. Connicle said heavily as she steered the girl—for she didn't look older than her middle teens—to the young housekeeper who had presented herself upon our entrance. "Go with Miss Porter now. I simply haven't the heart to deal with your fretting." Miss Porter, a pretty, slight, brown-haired woman meticulous in her deportment and dress, stepped up right on cue, ushering the quavering girl out of the room with a finesse that suggested she had done it before. "You must for-give me." Mrs. Connicle sagged into the nearest chair, her tiny, winsome frame nearly swallowed by its generous dimensions. "I'm afraid I am quite done in."

"Annabelle . . ." The portly man stood up and moved to us, adjusting a pair of glasses clinging to the bridge of his nose. I could tell at once, by both the suit he wore and the leather satchel he carried, that he was a doctor. "You have suffered a tremen-dous shock and I am certain these men understand that." He glanced at me before quickly flicking his eyes to Colin. "I take it Annabelle has retained your services to look into this . . . this business, Mr. Pendragon?"

Colin gave him a stiff smile. "And you would be . . . ?"

"Dr. Benjamin Renholme." He stuck out his hand but did not belabor a smile. "I've seen to Annabelle for years. Edmond less so. He could be quite dismissive of the medical arts."

"Past tense?" Colin fished idly.

A disapproving frown settled onto the doctor's face. "I take it you have yet to see the shed?"

Mrs. Connicle groaned and Colin gave her a gentle smile before turning back to the doctor. "Sometimes people say things they do not mean and other times they spill what they did not intend. It can be a razor's edge."

The doctor took a moment before he gave a stiff nod. "No doubt. I'll take no umbrage. All that matters is that you discern what has become of Edmond." His words elicited another moan from Mrs. Connicle that finally stole his full attentions as he swooped over to her. "Come now, Annabelle. I have prepared a tincture of laudanum to help you relax. There is nothing more for you to do but let these men have a look about. I must insist you go upstairs and get some rest."

"I cannot rest until I know what has happened," she mewled in the most pitiful voice.

"We will let you know the moment there is anything to report," Colin said. "The doctor is right; you must attend to yourself just now."

She gazed at Colin, her thin, drawn face a mask of pain. "All right," she muttered. "All right . . ."

Dr. Renholme shoved his glasses up onto his forehead as he bent forward to help her to her feet. She leaned against him and he guided her from the room with the gentle assurance of a man of his profession. Even so, the moment they disappeared Colin turned to me with a frown. "It seems to me that man is awfully full of himself."

I couldn't help chuckling. "You know . . ." I said as we were finally able to head out of the house for the side yard, ". . . there are those who would say the same about you."

He shot me an unamused scowl. "Little, pesky, small-minded people, I should think." And this time I did not try to suppress my laughter.

The moment we cleared the corner of the house the phalanx of bobbies milling about became instantly apparent, so many that the little gardener's shed was almost inconspicuous amongst the quantity of navy-blue uniforms. Oddly, it appeared that nothing more was happening than idle conversation and the general passage of time. If a crime had been committed, it seemed lost on this leisurely band.

"Do you see Varcoe?" Colin asked.

"No. But you know he's here somewhere."

Colin pursed his lips. "Pity," he bothered to say as we reached the nearest cluster of men. "Excuse me . . ."

The young officer we were nearest to turned from his companions with a frown. "Excuse yourself!" he snapped. "You can't be here. This is official Scotland Yard business."

His companions broke into laughter. "Don't you know who you're talking to, Lanchester?" clucked one of the older men.

Lanchester glared at Colin. "Should I?"

"You're a tosser." The older man snickered. "You're telling me you've never seen a picture of the renowned private detective Colin Pendragon?"

Young Constable Lanchester screwed up his face and gave a listless shrug. "I thought he was younger."

The men all brayed with laughter before one of them managed to halfheartedly say, "These young buggers don't have a lick of class. Don't let him bruise your ego. Not that he could."

"Pithy," Colin answered with a spectacularly forced smile. "But tell me, have you good men of the Yard managed to determine anything at all about Mrs. Connicle's missing husband thus far? Any explanation for all of the blood in the shed?"

Unfortunately, young Constable Lanchester found his tongue first. "I don't think that's any concern of yours, Mr. Pendragon," he shot back, punching Colin's name as though it tasted bitter on his tongue.

"Oh, lighten up," another of the more seasoned men cajoled, a sergeant I recognized by the name of Maurice Evans. "There's nothing much to see beyond about a pail of blood splashed across the walls. We can't even be sure whose blood it is."

Colin's eyebrows arched. "You mean to tell me you're discounting the obvious? How positively nouveau."

Sergeant Evans laughed. "You're a pip, Pendragon."

Colin managed another brief smile. "Mind if I take a look?"

"Suit yourself."

"You sure about that, Sergeant?" Constable Lanchester could not seem to keep from piping up.

"Keep an eye on him," Evans allowed, waving the young man off.

Colin nodded to the sergeant as we headed around the small building, Lanchester and one of his mates in our wake. No one paid us much heed now that we had our escort, either presuming we must belong or not caring so long as someone else was responsible.

Colin pulled up short as we reached the entrance to the shed, but his face revealed nothing.

"Don't touch a thing," Lanchester piped up from behind us.

To my amazement, Colin held his tongue.

I stood beside him and gazed inside, finding myself staring at an inexplicable scene of carnage. It was just as Annabelle Connicle had said; the blood was everywhere. Great ropes of it were suspended from the ceiling like viscous stalactites, and swaths were splattered in huge arcing sweeps across the walls and assemblage of tools and yard implements hanging thereon. The floor also contained its own multitude of coagulated puddles, making it look as though a veritable battle had been fought and lost here. The most curious thing of all, however, was the simple fact that there was no body. How anyone could have walked away from such a scene was unthinkable.

"It's quite a sight, isn't it?" Sergeant Evans said as he approached.

"Are you sure it's blood?" Colin asked.

The sergeant chuckled and shook his head. "You *really* are a pip, Pendragon."

"May I?" Colin bothered to ask even as he stepped forward.

"If you must. But I'll ask you not to touch anything. And you, Mr. Pruitt, may remain outside."

"Of course," I said as I took a step back. Colin caught my eye as he cleared the doorway and I knew what he meant for me to do. I shifted sideways as though ducking from the sun's intensity and stared out toward a copse of trees near the edge of the property where a great deal more bobbies were loitering about. "You've got quite a contingent of men down there," I noted pointedly, and was pleased when Sergeant Evans and his two constables swung their gazes around, allowing Colin to quickly dab at one of the puddles. "Have they turned up anything?"

"I wouldn't know," Evans said. "This shed is my concern. I don't really give a shite what they're doing over there."

"Have they found something?" I pressed.

He turned back to me with a sharp look. "I didn't say that." His eyes shifted to Colin, who was now innocently glancing about. "That's enough, Mr. Pendragon. Come out of there now. Nothing but a rash of blood, same as you can see from the doorway."

Colin complied at once. "Is that the official consensus?" he asked, continuing to stare inside.

"What's that supposed to mean? You see something else?"

"I'm sure I see exactly what you do, but what I perceive could very well be different."

"Listen to him." Evans wagged a finger at Colin and snorted at his two companions. "No wonder you pique poor Varcoe's nerves. Who dragged you out here anyway?"

"The mistress of the house."

"Well, that may be," Evans said as he beamed at his companions, "but she sent for us first." They all nodded smugly.

"Sending for the Yard is a formality," Colin responded blithely. "I'm here because she means to learn what's happened." He gave a rogue's leer and began walking around the periphery of the shed as Evans and his men laughed, assuming, it would seem, that Colin had meant it as a joke. As Colin was about to make a second pass around the small building a familiar voice blasted out from the trees on our left.

"What in the devil's tortured ass are *they* doing here?!"

Colin looked over, his smile drooping. "A pleasure to see you as well, Inspector."

Inspector Varcoe stormed toward us with four officers at his heels, his tall, slender frame accentuated by his endlessly disheveled white hair with his face its usual shade of plum. Whatever foraging he had been up to seemed to have stirred him quite thoroughly. "You're not needed here, Pendragon. Take your toady and go back to your hole."

"How you flatter me," Colin replied with a lopsided smile that lit his dimples.

"This is official Yard business." Varcoe planted himself between Colin and the shed, his arms folded across his chest even as the color of his face deepened. "We most certainly do not need the assistance of amateurs trying to sully the good name of Scotland Yard."

"Now, Emmett. I've only ever tried to be helpful whenever I've solved your cases for you."

"You're not funny, Pendragon!" he snapped back. "Just what the hell are you doing here anyway?"

"Mrs. Connicle fetched us," Colin answered with a note of relish. "Though I'm sure she meant no affront to you and your fine horde of merry men," he added with a decided lack of subtlety. "But tell me, what has led you and your men to prowl about the trees?"

Varcoe gave a sly smile. "Seeing as how this is a Yard investigation, I'm afraid you'll just have to piss off."

Colin's grin froze as his jaw tightened and his eyes degraded to slits. I seized his momentary silence to interject the obvious. "You will remember that we can get a magistrate to formally assign us to this case before day's end."

Emmett Varcoe fixed his eyes on me with a loathing I found absurd. He was well aware that Colin's father wielded enormous power in both Parliament and Victoria's court. Yet when Varcoe's harsh smile slowly snaked into something more righteous, I knew exactly what he was going to say.

"Then you go right ahead. Go visit your lackey and get your scrap of paper. By the time you get back here we'll be long gone." His smile widened. "You're always welcome to our castoffs," he sneered.

"I could solve the riddles of the universe with what I've seen you and yours leave behind!" Colin snarled.

I feared we were on the verge of being forcibly removed when one of the inspector's men suddenly came bounding out of the trees. "You'd better come, sir," he called with noticeable agitation. "You'll want to see this."

Varcoe's eyes narrowed, but before he turned away he set his glare on Sergeant Evans and said, "Get these two out of here. I'll not have them around while we're conducting an investigation. You had best remember that, Evans." And with that pronouncement Varcoe bolted back to the woods with the man who had summoned him—quickly, frustratingly, disappearing from view.

CHAPTER 2

While I am quite certain that there is no one of import who does not recognize Sir Atherton Rentcliff Pendragon as a force to be reckoned with given his lifetime of service to the Crown, it is still virtually impossible to get any bureaucracy to move at much more than a glacial pace. So it was with great relief that by dusk Colin and I had been granted a release from one of Sir Atherton's magisterial colleagues to conduct a concurrent investigation into the disappearance of Edmond Connicle. The moment we had that writ in hand we raced back to the Connicle estate just in time to catch the sun melting below the horizon as it gathered the last vestiges of its colorful skirts. Innumerable lanterns wagged in and out of the woods like so many lightning bugs, trundled to and fro by the bobbies still patrolling the area in spite of Varcoe's insistence that they would be long gone by the time we returned. It was unforgivable that he had cost us the daylight, but then Colin had hardly helped matters.

"You know," I spoke up as we picked our way down to the tree line behind the shed, "if you could be just a bit more tolerant of Varcoe once in a while, perhaps we wouldn't have to go through such machinations."

"I think I display the patience of a saint whenever I'm forced to deal with him," Colin scoffed. "After all, have you ever heard me enlighten him on what a bloody lout he is?"

"How that must burden you," I drolled.

He snickered as we reached the edge of the woods but got no farther before a small cadre of Yarders came hurtling toward us. Sergeant Evans, looking thoroughly wearied, was at their front. A look of surprise lit his eyes as he pulled up abreast of us, but before he could say a word Colin shoved the court's paperwork under his nose.

"Well, Mr. Pendragon." The sergeant heaved a sigh as he raised his lantern to read the hastily prepared document. "This didn't take you long at all. The inspector has only just left himself."

"Pity," Colin sniffed.

"Get on with your duties!" Evans snapped at his men. "You too, Lanchester," he added to the same young constable who had harassed Colin and me earlier. "I shall see to Mr. Pendragon and Mr. Pruitt." His men immediately struck off for the house with the exception of Lanchester, who paused long enough to furl his brow at Sergeant Evans before following the others. "He's a shite, that one. Forever trying to crawl up the inspector's bum. He'd better come around."

"God help you if he doesn't," Colin said.

The sergeant tsked as he turned and headed back toward the trees, his lantern held high out in front for us. "I take it you've come to see what we discovered down here."

"I'd wager it's the body of Edmond Connicle."

A crooked smile crept across Sergeant Evans's face. "So it is, Mr. Pendragon. And you'll be glad to see the body just as we found it, as I can assure you, you have never seen anything like *this* before."

Neither of us pressed him for additional details as we plunged into the stand of trees running along the periphery of the Connicle property. We would wait and see what there was to see ourselves. Beyond that, I doubted this body could be much worse off than the remains of Captain Trevor Bellingham on our most recent case.

We came out into a small clearing that sloped down toward a

gravel road overgrown with scrub and brush, attesting to how long it had been since its last use. Thistles sprouted randomly within the deep ruts left by carriage wheels and the grass covering the center berm had risen to several feet. These details were easily viewable as a result of the multiple stands of electric lighting being run off a portable engine bellowing from the back of a nearby wagon. Buckingham Palace had only been electrified eight years before and yet Scotland Yard was already finding the wherewithal to make use of this expensive new technology. Its value was undeniable considering how the evening sky was lit up like the sunniest day where the lights were focused.

"We really must look into electric lighting." Colin voiced my very thought as we made our way down the sloping field. "How extraordinary to banish the night so completely."

"We'll have to save our extra farthings," I answered as a large black swath midway along the road gradually came into view. It looked like a charcoal-blackened crater left behind after an explosion had torn it asunder. But as we drew closer we spotted charred remains lying at the center of the earthen wound, curled in a fetal position and recognizable only as being human, nothing more.

"That would be Edmond Connicle," Sergeant Evans announced as we stopped at the edge of the gouge. "There's a blackened ring on his finger that matches what his wife described. We haven't told her yet," he admitted. "We hear she's fragile. . . ." he added with a wince. Colin kept silent as he knelt down for a closer look at the remains.

"Is the coroner here?" I asked with feigned disinterest, though I was loath to run into Denton Ross.

"Mr. Ross and his assistant have gone back to their wagon to fetch a stretcher. The Yard's photographer just finished taking pictures, so they're ready to move the body to the morgue."

"May I steal a closer look?" Colin asked as he went ahead and stepped into the blackened depression. Sergeant Evans did not bother to respond.

"We're quite a way from the house," I said to the sergeant. "What made your men come down this far?"

He grinned as he answered. "The dogs." He took his hat off

and scratched the top of his thinning pate. "The inspector had us fanning out in every direction from that gardener's shed, but it took the dogs to finally drag us all the way out here. God only knows why he didn't head for the house."

Colin harrumphed. "Did anyone bother to look for signs of a trail while the dogs were mucking about?" He squatted down by the front of the body. "You know . . . drops of blood, bent grasses, broken twigs, the usual sort of tedium?"

Sergeant Evans laughed. "You really think remarkably little of us, don't you, Mr. Pendragon?" Colin didn't bother to answer as he poked at the cadaver's face with the handle of a small folding knife he'd extracted from his pocket. "I suppose there are times we deserve it, but not today. There's not a drop of blood outside that shed. No such trail to follow."

Colin stood up and moved to the far side of the depression, sweeping his eyes along the nearby ground. "Were there any other signs?"

"One of our men did finally notice a meandering sort of trail that leads down here. One man's footprints. As if he had hemorrhaged inside that shed and then wandered all the way down here to be a human bonfire." His face curled grimly. "None of it makes a bit of sense."

"Meandering?" Colin asked as he continued to scan the ground on the opposite side of the body, his every move amplified by the harsh electric lighting.

"He didn't come straight down here. It was like he was searching for something."

"I see," Colin said, but it was clear from his tone that he did not. Nor, most certainly, did I. Given the level of trauma evident in the gardener's shed, it was indeed impossible to believe that the victim of such an attack would go wandering through the woods with his house so near.

"*Hey!*" The cold, harsh voice tore up my spine like a streak of lightning. "*Get the bloody hell away from there!*" It was Denton Ross.

"It's all right." Sergeant Evans waved him off. "They've got approval from the courts on behalf of Mrs. Connicle."

"I don't care if the ruddy *Queen* has given her blessing!" he snarled back as he and his aide reached us. "I'll not have these prigs fouling my remains."

"Watch yourself, Mr. Ross," Colin replied tightly before stepping out of the ditch. "I'll not stand here while you slander Mr. Pruitt and me."

"Then sod off," Denton sniped. He and his cohort stumbled down into the trough and set the stretcher they'd brought next to the scorched remains. "And you'd better keep *that* one on a short leash," he added, squinting at me with a dour expression. "If he so much as breathes on me I'll have him back in prison before the moon finishes rising."

I rolled my eyes even as I heard Colin chuckle.

"Just do your job," Sergeant Evans cut in, "and be on your way. Some of us have been here all day and would like to go home." He turned back to Colin and me with a wink and dropped his tone. "My, but the two of you can get on the wrong side of people, can't you?"

Nevertheless, the comment was enough to finally focus Denton Ross. He signaled his man and the two of them slid on fouled leather gloves before delicately easing the ruins of Edmond Connicle onto their canvas stretcher. I thought the whole of him might snap in half or crumble to the touch, but they treated him with enough care that he was able to survive this additional violation without further misfortune.

"If you don't mind!" Denton Ross growled at me as he leaned out of the charred gully to grab a muslin sheet he'd tossed to the ground near my feet. I wanted to chuck some equally caustic reply his direction but knew I would only regret it when the time came to beg his aid again on this or some future case. So I held my tongue and watched as he and his assistant drew the cover over what was left of Edmond Connicle, and hoped I would never have to look upon it again.

"I'll be anxious to see your report," Colin said as he hopped back down to check the place where the body had just lain.

"You'll not get it from me!" Denton snapped.

Colin didn't even look up as he continued to poke around the nearly unblemished swath of earth. "I'm crushed," he said amiably.

Sergeant Evans laughed out loud as Denton and his man moved off with their laden stretcher. I could only shake my head, aware that it would be virtually impossible to get any further information from Denton Ross, magistrate's order or not. This case was already proving to be a challenge. I turned back to Colin just in time to see him withdraw his folding knife, kneel down, and plunge it into the earth at the spot where the body's sternum had just been. He scrabbled at the dirt with his knife and bare hands a moment, quickly opening a small fissure from which he abruptly extracted a jagged piece of crystal tied to a leather string.

"What the hell is that?" Sergeant Evans scowled.

"Indeed . . ." was all Colin said as he began rooting about in the earth again. A moment later he pulled out a small, white beeswax candle the size of his index finger that had been burned briefly at both of its ends. He handed the two items up to me before squatting back down and attacking the small hole in earnest. Within another minute he had extracted a crude doll made of thatch no larger than his palm, a tiny vial filled with a thick amber liquid, and a small leather pouch from which he poured an assemblage of pebbles, bits of shiny, broken glass, and several teeth.

"What in the hell *is* all of that?" the sergeant asked again.

"Fetishes," I answered.

"What?" He swung around and stared at me.

"Voodoo," Colin mumbled as he quickly pressed the other things on me before attacking the hole once more.

"Voodoo?!" The sergeant's scowl deepened. "You're talking about that African nonsense with snakes and witchery?"

"It's a religion . . ." I started to say.

"It's bloody superstitious twaddle," he shot back. "Good god, it's almost the twentieth century. If Her Majesty's government hasn't managed to lead her various peoples past this kind of rubbish, then I'd say we've done a ruddy piss-poor job of integrating her colonies."

"Maybe so," Colin muttered absently as he stood up and brushed himself off. "But whatever the case, Mr. Pruitt is right. These are voodoo fetishes planted beneath Mr. Connicle."

"For all you know they've been there for months," Sergeant Evans dismissed him brusquely.

Colin glanced up with a slim smile as he finally stepped out of the burnt hollow. "It was plain to see that the earth at that precise location had been freshly turned. That's what caught my eye when they removed the body. I'm sure you would have noticed had you been looking."

The sergeant seemed to approve of Colin's answer as he nodded his head. "Likely so . . . likely so . . ."

Colin plucked the little thatch doll from me and slowly inspected it inches from his eyes. "The question is, where might Edmond Connicle have come into contact with a practitioner of voodoo?"

Sergeant Evans pursed his face a moment and then lit up. "I know! He's got a couple of Africans working for him. Live-ins. I saw them lurking about when we got here this morning. Gave me a bad feeling right off."

Colin flicked a displeased gaze my direction. "Yes . . ." he said flatly as he passed the tiny doll back to me. "Make a note of those things, Ethan," he said as he began to pace around the area, inspecting the ground every few steps.

I did as he asked, jotting down the items on my pad and making a crude drawing of the doll. It was impossible to tell what, if anything, would have value later, and I couldn't be sure we would get access to these things again.

"What do you think, Mr. Pendragon?" Sergeant Evans asked when I finally handed the fetishes to him. "Have we solved the case already? Do you think it's those blasted Africans from the house?" He shook his head. "Inspector Varcoe will be enraged if you found the solution that quickly."

"He should be used to it," Colin answered with a tight grin. "But tell me something, Sergeant, if you were a practitioner of voodoo and in a murderous state of mind, would you leave such evidence behind?"

"What? Well . . ." He shrugged vaguely. "Maybe it's part of their custom. They did have it buried. Perhaps they thought that was clever enough."

"Leaving behind a freshly dug bulge in the earth is hardly clever."

Evans waved Colin off. "That lot isn't known for being clever."

"That lot . . . ?"

"The Africans. They're not exactly Oxford trained."

Colin sucked in a breath. "Given the lack of cleverness your Yard was able to summon on that Ripper case, you might want to be more considerate before you disparage an entire continent of people." He nodded at me and started back toward the Connicle home.

"You are quite the conundrum, Mr. Pendragon," Sergeant Evans chortled.

I smiled as though we had shared a good joke, though I knew Colin had not meant it to be. Nevertheless, if Colin was right about the fetishes being nothing more than a deception, I knew we would need Sergeant Evans to be an ally, magisterial order or not. And I had long ago learned that in matters such as these Colin was nearly always right.

CHAPTER 3

$\longrightarrow\!\!\bullet\!\!\longleftarrow$

The night sky was speckled with an ocean of stars by the time we pounded our way back through the woods to the Connicle house. Police lanterns continued to bob about the area and I noticed three bloodhounds being loaded into a wagon parked next to the gardener's shed as three more were brought out from another wagon nearby. "Now why would they be bringing more dogs in?" I asked.

Colin shook his head with a shrug. "I would hope to start searching for somebody else's tracks."

"You don't think they've been doing that all afternoon?"

Colin's nearer eyebrow arched as he looked at me. "You do give the Yard such credit." He chuckled as we watched the dogs blunder about in haphazard directions, their noses held firmly to the ground. "Now let's have another look at that shed." And with that he was off, cutting away from my side and charging back to the shed, nearly bowling over the young bobby currently stationed there.

"It's all right," I notified the young constable as I caught up. "We've a magisterial order."

"I heard," he replied with a decided lack of interest.

I mustered what I could of a smile and followed Colin inside.

Only two lanterns were lit, leaving the small space mostly dark and heavily cast in shadows. Colin had stepped to one corner and was staring at the fouled wall as though trying to decipher tea leaves. In the dim light the splatters of blood resembled black slashes, as if a bear or some other great creature had attacked the building with a manic savagery. I could still smell the metallic sting of the blood and suspected the building would need to be torn down and burned to purge the stench.

"What are you thinking?" I asked.

"I don't know."

"Should we tell Mrs. Connicle about her husband?"

"I'd sooner swallow my tongue. Let the Yard bear that news." He went back outside and pulled in a deep breath of night air. "I'll solve the case. That will be my contribution."

"And do you have any idea how to do that?"

"We shall start at once with the African couple," he said as we headed back across the side yard toward the house. "Once Varcoe hears about the fetishes he's sure to arrest them without a second thought. This will likely be our only chance to speak with them before they're put on their guard."

"It could be them, you know. It *could* be that simple."

He tossed me an amused look as we climbed the steps to the front door. "What would I do without you?" he asked before reaching out and pounding on the door. It was drawn open almost at once by the lovely young housekeeper, Miss Porter. "I do apologize for the intrusion," Colin said as he flashed her a quick smile, "but we've a need to get a bit of information from Mrs. Connicle about the household staff. The usual sort of thing really—"

"And how *is* Mrs. Connicle doing?" I hastily added in an effort to keep him from sounding completely mercenary.

Miss Porter shifted her eyes to me and I noticed both exhaustion and worry there. "I'm afraid she's still up in her room. She's been there since you brought her back this morning. The waiting is . . ." She let her voice drift off as her eyes slid toward the trees, making her fear obvious.

"Of course," Colin muttered, his brow knitting even as he held his tongue against what we knew. "We needn't disturb her then. Perhaps you might do us the favor of a few minutes of *your* time?"

The fatigue that ringed her eyes made me certain she would demur, so I was surprised when she rallied a smile and answered, "Certainly."

She ushered us into the same drawing room we'd been shown to that morning and proceeded across it to a swinging door on the far side, which she pushed open. "*Letty!*" she called out. "Fetch some tea for three of us, please." She released the door and came back to join us. "Do sit down, gentlemen. Mrs. Connicle would insist on your comfort and care were she able to see to it herself."

"You really mustn't trouble anyone on our account," Colin said as we settled onto the sofa across from her. "I would only like to know something of the staff here. Names, position, tenure . . . all very routine." He gave her an easy smile that earned him one in return.

"Of course," she answered, her polite grin reminding me how very striking she was with her delicate features accented by a froth of curly brown hair. I determined her to be somewhere in her mid-twenties, which struck me as curious that the Connicles had selected such a young woman to take charge of their home. "We are a rather disparate group," she acknowledged with some unease. "A few have been with the Connicles from the beginning of their marriage while the rest of us are rather new to their employ."

There was a clatter of dishes from the back corner of the room as the fretting girl we'd seen that morning pushed through the swinging door balancing a large silver tray. She had been quite beside herself earlier in the day and appeared little better now. Her face was ashen and she was clearly in some disarray. As she set the tray in front of Miss Porter I noticed that the girl's hands were trembling, leaving me with nothing but pity for the poor thing.

"You remember Mr. Pendragon and Mr. Pruitt," Miss Porter said as she leaned over and began preparing our tea.

"Aye," she answered at once, her eyes flitting down as she gave a well-practiced curtsy.

"They're here at the behest of Mrs. Connicle. We must give them every assistance."

"Yes, Miss Porter." Letty nodded, her eyes still on the floor.

"Thank you, Letty." The young girl took several steps back before giving another quick curtsy and fleeing the room. "You must forgive her. She is the newest member of the staff and is only just sixteen. Her mother is the Connicles' cook, Edna Hollings. She's been with them from the beginning. Almost twenty years now."

Colin flashed another smile. "We'll need to speak with her. Has Mrs. Hollings been with the Connicles the longest?"

"No. That would be their driver, Randolph. Randolph's been with the Connicle family since Mr. Connicle was just a boy. When Mr. and Mrs. Connicle married, Randolph's services were a gift to them from Mr. Connicle's father."

"A gift, you say?! How very provocative," Colin muttered, his poorly veiled disapproval not lost on Miss Porter as she averted her gaze with the thinnest of smiles. "And who else works in the household?"

"There is a couple, Alexa and Albert, who joined the staff about two years ago. They've been here the shortest if you don't count Letty. Alexa is the scullery maid and Albert is the groundskeeper."

"Alexa and Albert . . ." Colin repeated thoughtfully. "I would suspect those aren't their birth names."

"Why, Mr. Pendragon"—Miss Porter looked startled—"however could you know that?"

"I assume Alexa is short for Alexandrina, our dear Victoria's given name, making it too great a coincidence to have a married couple on-staff named after our sovereign and her late consort."

"How very astute." Miss Porter grinned. "I'm afraid I don't actually know their given names. I've heard them, but like everyone else found them quite unpronounceable, which is why Mrs. Connicle lent them those. They're not British, you see. They're from the Kingdom of Dahomey in French West Africa."

"Ah yes." Colin nodded solemnly. "I believe the French claimed that as their own just last year."

"After a brutal two-year war," I pointed out.

He tossed me a patient smile. "And what war isn't brutal?" I opened my mouth to respond before realizing he was entirely correct. "Is there anyone else on-staff?" Colin continued.

"No, sir. That's all of us."

He settled back on the sofa with his tea held close. "At the risk of being a nuisance, I should very much like to speak with the staff tonight. We shan't trouble them but a few minutes each."

Miss Porter acquiesced at once. "Shall I assemble everyone?"

"Individually would be best. I find people far more willing to speak their minds when given the opportunity to do so in private."

"Certainly," she said, and once again I could see the stress and anxiety lingering just beneath her movement and words.

The moment she stepped from the room I turned to Colin, who was already on his feet checking out a series of photographs atop the mantel. "She seems a bit unsure of herself," I said.

"She's too young to be running a household on her own," he answered without taking his eyes from the photographs. "Must have had immaculate references." A Cheshire's grin spread across his face as he moved to a pair of bookshelves on the opposite side of the fireplace. "Or else she knows the family secrets."

"Wouldn't that more likely explain how she *keeps* it rather than how she *procured* it?"

He chuckled. "You have a point."

The sound of a door opening behind me brought me to my feet as I turned to find Miss Porter ushering a short, heavyset middle-aged woman into the room. She wore a full-sized white apron and had gray hair shorn so close to her head that there was no need for a toque of any kind. This was clearly Mrs. Hollings. Miss Porter made the introductions and withdrew from the room, leaving Mrs. Hollings looking quite uncomfortable. After much cajoling Colin was finally able to coax her to sit down, but even then she would only perch on the edge of the chair closest to her kitchen.

"Miss Porter tells us you've been working for the Connicles since they married." Colin offered her a generous smile.

"Aye," she answered.

"Twenty years, is it?"

She seemed to consider the question a moment before answering. "Aye."

"They must be kind and equitable employers for you to stay so long."

She flicked her eyes between us. "Aye."

"Wonderful." Colin stood up and gestured her toward the door. "I think we've taken enough of your time. Perhaps you'd be kind enough to send your daughter Lucy—"

"Letty," I corrected.

"Letty." He smiled easily. "Will you have Letty come and see us?"

Mrs. Hollings looked befuddled as she got to her feet and nodded. I could hardly contain my laughter until the door swung shut behind her. "That has got to be the *shortest* interrogation I have *ever* seen you conduct."

He shrugged as he moved back to the fireplace. "We'll leave Varcoe to spend his time on her. She's got nothing for us."

Not a minute later her daughter reentered through the same swinging door, though this time far more hesitantly and without anything cradled in her arms. "Miss Hollings." Colin gestured her in with his usual grin, earning him yet another of her awkward curtsies in return. "We appreciate your time and promise to be brief. Will you tell us how long you've been working for the Connicles?"

"I started 'elpin' me mum in the kitchen a couple days a week when I were thirteen. But I've been 'elpin' more regular now for 'bout a year."

"Still in the kitchen?"

She shook her head. "I ain't much of a cook. That's me mum's

THE CONNICLE CURSE / 23

knack. I 'elp out wherever the missus needs me. She's a fine, delicate woman."

"How so?"

She pursed her lips and appeared to consider it a moment. "Just is," she said with a shrug.

"Right." Colin released a sparrow's sigh as he gazed into the fireplace with marked disinterest. "And Mr. Connicle? Do you ever assist him?"

"No, sir. He don't need me 'elp. Only the missus. I watch 'er when she has 'er spells."

"Spells?" Colin looked back at Letty.

"Well"—she shuffled her feet and stared down at the floor—"it ain't really me place ta talk. . . ."

"Certainly it is." Colin turned fully away from the fireplace and focused his attentions solely on Letty Hollings. "That's why we've asked to speak with you. Because we know you want to help your mistress. Now tell us about her spells."

"She 'as bad 'eadaches and dizziness and sometimes thinks she 'ears things when no one's talkin'."

"Hears things?" Colin repeated as his eyes slid over to me. And I knew, without the slightest hesitation, exactly what he was thinking.

"Mum says the missus is fragile. But she's been good ta me and me mum. She's never said a mean thing. Not once."

"How often does she hear things?" Colin pressed.

"She don't like ta say, but sometimes I see 'er turn white as a sheet and I know she's 'avin' a spell. It makes 'er look so sad."

"What sorts of things does she think she's hearing?"

"I don't know. I don't ask 'er nothin' like that. But I know she were in 'ospital for it once. Way back when I was first 'elpin' me mum. She were gone for quite some time. Least it seemed like it." Letty shrugged. "That's what I 'member anyway."

"You've been most helpful, Miss Hollings. May I impose upon you one last time to send in either Alexa or Albert?"

"Alexa's in the kitchen. I'll fetch 'er."

"Thank you." He nodded gallantly and she quickly hustled from the room after giving one last clumsy curtsy. As the door swung briskly in her wake Colin turned to me. "Whatever do you make of that?"

I knew what he was really asking. "It's certainly not a thing to be taken lightly," I tossed back, trying to sound blasé in spite of the coiled recollections of my mother that insisted on their due whenever such talk came up.

"Ethan . . ." he started to say, clearly about to extend some heavy-handed consolation in an effort to neutralize a past I had never been able to set right, when the sound of the opening door thankfully interrupted him. I turned to see the woman they called Alexa coming into the room. She had a flawless complexion the color of tea with a stout dose of cream, and raven-black hair that fell in tight ringlets to her shoulders. Her figure was both lithe and lean, and she stood just an inch or two shorter than Colin's five foot eight. It was evident by the way in which she carried herself that she was neither intimidated nor anxious about being thusly summoned. Which became ever more obvious when she said:

"Now what you be wantin' wit' me?"

"Mrs. . . ." Colin stood up and smiled broadly as he gestured to a chair.

"Alexa. Jest Alexa. Dat's what dey call me." Her tone was cool but without a touch of artifice as she sat down in the chair next to the one Colin had pointed her toward.

"Alexa then." He held his smile even though she did not return the pleasantry. Rather, her face remained blank, without reproach, making it clear that she was waiting for some sort of explanation. "I would like to ask you a few questions about your time here with the Connicles."

"Me time 'ere?" She clucked dryly. "Ya make it sound like I'm on 'oliday. I work for 'em, ya know."

"Yes," he answered, his smile faltering at the corners. "That's what I'd like to speak with you about."

"Then get to it. I got t'ings ta be doin'."

Colin's brow curdled as she stared back at him expectantly. "Are you really so unconcerned about the welfare of your employer?" he snapped.

To my surprise she smiled. "Now wot makes ya say dat? 'Cause I ain't weepin' all about? Ain't ya never seen a rainbow after a terrible storm? Dat's wot dey call 'ope. Ya see?"

Colin stared at her a minute before turning to me and grousing, "Is she bloody starkers?"

And before I could even think to respond, Alexa leapt up and scowled at me with fire in her eyes. "Is 'e talkin' 'bout me like dat? 'Cause I won't 'ave it."

"He was joking," I said, braying the worst sort of laugh. "It was only a joke." Fortunately, he had turned his back to us as he stood gazing into the fireplace, for I knew she would find no smirk upon his face. "How long have you been working for the Connicles?" I asked, trying to ease the strain.

"Two years. Two years last April," she sniffed.

"And before that?"

She pursed her lips and sat down again. "Me 'usband and I worked for an old couple in Notting 'Ill. Dey brought us 'ere 'bout a dozen years ago. We were starvin' ta death back 'ome and da blasted French were already sniffin' about for control."

"And the Notting Hill couple?" I pressed. "What happened to them?"

"Dead. Left us a bit a money, but it weren't enough ta live off, so we 'ad ta come 'ere."

"You don't like it here?" Colin interrupted, finally glancing around.

"Dey good people. But I'd rather work for meself. Missus is a poor soul and I don't 'ardly see da mister."

"What did you do back in Dahomey?" Colin leaned against the mantel with a studied indifference.

Her deep brown eyes momentarily betrayed surprise that Colin knew where she was from, but a practiced coolness quickly settled over it. "Stay alive," she said offhandedly.

"Are you a Christian woman?"

She studied him before answering. "Now why ya askin' me dat?"

"I am conducting an investigation into the disappearance and possible murder of your employer. I'm likely to ask you anything."

"I go ta church wit' me 'usband when it suits me. I know da stories. Dat make me Christian?"

"Better than some." He flashed a tight smile. "And in Dahomey?"

"Ain't no Christians dere," she said flatly. "'Cept dem French."

"Yes . . ." he muttered. "And what's the name of the traditional West African religion?"

"Dere are many traditions in Africa."

"What about yours?" he pushed. "What is *yours* called?"

She settled her eyes on him, but I couldn't otherwise tell what she was thinking. "We call it Vudun," she finally answered. "It means *spirit*. Da belief of a single, divine Creator named Mawu. So we ain't so very different. We jest use different names."

"Vudun," he repeated as if tasting the word. "I believe it's more commonly known here as voodoo. And while the precepts may be similar, we don't have fetishes in the Christian faith."

She looked wholly amused as she let out a laugh. "Ya 'ave saints carved in wood and stone, and shiny crosses 'angin' round yer necks. We jest prefer our t'ings from da earth. But it don't make much difference 'cause it all means da same t'ing: blessings and good life. No." She chuckled. "We ain't so different at all."

"Perhaps we're not." He nodded stiffly, pushing himself away from the fireplace and crossing to one of the large windows overlooking the grounds. "I think we've taken enough of your time for now. Would you be so kind as to ask your husband to come and see us."

"As ya wish." She stood up and headed for the same door that led to the kitchen. "You jest let me know if ya wanna talk more about religion." Her deep chuckle followed her out as the door swung shut behind her.

"I doubt she'll find our next conversation half as entertaining," Colin grumbled.

"Nor the one she's likely to have with Inspector Varcoe before this night is through."

Colin shrugged. "She'll deny everything. By the time he gets through haranguing her he likely won't even be able to get her to admit she's from Africa."

"Well, you almost trod upon her good nature yourself by accusing her of being daft. Must you always say whatever comes into your head?"

He shifted his eyes to me with a sly grin. "I'm not saying what I'm thinking this very minute."

Not a moment later Alexa's husband, Albert, pushed his way into the room through the kitchen door. He was a short, thickly muscled man, attesting to a life spent in labors of one sort or another. He appeared slightly older than his wife and in marked contrast to her was as dark as the night itself. His clothing was worn, as one would expect of a groundskeeper, yet it was pressed and clean. He clutched a small navy cap in both hands that he was twisting as though trying to wring it of water, making it obvious that he was nowhere near as confident as his wife.

"Thank you for coming." Colin smiled and gestured to the same chair he had offered everyone else. "Please sit down."

Albert shook his head and cast his eyes to the floor. "No t'anks."

Colin pursed his lips and took a seat himself. "I understand you were born and raised in Dahomey."

He nodded tepidly, wringing his cap first one way and then the other, his eyes remaining down.

"And you have been working for the Connicles a little over two years?"

He gave another nod, all the while twisting the cap.

"Do you like working here?"

Another nod.

"Do you use the shed on the side of the house?"

I thought Albert was going to rend his cap in half as he dropped his chin almost to his sternum. "I didn't do nothin'."

"I'm just asking whether you use the shed. Do you keep your tools in it?"

It took a minute, but Albert gave yet another nod.

"Were you the one to discover all that blood this morning?"

His head shot up and his eyes locked on Colin's. "I didn't do nothin'," he repeated, this time with force.

"I didn't say you did." Colin stood up and wandered around behind where Albert was standing, his movements slow and casual even though his words bristled with expectancy. "Tell me, Albert, are you a practitioner of voodoo like your wife?"

"Wot?!" His eyes shot over to Colin as his hands went still.

"Voodoo. Your wife tells us she was a practitioner in Dahomey. Were you as well?"

He shrugged, his gaze drifting back to the floor in front of him.

Colin waved him off. "It doesn't matter. What time did you go out there this morning?"

"'Bout five. Same as always."

"Did you go directly to the shed?"

"Yeah. But there weren't nothin' wrong."

"No blood?"

He nodded.

"Did you see anyone else?"

He shook his head.

"And what did you do after you went out to your shed?"

"I got me shovel and took it down past da trees ta fix da fence. A couple posts was knocked down yestaday."

"Beyond the trees on the eastern edge?"

He shook his head. "No. Da west."

"The west . . ." Colin repeated, and it struck me at once that Albert would have been on the opposite end of the property from where the murder and immolation of Edmond Connicle had taken place. "And what time did you get back to the house?"

Albert shrugged his broad shoulders. "Eight? . . . I don't see da time."

"Did you go right back to the shed?"

It took him a moment before he nodded again.

"And before you looked inside and saw the blood, could you tell that someone had been there? That anything had happened?"

"No."

"Are you sure?" Colin stepped toward him, forcing Albert to look up.

He shook his head vehemently as he began winding his cap again.

"Very well. If you remember something, anything at all, I should very much like to hear it."

The man looked pained as he turned and stared outside. "We done?"

Colin watched him a moment, taking his time before finally answering. "For now." And as soon as Albert was gone Colin turned to me with a broad grin and announced, "He's lying."

CHAPTER 4

Inspector Varcoe's coach drew up under the portico of the Connicles' house just as their driver, Randolph, brought a carriage around to take Colin and me back to our flat. I was relieved to be leaving, as I knew the only reason Varcoe and two of his nattier men were arriving was to deliver the terrible news to Mrs. Connicle about her husband. Colin and I could serve no further purpose for her tonight, so we climbed aboard the Connicles' carriage without exchanging more than the briefest of nods with Varcoe and his men.

As we started the journey home Colin leaned forward and began to engage Randolph in easy conversation, though I knew he was being precise in his seemingly amiable banter. Randolph was a tall, hawkish-looking man with sharp features and a gaunt frame who quickly proved to be a warm and congenial person. He seemed pleased to talk about his employer, confiding that he had been working for the Connicle family since he was seventeen—and given that he appeared to be in his mid-fifties, it was clear that he had known Edmond Connicle the whole of his life.

"... The mister does go ridin' from time ta time but never the missus," Randolph told us. "He prefers the big, black stallion, but I don't trust that one. He's too skittish if ya ask me. Now

Mrs. Connicle . . ." He made a clicking sound with his tongue. "She's delicate, ya see. She has spells and gets weak as a baby in the blink of an eye, so she can't be gettin' up on no horse. Horses are crafty buggers. Ya can't never let 'em think they're smarter than you is. Ain't that right, ya ol' nag!" he called out, jiggling the reins of the beautiful chestnut pulling us home.

"What sort of spells does Mrs. Connicle suffer?" Colin asked, managing to sound more concerned than interrogational.

"Oh . . ." Randolph rubbed a hand through his thin gray hair. "Women things, I s'pose. Ya'd best ask Miss Porter. If it ain't got four legs I don't know much about it." He shrugged easily. "Besides, weren't nothin' Mr. Connicle didn't know about. He was always sufferin' over her through the years. He'd look about ready ta cry sometimes. And her . . ." Randolph pursed his lips and released a slow whistle of air. "Most a the time she's fine, but there are days when she creeps around like she's hidin' from a ghost, and sometimes she don't even come outta her room. It's sad. Some years back he had ta send her ta hospital. Poor thing needed rest. Spent a couple months there." He shook his head and made a low tsking sound. "Thing was, when she came back she looked the worse for it. Pale and so thin her face weren't nothin' but skin and bone. Mrs. Hollin's set right ta fattenin' her up. Didn't speak for weeks when she first returned." He heaved a wearied sigh. "But eventually she came round."

"Where did he send her?"

"Needham Hills. Looks like a regular estate 'cept there ain't nothin' but nurses and attendants and hollow-eyed people walkin' about. Awful place."

"I'm familiar with it," Colin answered brusquely, taking care not to look in my direction. "You seem very fond of her," he added.

"She's a kind and gentle woman. She don't deserve all the unhappiness she's had. And now this . . ." He let his voice trail off.

"Yes." Colin's tone matched Randolph's with remarkable accuracy. "When was the last time you saw Mr. Connicle?"

"He went out ridin' last night. Right after dinner. Wasn't gone very long, but his horse was knackered by the time he got back. I didn't see him this mornin'. He gets up early. Not that I don't, mind ya. If I don't feed them horses right off they'll set up a racket kickin' the walls a their stalls. It's enough ta make ya feel sorry for 'em if ya didn't know better."

"No doubt." Colin gave a quick smile. "And when you were attending to them this morning, did you notice anything unusual? See anyone about?"

"Nah. It's only ever just me and Albert once the mister heads out."

"Was Albert about last night? After Mr. Connicle came back?"

"Albert's always about. It's his job. He's got a lot a property ta keep up. He don't get paid ta lay about on his arse." Randolph chuckled. "I see more a him than anybody else round here. Seems a good sort. Don't know where the mister found him and his Alexa, but I don't hear no one complainin' about 'em, either." He guided the horse onto Gloucester Road as we drew close to our flat.

"Did you see the shed before Scotland Yard arrived this morning?"

Randolph's posture stiffened as he steered the carriage down our street. "I saw it," he said after a moment.

"What do you suppose happened?"

He shook his head as he pulled the carriage to a stop in front of our flat. "I don't know. I'm hopin' the mister will show up and tell us before another day goes by." He craned around as we climbed out. "Ya think he'll be doin' that?"

Colin's expression softened as he settled his gaze on Randolph. "I'm afraid we should prepare ourselves for the worst."

Randolph dropped his eyes and shook his head. "I remember the night Mr. Connicle was born. It's not right. It jest ain't right."

I longed to offer some words of encouragement but knew that I mustn't. He would learn the truth soon enough and, until then, could bind himself in the comforts of hope. Many times I had sought refuge there myself.

We bade him good evening and went inside, the scent of roasted chicken caressing my nose and stomach, reminding me that we had never stopped for lunch. Colin clearly had the same thought, as he bypassed the stairs and headed straight for the kitchen, me tagging eagerly in his wake. But as soon as he pushed the door open I knew we were in trouble. A fully cooked chicken stood coagulating on a platter on the wooden table. The chicken had been picked apart, leaving it as forlorn looking as my stomach felt.

"Well . . . look 'oo finally bothered ta show up," Mrs. Behmoth grunted as she came out of the larder with a biscuit tin in her arms. "I 'ope ya ate 'cause *I* ain't fixin' ya nothin'. This meal were done an 'our ago. Just like every night." And true to her word she dumped the carcass into a pot of simmering water and slammed a lid onto it.

"We have *not* eaten!" Colin barked sourly. "And while we are sorry to be delayed in getting back to your meal, I will thank you to rummage something up for us."

She picked up a small bowl and waved it at him. "You can eat the cold Brussels sprouts. I can't reheat 'em anyway."

His eyes narrowed. "There must be some chicken left."

"I'm usin' it for soup."

"Then use a little less."

"I work 'ard plannin' meals."

"I know you do. I said we were sorry."

She glared at him and I knew she would give in. Eventually almost everyone gives in to him. She brusquely turned and started pulling dishes out of the cupboard, all the while grousing under her breath. "I'll make ya some porridge, but ya ain't gettin' any chicken!" A sudden pounding on the front door brought us all up short before she said, "And I ain't gettin' that, either." Then she turned and headed back to the larder.

I suppressed a laugh as I headed out to the foyer while he stayed behind to protest her choice for our evening meal. I most certainly wasn't going to have any impact on her. She had raised Colin from the age of seven, not me. I had long ago decided that the only reason she even tolerated me was because Colin insisted on it.

By the time I reached the door I realized the pounding had become decidedly persistent. I yanked it open and found myself facing a broad, angular-faced Indian man of middle age and medium height with jet-black hair and coal eyes.

"Mr. Pendragon?" he blurted at once.

"No. He's"—I gestured into the flat, uncertain what to say— "indisposed. I'm Mr. Pruitt."

"I must speak with him," he implored over my introduction, staring at me with such determination that I found myself feeling oddly uneasy.

"Is he expecting you?" I asked, though I knew he wasn't.

A thin sigh escaped his lips, but his eyes never left mine. "He is not. But Mr. Pendragon grew up in my country. He is a friend to my country. I require such a friend now. Will he not agree to speak with me for that reason alone?"

He would. Colin held a special affinity for India and her countrymen despite having left the country at the age of thirteen to attend the Easling and Temple Senior Academy, where our paths had first crossed. Never mind that his interest would be piqued by the way this man was holding me in the thrall of his unwavering gaze anyway.

"Please come in," I said, stepping aside and bidding the man enter. I led our guest up to the study and got him settled on the settee before quickly stoking the fireplace embers back into a soothing blaze. "You will excuse me while I fetch some tea and Mr. Pendragon," I said before heading back downstairs.

By the time I pushed my way back into the kitchen I found Colin hovering behind Mrs. Behmoth in the larder, obviously still trying to coax her to reheat some chicken. "We've a gentleman who seems most anxious to speak with you," I announced, interrupting their joust.

"Did you tell him I'm busy?" he shot back gruffly.

"I did."

"Then why did I hear you take him upstairs?"

"Because he was insistent," I said calmly. "And because he is from India."

"India?!" Colin's face lit up as he stepped out of the larder. "Outstanding."

"I thought you might think so." I smiled. "Bring some tea

when you come, won't you?" I added glibly before turning to leave.

"That would be Mrs. Behmoth's job," I heard him bluster, but I didn't stay to hear her response.

Our guest was right where I'd left him, his posture ramrod straight and his face an unreadable canvas of rigid formality. I figured him to be some ten years older than Colin, putting him in his late forties, and was certain, given the stiffness of his bearing, that he had been born to wealth and class. His suit was immaculate, if traditional for this part of the world, leaving me to surmise that he had been in our city for quite some time. He wore a thick gold band on his finger and a heavy gold chain disappeared down the collar of his shirt.

"Mr. Pendragon will be right up," I said as I took my usual seat.

"You're very kind. Have you ever been to India?"

"I'm afraid I have not, though I would very much like to go. Mr. Pendragon speaks most fondly of it."

"That is a blessing to hear. His father is still a revered man there. I am sure you know he was the Queen's emissary in Bombay for over thirty years."

"I do. Sir Atherton remains devoted to India."

"He left a deep void when he returned to England. He was a man of great integrity during a most tumultuous time for our people. A lesser man would not have been successful. I am hoping his son will be his equal."

"I believe you will find that to be true," I said as I finally heard Colin's sure, hard footfalls on the stairs.

"Thankfully," the man replied with the same solemnity with which he had approached our entire conversation.

As Colin reached the landing I noted with amusement that he was bearing the tea tray. Dear Mrs. Behmoth had an undeniable way with him. Even I could not claim such abilities against his will. So once again I found myself suppressing a chuckle as he set the tray on the table and stuck a hand out to greet our guest.

"Colin Pendragon at your service."

The man popped out of his seat, his eyes filling at once with warmth and gratitude. "Mr. Pendragon . . ." He sounded notice-ably relieved. "My name is Prakhasa Guitnu." He bowed his head slightly, but his eyes remained riveted on Colin.

"Guitnu?" Colin repeated at once, the name immediately familiar to me as well. "The jeweler?"

"I am humbled that you have heard of me."

"Your designs are renowned. Victoria has been a devotee for years."

"Her Majesty has done me a great honor."

"Sit down, sit down," Colin said as he set to pouring tea for the three of us. "Do tell us what has brought you here this evening?"

Mr. Guitnu cleared his throat with evident discomfort. "I am being robbed, Mr. Pendragon, by a member of my household staff."

Colin's eyebrows sprang up as he passed out our cups. "A member of your own staff? Are you certain?"

"It can be no other way," he answered, and I realized it was embarrassment that was coloring his tone. "It has happened many times over the last several months. I did not think it true at first, certain it was my own forgetfulness, but then I had to admit the truth. I have invited a common thief into my home."

"Why don't you start at the beginning."

"Of course." He shifted as though to make himself more comfortable, yet did not pick up his tea. His distress, or perhaps it was something more like humiliation, felt palpable. "I often bring loose gems home when I am designing a new piece or seeking inspiration. It helps me to look at them, glittering like winking stars in the evening sky, until I can see the pattern they belong to. I always have many stones at the house for that purpose. My wife also has a pleasant collection of jewelry," he added with a shy smile. "It makes her happy. And even she has lost many bracelets, necklaces, and rings in the last several months." He shook his head and heaved a sigh. "I have no idea how many items are missing. I am ashamed at my carelessness."

"Where do you store them at home?" Colin asked, idly snatching a crown from his pocket and flipping it between the fingers of his right hand.

"I have a hidden safe."

"And who among your staff knows of it?"

"Until now I would have told you none of them. But I have clearly been a fool. Whoever has discovered it has done so with great evil of heart. Stealing a little here, a little there, thinking I would not notice. I want you to find this man, Mr. Pendragon, so I can cut off his thieving hands."

Colin smiled evenly as the crown continued its steady rotation between his fingers, as though he had been told something in jest. Yet I could see by the pinched expression on our visitor's face that he had meant his words. "Mr. Guitnu . . ." Colin said after a moment, tossing the crown about a foot and snatching it out of the air, "I shall find the perpetrator of these thefts, but not for you to extract your own sort of revenge." He shoved the crown back in his pocket. "There will be no loss of limbs unless the British courts decree it. Are we in agreement?"

Mr. Guitnu scowled. "So you will take the case?"

"I shall have your word, Mr. Guitnu. . . ."

"Yes, of course." He waved Colin off, his displeasure evident. "As long as the scoundrel lives under my roof he will be safe. But when he becomes a ward of the prisons I shall pray for his dismemberment every day."

"As you wish." Colin chuckled. "Mr. Pruitt and I shall come by your home tomorrow morning. Will your full staff be in attendance?"

"Most certainly."

Colin stood up and wandered over to the fireplace with his teacup clutched in his hand. "And how many would that be?"

"Eight. And you may consider every one of them a suspect. I will not speak for one of them."

"Do you have any children?"

"Three daughters. Vijaya, Sundha, and Kajri."

"Is there anyone who comes to your home on a regular basis?"

He shrugged slightly. "We get deliveries. There is the boy who brings the *Times*, for one."

Colin smiled. "A man of detail. That will make things easier." He crossed over to the landing and glanced back. "I should think that will be all for now, Mr. Guitnu. Until tomorrow then." Before our new client could even rise to his feet Colin turned and pounded down the stairs.

Mr. Guitnu looked at me with surprise.

"There will be many more questions tomorrow," I said by way of reassurance.

"Of course." He nodded with his usual seriousness and stood up. "My wife did not wish me to come at all, but I have had enough of this thief. I pay a fair wage and will not be made a fool of by that caste."

I cringed at his reference but let it pass, quickly settling on a fee with him even as I became aware of the rising murmur of voices from beneath our feet. Mortified at what I feared was happening in our kitchen, I hurried Mr. Guitnu down the stairs and out the front door. "Tomorrow then," I called as he climbed into his large, black coach.

"I shall send my carriage round to fetch you. What time shall we say?"

"Ten," I answered hastily, eager for him to be on his way.

"Very well. Thank you." Mr. Guitnu ducked into his carriage and it immediately pulled away.

"*Ethan!*" I heard Colin shout before I could even get the door shut. "Grab our coats. We're going to Shauney's."

Not thirty minutes later we were seated at a back table in Shauney's pub mopping up the remains of a heavenly chicken stew with thick chunks of bread. Colin had long since hit the bottom of his ale tankard and was generously helping himself to the rest of mine. I leaned back on the worn wooden bench and stretched my legs out with a sigh. "It has been quite a day."

"There will be much more tomorrow. We'll go back to the Connicles' at dawn. I should like to speak with Albert once more before Varcoe locks him away."

"He seemed suspicious to me."

"Suspicious?" Colin pushed the bill Shauney had left us toward me. "I don't yet know what is driving him, but he certainly knows more than he was letting on."

"Are you sure?" I asked as I tossed a handful of change onto the table.

He grinned and snatched up a shilling, flinging it into the air. "As certainly as Victoria is our sovereign, my love." He grabbed my hand and flipped it over so that the coin landed in my open palm, Victoria's stern profile shining up at me from the silver planchet.

CHAPTER 5

The moment our hansom cab pulled into the short drive of the Connicle estate, just as dawn began to stretch up from the horizon, it was clear that Colin had been right, if woefully mistaken about the timing. Though the sun had not yet crested above the horizon, the house was already ablaze with light and there were half a dozen police coaches parked near the front door. It was astounding to find such a contingency of force. Was there any wonder the Yard's reputation had receded over the years if this was how many men they determined were required to question the scullery maid, Alexa, and her husband, Albert? It seemed inconceivable, even for Inspector Varcoe, to have mucked up such a straightforward task.

"They cannot still be here from yesterday," I grumbled into the early morning chill.

"No," Colin muttered. "They aren't."

I turned to scowl at him, annoyed that he could be so certain at this hour, and that's when I spotted the coroner's wagon parked on the far side of the house. The opposite side from where the bloodied shed stood. Not a word was spoken between us as we cut across the front of the property, Colin's eyes set rigidly on that gray wagon with its seven black letters etched across its side: CORONER. What, I began to fear, was Denton Ross doing here?

Colin and I skirted around the corner of the house and noticed a cluster of police along the tree line. Most seemed to be milling about, some with their arms crossed and others with their rounded navy caps pushed back on their heads, but there were several kneeling in the grass beneath a tree as though foraging amongst the roots for truffles or mushrooms. Inspector Varcoe was one of them.

"What can they possibly be up to . . . ?" I started to say, but let my voice fade out as I caught sight of the twisted legs lying prone there.

"It's Albert," Colin said, the astonishment in his voice unmistakable as he suddenly rushed ahead.

I hurried to catch up, the sight of Albert's misshapen and bloodied body coming into view as I drew closer. He was lying on his stomach, though his head was turned to one side, his visible eye staring toward the horizon as though fixed on the blossoming dawn.

"Pendragon!" Varcoe barked as he stood up and brushed his hands along the sides of his slacks. "You investigating every ruddy accident now? 'Cause I got a boy stubbed his toe a couple houses down. Perhaps you could do some of your fine work on that situation," he snorted.

Colin's brow curled into a tight frown. "What are you talking about?"

"This dumb sod who fell out of this tree!" he snapped. "What the hell do you *think* I'm talking about?"

"Fell out of the tree?!" Colin repeated with stark disbelief.

Varcoe's face went dark, which was offset by the blinding whiteness of his hair. "That's what I said, you pompous shitheel." He glared at Colin a moment before abruptly stepping back, crossing his arms over his chest, and allowing a crooked grin to slide onto his face. "Why don't you tell these two tossers what you've determined so far, Mr. Ross."

My stomach clenched as Denton Ross stepped forward, his pasty complexion, stringy hair, and unkempt form maintained in defiance of anything good or proper. "Must I?" he groused.

Inspector Varcoe's smile faltered slightly as he gritted his teeth. "If you *please,* Mr. Ross."

An irritated sigh escaped his blubbery lips as he began clipping off his official report as though under duress. "If you must know, my preliminary determination is that this man fell out of this tree from a height of some fifteen feet as evidenced by the contorted position of his body, the multiple fractures to his left arm, and the complete dislocation of the same shoulder. It wasn't the fall that killed him, however." He glowered smartly at Colin. "It was a blow to the left temple sustained from a rock when he struck the ground. In short, an accident," he added with disdain.

"I see," Colin sniffed. "And do you have this murderous rock? I certainly don't see it by his head."

"What?"

Colin's eyes flashed darkly. "Where is the wretched stone upon which your supposition lies? Or are you merely espousing the basest possibility?"

"How dare you—"

"Answer the damn question," Inspector Varcoe cut in.

Denton Ross flicked his eyes between Colin and Varcoe, a look of distaste pinching his mouth. "We'll find it once the sun comes up."

"Oh, bloody hell!" Varcoe growled as he waved a couple of his men over. "You lot start looking for a rock around here with blood and god knows what other kind of matter on it. And you, Mr. Ross . . ." He leveled a damning gaze at Denton. "I don't give a ruddy shite what you *think*. I want the *facts!*" He shoved himself past all of us before suddenly turning and adding, "And don't you or your toady touch a damn thing, Pendragon. I'll not have you fouling this scene to prove your conjectures."

"Conjectures?"

"There is currently *NO* indication of *any* connection between this man's death and the ritualistic killing yesterday of Edmond

Connicle," he seethed. "And I will thank you to remember that."
He shifted his gaze to Denton Ross and stabbed a finger toward
him. "I want your full report on my desk by midday. Do you understand?!" He didn't wait for an answer but instead stalked off
toward the driveway muttering his fury.

"I've hardly slept this entire night," Denton Ross fumed in
the inspector's wake. "And now, because of you, I have a blasted
deadline. So *piss off!*" To my surprise Colin immediately stepped
back, so I did the same. While I was certain Denton hoped we
would move off completely, I knew he was grateful to get whatever he could.

The young man who assisted Denton slumped forward with a
stretcher rolled up under one arm. He set it on the ground next
to Albert's remains and kicked it open with an irrefutable look of
disinterest. "Ready," he muttered before they knelt down and
grabbed Albert's body, Denton at his shoulders, the assistant
grabbing the twisted legs. Rigor mortis had already begun to set
in, leaving Albert looking like a broken wooden doll, stiff and
contorted in ways he was never meant to bend.

"You must forgive me," Colin spoke up delicately once they
had set the body onto the stretcher. "I didn't notice any particular sort of trauma point on the prone side of the face. Where did
you get the idea that he struck a rock when he fell?"

Denton's face puckered. "I am not about to explain my process
to an amateur and his sycophant."

Colin allowed the ghost of a grin to settle on his face. "Specu-
lation can hardly be called a process. Surely you can see that this
man did not die as a result of blunt trauma to his head. He was
murdered elsewhere and quite deliberately placed in that de-
formed position to make it appear that he had fallen from that
tree."

"You don't know anything."

Colin sighed with unaccustomed patience. "Have you asked
yourself why he was in the tree? I don't see any shears or a saw,
so he couldn't have been trying to prune it. Do you suppose he
was just up there waiting to enjoy the sunrise?"

"Well, how the hell would I know that?!" Denton bristled with annoyance. "It's not my job to explain the whim of every nutter who runs into trouble."

"Runs into trouble? He's dead, man."

"I know what he is!" Denton snarled, spittle flying from his lips. "*Lift!*" he shouted at his aide, and the two of them roughly hoisted the stretcher up.

As they began to move off, Colin spoke up once more. "You will find abrasions on the prone side of Albert's face and chest consistent with having been dragged behind a horse. I'd say you'll also find contusions from a rope around one or both of his ankles or wrists. That man was murdered and dragged here, Mr. Ross, as surely as this day is upon us."

Neither Denton nor his assistant gave so much as the whiff of a response as they headed for the corner of the house where their wagon was parked. I knew it would be too much for Colin to stand and after a moment was not surprised when he could not stop himself from calling out, "I look forward to reading your findings!"

"Well . . ." I said as they disappeared from view, "it would appear you were right about Albert keeping something from us last night. I can think of no other conclusion to draw."

"Indeed," he grumbled irritably. "Only Varcoe and that morgue monkey could be fooled by such a thing. And even Varcoe appears to be having second thoughts." He glanced back to where Albert's body had lain before turning and starting for the house. "Let's get inside and speak to Alexa and Mrs. Connicle before Varcoe manages to pollute the whole of this confounding investigation."

"*Pendragon!*" The inspector's voice assaulted us again before we could reach the portico. Even so, Colin kept moving, his chagrin evident as we climbed the porch. Only then did he bother to glance back at Varcoe and the two bobbies bearing down on us. "Where the hell do you think you're going?"

"To knock on the door," he said as he did so. "I am under the employ of Mrs. Connicle and would like to pay my respects to her."

"The hell you are. You're going in there to ferret about and I won't have it."

"We have a magisterial order allowing us great latitude to—"

"*I know what you have!*" he howled back. "But that won't stop me from hounding your every blasted move." He abruptly leaned forward and pounded on the door himself. "And that's precisely what I intend to do."

"Oh, come now, Inspector—"

"Do *not* be impudent with me, Pendragon, or you will need a magisterial order just to wipe your buggered nose!"

I could tell Colin was on the verge of an unfortunate reply just as the door was swept open by Miss Porter, wearing a surly frown that blemished her otherwise lovely face. "Gentlemen! We are a household in mourning," she scolded. "Must we suffer additional disregard with such a racket?"

The inspector reddened as he puffed out his chest and gave a rudimentary nod. "Of course. My men sometimes forget themselves in the midst of an investigation," he blustered inanely, as neither of his men had accompanied him onto the porch. "Just the same, this is an investigation and we shall require the household to rally in order for us to proceed."

Miss Porter's eyes narrowed the slightest bit as she took a curt step back to allow us entry. Whatever she was thinking, her decorum remained intact as she showed us to the library. Varcoe had waved one of his men to follow, which meant there would be four of us confronting whomever Colin meant to query. Hardly the sort of informal environment conducive to confession.

"Who is it you wish to see, Inspector?" Miss Porter asked as she prodded a fire back to roaring life.

"Not me," he answered with pointed artifice. "Mr. Pendragon here. Who will it be, Pendragon?"

Colin's displeasure was evident from the vitriol in his eyes to the rigid way he was standing. Still, his voice remained smooth and cordial as he turned to Miss Porter with a smile. "Perhaps *you* would be so kind as to speak with us a moment?"

Miss Porter sucked in a breath that seemed to carry the weight of the day. Nevertheless, she gestured for the three of us to sit, Varcoe's man having remained at the door, as she perched herself on the edge of a settee.

"How is your mistress faring?" Colin asked.

"It was a terrible night. We had to send for the doctor after she learned about her husband. She was inconsolable and I feared for her safety." She brushed a wayward hair from her eyes and seemed to grow smaller. "The doctor spent an hour with her and gave her something strong for her nerves, but it was still quite some time before she fell into sleep. She is not awake yet and so is unaware of what has occurred this morning. We have already sent for the doctor to ensure he is here when she arises. I am certain she will not bear this second shock at all well."

"I'm sorry." Colin nodded. "I know this is hard on all of you, but I must impose a few questions so that we may bring these terrible events to a swift and just conclusion."

"I understand."

He offered her a tight smile as he began. "Did you see Albert this morning before he went outside?"

She shook her head. "Albert is on to his chores long before I'm about. There are days when I don't even see him until supper."

"Do you know what time his day usually begins?"

"You'd have to ask Alexa or Mrs. Hollings. Mrs. Hollings sees that he gets something to eat before he heads out."

Colin nodded. "Very good. One last question. Were you aware that Albert was planning on trimming trees this morning?"

She shook her head. "He didn't confer with me about his work."

Colin flashed a thin smile as he fished a crown out of his vest pocket. "Then I thank you for your time," he said as he began to coax the crown effortlessly between the fingers of his right hand. "May I trouble you to ask Mrs. Hollings if she would speak with us a moment?"

"Certainly." She stood up and brushed idly at her skirts. "Gentlemen . . ." she said as she excused herself.

"You're about as smooth as a baboon's behind," Varcoe snorted once Miss Porter was gone. "It's a bloody wonder you can solve a case with that kind of piffle."

Colin grinned as the shiny coin continued to glide between his fingers. "Perhaps you'd care to compare our rates of success?"

The inspector's face pinched and his brow furrowed. "Awfully full of yourself, given you've nothing but treacle and fluff to show for your efforts." He swiveled toward the young constable still hovering at the door. "I hope you're taking notes," he blustered. "Pendragon's every word is priceless."

Colin's face tightened, but he managed to keep silent for the few minutes it took before Mrs. Hollings finally came ambling into the room. She moved like her feet hurt, listing from side to side as though improperly balanced. And though she was generous in size, she was not nearly as ample as our Mrs. Behmoth. Her long white apron was surprisingly smudged given that it was not yet eight, which implied that she was a woman very much into her work.

"It is a pleasure to see you again, Mrs. Hollings," Colin said as she came to a halt at the room's center. "I only wish it were under better circumstances."

"As do we all," she sighed heavily.

"Please . . ." He gestured to the chair next to me.

She flicked her eyes between all of us, her expression vacant, before tsking and dropping herself onto the edge of the proffered seat.

Colin fluidly slid the coin back into his vest pocket and asked, "Did you see Albert this morning, Mrs. Hollings?"

"Course."

He allowed something of a smile. "I take it you see him every morning then?"

"Well, 'e don't feed 'imself and I don't let nobody putter about in me kitchen."

"What time was that?"

"Four thirty. Same as every day."

"And how did he seem this morning?"

She gave Colin a curious look as though she thought he were balmy. "Same as ever," she said flatly.

Now it was Colin's turn to pause, though at first I could not tell if it was frustration or disappointment clouding his eyes. "Did he mention what sort of chores he was planning to attend to today?"

She snorted. "I made 'im a crock a porridge. I didn't pester 'im with questions."

Colin's mouth flat-lined. "Naturally. Then there was nothing particular about this morning?"

"Nah," she answered at once.

Varcoe's surly chuckle intruded into the brief silence.

"Was climbing into trees to trim them a regular part of Albert's duties?"

She shook her head. "Nah."

"Do you ever remember him climbing into the trees?"

Mrs. Hollings stared straight at Colin. "I don't know what 'e were up to 'alf the time, but I don't remember 'im climbin' no trees. Wot's the point in that?"

Colin's face gradually relaxed into something I recognized as satisfaction. "How many years has he been here?"

"Close ta three, I guess." Her expression began to curl in on itself as she seemed to consider her own words for the first time. "So wot *was* 'e doin' up there then . . . ?" she asked.

"Can you say for certain that Mrs. Connicle didn't tell him to get out there and clean those trees up?" Varcoe cut in.

"She 'asn't been outta 'er room since you came by with the news 'bout the mister last evenin'." She wagged an accusatory finger at him.

"Maybe she told him the day before. Or Mr. Connicle perhaps. . . ."

"Inspector . . ." Colin piped up. "Don't you think it's a bit much if we're both peppering this good woman with questions?"

Varcoe scowled at him before settling back in his chair. He gestured to his constable in the doorway and I saw the young man jot something down in his notebook. It seemed the inspector meant to have his questions answered at some point or another.

"Now, Mrs. Hollings"—Colin looked back at her and flashed

a gentle grin—"I want to ask you to think hard about this morning one more time. Did Albert seem different in any way? Agitated perhaps? Distracted? Particularly quiet . . . ?"

" 'E were always quiet." She waved him off. "I don't think 'e spoke the Queen's tongue all that well. But 'e did do somethin' strange now that ya mention it. 'E stood at the back door and stared out a couple minutes like 'e were lookin' for somethin'. I thought it were 'cause a what 'appened yesterday, but 'e weren't starin' toward the shed. 'E were lookin' at them trees on the other side." She shrugged. "Maybe 'e were thinkin' 'bout cuttin' 'em."

"And there it is," the inspector pronounced grandly.

Colin shifted his gaze toward Varcoe but held his tongue. It took better than a moment before he finally turned back to Mrs. Hollings with what remnants of civility he seemed capable of mustering. "I'd like to ask you one last question, Mrs. Hollings. Did Albert's wife confide in you over the last twenty-four hours that she was concerned for her husband's safety?"

"Nah. Bless that poor woman. Alexa never said nothin' ta me."

"Thank you." Colin settled back, his face softening. "We appreciate your time."

"It's all so 'orrible," she muttered as she stood up and made her way out of the library.

"This is ridiculous!" Varcoe snarled in her wake. "You're wasting time." He stood up as though to punctuate the veracity of his claim but did not otherwise make a move to leave.

"You needn't stay on my account," Colin urged.

Varcoe scowled. "I'll stay." He did not, however, sit down until Miss Porter had returned and Colin requested that she send Alexa to see us.

"She has just lost her husband," Miss Porter reminded us needlessly. "I hope you will be considerate of that fact."

"It is that very fact that causes us to wish to speak with her." Colin met Miss Porter's gaze and held it. "I shall be the only one to question her. The others will be as quiet as church mice." He turned toward Varcoe. "Isn't that right, Inspector?"

Varcoe's face flushed pink. "For now," he blustered, glowering at Colin until Alexa finally came to join us.

She stood silently in the doorway, none of us even aware she was there until Varcoe's man cleared his throat and we all turned to find her right beside him. I had forgotten how solid of build she was, tall and lithe with wide shoulders and hips. And though her face was set and proud, the pain in her eyes was undeniable. "Ya sent for me?" she said.

Colin jumped off the sofa so quickly it looked as though something had surely bitten his backside. He moved to her and extended his hand, guiding her to the same seat Mrs. Hollings had just vacated, though when Alexa sat down she did so with the dignity and grace of someone we had come to visit in her own home. "Thank you for speaking with us," Colin said. "I know how difficult this must be." He moved around the room ticking off our names before settling in and asking whether she had spoken with her husband this morning.

Alexa eyed Colin warily. "I shared a room wit' him. It'd be hard not ta."

"Forgive me." Colin nodded. "And how did he seem? Was he at all worried or anxious . . . ?"

"He was tired," she answered back, sounding very much so herself. "Workin' 'til late and gettin' up before da sun. He was always tired."

"Did he tell you that he was planning on trimming trees near the edge of the property this morning?"

Her face puckered and her eyes flared angrily. "Now what's da sense in trimmin' trees ain't even near da house?" She glared at each of us in turn. "Someone tol' ya dat don't know what dey talkin' 'bout."

"Did he say what he was intending to do?"

"He didn't have ta. He did da same t'ing every day: planted, cleaned up da yard, cut bushes against da house, minded da garden. 'At's why dey paid him."

"Indeed." Colin nodded as though she had clarified some great mystery. "Then I must ask you again. Given what happened yesterday, did he confide any particular concern about his safety?"

She glanced down a moment and it looked like much of the

anger that had held her so steely was deserting her. "He was worried 'bout me," she answered in a thin, halting voice.

"And why was that?"

"'Cause a him." She stabbed her chin toward Inspector Varcoe. "He was afraid dey guon arrest me for killin' Mr. Connicle. We heard 'bout dem t'ings you found buried wit' him. Dat weren't me. I ain't callin' on nothin' ta harm nobody. Vudun ain't like dat. It's about da spirits dat govern da earth. But I don't 'spect you would know nothin' 'bout dat."

"I was raised in India," Colin said softly. "Alongside Hindus, Buddhists, and Muslims. In my thirteenth year we spent the summer in West Africa on our way to Britain. We were almost three weeks in Dahomey. I still remember the sight of the fierce female warriors, something I had never seen before. But mostly I remember the simple beauty of a religion steeped in the essence of nature." He leaned forward and held Alexa's eyes, which were no longer guarded but filled with a raw pain. "Were you worried for your husband's safety? Did you have reason to believe he might be in danger?"

She dropped her gaze to the floor, but I could still see the tears beginning to form in the corners of her eyes. "He tol' me he saw a man real early yesterday when he was headin' out ta fix da fence. A man on a horse ridin' up past da trees where Mr. Connicle was found. He said da man chased after him, but Albert was dark as night and hid away easy. Least dat's what he thought." The tears began to leach down her cheeks. "Dat man knew who Albert was. He knew. And now Albert's gone. . . ."

CHAPTER 6

The sound of rain spattering against the windows of our flat could be heard over the popping of embers in the fireplace. The clouds had waited for the completion of our journey home before beginning to let loose in earnest, saving us from having to huddle within the hansom cab with little more than a quarter-round top to cover the best of us. Though we were soon to be voyaging out again, I knew the carriage Prakhasa Guitnu was sending had a proper roof.

I was attempting to jot some notes in my journal even though Colin was prattling on about the case while simultaneously pressing a set of dumbbells across his chest as though they were fashioned of cardboard. "Varcoe hasn't the kernel of a notion about what's going on out there," Colin grumbled as the weights continued to fly across their effortless arc. "But it did seem even *he* was finally starting to realize how ridiculous it is to believe Albert fell from that tree." He flung the dumbbells onto the floor and stood up, quickly rolling down his sleeves. "Get yourself ready. There's a carriage just pulled up downstairs."

"So I heard," I answered with some satisfaction.

And not thirty minutes later we were delivered to a large

brick home in Holland Park with an emerald lawn that sloped down from the face of the house to the street. Crisp lines accentuated the clean, Federalist design that nevertheless hinted at a greater wealth than was initially perceived from its tidy size. There was clearly money here, and it made me begin to wonder how extensive Mr. Guitnu's loss might truly be.

The rain had once again subsided to little more than a sputtering annoyance, so Colin asked that we be dropped at the curb. We made our way up to the house along a curved stone path that ascended the gentle angle of the lawn, and as we climbed the porch I could not take my eyes from the metal door knockers shaped like elephants, lacquered in brilliant jewel-toned colors where the headdress and mantle fell below their sides. Tiny gems were fitted for the eyes, though whether they were diamonds or crystals I could not say.

Colin smiled. "Spectacular. These certainly remind me of a simpler time." He grabbed the nearest one and gave it a resounding *thwack!*

"I think your memory is playing tricks on you," I said.

He chuckled. "Leave me my delusions."

Before I could say anything further a tall, striking Indian man with a burst of white hair, dressed in an impeccable black suit and white gloves, pulled the doors open and bade us enter. "Mr. Pendragon . . . Mr. Pruitt . . . the family is expecting you." He led us through an exquisite foyer paneled in what looked to be a deep mahogany or red oak that soared two stories above our heads. It was clearly meant to impress and so it did. A staircase of the same wood sprawled along the right side of the space, further accentuating the unexpected grandeur of the home.

We were ushered into a large sitting room that was surprising in that its furnishings were British, with nary an Indian artifact to be seen. Deep burgundy brocade covered the traditional couches and wing-backed chairs, and there were two hutches and a long wooden bar that looked like they had come straight from one of the shops near Leicester. Mr. Guitnu was seated in the chair nearest an ornate fireplace of geometric design, while Mrs. Guitnu and three young women, presumably their daughters, sat across from him on one of the couches.

"Gentlemen . . ." Mr. Guitnu stood as we entered. "It is a pleasure to have you in our home. I am only sorry it is for such a circumstance as this." He turned with a smile toward the women. "May I present my family. My lovely wife and our daughters: Vijaya, Sundha, and Kajri."

"A pleasure." Colin gave a generous, dimpled smile as we both nodded to each of the women in turn. Mrs. Guitnu was a handsome woman of diminutive height with dark features and black hair who, in spite of having borne three children, was very slight of frame. Yet it was the daughters who truly drew and held my attention. The eldest, Vijaya, looked to be just out of her teens. She was tall and lithe and the most beautiful shade of pale olive and had the finely chiseled features of a delicate work of art. The middle sister, Sundha, who I presumed to be no more than a year or two younger, was not graced with the fragile refinement of her older sibling but looked sturdier built, with plainer features, though she too shared the same flawless olive complexion. I decided Kajri was the youngest by three or four years, as her face still held the roundness of receding childhood, and while she was a darling girl, with bright features and a ready smile, was still more cherubic than polished.

Mr. Guitnu gestured us to sit and did so himself. "Now please tell us how we can help put an end to this terrible circumstance."

"I should first like to see where you store the jewelry. After that we shall need to meet the members of your household." He glanced at the three girls a moment and then looked back at Mr. Guitnu. "I'm afraid we will also need to speak with each of your daughters. Alone. I trust, under the circumstances, that will not cause offense?"

"That is out of the question," he answered at once.

"Oh, come now, Father." The youngest girl, Kajri, rolled her eyes. "Must you be so old-fashioned?"

"That is quite enough." He leveled a scowl in her direction.

"Forgive me," Colin spoke up again. "I am being thoughtless. Perhaps one of the women on your staff could remain in a far corner of the room?"

Mr. Guitnu frowned uncertainly before finally nodding his agreement. I noticed that he never once deigned to look at his wife. If she had any considerations on the matter he did not seem concerned in the least. "Let us show you what you have come to see then," he said.

Colin and I followed him back through the astonishing foyer and up the stairs to the second floor. He led us down a long hallway adorned with photographs of places in India, so it was hardly a surprise when Colin stopped in front of the picture of a massive Gothic building that looked at first like a structure in London, until the teeming throngs of people in traditional Indian dress became apparent at the bottom of the photo.

"Isn't that the Victoria Terminus in Bombay?" Colin asked.

"It is!" Mr. Guitnu grinned. "It is a marvel, is it not?!"

"They were still planning it when I left. Hadn't even broken ground yet." He studied it a moment more. "I must admit I prefer your country's more fluid architecture to this."

"Psssh." Mr. Guitnu dismissed this comment. "This is modern and strong. This is the coming century." He beamed proudly before turning and escorting us the rest of the way down the hall to a large bedroom. "Look for yourself," he invited with a coy smile. "Can you spy where we keep our sparkling treasures?"

I let my eyes rove about the room. Beside the bed stood a small table on either side with a crystal lamp atop each. Two large armoires straddled the doorway and there was a large standing mirror leaning against one wall. Two banquette seats were built into the square, floor-to-ceiling bay windows, and there was a small adjoining room off to one side within which I could see shelves of hatboxes, ladies' shoes, and endless women's clothing and linens. It seemed a veritable abundance of possibility, so it was with great interest that I watched Colin begin a slow rotation around the space, stomping on several floorboards near the walls and giving a cursory look into the side room before coming to a halt in front of the banquette farthest from the door.

"My guess is that you've either fitted a false bottom into one of your armoires, a costly and rather predictable choice, or one of these banquettes conceals a built-in safe. And if that is the case, then I choose the one farthest from the door."

"Why, Mr. Pendragon!" Mr. Guitnu's smile came easily again. "And I thought I was being so clever."

"You really mustn't judge your cleverness by Mr. Pendragon," I said.

Mr. Guitnu laughed. "Perhaps not, but he is most certainly correct. I thought it would provide us the best protection." He shook his head and walked over to Colin. "I never imagined a thief could come from within our own home."

He removed the thick seat cushion and lifted a tiny rectangle of wood in one corner. Within was a small lever that he twisted like a spigot, releasing a spring that popped the seat up about an inch. He swung it up toward the window, revealing the dial of a long, slim metal safe inside.

"Ingenious," Colin marveled.

"Yet not enough." Mr. Guitnu reached down and spun the dial quickly back and forth before pulling back the door to expose stacks of trays filled with loose gems and exquisite pieces of jewelry. "I thought I was a clever man, but now I see I am only a fool." He lifted several of the trays out, but as he reached in deeper it became obvious that the trays farther in were sparser in their bounty. "The thief is no fool. He takes only things from the bottom. Harder to notice. Items my wife seldom wears. But I noticed." He stood up and backed away from the safe to allow Colin to peer inside.

"Who knows the combination to this safe?" he asked as he ran his fingers along the door and locking mechanism.

"Only my wife and our eldest daughter, Vijaya."

"And who else knows about the safe?"

"All of our daughters. My valet, Damish, who met you at the door, and the girl who tends to the upstairs. No one else."

"You seem very certain," Colin prodded, "and yet someone is helping themselves to your hoard."

Mr. Guitnu's smile wilted. "And so he is." He took the trays and laid them back in the safe in the same order he had removed them before closing the lid and whirring the dial about haphazardly. Appearing satisfied, he pressed the wooden seat back down upon the top and set the heavy cushion back in place. "Shall we go back down so you can ask your questions and sort this matter? I cannot abide this scoundrel living under my roof one more night."

Colin's eyebrows arched up. "I'm honored by your faith in me but cannot promise a resolution in a single day. These types of crimes can be difficult and I do not want to accuse someone wrongly."

We made our way back to the sitting room and within half an hour Colin and I had questioned both the valet, Damish, and the upstairs housekeeper, a pretty freckled Irish girl named Molly. Both admitted knowledge of the safe and yet neither recollected having ever seen it open, a contention Mr. Guitnu and his wife ultimately verified. While Damish had proven to be collected and succinct in his demeanor, poor Molly had been nearly undone by nerves as her dark eyes darted about and her already-pale complexion grew almost transparent.

"That . . ." Colin said as she hastily made her way from the room, "is either the guiltiest woman I have ever confronted or the most timid."

A moment later the Guitnus' eldest daughter, Vijaya, came into the room followed by a plump older woman whom she introduced as Miss Thurman, the caretaker for her and her sisters. We all sat down, Miss Thurman relegated to a chair just inside the door, leaving quite a bit of space between her and the three of us.

"I hope," Colin spoke quietly, "that you will accord us nothing but the truth in spite of Miss Thurman's proximity."

Miss Guitnu looked over and twisted her graceful features into a sour glare. "Yes." She turned back to us. "I am already twenty and hardly need a caretaker any longer."

"A father's desire for propriety can hardly be undervalued," Colin said with a smile as he fished out a crown and began shifting it smoothly between his fingers.

She flashed something of a labored grin, her dark eyes sparkling fiercely. "I find it stifling."

"I should think you're supposed to." He winked. "So tell me, what do you make of this business with the missing jewelry?"

She heaved a ready sigh. "I don't know. I wonder if they're not simply mistaken."

"Do you suppose?"

She scowled at Colin. "It's perfectly conceivable. They just throw things in there. I don't know how they could possibly know what they have."

"Does your father keep an inventory?"

"Has he told you he does?"

The coin skating between Colin's fingers hesitated slightly as he looked at her. "I haven't asked him."

She waved him off. "I should think you'll find that he doesn't. I don't even think he knows what's really gone. After all, only my parents and I know the combination and I certainly haven't given it to anyone."

"Then if things truly are missing," Colin muttered as though deep in thought, "are you saying I have no further to look than you and your mother?"

"What?!" Vijaya's spine went rigid as her black eyes bore into him. "Do you mean to accuse me?"

"I mean only to understand what you make of all of this."

"What is there to think?" she said blithely. "How would I know if someone is pilfering from their safe? I've only opened it once or twice. If I want something I ask for it. I've no need to rifle through their things."

"Does anyone amongst the household staff give you pause?"

She pursed her thin, dainty lips and turned toward the fireplace, whether considering an answer or lost in thought I could not say, but it took several minutes before she finally spoke up.

"I don't know these people any more than they know me. I couldn't even tell you Miss Thurman's given name and I've known her all of my life." She flipped her gaze back to Colin. "What gives me pause, Mr. Pendragon, is my father's ability to find a crime where one might not even have been committed."

A slow smile spread across Colin's face as he slid the crown he'd been tossing back into his pocket. "I appreciate your time, Miss Guitnu. Perhaps you wouldn't mind sending in one of your sisters?"

"As you wish." She stood up and swept from the room without another word, leaving Miss Thurman to remain settled in her seat by the door. In spite of Miss Guitnu's having been perfectly content to speak candidly in front of her caretaker, I found that I could not, as did Colin, so we remained silent until the middle daughter, Sundha, wandered in.

"Mr. Pendragon . . . Mr. Pruitt . . ." She nodded as she took the same seat her sister had just vacated, moving hesitantly and without the subtle elegance of her sister.

"Miss Guitnu." Colin smiled.

"Please," she said, a tight, fragile smile ghosting across her lips, "call me Sunny. Everyone does."

The incongruity of her nickname from the somber girl before us struck me at once. Though she shared the same dark eyes and long, black hair of her sister Vijaya, Sunny's features were not as finely chiseled, giving her a softness that her older sister did not possess. And I suspected, given the reticence in her movements and manner as compared to Vijaya, that she was aware of that fact as well. I was also fairly certain she was the quietest of the three girls, sharing neither her older sister's confidence nor young Kajri's girlish charm.

"I trust," Colin began just as he had before, "that Miss Thurman's presence will not keep you from speaking freely."

"No," she answered at once, her eyes flicking down to where her fingers fidgeted in her lap. "I trust Miss Thurman with my life."

I snuck a glance in Miss Thurman's direction, but if she heard what Sunny had said, she showed no reaction whatsoever.

"May I presume, then, that you would not suspect her of the thefts your father has brought us in to investigate?"

"Never."

"Might there be someone you *do* suspect?"

She shook her head slightly. "I don't know. No one has access to their safe. I've never even seen inside it myself."

"Your sister Vijaya admits to having the combination."

"My parents have no son and Vijaya is the eldest. Of course she would know such a thing."

"Yes." Colin smiled deferentially. "Might there be some reason your sister would have removed items?"

"I don't think so," she said, her eyes flicking back down to her hands.

"And what about your younger sister?"

"Ka?!" She glanced up at Colin with the hint of a scowl. "She's only fourteen. She's just a girl."

"And so she is," Colin demurred yet again. "Do you think it possible your father could be mistaken about the thefts?"

Sunny looked at him a moment, as though the idea were trying to take form in her mind, before answering, "Perhaps . . ." with a distinct vagueness in her tone.

Colin gave an easy smile. "Very well then. Would you please find Kajri and ask her to spare us a moment of her time?"

She nodded, just as she had done upon entering, and was out the door like the ghost of a shadow. Miss Thurman still did not move from her position at the door, leaving the three of us sitting there, silent and awkward, avoiding even the most furtive eye contact until Kajri Guitnu suddenly came bounding into the room.

"Sunny says it's my turn for the inquisition." She giggled as she heaved the door shut with the heel of a shoe. "Am I a suspect? Are you going to search my room and rummage through my undergarments?" She plopped down in the chair across from us and smiled broadly, her round face alight with mischief.

"I should think not." Colin laughed with her. "We would only like to ask you a few questions. We shall leave your undergarments to a better suitor."

She clapped her hands with delight and howled laughter. "Well, all right then. What is it you wish to know?"

Colin gestured toward Miss Thurman. "I only ask that you not let Miss Thurman's presence keep you from telling us the truth."

She continued to laugh. *"Miss Thurman!"* she called out in full voice.

"Yes, Miss Kajri."

"If you listen to anything I tell these gentlemen then I shall never speak to you again."

"Yes, Miss Kajri," the woman answered without the slightest inflection.

"So what shall it be?" She turned back to Colin with her ever impish grin.

"Are you aware of the jewelry your father has reported stolen?"

"Aware? It's all my father has been talking about. He thunders around here cursing the staff for their thievery and malfeasance. Isn't that right, Miss Thurman?"

"Pardon, Miss Kajri?"

"Splendid." She grinned effusively as she looked back at Colin, her honey-brown eyes sparkling with amusement. "I think we've a fine staff."

"Then what do you make of your father's assertions?"

"It's making him potty to think that somebody has gotten into his safe. He believes himself so clever, but that hasn't worked out well for him at all." She did not try to control her giggling.

"Is it possible your sister might have revealed the combination to someone in the household?"

Kajri laughed as though the two of us were fools. "Vijaya?! She thinks she's the empress around here. Always walking around with her nose in the air. There's not even eighteen months between her and Sunny, but you'd think they were ten years apart.

Believe me, she won't whisper a hint to either one of us, so why would she tell one of them?"

"Of course." Colin nodded. "Then what do you make of the missing items? Who do *you* suppose might be culpable?"

She thought for a moment before her oval eyes came alive with merriment, her face a study of excitement as a huge smile lit up her already-beaming features. "My mother!" she squealed. "She's keeping a dashing expatriate holed up in the East End. He's young and poor and *madly* in love with her, and she's giving him just enough to keep him beholden until she tires of him," Kajri rattled off breathlessly. "Oh, isn't it romantic?!" She stared at us expectantly before suddenly bursting into a wave of giggles.

Colin raised an eyebrow as he clung to the spurious grin he had pasted to his face. "Do you suspect such a thing could be true?"

"Oh, never." She rolled her eyes as though it were the largest disappointment she'd yet had to face in her young life. "She dotes on my father as though he were quite without fault, which I can assure you he is *not*. When I get married someday my husband had better not expect any such thing. I'm going to be a modern woman, you know."

"I have no doubt of that." Colin snickered as he quickly drew the conversation to a close and asked Kajri to fetch her father. This time, when Kajri left, Miss Thurman thankfully went with her.

Mr. Guitnu returned at once and walked us back to the street, gently needling Colin to see if he had any immediate thoughts. Given what little I had perceived of our enquiries, I was quite surprised when Colin informed him that it would not take long to put an end to the mystery of his missing jewels.

Mr. Guitnu's eyes went wide just as I suppose mine must have. "Do you suspect someone already?" he asked.

Colin's face remained inscrutable. "We shall know more in a day or two. But in the meantime I would suggest you have a locksmith change the combination on your safe and tell no one." He gave a curt nod before stalking off to hail a passing cab.

As I climbed aboard, watching Mr. Guitnu shuffle back up his driveway like a man condemned, I finally had the chance to ask what Colin had managed to ascertain from such a worthless series of conversations.

"Young Kajri has put an idea into my head." He turned to me with a keen smile. "And you, my love, are just the one to prove it."

CHAPTER 7

——➤◦◄——

By the time the hansom cab returned us to our flat we found a young messenger huddled beneath the half-moon canopy over our front steps. While the sky had temporarily eased its incessant spattering, the chill of the wind had refused to relent in the least. The lad was wearing a regrettably thin coat pulled tightly around his scrawny shoulders and what was left of his scarf appeared to be doing its best to protect his face and neck. Which made me wonder just what sort of news he could possibly be clutching in the envelope in his hand. Why Mrs. Behmoth had left him to wait outside was no mystery to me.

Colin was the first to charge from the carriage while I paid the driver. "Young man," Colin blustered as he dashed to the door. "You should be warming yourself by the fire, not standing out in this mess."

"I don't think yer lady likes me," he muttered. "You Mr. Pendragon?"

"I am," he answered as he ushered the youth inside.

I rushed in after them, but before I could even get the door shut Mrs. Behmoth hollered from the kitchen, "Did ya see that scrubby little bit a shite outside?" She poked her head out the swinging door and caught sight of the three of us heading up the stairs. "Oh." She scowled. "I s'pose you'll be wantin' tea then."

She got no answer as Colin and I took the boy up and settled him before the fire. The tea followed promptly, without further comment from Mrs. Behmoth, and only after she had thundered back downstairs did Colin ask the boy for the letter he'd been so carefully guarding. "I was sent by a Miss Porter wot lives in a house in West Hampton. Real nice place. She gave me two crown ta make sure I give it ta no one but you."

"The Connicle residence," Colin mumbled as he slit the envelope open with the smaller of the hunting knives he kept on the mantel. His eyes were alight and there was no denying his enthusiasm. He pored over the note while the boy and I quietly sipped at our tea, though I admit I wished the boy had left so Colin would have read the letter aloud. My curiosity was threatening to get the best of me, and just as I thought I might be unable to contain it any longer, Colin finally set the letter on the table and smiled at the boy. "You have done a tremendous service for us, lad, and I'm wondering if you might be available for an additional moneymaking venture?"

The boy's hazel eyes blazed eagerly. "I'm yer man fer whatever ya need."

I figured him for eleven or twelve, the same age I had been when I'd begun losing myself amongst the alleyways of the East End. Yet this boy had a fire in his eyes that I never possessed and I couldn't help admiring his confidence. "What's your name?" I asked.

He turned his gaze to me with a smile. "Paul. Like the cathedral."

"Ah . . ." Colin stood up and went to the bookshelves where we kept a handful of crowns in an old tea canister. "Your mother a religious woman?"

Paul gave him a vacant stare and I knew at once what his answer would be. "I ain't got a mum. Just me and me da. And he ain't around much, so I take care a meself." There was great pride in his voice as he spoke without the barest hint of self-pity.

Colin faltered slightly as he dove his hand into the canister and withdrew three crowns. "Well, neither Mr. Pruitt nor I have a mum, either, so I'd say that makes us all very much the same." He came back over and handed one of the crowns to the boy. "Here's what you've earned for bringing us that note." He held the other two aloft. "These can be earned for your further endeavors."

"Whatever ya need." The boy beamed.

"There are three young ladies living with their parents in Holland Park. I should like to know where they go when they leave the house and with whom they meet. And should the mother ever venture out on her own, I would ask the same thing of her. But they mustn't know you're following them."

"I'll be like a ghost," he fired back at once.

Colin laughed. "Perhaps you have a chap who could help you? It is four women after all."

"I got a mate. He ain't as good as me, but 'e'll do what I tell 'im."

"Very good." Colin handed over the second crown. "Come back at nightfall with your report and I shall have two more crowns for your friend and one more for you."

"We'll be 'ere." He leapt up. "Wot's the address?"

I jotted it on a slip of paper while Colin went over to the hall tree and pulled off his black cashmere scarf, tossing it at Paul. "Take this and give me your old scarf, and you'll take one more thing." Colin disappeared down the hall a moment before striding back with one of his old coats flung over his arm. "This will be a bit big for you, but it'll keep you warm if you put it over what you're already wearing." He snatched Paul's old threadbare scarf and flung it into the fireplace. "You'll not be cold on our watch." He smiled at the bright-eyed boy. "Now get out to Holland Park," Colin said as he handed young Paul the slip of paper I'd filled out.

"Yes, sir!" The boy was practically aglow as he turned and bolted down the stairs, the front door slamming in his wake.

CHAPTER 8

As we neared the West Hampton residence of Mrs. Connicle I handed the note back to Colin that had brought young Paul to our doorstep. Mrs. Connicle's tight, tiny, haphazardly slanted writing looked like the work of a feeble mind, scribbled with less care and attention than what I imagined Paul could have produced. It portended the frame of mind we were likely to find her in.

"What do you make of it?" Colin asked as he stuffed it back into his coat pocket while keeping a crown absently swirling between his fingers.

"She sounds quite undone," I answered with a sigh. "Not that I blame her. I understand her fears for the safety of herself and her staff. But demanding our immediate return?" I shook my head. "We were just there a few hours ago. If she thinks us her bodyguards—"

"Perhaps she has a suspicion." He eyed me keenly. "To have awakened this morning and learned that both her husband and groundskeeper are dead. . . ." He slipped the crown back into his pocket as the cab pulled under the portico. "It may well have spurred her to considerable thought."

"How could it not?" I said as I handed the fare to the driver and Colin and I climbed out. "Nevertheless, I worry what her expectation of us might be."

"Her expectation . . . ?!" He looked at me as though my sense had fluttered off with the late morning winds. "Her expectation is that we will solve these murders at once," he said as he rattled the great ringed door knocker.

I was scowling at the obviousness of his words as the door was hauled open by Miss Porter. She still looked quite scattered and worn. "Mr. Pendragon . . . Mr. Pruitt . . . thank heavens you have come." She sounded breathless as she quickly motioned us inside. "Mrs. Connicle is not well . . . not well at all. . . ."

She revealed nothing more as she led us to the rear of the house, where a vast sunroom that stretched almost the length of the structure looked out onto the back of the property. Replete with twisted bamboo furniture topped by overstuffed cushions in a bright palm leaf pattern, several large jute rugs, and enough towering potted ferns to affect the out-of-doors inside, the space struck me as quite charming. With the day's burgeoning sunlight beginning to stream in through the walls of glass, it was hard to believe that anything untoward could have touched this home.

Miss Porter gestured us to seats, and only after I had settled into one of them did I realize that Mrs. Connicle was huddled on the nearby settee beneath a thick blanket, nothing more than her ashen face visible from within its enfolding embrace. "You will forgive me," she murmured in a barely audible voice, "if I do not rise to greet you."

"I wouldn't hear of it," Colin soothed.

"I have tea prepared," Miss Porter announced. And true to her words she returned with a tea service and plate of ginger biscuits before we could even commence to speaking.

The three of us stayed silent until well after Miss Porter had left again. I was beginning to wonder if Mrs. Connicle only wanted our company, so I could not stop myself from finally saying, "We are terribly sorry for your losses."

"Yes," she answered with an odd bluntness.

"We will see to it that justice is brought to bear for both your husband and your groundskeeper without delay," Colin assured her.

"Of course," she muttered, her gaze fixed somewhere out the window along the rolling expanse of her back lawn with the same rigidity that seemed to be holding her slight, drawn figure upright.

"You summoned us here to give us news?" Colin spoke gently, clearly also aware of the brittleness of our hostess.

"Yes," she answered again in that vague, hollow tone. "An inspector came and arrested Alexa several hours ago. She has been charged with the murder of Edmond." Her eyes shot down to her lap as tears began to streak across her face, making her look even more sorrowful, as she did not move to wipe them away. "He said there could be more charges once they have completed the autopsy on Albert."

"And what do you think?"

"I don't know anymore. . . ."

"Do you have any reason to believe Alexa would do such a thing?"

"I do not," she answered immediately but without conviction, her voice barely above a whisper. "I don't know what to think." She drew even farther into the couch as she finally wiped at her eyes. "You see, Mr. Pendragon, I am not a woman of great reserves of strength. In fact, I spent some time in hospital some years back." Her eyes grazed across our faces, revealing a vast pain that made it clear she was willing herself to continue. Neither of us breathed a word that her driver had already confessed as much to us. "I am visited by spells that leave me . . ." Her voice cracked. ". . . unwell."

"Spells?" Colin repeated, and I could not help but cringe.

"I am sometimes nettled by thoughts . . . voices . . . they pick at the very fabric of my mind. So I am not the one to ask about reason and belief." Her words so startled me that I could not move as she began to weep again, leaving Colin to finally lean forward and hand her a handkerchief. "If you think me mad," she managed to say, "you are not the first."

"You have nothing to fear from us." Colin glanced over at me with a pointed look that made it clear what he meant for me to say.

"I have seen true madness, Mrs. Connicle," I began. "I can assure you that you display nothing of the same. You see, my mother was thusly plagued. I watched her struggle with things no one else could hear or understand. It was"—my own thoughts quite suddenly seized as though I were a nine-year-old boy once again—"difficult," I finally managed.

"Then you understand," she muttered thickly as she dabbed at her eyes. "And how has your poor mother fared?"

Her question hung in the air as I tried to think how to answer, for I dared not admit the truth to this sad, broken woman.

"She found her peace," Colin thankfully spoke up. "And I should very much like to hear what you think about every facet of what has happened. Now tell me about Alexa."

"She has always been proper," she answered vaguely as she handed Colin's handkerchief back to him. "And Edmond rarely spoke with her anyway. What need did he have to converse with our scullery maid?"

"Indeed," Colin answered with a smile, but I could see that his thoughts were already leading him elsewhere. "And Albert? Did you have any sense of the union between Albert and Alexa?"

Mrs. Connicle turned her eyes to Colin with confusion. "Why would I?" And then, without a note of warning, she flicked her eyes back to me and asked, "Did your mother take her own life, Mr. Pruitt?"

I felt myself physically cringe, though I do not believe she noticed me do so. My throat clutched and I feared how my voice would sound, so I did nothing more than nod once. My silence, I was certain, had been answer enough anyway. But I did not mention the lives of my father and infant sister that my mother had taken with her. Little Lily, barely past her eighth month when the end came, and yet she remains forever in my heart and conscience. Her beautiful round face and huge blue eyes, bluer than Colin's, bluer than the daytime sky when the sun is at its peak, with short, curling wisps of white-blond hair like fluff across the top of her sweet, soft head. She had been beautiful and innocent and I still could not justify how she could be lost when I had lived. Lived because of my cowardice.

"Of course," Mrs. Connicle said with harsh finality. "Of course." She turned away and stared out the large windows onto the expanse of her back property again.

I understood that she was lost to her own demons once more, and it made my heart sink even further. It was a look of untenable grief and anguish that I had seen on the face of my father too many times to ever forget. I had always thought him aloof and brusque—I knew he loved me, but I also knew that he carried the burden of a wife who was as fragile as gossamer. He needed me to be strong, to behave—and so he had told me as far back as I could remember. Yet in the end, when it had mattered the most, he had put himself in the path of my mother's final undoing. I have always wondered if he knew, if he realized what might happen that evening, if the years of torment had taken their final toll and he had shielded me as the last vestige of his own life. It is a thought that has haunted me ever since.

"I believe . . ." Colin suddenly spoke up, startling both me and Mrs. Connicle, ". . . that we have taken up enough of your time today." He stood up and gave an ill-fitted smile, aware, I was certain, of what I had been thinking.

"Where will you be going then?" Mrs. Connicle asked with little real interest.

"We shall spend some time walking your grounds and check in with your neighbors. Critical bits of information can come from anywhere."

"I see," she answered flatly. "The Astons are a fine family. They're blessed with seven children and their house is always filled with such joy. But the Huttons . . ." Her voice trailed off a moment as her eyes drifted toward the north. "They have had a difficult time. Their young boy, William, is not right." She looked back at us and I could see that her eyes were rimmed in red again. "Please, Mr. Pendragon, you must promise to come to me as soon as you know something. I cannot bear this for long. I simply cannot."

He nodded solemnly. "You have my word."

CHAPTER 9

We circumnavigated the Connicle property to little effect before finally cutting south and heading for the Astons' home. I don't know whether Colin purposefully chose to head to the Aston family first, but after the intensity of Mrs. Connicle's grief I know I was looking forward to a household filled with something closer to joy.

We turned off the road and began trudging up the gravel drive toward the stately three-story brick home when a pack of massive dogs suddenly came barreling toward us, barking and scrabbling, from around the far side of the house. "How magnificent!" Colin laughed as he held out his arms as though to hug the lot of them.

"They're bloody huge," I noted with much less fervor.

"They're Irish wolfhounds. They're supposed to be. But see how their tails wag?!"

Before they could reach us, an authoritative male voice blasted out a single command, to my immense relief. "Down!" And just like that the mighty beasts dropped mid-leap as a tall, slender, sandy-haired young man came jogging around the same corner they'd appeared from. "You must forgive them," he said with a laugh, "but they're quite incorrigible around visitors. I'm afraid they've no idea the sight they make bounding at people. I trust they haven't addled either of you?" His eyes shifted to me.

"Not in the least." Colin grinned happily. "Do let them up then."

The young man had a sharp nose, the smooth skin of late boyhood, and large brown eyes. I guessed him to be in his late teens and, given the impeccable manner of his dress, determined him to be one of the Aston progeny, assumably one of the older. He laughed at Colin's enthusiasm and gave a short whistle, and the three dogs instantly burst up and closed the remaining distance between us. I could not stop myself faltering back a half step as the hounds surrounded Colin, licking and nuzzling and welcoming him to their property. They seemed as pleased with him as he was with them, allowing me to get by with little more than a few cursory sniffs from the lot of them.

"I take it you've owned wolfhounds yourself?" the lad asked as he reached us, his face alight with a smile.

"Not yet." Colin tossed me a sly wink. "But I know them to be nothing less than big kids." He stuck out his hand. "I am Colin Pendragon and this is Ethan Pruitt."

"Phillip Aston," he replied, stabbing out his arm like a proper gentleman. "You cannot imagine the number of people reduced to hysteria at the sight of them." He laughed again as he scratched the head of the nearest one.

"No doubt," I answered, trying to sound cavalier but not even fooling myself.

"We have been hired by Mrs. Connicle to look into the deaths of her husband and groundskeeper," Colin said. "Might your parents be at home?"

"They are," Phillip answered, his face clouding. "I hadn't heard about their groundskeeper."

"He was found this morning. It is too soon to say much more." Colin flashed a stiff grin as he cuffed the hound closest to him.

"I saw Mr. Connicle just yesterday," Phillip said as he led us back toward the house, the hounds trailing eagerly in our wake.

"I go out riding first thing every morning to keep in shape because I'm hoping to get into Sandhurst in the fall."

"An admirable goal," Colin replied, eyeing the boy with renewed interest. "And where did you see Mr. Connicle?"

"I did more than see him," Phillip said as he swung the front door wide and bade us enter. "I spoke with him as well." He ushered us inside, skillfully managing to keep the dogs from entering behind us. "Susan . . ." he called to a young girl hopping down the main staircase. "Would you tell Father and Mum that we've company in the study. They work for Mrs. Connicle." The girl's face went flush as she abruptly turned and hurried back up the stairs.

We followed him through the elegant white foyer and down a hallway at the left side to a grand study near the back of the house. It was filled with books and held two large rolltop desks and a great rectangular table that I envied for all the paperwork that could be strewn across it. How easily I could organize my chronicles upon it. Two settees faced each other near the center of the room with four stout wing-backed chairs arranged around them. All faced a fireplace at the center of the outer wall that looked large enough for the girl we'd seen on the stairs to walk right beneath its mantel. Yet even with all these furnishings there was still plenty of space, keeping the room from feeling the least cramped.

"Tell me," Colin said casually as we took the seats Phillip had gestured us to. "What did you and Mr. Connicle speak about yesterday morning?"

"He wanted to warn me off."

"Warn you off?"

The boy gave a slight shrug. "He'd seen me riding along the ridgeline between his property and ours and came charging after me. It gave me something of a start."

"Did you see him often during your predawn rides?"

"Never. But I knew it was him right away. So I slowed down and let him catch up. I could see he wanted to speak with me."

"And what exactly did he warn you about?"

"He told me to keep away from their property. Said their man Albert was bringing supplies and equipment in to replace a good part of their fence. He didn't want me to get caught unawares in the darkness."

"And did you heed his advice?"

"Of course," Phillip said simply, with the grace of youth.

Colin's grin tightened ever so slightly. "How did he seem when you spoke with him? How were his spirits?"

Phillip's brow knit almost imperceptibly as he seemed to consider the question. "A bit agitated as I remember it. But then it seems understandable, given all the work he was talking about."

Colin nodded as though in agreement. Just at that moment a noise at the doorway caused us all to turn. "Father . . . Mother . . . !" Phillip called out as we all rose. "These men are working for Mrs. Connicle." He turned to us with a mortified expression. "I'm afraid I have forgotten your names. . . ." He let his voice trail off as his parents entered. His father was tall and slender, with the same sharp nose as his son, though his hair was black and he sported a full, bushy mustache. Phillip's mother stood nearly half her husband's height and had a thick figure and waves of auburn hair pinned up.

"Colin Pendragon," Mr. Aston filled in for his son. "I recognize you from the papers." He glanced at me. "And you must be Mr. Pruitt."

"Indeed I am." I smiled as we all sat down with the exception of Phillip.

"You will excuse me then. . . ." the young man said.

"Please have Bridget bring us some tea," his mother commanded.

Phillip gave her a ready smile. "Of course."

He had barely left the room before a lovely young maid with a great mane of sunny yellow hair brought us tea accompanied by a generous plate of shortbread, about half of which were partially covered in chocolate. Such an indulgence kept us all quiet for several minutes before Mr. Aston finally settled back in his chair and posed the inevitable question. "So how can we help you gentlemen with this awful Connicle business?"

"Not business, Hubert," his wife corrected at once. "The paper says it's murder."

"Yes, yes, of course. Poor Edmond."

"Poor Annabelle," she corrected again. "That poor woman has been through so much."

"Has she?" Colin asked with a casualness that, in spite of his best efforts, still sounded heavy-handed. "In what way?"

Her eyes shot over to her husband as she fussed with the folds of her dress. "She is a delicate woman, Mr. Pendragon, and has not always been well."

"Yes. She told us she spent time in hospital a few years back. . . ."

Once again Mrs. Aston flicked her eyes to her husband. "Go ahead, Genevieve." He released a begrudging sigh.

"It wasn't a hospital," she said in a near whisper, her pretty, round face marred by both regret and the weight of a secret needing to be told. "It was an asylum. It was Needham Hills."

"I see." Colin sipped at his tea, taking care not to glance in my direction so he did not see me wince. "Do you know why she was sent there?"

"Oh . . ." Mrs. Aston shook her head and glared at the floor. "It's all so awful."

"Don't trouble yourself," her husband said as he glanced at us. "Mrs. Connicle is unable to bear children. There was one, but it died the day of its birth and she would not willingly surrender it. Edmond had no choice. It was a tragedy. I don't believe she ever recovered from that."

"It about killed her," Mrs. Aston added, her voice catching with emotion. "A woman loses a piece of herself when she bears a stillborn. It happened to me once." She pressed her eyes shut as her husband leaned over and squeezed her arm. "When poor Annabelle came back from that terrible place I could see she was changed."

"I'm very sorry," Colin said. "And what of Mr. Connicle? How has he handled his wife's difficulties?"

"Edmond worried about her," Mr. Aston answered. "It took its toll on him." He shifted a quick glance to his wife before continuing. "And that wasn't his only burden with her."

"Oh, Hubert . . ." his wife protested.

"No." He waved her off. "They should know all of it. She thinks she hears things. Voices . . . sounds . . . I don't know what all. It's madness. The woman suffers from madness and Edmond stood it longer than I would have."

"*Hubert!*"

"No, Genevieve, I am stating a fact."

"What do you mean to imply?" Colin asked in a tone of indifference, though I could sense the pulse of his ratcheting thoughts by the clenching of his jaw.

"I should think I have made myself clear."

His wife stood up and brushed at her dress as though trying to sweep the thrust of our conversation away. "You will excuse me." She looked pained as she spoke. "Annabelle Connicle has suffered terribly and Edmond always stuck by her just as one would expect a husband to do. I have nothing more to add."

"Of course." Colin stood up and bowed his head slightly. "But may I trouble you with one last question?"

She looked leery as she nodded.

"Are you familiar with their scullery maid, Alexa?"

Her brow crinkled. "I know who she is. Why do you ask?"

"She was arrested this morning. The Yard believes her complicit in the murder of Mr. Connicle. I wondered if you had any impression of her?"

She flicked a quick scowl over to her husband and appeared to noticeably deflate. "I don't know anything about her. Now if you will excuse me." She did not wait for a response the second time but made a swift exit, swinging the study doors shut behind her.

"You must forgive my wife," Mr. Aston said as we all sat back down. "She does not approve of the ways of most men."

"There is often much to disapprove of." Colin chuckled as he returned to his tea. "May I presume your inference is that Mr. Connicle had taken a mistress or two over the years?"

"Well, of course he had. I think the world of his Annabelle, but the woman is damaged goods. He did everything right by her; she can have no complaints. But you cannot expect a man to be monastic in light of such frailties."

"Do you suppose his wife knew?"

He made a great effort of shrugging. "It's hard to say what that woman knows. At times she seems quite sharp, yet at other times it's as though she folds herself into a cocoon. I don't know how Edmond stood it."

"Did he confide in you?"

Mr. Aston laughed. "We are not gossiping women, Mr. Pendragon."

Colin gave a halfhearted smile as he shoved a hand into his pocket and pulled out a crown, swiftly shuffling it between his fingers. "Do you make anything of the arrest of Alexa?"

"Is that the African woman?"

"She is."

"Well . . ." He cleared his throat and chuckled slightly. "She is surely a comely woman and most certainly exotic."

"Are you saying she was his mistress?"

He shrugged. "How would I know such a thing?"

"What if I told you Alexa's husband was found dead this morning?"

"*What?!*" He bolted upright and glared at Colin. "That puts a spin on it all, doesn't it? Are all the men around that African wench being murdered?"

"I didn't say he had been killed," Colin corrected as he caught the spinning coin in the palm of his hand.

"No?" Mr. Aston reached for a shortbread and fussed with it a moment. "Well, I really don't know why he hired that couple in the first place. He knew nothing about them. They're uneducated barbarians hardly different than the beasts they used to dwell amongst." He stood up. "And now you must forgive me, as I have matters that need attending."

"Of course," Colin said. "We appreciate your time."

Mr. Aston nodded tightly as he scurried us back to the front door. "If there is anything further we can do . . ." he said flatly.

"Thank you." Colin flashed a mirthless grin. "I am sure we will be back."

Mr. Aston managed a smile, but I could see there was no pleasure behind his eyes.

CHAPTER 10

Arthur Hutton looked to have ten years on Colin, putting him in his late forties. He stood slightly taller than Colin, though not as tall as me, and had a broad, square face with thinning hair at the back of his head. He seemed agreeable enough, even if his greater years lent him a gravitas that could not be denied. Certainly he had allowed us to be invited into his home without prior notice and asked that his wife be summoned in spite of his contention that they had fairly little to do with their neighbors the Connicles.

"We'd run into them at the occasional social event, but I would hardly call them friends," he was telling us. "Mr. Connicle was a nice enough chap, but I always found his wife peculiar. She struck me as being a frail, rather morbid woman. I suppose that's understandable, given her inability to successfully bear children. That sort of thing does something to a woman. Unhinges them, I think. After all, if they can't fulfill their duty, what else is left for them?"

"I hear some of them have thoughts and ambitions," Colin parried back.

"That they do." Mr. Hutton smirked. "There's no telling the trouble we'll be in if anyone starts paying them heed."

"I should think great heed is paid our Victoria."

Mr. Hutton waved him off. "Now you're being obstinate. I know what I'm talking about." He leaned forward. "After my own wife bore me a damaged son it left her all at ends," he hissed. "And I would tell you she is no better for it these six years later." He sat back again, his face soured. "Thankfully my daughter was born first and is a jewel, but I shall never have a proper heir."

"Arthur . . . ?" A warm, honeyed female voice brought us to our feet. "Have you not sent for tea for our guests?"

"I have," he answered gruffly. "Gentlemen, my wife, Charlotte."

She stood tall and slender and had remarkable curves just where they belonged. Her hair was a true golden blond that looked like a puff of spun sugar atop her head. I guessed her age to be no more than my thirty-five years, given the luster of her skin, as pale and unblemished as Devonshire cream. All of which accentuated her exquisite cheekbones and delicate features set off by eyes every bit as sapphire blue as Colin's own.

"Mrs. Hutton." Colin nodded politely. "You must forgive our intrusion. We have been hired by Mrs. Connicle to investigate the murder of her husband."

"Investigate . . . ?" she repeated as she came into the room, settling in a chair near her husband. "I heard an arrest had been made?"

"An arrest *has* been made," Colin acknowledged. "They have taken the Connicles' scullery maid into custody. But an investigation is never concluded until the magistrate's gavel has made its final descent."

"Yes, of course. And how might we help you?"

"Your husband tells us the Connicles were little more than social acquaintances?"

"They were pleasant enough." She cast a glance toward the fireplace before looking back at Colin. "But in truth I found the wife rather morose and the husband"—she seemed to struggle for the right word before finally settling on—"boorish. I don't mean to speak ill of the man, but I found him overbearing and brusque with his wife. And she *is* such a frail thing."

"I think some men struggle with their rougher edges," her husband announced with an amused smile.

"Some men are nothing *but* rough edges," she shot back slyly, seeming to freeze the grin on her husband's face. "I realize he was a man of considerable wealth, but that does not excuse indecorous behavior."

We were interrupted by a young, redheaded woman rushing into the room balancing a tray of tea things, and it was obvious by the careless way she did so that this was not normally her task. "My apologies for the wait," she said in a soft Scottish burr, without making eye contact with either of the Huttons as she set the things on the table before them.

"That will be all," Mrs. Hutton answered crisply as she took over the task of preparing our tea.

"Janelle is our son's nurse," Mr. Hutton informed us. "Though we are forced to press her into other services from time to time." He shrugged. "Decent household staff is so difficult to come by anymore." He gave an odd chuckle as his wife doled out our teacups, the crease on her brow not escaping my notice.

"Were either of you aware that the Connicles were having work done to the fence separating your properties?" Colin asked, apparently oblivious to whatever had just transpired between the couple.

"That was my doing," Mrs. Hutton answered. "Our boy tends to wander if Janelle doesn't keep her eyes on him and I worried he might stumble through a breach in their fence. I understand there were many such breaches."

Colin nodded as he sipped at his tea. "Did you pay them a visit to discuss their repair of it?"

"I sent them a letter. I must admit to not being particularly comfortable in their company."

"Yes." Colin allowed a slight grin to stretch his lips. "You will be pleased to know that their groundskeeper, Albert, had begun work on it."

"I am certain Mrs. Connicle appreciated my concern."

"Were you familiar with their groundsman or his wife, Alexa?"

"Whyever would we be?" she asked, staring at Colin.

Colin's mirthless grin extended as he slid his eyes to her husband. "Did you, by any chance, happen to go riding along your property line before dawn yesterday morning, Mr. Hutton?"

The question brought immediate laughter from the man. "While there is much that demands my attention each day, Mr. Pendragon, I am rarely up to greet the dawn and was certainly not yesterday."

"Why would you be asking such a thing with an arrest already made?" Mrs. Hutton spoke up.

"We were told the Connicles' groundsman, Albert, may have seen a man riding along the ridge between your properties before Mr. Connicle was discovered to be missing. With Albert now deceased—"

"What?!" Mr. Hutton sat forward. "There's been another murder over there?"

"The Yard is calling it an accident at this point."

"Do you mean to say you harbor doubts about the Yard's conclusion?"

Colin set his teacup down and stood up. "When it comes to that lot I harbor doubts about their ability to saddle their horses in the morning."

"Mr. Pendragon . . ." Mr. Hutton also stood up, chuckling in spite of himself. "You jest at the expense of our police staff."

"I make no jest."

Mrs. Hutton's brow knit. "Then you believe that African woman to be innocent simply because you distrust Scotland Yard?"

Colin's lips pursed as he looked at her. "I do not mean to believe her guilty simply because she *is* African." He stuck his hand out to her husband. "We've taken enough of your time today."

"Very well, gentlemen. Let us know if we can provide any further assistance."

"I hope you don't mean to prolong this terrible affair." Mrs. Hutton glanced from Colin to me. "Mrs. Connicle hardly seems up to such political gamesmanship."

Colin's brow instantly collapsed, so I quickly muttered something offhanded and got him out of there before he could say anything regrettable. We had barely gotten off the porch before he growled, "How dare that woman presume that I would play games with the bloody Yard instead of solving these crimes!"

I chuckled. "She doesn't know you, Colin, and besides, her husband warned us that she's been at ends since the birth of their son."

Colin scoffed. "A woman like that was born at ends."

CHAPTER 11

———⟫•⟪———

Colin did not say a word as we pounded back to the Connicle estate, the scowl he'd adopted in the Huttons' home appearing to have permanently embedded itself on his face. I kept quiet even as we came to a halt beneath the tree from which Albert had supposedly fallen to his death. Colin took several steps to one side before abruptly kneeling down and pawing at the crushed grass. If he was looking for something, I couldn't imagine what it might be. Instead, I decided to busy myself studying the bark of the tree for signs that Albert had climbed it at all.

"Are you finding anything?" The sound of Colin's voice startled me after such a length of silence.

"No." I heaved a sigh. "Not even the scuff of a shoe. If he climbed this tree he did so with extraordinary skill."

"Preposterous," Colin sneered as he stood up and started stalking off toward the trees behind us, away from the house. "Denton Ross is a bloody, buggery fool, as is Varcoe if he believes the sod." And that was the last thing I heard Colin say before he plunged in among the trees.

I felt instant relief at being left alone for a minute. I couldn't be sure whether it was the case, the people, or the character of those people that had left Colin in such a mood. Whichever it was, I decided my time would be best spent trying to discern what Albert might or might not have done at this tree.

Releasing another sigh that surprised even me, I began to study that tree trunk as though it might contain veins of gold in amongst its crackled surface. I touched it, poked at it, and searched for signs of recent rupture or breakage before finally coming to the conclusion that there was only one way I could be *certain*. I was going to have to climb one of these old souls myself. I knew I could do it. I'd been quite the climber as a lad. And while I didn't have the musculature of Colin, I was still in shape.

I glanced around and spotted a large elm not twenty feet away that looked to be the ideal comparative. Its girth was nearly identical and its lowest branch appeared to be about the same height as the one Albert had supposedly fallen from. That meant I would need to hoist myself up about a dozen feet before I reached the nearest plateau.

An unbidden doubt curled around my brain as I studied the chosen tree a moment, trying to decide whether I had lost my good sense. Keener instincts swiftly kicked in, however, as I realized there would be little to gain if Colin returned and I was found standing idly by without having formed a compelling opinion. So without allowing a second thought I stripped off my jacket and laid it neatly away from the base of the tree.

From this relative distance I determined the smartest way to make my assault was with a running leap. For what I lacked in brute force I made up for in height. A running start and a jump would serve me well.

I sucked in a deep breath, took another half-dozen long strides backwards, and gave a quick scan behind me at the trees to ensure Colin would not suddenly reappear and scold me for being daft. There was no sign of him. Banishing all hesitation, I launched myself forward like some great vaulter at the Easling and Temple Academy Fitness Games, at which I never once participated. With singular concentration I hastily closed the gap, my eyes never once leaving the branch that was my goal. At just the right moment I hurled myself upward and stretched as far as my six-foot frame would allow, missing the blasted branch by an easy four feet. I slammed back to the earth entirely off balance and went skidding across the ground on my rump. *"Bloody hell..."* I cursed.

Stealing another furtive glance at the trees, I was grateful to still find no sign of Colin. I hurried back to my feet and reassembled my dignity, though the seat of my trousers would never be the same again. Nevertheless, I knew it was time for a more sensible approach. So I removed my shoes and set them carefully next to my jacket. If I killed myself in this endeavor it would be a wonder what anyone would make of my precise little arrangement of shed clothing.

More determined than ever, I approached the tree and reached high above my head, forcing my fingertips into tiny crannies in the craggy bark. Hugging the tree like the desperate man I was becoming, I clawed at the base of the trunk with my stocking feet feeling for any purchase I could gain. To my amazement, both feet found outcroppings of bark that allowed me to begin hoisting myself upward. With the tree slowly scraping along my chest and thighs, I was able to move my hands farther up and seize a new hold, scrabbling my unhappy feet along in spite of the shards of bark they persisted in raining down as they sought what purchase they could.

My movements were painstaking, and more than once I heard the muffled tear of fabric, but before I knew what was happening, as though in a dream, the branch I had been aiming for skinned the knuckles of my right hand. I struggled to hook an arm around it, my feet flailing absurdly beneath me, but I didn't care. I had an arm curled over the branch and was able to swing the other up to join it. After that it was almost easy to bring my legs up and hook them over the branch until I was hanging upside down like the inveterate tree sloth.

"What in the *hell* are you doing?"

I refused to answer Colin until I had righted myself, managing to foist myself into the sitting position I had been aiming for in the first place. "Proving a theory," I said with pique.

He shook his head with a smirk. "You're in the wrong tree."

"I know that!" I snapped.

"And what have you proven?"

"That Albert didn't climb that tree."

"And just how have you managed that?"

"Handily," I fired back. "For one thing, you will recall that Albert had shoes on. I can tell you that it was all I could do to get up here in stockings. It would have been impossible with leather soles on."

He gave a noncommittal shrug.

I could feel my cheeks burning with embarrassment and was glad I was so many feet over his head. "And if you look around the base of the tree," I continued defiantly, "you will find a veritable storm of broken bits of bark as a result of my scrambling up here. There is nothing of the kind beneath the tree he's supposed to have climbed."

"Suppose he was just better at it than you?" came Colin's infernal reply. I thought I heard a snicker as he moved over to the base of the actual tree. "You are right about the bark, though. And Denton Ross's autopsy should prove the rest." He looked over at me with a laugh. "I concede your point. Now come down here, as I've found something myself."

"You've found something?" I parroted, suddenly aware that I hadn't the slightest notion how to get down.

"Indeed," he muttered as he headed back toward the trees again. "Come and I'll show you."

He plunged into the brush without a backward glance as I stared down at the ground far below my dangling feet. What had I been thinking shimmying up here? I might have proven my point, but I looked about to lose the argument.

"*Ethan!*" he bellowed from somewhere out of sight.

"I'm coming!" I hollered back, leaning forward and wrapping

my arms around the branch before slowly easing my body out into the abyss. I loosened my grip until I was dangling precipitously, swinging uncontrollably back and forth with only blind terror as my companion. Unable to think of any better plan, I finally released my hold and hurtled back to the earth like a sack of rocks. It was only when my feet slammed into the ground that I remembered I wasn't wearing any shoes. My legs gave way without a thought, crumpling me all the way over until I was facedown in the dense grass. It tasted just as it smelled.

"Are you all right?" I pushed myself up to my knees to find Colin racing back toward me.

"I'm fine," I answered with far more humiliation than pain.

He knelt down beside me with a lopsided grin. "The side of your face . . ."

"What?"

He reached out and peeled away a small piece of bark that had embedded itself near my temple. "It's bleeding. . . ."

"I'm fine," I said again, batting his hand away.

He chuckled as he leaned forward and gave me a peck on the forehead. "Then come along, my foolish boy." He hopped up and headed back for the trees.

I wiped a small smear of blood from my head and glanced about to be certain no one had seen us before standing up, stabbing on my shoes, tossing my jacket over one arm, and hurrying after him. He led me through a copse of trees that opened onto a small field of knee-high brush ending at a narrow hillock. The same tall grass covered the mound save for a narrow swath that ran more than fifty yards downhill, ending in a stomped, circular plot that looked like a herd of deer or pack of wild dogs had spent the night there. "What do you make of that?" Colin asked.

"It looks like somebody rolled a log down the hill."

"Look closer," he said, nudging the small of my back.

This game was rapidly fraying my patience, as I did not relish being tested after having so valiantly unhinged myself with the elm tree. Nevertheless, I gamely moved forward until I came alongside the trampled path, and that's when I realized what I was looking at. "Albert . . ." I gasped.

"Precisely," Colin agreed, his tone dropping precipitously.

The imprint of a horse's hooves could be seen at the center of the flattened trail, yet there were no wheel ruts to suggest a carriage or wagon had been drawn behind. It looked very much like a log had been dragged except for the fact that there was no downed tree nearby or lying at the bottom of the hill. "You said you thought Albert had been dragged to his death. This would seem to suggest you were right."

"We should know soon. Assuming we get a look at his autopsy report and that Denton Ross doesn't misconstrue the damage to Albert's anterior as having been caused by the tree."

"That would be absurd." I shook my head. "Even for Denton."

"Well"—Colin nodded his chin toward me—"given your current state, I'd say there is considerable damage done in climbing a tree. . . ."

"What?" I looked down and noticed for the first time how badly I had scruffed my clothing, tearing my shirt and pants in several places. While I looked the worse for my endeavors, I knew it was nothing compared to what Denton must have seen when he had rolled Albert fully over. "You're not amusing."

"I am not trying to be," Colin said, stepping into the large patch just where the bent grass came to an abrupt halt. "Whoever did this dragged Albert along here before throwing him over the back of the horse and climbing up himself. See how the hoofprints deepen near the edge here?" I noticed not only the heavier markings but also a thin parting of the surrounding grass that revealed the direction the horse and its burden had traveled: back toward the trees we had just come from.

We crept back along the faint trail, Colin in the lead, taking care to step directly in the horse's tracks in order to keep the path as pristine as possible. I kept watch along our flank as we went, searching for any further signs of what had transpired here, and was rewarded after not more than two dozen steps by something so obvious I was surprised Colin had not seen it. "Colin." I pointed toward a small cluster of frothy gold grass off to our right side that was marred by small black blotches as though bearing the blight of some deathly fungus. "Look at those stains." It was all I needed to say.

"Blood," he murmured. "Almost certainly Albert's. He was attacked out here and dragged up that hillside, and then left for dead at the bottom of that tree to make it look as though he'd had an accident." Colin took off along the horse's trail, taking less care now, plunging through trees and undergrowth that led us, finally, back to the place where Albert's body had been found. "I'd wager Albert was tethered on the horse faceup so that when he was shoved off he would land facedown and the story of his death would seemingly tell itself."

"Then he must have seen something . . . someone . . . the morning Edmond Connicle was killed."

"Whatever it was, it cost him his life." Colin started kicking at the ground where Albert's body had lain, and just as he had done before, he suddenly dropped to his knees and began clawing at the earth like a feral dog.

"What are you looking for?"

"I don't know," he said with evident frustration. "I just thought . . ." but he let his voice trail off as he sat back on the bare earth, his hands and shirtsleeves thickly smudged with dirt. Even so, I knew he had been checking for fetishes. Yet this death was meant to seem an accident. There would be none here, and as Colin ran a hand through his flaxen hair, leaving a dirt streak down the middle like the reverse of a skunk, I knew he had accepted the same conclusion.

I turned my head to keep from snickering at the sight of him and as I did my eye caught the glint of something shiny just beyond where he sat. I stooped to pick it up, having to finger the earth slightly to loosen the object before finally extracting a small, gold man's pinky ring with the initial *H* on its face in tiny diamonds. "Maybe this is something?" I said as I passed it over to him.

"*H?* How many men have we met with the initial *H?*"

"Arthur Hutton and Hubert Aston," I answered at once.

"A seeming embarrassment of riches." He gave a smile as he stood up, looking almost as disheveled and grubby as I.

"I wonder who the lucky owner is?"

His smile turned rogue. "It should be easy enough to find out."

CHAPTER 12

By the time we let ourselves back into our flat I couldn't honestly say which of us looked the worse for wear. While my clothes were torn, abraded, and smudged in a fair many places, Colin looked as though he had been up to his knees and elbows in muck. Yet having all but confirmed Colin's supposition around Albert's death kept either of us from caring a whit about our appearance, even in light of the frown the cabdriver had leveled upon us.

"*Wot in the name a me cursed mother's ruddy arse did you two get into?!*" I hadn't even noticed the kitchen door swinging open before Mrs. Behmoth was standing in the hallway, hands on hips, glaring at us foully. "Ya look like a couple a poxy urchins. Ya ain't goin' upstairs like that."

Colin glanced at me, his eyes rolling. "Why don't you go draw us a bath."

I curled my nose up. "I'm not getting in a bath with you. You'll turn the water black."

"Do I really need ta 'ear this? Ain't there no end ta wot I put up with?" She scowled and shook her head. "Get upstairs and don't make a bloody mess."

Colin took two strides forward and bussed her cheek before she could recoil. "We'll be tidy."

"'E may be," she said, nodding toward me, "but I ain't never seen the day you was." She shook her head and tsked before bustling back into her kitchen.

I had not truly realized how done in I was until I was reclining in the tub, Colin slumped behind me with his chin resting atop my head. There was no doubt that I had wrenched several muscles during my foray into that wretched tree, but at least the outcome had been decisive. While we didn't have much to show for this case yet, we knew someone was working hard to cover their tracks.

"What do you make of Hubert Aston's assertion about Edmond Connicle having an affair?" I mumbled in spite of the lulling effect the hot water was having on my body and brain.

"Hmmm . . . ?" came Colin's lazy reply. "Oh . . . I'm sure it's true. Entitled men consider a mistress a right. I've little doubt that Mr. Aston is similarly engaged himself."

"And him with his fine, proper wife," I scoffed. "Does he owe her nothing after she bore him seven perfect progeny?"

Colin laughed. "Don't be balmy. She's living in grand style and wants for nothing. By now she'd probably rather watch snails race than shag him anyway." He slid his hands beneath the water with a snicker. "Unlike me."

"Fancy him, do you?" I teased.

He responded by pelting me with a faceful of water. "You're vile!" he growled.

I burst out laughing just as a sudden pounding rattled the door. "When you two are done 'avin' yer jollies in the w.c.," Mrs. Behmoth barked, "that scruffy lad is 'ere! Says ya owe 'im a crown for spyin' on people 'alf the day."

"It's Paul!" Colin bolted upright. "He'll have news about the Guitnu girls. We'll be right out," Colin called. "Settle him in the study."

"If ya insist, but I ain't entertainin' the little shite."

"We'll be right out!" Colin blasted back as I tugged the drain plug out and he grabbed for the towels. "Bring him up and fetch some tea."

I heard her mutter something as she ambled off, but neither of us paid her any mind as we dried off and quickly dressed in clean clothes. In a matter of minutes we were back in the study before a roaring fire, tea and biscuits served, settled into our usual chairs across from the settee where Mrs. Behmoth had directed Paul.

"I see you're a man who takes his responsibilities seriously," Colin remarked with the hint of a grin. "I knew I was right about you."

"Yes, sir." Paul beamed with pride. "'At's why ya won't catch me pickin' pockets on the street."

"I'm sure a conscientious young man like you is far too clever to get caught," I agreed, letting him know he didn't fool me.

"'At's right." He puffed out his chest before the true meaning of my words sank in. *"No!"* he snapped far too harshly.

"Never mind." Colin waved him off and tossed me a scowl. "What I'd like to know is what you observed this afternoon at the Guitnu residence."

"I seen plenty," he said, his voice immediately charged with excitement again. "I got one a me blokes ta help and it were a good thing I did too 'cause we had ta split up fer part a the day." His face was aglow with fervor, much like a carriage salesman hawking the latest model as though there truly were nothing else like it. "I promised 'im two crowns like ya said I could."

"Excellent." Colin smiled as he dug three crowns out of his pocket and poured them enticingly from hand to hand. "So what did you boys see?"

"We seen one a them girls go out with 'er father. Me chum followed 'em and said they went ta a jewelry shop and set about workin' there." He shrugged. "Didn't seem there were nothin' else ta see, so 'e came back. I followed an ol' woman who must a been the cook, 'cause she went to the market and bought all sorts a food. She were real stingy too, yellin' 'bout the prices and puttin' as much back as she bought."

"I'm sure you're right. And was there anything else?" Colin asked, a note of disappointment creeping into his voice.

"I followed another a them girls off ta school," he said as he snatched up several biscuits. "She walked part a the way and then a cab stopped without 'er even askin' and took 'er the rest a the way."

"She didn't hail it? You're certain?"

"I know what I saw! She were just walkin' down the street and it pulled right up beside 'er and she climbed in like she owned it."

"Was anyone else in it?"

He shook his head and popped a biscuit into his mouth. "Not that I saw."

"How about when it got to the school? Did anyone get out with her?"

He shook his head. "Just 'er."

"Which daughter was that?"

He shrugged, a peppering of crumbs drifting down to his lap.

"Did she look older or younger than the one who went to the shop?"

He seemed to think about it a minute before finally saying, "I dunno."

"Fine." Colin exhaled, giving a broad smile to the lad anyway. "And was there anything else?"

"Some man brought a delivery of bread and another milk and eggs."

"Was either let into the house?"

"Nah."

"Did anyone from the house give either man anything? Anything at all?"

The boy screwed up his face as though with great thought, casting his eyes to the windows a moment. But all that came of it was another "Nah."

Colin stood up and finally passed the three crowns to Paul. "You've done us a fine service today," he said. "Here's a crown for you and two for your mate, just as promised." I fought the scowl trying to crease my forehead at the cost of this scant information, so was even more chagrined when Colin added, "And might we impose upon you for a bit more of your time tomorrow? Mr. Pruitt will need to know which daughter went where, so he'll meet you at the house tomorrow morning. Shall we say for another couple of crowns . . . ?"

"Blimey!"

"What time did the girl leave for the shop with her father?"

" 'Bout ten, I guess."

"And the young lady to school?"

" 'Bout eleven."

"All right. Then if you'll watch the house through the morning, Mr. Pruitt will meet you there shortly before eleven."

"I'll be there." He jingled the coins with a toothy grin before bounding down the stairs and out the door.

Colin stalked over to the window and peered through the drapes. "I hope you don't mind me volunteering you for duty tomorrow."

"You know I don't. But what is it I'm supposed to do?"

"First you must stop by the Connicles' to speak with their driver, Rudolph."

"Randolph."

He waved me off. "Whichever. If anyone might know about Edmond Connicle's infidelity, it would be he. I'm most interested to see if he suggests any such link between Mr. Connicle and their scullery maid, Alexa. Then go see which Guitnu daughter is getting into unbidden cabs on the street."

"And what will you be doing?"

"Our Paul is turning out to be quite the entrepreneur." Colin chuckled as he came away from the window and snatched up his dumbbells. "He only handed one crown over to his mate. A crafty boy like that could well end up in Parliament one day." He hoisted the weights over his head and began pressing them up and down. "For my part, I shall find out whether Arthur Hutton or Hubert Aston has lost a pinky ring. Needless to say, I will be asking their wives or one of their children." He chuckled as he kept the weights moving effortlessly. "And then I'll head over to Columbia Financial Services, where Edmond Connicle was a founding partner. I shall see if I can ferret anything out about his indiscretions from one of his chums."

"So what are you thinking?"

"Perhaps he picked the wrong husband to cuckold. Or maybe his dalliance *was* taking place in his own home."

"You mean Alexa?"

He tossed me a pointed look as he kept the weights flying back and forth. "Alexa . . ." he muttered airily. "Or suppose his wife found out and her brittle mind snapped. . . ." He stopped himself and lowered the weights at once, staring at me. "I didn't mean . . ."

"No." I waved him off, stung by the inevitability of something I had not even considered myself. "You're right. We would be foolish not to consider it."

He set the weights down and came over, curling his arms around me. "We'll know more tomorrow," he said.

And I hoped we would, though I knew it would take time for the memory behind his words to let go of me again.

CHAPTER 13

The Connicle household was in a state of near hysteria by the time I arrived there just after ten. It was all the more overwhelming in that I had slept little the night before, my brain unrelenting in its determination to painstakingly relive my mother's own devastating snap from reality. I could not recall a time when she had ever been truly right with the world around her. Even when I was a child I could remember my confusion when she would swing from great heights of joy to near-total catatonia within the matter of a day. It was painful to see, even as a boy. How well I still remembered the morning she and I had gone to Green Park. I couldn't have been more than five or six. We had romped in the too seldom seen sunshine, my mum chasing me about with peals of laughter, tickling me every time she caught up with me until my sides ached with pleasure.

We had turned to hide-and-seek at some point and I was sure I was well hidden in a nearby bush, so when she did not find me I was entirely proud of myself. I fled my hiding place and went to look for her and found her on a nearby park bench, her gaze fixed far into the distance in front of her, her posture as rigid as though she had been staked there. I had crawled up next to her and laid my head on her lap. She did not touch me or respond, but I had not expected her to. And that was where my father found us that night, well after darkness had fallen.

My mother had gone to Needham Hills for a while after that. Though it was the first time that place entered my life, it would not be the last. I thought she seemed better when she returned—more lively, more beautiful, more at peace. That's how I remember it. And sometimes she was. Sometimes she would read to me at night until I fell asleep, or she would walk me to and from school peppering me with questions about my day. But those things eventually gave way to more incendiary moods. She would not speak for days, oftentimes never leaving her room, or accusing me of watching her, or stealing from her, or trying to cause her harm, when I had done nothing of the kind and given her no reason to believe so.

All of which left me wondering how I had failed to conceive of the possibility that Mrs. Connicle might also lose the fragile bond that seemed to connect her to the world. Was she capable of murder? I had never conceived of the possibility in my own mother.

I had arrived at the Connicle estate with my thoughts in such dogged turmoil that I missed the significance of their carriage idling by the front door with no one around. A beautiful golden-maned horse was tethered to the coach, its breath coming hard and fast and its coat slick with perspiration. I saw it, but it made no impact on me. Instead I remained mired between my own disquieting memories and wondering how I would ever coerce Randolph to confide in me, so I was quite startled when Randolph himself opened the door. For an instant I even thought perhaps he knew I was there to speak with him. But my better senses quickly rallied, alerting me to the fact that something was dreadfully wrong.

By the time I stepped in, Miss Porter had come up behind Randolph and hastily bade me to follow her. When I didn't seem to be moving quickly enough, she seized my arm and hurried me along the hallway to the library. The moment I crossed the threshold I spotted Mrs. Connicle balled up on the couch. She was whimpering like an injured animal and had a damp cloth spread across her forehead. Her face was so pale that her lips looked bluish and I could see at once that she was shaking ever so slightly. Mrs. Hollings was kneeling at Mrs. Connicle's side, dabbing at her cheeks with yet another wet cloth, and Letty hovered just behind, looking nearly as pale as Mrs. Connicle herself.

"Your mistress needs to be covered with a blanket at once," I said to young Letty as I dashed across the room. "And give her some air, ladies." They both moved back at once, allowing me to reach her side and get a proper look at her. I was pleased to note that while she was still weeping, her breathing was neither labored nor irregular, and as I knelt at her side and saw that her pupils were full and round I knew she had not succumbed to shock.

"Get back over to Dr. Renholme's, Letty," Miss Porter spoke up. "Find out what's keeping him."

"Right away," the girl answered, dipping her head and running out, all the while looking very much relieved to be doing so.

Miss Porter finally snatched a chenille throw off the back of a nearby chair and draped it gently over Mrs. Connicle. She stepped back and glanced at me, a well of pity evident in her gaze, before moving over to the fireplace, where she began to restoke the flames.

"Whatever has happened?" I asked as I came up beside her.

"She thinks she has seen a ghost," she mumbled under her breath.

"Do you betray me too?" Mrs. Connicle's frail voice drifted accusingly between choked sobs as her eyes pleaded with Miss Porter. "How can you?"

"Hush now, mum," Mrs. Hollings said as she crept forward, adjusting the compress still pressed to her mistress's forehead.

"It was no ghost," Mrs. Connicle managed in a voice faintly stronger. "I saw him, Mr. Pruitt. In Covington near the marketplace. It was he." Her face began to collapse as she started to whimper again. "I know it was he."

"Ssshhh, mum. Ya mustn't fret," Mrs. Hollings persisted.

"Who . . . ?" I asked foolishly.

Mrs. Connicle stared over at me, her face so drawn and

swollen she appeared to be succumbing to some disease. "Edmond!" she sobbed.

"You mustn't, Mrs. Connicle . . ." Miss Porter started to say as she began to move back to her mistress's side.

"*No!*" Mrs. Connicle howled, listing up and sending Mrs. Hollings tumbling backwards. "It was he. *It was Edmond!* Am I so broken that you find it easier to doubt me than believe me?" Neither of the women said a word nor so much as moved as Mrs. Connicle shifted her gaze back to me. "I tried to run after him, but there were too many people and he was so very far away. . . ." She sagged back against the couch, tears streaking down her cheeks as though driven by their own resolve. "And then he was gone. . . ."

"Now, now," Miss Porter muttered as she fussed the blanket back over Mrs. Connicle. "Sometimes we wish a thing so deeply that we can convince ourselves—" But she got no further, as Mrs. Connicle suddenly lunged at her, lashing out at her head and face with balled fists in a rain of fury.

"*You horrible woman,*" Annabelle Connicle shrieked. "*You horrible, hateful woman!*"

And then I was in motion, racing forward and pulling Miss Porter out of range. The poor young woman was shaking as I held her a moment, her eyes filled with shock and horror. "You mustn't think anything," I whispered to her. "These are extraordinary days." I glanced up to find Mrs. Hollings staring at us and gestured her over. "Take Miss Porter and get her some tea," I said to the older woman. "I shall stay here and tend to Mrs. Connicle." She nodded and dutifully led Miss Porter out of the room.

As the kitchen door swung closed behind the two women I quietly settled into a chair across from the couch Mrs. Connicle was huddled upon. She had curled back up beneath the blanket, her tiny form taking up no more than a small slice of a single cushion. She was still sobbing and I could tell by the movements of the blanket that she was shivering with either cold, grief, or both.

"I believe you, Mrs. Connicle," I said after a moment, holding my voice low and calm. "You know your husband better than anyone. How far away from him were you?" I knew it would be foolish to try to convince her of other than what she believed. All I could do was try to guide her to consider the improbability. How many times I had watched my father do the very same thing with my mother.

"I know what you mean to do, Mr. Pruitt," she answered at once. "I appreciate it. I do. But I know what I saw and it was neither an apparition nor an illusion. Believe what you will. I shall not be dissuaded otherwise."

"I wish to dissuade you of nothing," I said. "You are our client, Mrs. Connicle, and if you wish us to search the whole of Britain for your husband, then we shall do so."

She looked over at me, her eyes as hollow as her voice. "You told me once that you knew madness in your own family. So tell me . . . do you think me mad?"

CHAPTER 14

Randolph steered the Connicle carriage toward Holland Park with the assurance of a man who has been doing so for the whole of his life. He seemed relieved when I had asked him to ferry me back to the city, obviously as uncomfortable in the house as I felt. He also had no idea that I really just wanted an opportunity to ask him about Mr. Connicle's connubial wanderings, even after I shunned the interior of the carriage and climbed up beside him as though we were great old chums. The city's crystal-blue sky and warm, indifferent breeze did give me a compelling argument for my actions, but I was still glad to have him off his ease. I hoped it might give me an advantage in our discussion.

As the scenery slowly began to alter, large landed estates gradually giving way to abbreviated properties that in turn let on to homes of barely more than the land beneath them, I considered my words carefully. It was only as the Guitnu home drew closer that I decided to lead with the banal. "Do I remember correctly that you've been working with the Connicles since they married?"

My sterling conversation starter earned me a silent nod.

"It speaks well of them to have such loyalty from a man like you."

He tossed me a curious glance and I suspected he was wondering how I could possibly have any idea what kind of man he was. "I s'pose." He shrugged.

"It's such a shame how poor Mrs. Connicle suffers so. That must have been difficult for Mr. Connicle."

Randolph slid his eyes back to me for the whole of an instant but otherwise offered nothing else. I was clearly having no impact on him and all the while Holland Park was drawing inevitably closer.

"My mother suffered bouts of hysteria when I was a boy. Voices . . . Hallucinations . . . They caused my father an infinite sorrow."

"I'm sorry," he muttered.

"It was a long time ago," I said too glibly, and was rewarded with a fleeting stab of shame that I quickly tamped down. "My father would sometimes seek solace in the company of a diffident widow who lived near us. I believe she helped afford him the fortitude to remain by my mother's side during the worst times." The lie caught in my throat and I was forced to look away from Randolph to ensure my composure. "No one could fault Mr. Connicle"—I plunged ahead after sucking in a quick breath— "for having done the same."

Randolph kept his eyes focused straight ahead as he steered us down the Guitnus' street. I knew he had no reason to answer me and even less to betray the confidence of his employer. Even so, as he pulled the carriage to a smooth stop he spoke up. "I wouldn't know about that," he said.

I noticed my young accomplice down the path, half-hidden in a cluster of bushes, watching my arrival with a grand smile. "Thank you for bringing me." I looked back at Randolph, fighting to keep the disappointment from my face.

"Mr. Pruitt?" he said after I climbed down. "Ya ought not discount Mrs. Connicle too quick. I saw the man near Covington Market that got 'er all roused up. It did look like 'im. I'm just sayin' . . ." He stared off down the street. "Ya ought not discount 'er too quick."

CHAPTER 15

⸻◆⸻

Entrepreneurial Paul was clearly not pleased that I was almost an hour late in meeting him at the Guitnu home, or that I had ceased listening to him prattle on while I endeavored to procure us a cab. To be fair, I was still very much caught up on Randolph's parting words as I tried to determine precisely what it was he had wanted me to understand.

"*Mr. Pruitt!*" The exasperation in the lad's voice finally sliced through my preoccupation as I turned to find myself staring at a boyish scowl.

"What?" I barked back with a woeful lack of patience.

"Ya 'aven't been listenin' to a bloody word I been sayin'. Yer moonin' all over the place."

"I am *not* mooning," I corrected brusquely, further angering myself for treating this well-meaning boy thusly. "All right . . ." I took a breath and forced what I could of a smile to my face. "What were you saying?"

"The girl you was wantin' ta follow . . . ? She came out at eleven jest like yesterday, only you wasn't 'ere. So I tailed 'er back to 'er school like before, but this time she weren't picked up by no cab. I left me mate there and told 'im not ta lose 'er." He shook his head gravely. "But that were near an 'our ago. Where the 'ell were you?"

"I was *working* and got unavoidably delayed!" I groused sharply, and then made it worse by adding, "And may I remind you who is working for whom."

His eyebrows shot up and he dissolved into laughter. "I ain't workin' fer you. I'm workin' fer Mr. Pendelwagon. You can bugger off."

"It's Pendragon," I said with a scowl. "And must you talk like a guttersnipe?"

"Well, I weren't born with a silver spoon up me arse."

I shook my head. "Fine," I muttered, scolding myself for behaving so badly. "Do you suppose your chap has been able to keep an eye on the girl?"

He shrugged noncommittally and I decided I deserved that.

"You said she went back to her school?"

"Yup." He finally slid his gaze back to me and I could already see enthusiasm coloring his face again. "She went right to the library and that's where I left 'er. Tol' me chum not ta lose 'er. Maybe they'll still be there." He shrugged again. "We'll 'ave ta see."

A cab carried us the short distance to the school, where, upon our arrival at the grand library, Paul nearly dragged me to an end stack at the rear of the huge main floor where he had already spotted his mate. It was astonishing that I hadn't noticed the boy myself, given that he was as conspicuous as a fly in ointment. He was shorter than Paul, with black, wiry hair tucked haphazardly beneath a well-worn cap, and was wearing rumpled, ill-fitting clothing that looked old enough to have belonged to his grandfather. It seemed a veritable miracle that the Guitnu girl hadn't caught sight of this ragamuffin tailing her. I took it as an indication of her state of mind.

"You lads have done a fine job," I whispered as Paul and I sidled up to his friend. "But you'd best let me take it from here."

"You can take it anywhere ya want, but I'll have me crown first," Paul responded with an upturned palm.

"I thought ya said it were a farthing. . . ." His pal scowled.

"Hush up," Paul warned as he shook his empty hand at me.

I dug into my pocket and gave the boys a crown each, but not before asking Paul to wait for me outside. "There'll be a half crown in it for you," I added, and of course he agreed.

With the boys dispatched I turned my attentions to the person I had come here to see. I crept down the parallel aisle from where I knew the Guitnu girl to be, and as soon as I caught the sound of her sibilant whispering I stopped. Carefully tugging a book from the shelf, I peeked over the tops of several disparate volumes on the other side and spotted the Guitnus' middle daughter, Sunny. She was deep in conversation with a tall, skinny, red-haired young man with a complexion like parchment and a cabbie's coat and hat clutched in one hand. Her voice kept cracking and I could tell that she was choking back tears, but I could not decipher exactly what either of them was saying.

I was about to try moving closer when I saw Sunny suddenly reach out and drop something glittering into one of the young man's hands. He closed his fingers around it so quickly that I couldn't see exactly what it was, but I had no doubt that it was certainly some piece of jewelry. Then, just as suddenly, Sunny turned and raced away from the young man, her muffled sobs echoing through the otherwise silent space. Extortion, I realized. This pasty young pissant was up to some manner of extortion against poor Sunny, though what she could have done to elicit such a thing bewildered me. Before I could give it the faintest consideration, however, he abruptly turned and charged up the aisle after her. Without a second thought I launched after him, managing to collide with him as he came barreling out of his aisle and sending him sprawling to the floor.

"Pardon . . ." I sniffed as Sunny made good her getaway.

CHAPTER 16

"We are wasting away up here, Mrs. Behmoth. Any chance of getting some lunch before nightfall?" Colin's evident frustration had boiled beyond the point of civility the moment I told him about Randolph's illusory comment concerning Mrs. Connicle and what she may have seen near Covington Market.

"Ya ask me that way again and I'll bloody well toss this tray out the winda," came the hurtled reply.

"So you've got it on a tray then?" he snapped back, pounding away from the landing and dropping back to the floor to blast out several dozen more push-ups. He admitted to having been doing them since returning from the Hutton home, where Charlotte Hutton had readily acknowledged that her husband had indeed lost a pinky ring with a diamond *H* several weeks ago. Rather than being unnerved, however, Mr. Hutton had apparently dismissed the episode with a blistering glance at his wife. It had obviously annoyed Colin and I knew Mr. Hutton would likely come to regret that.

"We know Mrs. Connicle is prone to hysterics!" Colin groused with unreserved agitation as he bolted up from the floor the moment Mrs. Behmoth came into the room. "But to have her driver say such a thing makes me wonder if he's not trying to lead us astray. Or perhaps he has some motive in ensuring she believes such a thing could be true." He swept the tray of finger sandwiches, cut fruit, and tea from Mrs. Behmoth and set it skittering onto the table near me.

"Mind how ya treat the ruddy dishes," she griped, her meaty fists on her hips.

"I promise to get it all back to you in one piece," I said.

"See that ya do." She scowled at Colin before thundering back downstairs.

"I need to see Edmond Connicle's autopsy report," he grumbled, snatching up two of the sandwiches and downing them almost without chewing.

"You've got the magistrate's order," I reminded. "You can see whatever you wish."

"Yes, yes," he muttered absently as he handed me a napkin full of sandwiches. "We'll just have to go and visit that twit, Denton Ross. I despise him and his morgue." Colin turned and glared at me, and I knew what he was going to say next. "We'll go and get the report. Together. Maybe take another look at the remains. If our client is going to start seeing her husband's ghost then we've got to give her proof of his death."

"And what of Randolph?"

"What indeed . . ." Colin gave me a scowl and grabbed another sandwich and his tea as he stalked over to the fireplace. "I'll speak with him. I'll find out what the hell he's blathering on about. He's probably just gotten caught up in his mistress's hysteria. I hope so for his sake."

I nodded. The thought that Randolph might have some ulterior motive had not occurred to me. "And when do you intend for us to go to the morgue?"

"At once." He gulped down his tea and fairly slammed the cup onto the mantel.

The watercress sandwich I'd been chewing curdled in my mouth. I loathe the stench and sight of his morgue but have even less enthusiasm for Denton Ross himself. "I haven't even told you about Sunny Guitnu yet," I said, set on stalling him as long as I could.

"Let's be off." He tugged on his jacket. "You can tell me on the way."

As much as I wanted to protest, to find some way to delay the inevitable, I knew there was no sense in it. So, quicker than my heart was ready, we were in the back of a carriage heading to the drab, stone-block medical building that housed the County of London morgue in its bowels. I relayed everything I had seen of Sunny Guitnu, and just as I had suspected, the first thing Colin said was, "We must find this detestable young cabdriver."

I could not suppress a smile. "I thought you might be interested in him, so I gave your little underling an extra half crown to follow the young man when he left. See where he goes. Where he lives."

"Brilliant," he muttered as he gazed out at the soot-blackened buildings crowding past as we drew nearer to the morgue. I could see that he was deep in thought and wondered if he too was considering how unpleasant this was going to be. That Denton would most certainly do his utmost to try to find a way to thwart us.

I kept quiet until we had pushed our way through the double doors and, as always, the pungent scent of death struck us like a physical blow. It cloyed inside the nostrils with such intensity that it seemed every pore had to be absorbing the stink of it. My eyes stung and my tongue felt like it was swelling with the effort to keep my throat from becoming coated with it. I fought the urge to gag as I glanced at Colin and noticed that he had taken on a grayish cast himself. "I hate this place!" I growled.

"It serves a purpose," he bothered to reply before pounding the bell on the front countertop. That singular note, high-pitched and jarring, was enough to momentarily shift my brain from the distastefulness at hand. It would do no good for Denton to find us with our lips curled and eyes glazed.

A moment later a tall, painfully thin man with a heavily pocked, angular face shoved through the doors behind the counter and leveled a spare, disinterested look at us. He was wearing a leather apron atop a white smock that was splattered with all manner of unrecognizable effluvium. "What?" was all he said.

Colin gave a warm, easy smile. "I'm Colin Pendragon and this is—" But he got no further before the sour man interrupted him.

"I know who you are."

Colin's smile widened unnaturally. "Very well. Then I presume we can dispense with the frivolities and get right to the business at hand."

"What's going on, Mr. Armsted? Who is it?" Denton Ross's pinched, nasal voice drifted out from the back, setting my stomach on a round of dissent. Before his assistant could respond Denton pushed his way through the doors with his usual display of irritation. He too was wearing a gore-smeared leather apron over a long white smock, but he also had on gloves that were coated in a rust-colored ooze from the tips of his fingers to the middle of his wrists. "Oh." His lips curled. "You two."

"Well . . ." Colin glanced from the unmoving face of Mr. Armsted to the disapproving visage of Denton Ross. "Hardly the welcome we were hoping for."

"Whatever would make you think you'd be welcome?" Denton sneered.

Colin plastered on his smile again. "I would agree there is much mileage between us, the enchanting Mr. Armsted notwithstanding, but I thought perhaps it time for us to put such things in the past."

"Such things . . . ?" Denton seethed. "Is that how you characterize your treatment of me? Playing me for a fool and ridiculing my character?"

Colin seemed to ponder Denton's words a moment, though I doubted he did so in earnest. After all, we did still have the magistrate's order. "When I suggested you might be mistaken about the cause of death of the Connicles' groundsman," he said with much forced integrity, "I never meant to offer up any sort of ridicule—"

"A pox on you, Pendragon!" Denton roared. "You and your blasted Pruitt!"

"Now you see . . ." Colin maintained his dubious grin as he took a single step forward. "One moment you are lamenting your fine character and the next you're attacking the one person for whom I would gladly disembowel you."

Denton's bulbous eyes stretched the boundaries of their sockets even as Mr. Armsted feinted back slightly. *"Get out!"* Denton seethed. "Or I'll have the Yard toss your ass in jail again!"

"Really?" Colin scowled. "Can we not find some modicum of civility here?"

"Piss off."

"You know we have a magistrate's order." He turned to me. "Show it to him."

My heart seized as I stared back at Colin blankly. "I thought you had it."

Colin's lips pinched as he swung back on Denton. "You saw it at the Connicles' house yesterday. Don't be a ruddy ass."

Denton shrugged with a jackal's smile. "Did I? I'm sure I don't recall. You'd best toddle on home and fetch it." He glanced at the clock on the far end of the counter. "Of course we close at three. You'll likely have to come back tomorrow. Pity that."

"Bollocks!" Colin snarled. "Are you really going to be such a bloody tosser?"

"Oh." He gave a dry chuckle. "Quite."

Before I could think to raise my own protest, Colin turned on his heel and stormed from the room. Only then did I once more become aware of the cold, putrid air as I stared mutely across the counter at Denton Ross's ecstatic smirk.

CHAPTER 17

Paul's eyes were riveted on Colin's right hand as he carelessly spun a crown between his fingers. He was clearly deep in thought as he stared out the carriage window, his hand moving without the slightest hint of consciousness on his part, while Paul watched his movements as though they were an endlessly profound bit of magic. At first I figured the little urchin merely yearning for the coin, but then I noticed him trying to mimic Colin's actions with the half crown he'd just earned. It was a clever trick for a street lad to learn and I knew the rascal appreciated that fact as well.

"It isn't good to pick up bad habits," I admonished.

"What?" Colin turned back and stared idly at the two of us.

"Paul is studying how you flip that coin about."

He glanced down at his hand with a vacant look. "Oh." He shoved the crown back into his vest pocket. "Helps me think," he muttered as he set his gaze outside again. "I can teach you sometime if you'd like."

I was about to protest when Paul abruptly slammed the roof of the coach with his fist and announced that we had arrived. We had come all the way up to Lisson Grove, where one slim four-story tenement hugged the next and the only nod to there ever having been groves was the postage-stamp-sized bits of weed and dirt out front.

"You followed that young cabbie from Sundha Guitnu's school all the way up here?" Colin turned to Paul with a dubious gaze.

"'Oo?"

"The young lady at the library," I answered.

"Bloody well right," he said as he shoved the coin he'd earned up his left sleeve. "'At's why I were tellin' ya I oughta earn a shillin' or two more. Cost me a sack a change ta come all this way."

I tossed him a skeptical look. "I'll bet you stole your transportation on whichever back bumper suited the direction you needed to go."

Paul scowled at me even as Colin waved us both off. "Why don't we make sure this is the right place before you start bartering for more money."

"Oh, it's right as rhubarb," Paul said as he shoved past Colin to jump out of the carriage first. "Ya got nothin' ta worry 'bout."

Colin chuckled as he climbed out. "Right as rhubarb?"

Paul led us to a flat on the second floor near the back. The building was well cared for, if modest, and looked aged by some forty or fifty years. This cabdriver, whoever he was, obviously came from solid working-class stock.

Colin gave Paul another shilling before shooing him off, with the promise of further recompense if everything bore out as he'd said it would. As soon as the boy scampered away, Colin turned and knocked on the door. It took several moments for someone to answer, but as the door yawed open I saw at once that Paul had indeed earned his fee. Before us stood the same pasty, red-headed rogue with the long face and aquiline nose that I had seen extorting jewelry from Sunny Guitnu at the university library.

Colin slid his eyes to me and I gave the slightest nod. "Good afternoon," he said, offering a warm smile. "My name is Colin Pendragon and this is my associate, Ethan Pruitt. I'm a detective working on behalf of Mr. Prakhasa Guitnu regarding a most insidious theft—"

"Who?" The young man cut Colin off with a frown, though I could see that his fingers had tightened around the doorknob.

"He has a daughter named Sundha," Colin went on. "I understand you are acquainted with her?"

Before he could answer, a worn woman of middle years came up behind him, peeking over his shoulder at the two of us. "Who is it, Cillian?"

Colin's face lit up as he offered the woman his best dimpled smile. "Colin Pendragon and Ethan Pruitt at your service."

"*Colin Pendragon?!*" Her hand went up to her mouth as she gasped. "I know ya from the papers. I dun't believe it!" She elbowed poor Cillian aside as she swung the door wide. "Come in." She flushed as Colin and I crossed the threshold. "I jest dun't believe it. Wait'll me girls hear about this." Her smile looked about to rend her face as she waved us into the sparse but immaculate sitting room. "I never thought we'd have a famous man in our little flat." She turned back to Cillian, still hovering at the door. "Come away from there and fetch us some tea, boy. Where're your manners?"

"You mustn't fuss," Colin said as he took a seat across from the woman. "In truth, it's your Cillian we've come to see."

"Cillian?!" She shifted her eyes to him and her brow curled down. "Has he done somethin'? I'll clock his arse if he has. He knows better."

"Not at all." Colin gave an easy laugh that seemed to assuage her. "In fact, your boy's done a great turn on a small case we're involved with. You must be quite proud of him."

"Most days," she answered warily. "He is a good lad. Been helpin' provide for us since his da passed away when he were jest a tot." Her smile began to waver. "Is this anythin' I need ta be worried about?"

"Not in the least. But we would appreciate just a few minutes with your son alone. I'm sure you understand." He glanced at Cillian, who had still done little more than take a single step from the door, making me wonder if he was considering an attempt to flee.

"A course." She exhaled as she stood up. "Then I'll be the one ta fetch the tea. Ya make yerselves ta home. Dun't mind me." She scuttled out of the room but not before jerking her chin at her son in an obvious effort to get him into the room.

"Please don't trouble yourself," Colin called after her. "We won't take a moment more of your Cillian's time than we must." He glanced back at the young man and dropped his voice. "Will you *please* come in here and sit down."

"What's this about?" he shot back, his eyes darting nervously even as he finally came in to join us. "I don't know about any theft."

"You were seen by Mr. Pruitt this very day with Sundha Guitnu at the university library."

"So?"

Colin's eyebrows drifted up as he glanced at me. "Ah. A step in the right direction."

"You were arguing with her," I said. "And after a minute she paid you off with a piece of jewelry. Most certainly one of her father's pieces. That is called extortion."

Cillian's face went slack as he looked from me to Colin before leaning forward and rubbing a hand across his forehead. His fiery hair contrasted sharply with the waxen discomfort that had settled on his face, and suddenly I found myself feeling unaccountably sorry for him. "You have it all wrong," he muttered in a near whisper. "I love Sunny." He lifted his eyes back to us and I could see a kaleidoscope of pain, fear, and yearning in them. "I've asked her to marry me."

"Oh . . ." Colin said grimly as I felt my own heart sink, mortified that I had been so wrong about what I thought I had seen.

Cillian seemed unable to continue, so it was a great relief when his mother ambled back into the room with a tray. "Here you go, gentlemen." She smiled proudly as she placed the tray of tea and ginger biscuits on the table between us. "Take yer time. I'll be in me room should ya need anythin' else." Her eyes flicked to her son as she left, and I could see the concern in them.

"Your mother is a fine woman," Colin said as he picked up

his tea and sipped at it a moment. "Now tell us about you and Sundha."

"Sunny and I . . ." His words came uneasily, his eyes remaining fixed to the floor. "We are in love." He spoke with immense gravity as though determining the fate of the world, and in a way I suppose for him that was true. "It is the simple truth." He pulled an old, heavily creased piece of paper from his wallet and handed it over to Colin. *I love you forever, Cillian,* it said in a florid girl's handwriting, *come what may*. It was signed by Sunny.

"*Come what may,*" Colin read aloud. "I suppose that includes stealing from her father?"

"What does he care?" Cillian yanked the note back as though Colin's very breath might soil it. "He has plenty of money. Have you seen the way they live? And he's certain to disown Sunny when he finds out. So I'm saving him a costly dowry. He ought to thank me."

"I very much doubt he will see it that way."

Cillian spun on Colin with a savage glare. "And what do you know about any of it? A stodgy old sod like you hasn't any idea what it's like to be in love. To feel passion so intense it threatens to burn your very soul. I'll not live without Sunny and she feels the same about me."

Colin looked as stunned as I felt by the young man's sudden outburst. However, I was still surprised when all he said was, "Stodgy old sod?!"

The fire that flushed Cillian's cheeks dissipated as he stared at Colin, and it took only a moment more before he sagged back into his chair and dropped his gaze to the floor. "I *love* Sunny. I think about her all the time and am only happy, *truly* happy, when we're together. She's the first thought of my day and the last at night. If I can't be with her . . ." He let his voice trail off pitifully.

Colin heaved a sigh. "How old are you, Cillian?"

"What difference does it make?"

"Answer the question."

"Nineteen!" he snapped. "Responsible enough to be driving a cab for over a year now."

Colin smiled. "If only being married were like driving a cab."
Cillian's face went dark, but before he could say anything Colin's
hand came up to hold him off. "The point is . . ." Colin went on
in a calm, measured tone, "I did not fall in love until I was
twenty-four. Can you imagine? I was already resigned to spending the whole of my life alone. Then the most wondrous person
came back into my life and I thought I would lose my mind if we
could not be together. And there was much against us at first, but
I knew . . . we knew . . . there could be no other way for us. So
yes, even though you perceive me a stodgy old sod, I do understand the depths of what you feel. But I also know that love will
not provide you shelter, nor put food in your babies' mouths,
nor shield you from the stares and judgments of those who despise what they perceive you to be. So do not *ever* underestimate
the realities of the decision you are making. For yourself and for
Sundha.

"Ask yourself what will happen when your passions abate?
Or how she will feel when her family refuses to acknowledge
her? Or when your babies come and you live in a flat smaller
than the room Sundha now sleeps in?" He leaned forward. "But
most of all, how long do you think either of you will be able to
tolerate the glares of people who revile you simply because the
colors of your skin do not match? What do you imagine will
happen to all that love you're drowning in then?"

"What about that love of yours?" Cillian shot back defiantly.
"You said there was much against you at first, but neither of you
cared. Why should you be able to marry and fulfill your desires
when we should not?"

Colin kept his eyes locked on Cillian. "I am not married. My
decision to be with the person I love is fraught with risk every
day. But it is one we made together, knowing what the consequences were."

My heart froze as I watched Cillian's brow furrow, hoping
Colin's inference had been lost on him. "And so it is with us," he
finally announced with great surety. "Nothing you can say will
dissuade us."

"Very well." Colin leaned back with a tight smile. "You may

do as you wish, but you cannot start your lives together by having Sundha steal from her father."

"I am not having her do anything," Cillian insisted. "It was *her* idea."

"Whichever the case, the outcome remains the same."

"You think we are foolish and without a proper thought, but we have already considered everything you seek to frighten us with. Sunny knows I drive a cab just as she is aware that her father has more money than he can ever use. A third of which would be hers one day were she to accept his every dictate. So she is taking a small part of what already belongs to her to help us get a modest start. I don't see where that is so wrong."

"It is stealing," Colin answered plainly. "A third of the Guitnu estate belongs to Sundha only if her parents decide it is hers. It is not for her to take as she wishes. Especially when she knows with every certainty that she is defying their will. Tell me your mother didn't teach you that long before you knew anything about the unreasonableness of love."

Cillian's jaw set tight as he gazed off between us and I could tell he was struggling with how to respond.

"Does your mother know about you and Sundha?"

"I will tell her when everything is ready. She'll stay with us. Sunny and I have already decided it."

"I should think she will be greatly disappointed to hear what the two of you have done," Colin said.

"It's all very easy for you," Cillian responded with great defense. "You got what you wanted. Yet you would have me and Sunny turn away from each other to settle for a life of regret."

Colin shifted in his chair as he leaned toward Cillian again, his eyes holding the younger man's with an inescapable intensity. "Have I once told you to turn away from Sundha?"

Cillian blinked but did not respond. And even as I reconsidered Colin's many words of caution, I realized that he had not.

"I am only asking that you search your brimming heart and decide whether it is the young lady you truly love, or her father's sparkling gems?"

Cillian recoiled as though he'd been struck. "I love *her*," he seethed.

"Then you must return the jewelry. It does not belong to either of you. You and your mother appear to be surviving without such things. If you and Sundha love each other as much as you insist, then *that* must be the foundation for your lives together, not ill-gotten gains. Is it not enough that you're already taking one of the three most valuable things the Guitnus have to give? Is Sundha not worth more than all the rest of it?"

"But the things you said earlier . . ." He rubbed at his face and looked about to weep. "If those things come true . . ."

"There is no if," Colin said as he stood up. "They will happen and either they will make your union stronger or they will rend it. But you have already lost if you start with a legacy of malfeasance." He sighed and tossed me a glance as I got to my feet, my head and heart reeling. "You and Sundha have much to discuss, Cillian. I will give you three days to bring me your mutual decision, but know that I will *not* be hindered in the solution of this case. And do not seek to disappear before our next meeting as I shall have eager eyes on your every move until then." He flashed a tight grin and took a quick step back before abruptly stopping. "You spoke about regret," he added. "I would caution you to remember that it encompasses both ends of the spectrum. Regret for the choices you did not make, as well as for those that you did."

He nodded curtly, leaving Cillian looking quite feeble and done in as we headed for the door.

CHAPTER 18

Colin's steady breathing beside me should have lulled me to sleep hours before, and yet I remained wide awake. One of his legs was astride my hip and he had an arm flung across my chest, and all I could think was how fortunate I was and how very sad I felt for Sunny Guitnu and Cillian. It made me wonder where I might be had Colin and I not come together in spite of the law, convention, and, in my case, a self-imposed abuse driven by the opium that soothed my fears and ceased my doubts.

I had been aware of opium as a boy, but it wasn't until I was sent to Easling and Temple Academy that I had my first taste. It was a dare from an older boy, as such things so often are. But while he and his mates determined it great good sport to addle the minds of a few twelve-year-olds, I was delirious with relief at the anesthetizing of my every thought. Neither the spectre of my mother's broken mind nor my own growing sense that I was, in fact, somehow different from every other boy could hunt me under the gentle stroke of opium's comforting release.

How I would like to say that it was a slow and stealthy process, but I would be lying, for it was not. Within weeks I was stealing small amounts from classmates whenever I could, and long before that year was out I had become a regular in the East

End, prowling about like a spectral waif, picking pockets, begging, plying whatever trade I needed to get the one thing I valued more than any other: relief. Fleeting though it was—sporadic, destructive, debilitating—nothing mattered more.

By the time I was fifteen Maw Heikens had taken me into her club to watch over her girls and tend to chores. For this she had given me a tiny room in her cellar and enough food to keep me alive. Food had ceased being much of a concern for me anyway. By then I was spending far more time in her establishment than at Easling and Temple, but since my grandparents sent their generous payments to the school without fail, no one said a word. I was certain no one knew or cared, but I was mistaken. Colin had been there, always on the periphery, but there just the same. He was not of my league and I paid him little mind, but fate would not leave it be so. Or perhaps it was more than fate. I do not profess to know. But what I am certain of is that without Colin's interference there is little chance I would have survived very much longer.

The relentlessness of my thoughts finally drove me from our bed. I slipped on a nightshirt and crept downstairs to warm some cocoa for myself even though I knew I risked the wrath of Mrs. Behmoth if caught. With the stealth of a mouse I tiptoed into the kitchen and lit one of the lamps near the stove. I painstakingly lifted a small saucepan from the rack overhead, my bare feet masking my every footfall, and almost dropped it when there came a sudden pounding. My jaw unhinged, as I thought it impossible for Mrs. Behmoth to have heard me. It wasn't until the pounding came again, more pronounced than the first, that I realized it wasn't Mrs. Behmoth at all. Someone was at the front door.

"What the bloody 'ell . . ." I heard Mrs. Behmoth curse from her room.

"Don't trouble yourself," I called back as I hurried from the kitchen. "I've got it." And not a moment later I was pressed against the door asking who it was at this hour, though, in truth, I had no idea what the hour was.

"Pruitt . . ." I recognized the voice at once and knew that it could not possibly bode well. "Pruitt, I need to speak with you and Pendragon."

"Now?" I answered in lieu of a proper thought.

"I wouldn't be here if it wasn't critical," he hissed through the door, and there was something in his voice that made me pull it open even though I was wearing nothing but my flannel nightshirt, my hair wildly askew.

Inspector Varcoe stood there looking drawn and nervous, Sergeant Evans and another policeman off to one side behind him. "This is most unorthodox," I muttered needlessly.

"I know, I know . . ." Varcoe said, signaling his men to remain where they were before he stepped inside.

"Do you mean to leave them outside?"

"They're fine," he dismissed as he gazed up toward our study with a look of unmistakable trepidation.

I gave a meager shrug to the two men as I shut the door. "I s'pose you'll be wantin' some tea," I heard Mrs. Behmoth grumble from the darkness of the kitchen hallway, and immediately took her up on it.

"You'll need to give me a minute while I get Colin," I said as we trudged up the stairs.

"Fine, fine," Varcoe muttered vacantly.

I deposited him in the study, lit several lamps, and prodded a fire back to life before I went to wake Colin. He remained just as I had left him, so it took several minutes to get him roused and moving about. Before I headed back to the study I pulled on a robe and slippers, arriving just as Mrs. Behmoth was bringing up the tea.

"We got vermin in the kitchen." She glanced at me as she set the tray on the side table. "Lightin' lamps and throwin' pans on the floor." She handed the inspector a cup. "Guess I'll get me a couple a traps."

"That will be all," I answered without a trace of humor. "We will see you in the morning."

She was about to fire something back at me when Colin swept into the room, fully dressed, with his tawny hair immaculately slicked back. He looked like he had been lounging by the fire just waiting for this call. "Inspector..." Colin gave a warm smile as he sat down. "To what do we owe this pleasure?"

I thought surely Varcoe was going to sneer some answer back, but he did not. Instead he released a burdened sigh before setting his teacup back on the table and turning to the fireplace as though he might find some solace there. "It's this bloody Connicle case." His voice sounded thin and drained. "There's been another murder."

"What?" Colin bolted forward, slopping his tea. "Who?"

The inspector rubbed his forehead a moment and then turned his weary eyes to Colin. "Arthur Hutton. He's one of the Connicles' neighbors—"

"I know who he is," Colin interrupted, springing to his feet and stalking over to the fireplace. "I spoke with him just this afternoon."

"You did? Why?" Varcoe's curiosity arced in spite of his fatigue.

"Never mind that now." Colin waved him off. "What happened?"

I'd have wagered that Varcoe was going to censure Colin for his usual lack of diplomacy, but instead he ran a hand through his shock of white hair with a labored sigh before answering. "We found him about an hour ago on an overgrown trail that borders his property and the Connicles'. He was on the Connicles' side. That's when I knew—"

"How was he killed?" Colin cut Varcoe off again, shoving his teacup onto the mantel and picking up a small derringer that he began repeatedly clicking open and closed. "Was it the same as with Edmond Connicle?"

"It is," Varcoe answered rather pitifully. "Beaten and set afire."

"What in the *hell* is happening out there?!"

"My point exactly!" Varcoe said as he stood up, keeping his eyes affixed on Colin. "Which is why I'm here." He took a hesitant step toward the fireplace, the firelight catching his ashen face and making him look haggard and defeated. "We cannot have another serial killer," he moaned. "It cannot be. We're still taking heat off the damn Ripper case even though it's been almost eight years since they found the body of that blasted Mary Kelly." He rubbed his forehead and for a moment I thought he might be about to cry. "When the papers find out we've got three murders likely connected . . ." He shook his head and sagged. "We'll be crucified when they learn it's happening in West Hampton."

Colin glared at the inspector. "So you have finally given up the notion that the Connicles' groundsman fell to his death?"

The inspector looked crestfallen and worn as he nodded.

Still, it was not enough for Colin. "And are you concerned about the killings of these three men or just the reputation of your band of incompetents?" he pressed.

I could not help cringing.

"I worry about both," Varcoe answered in a small voice.

"And what is it you want from me?" Colin asked as he delicately set the derringer back on the mantel. It was the question I had been waiting for from the moment I'd found Varcoe on our doorstep.

I watched the inspector grip the back of the settee before he spoke, but when he did his voice was clear and firm. "I need your help. I need you to work with the Yard on this case. Help us to solve these murders at once."

"I thought you already had your suspect," Colin remarked without cheek. I credited it to the hour, which, when I finally glanced at the clock, was stunned to find gliding toward half past two.

Varcoe reddened slightly, apparently chagrined in spite of Colin's moderated temperament, and cast his eyes down. "We're still holding the African woman. We've had her in custody since we found her husband's body yesterday morning. She is obviously not the killer. But that doesn't mean she isn't still involved somehow. Perhaps the mastermind . . ." he muttered with a shade of his familiar defensiveness, though he let his voice trail off just the same.

Colin gave a shrug as he picked up his teacup and settled back into his chair. "Perhaps," he conceded, though without much conviction. "And just how is it you propose that I should"—he hesitated—"work with the Yard?"

"You will have full access"—Varcoe's face went hard as he perched back on the edge of the settee—"to *everything*."

"I've got a magistrate's order," Colin reminded. "I already have access."

"I'll see that you get full cooperation whenever and wherever. No waiting around while your court order wends its way down to the little pricks on the front line. *Nobody* will stand in your way."

"You're being very seductive." Colin gave a roguish grin.

"I mean to be."

"And if I deign to test your goodwill right now?"

"Try me."

Colin's grin blossomed. "I should like to see Arthur Hutton's body before anyone touches it."

"I assumed you would ask for that." Varcoe allowed his own sly grin. "He's right where I left him, waiting for you to have a look. I've even ordered the men to keep off the ground nearby so you can get a *real* look, a *proper* look, like you're always badgering about."

Colin chuckled. "Do I badger?" He set his tea down. "But what I'd really like . . . after I've inspected this murder scene . . . is to go to the morgue and view the files for both Edmond Connicle and Albert. And I should like to inspect Albert's remains as well."

"Anything at all!" The inspector leapt up as though loaded with a spring. "*Sergeant!*" he hollered down the stairs.

"Ya tryin' ta wake the bleedin' dead?!" Mrs. Behmoth yelled back.

"My apologies," Varcoe blustered as he quickly scrambled partway down the stairs. "*Evans!*" he called out in a hissed sort of bark, and I heard the front door immediately open in response. "Go find that pox, Denton Ross, and tell him to get over to the morgue at once and prepare the body of the African for Pendragon to view."

"Yes, sir," came the succinct reply. And as the inspector returned to the top of the stairs I heard the sound of a horse galloping away.

"Are you with us then?"

Colin gave a wary smile. "We are."

Varcoe's eyes slid over to me and he nodded his head. "Of course."

"You had best make yourself presentable," Colin said to me. "The inspector and I will meet you downstairs."

Knowing the two of them were waiting got me dressed and in the inspector's carriage with undue haste, surprising even myself. Though still a bit disheveled and certainly not as focused as I would have liked to have been, I seemed to be the exception among us. Colin looked keen and alert and, in spite of Varcoe's obvious fatigue, I couldn't deny a sharpness lurking behind his eyes. I marveled at the toll to his ego coming to us must have cost him. Greater still, I wondered if his détente would last.

Once we reached West Hampton we followed a slight curve in the main road before abruptly leaving the macadam for a dark, rutted path through the woods near the Connicle home. Almost at once I could see the glow of startlingly bright electric lights ahead. The deepest part of night appeared to be unveiling the very heart of day as we drew closer, bouncing and jostling along a trail that had clearly not been used in some time, given the brambles rubbing against the underbelly of the carriage. By the time we rounded the last curve and drew free of the trees I had to squint to keep from being momentarily blinded.

"It's just as we found it," Varcoe said as we came to a stop.

It was hard to believe, given the number of uniformed men milling about, stomping on potential clues that could lie anywhere within the broader radius. Only the ground nearest the remains was wholly undisturbed, a plot of some twelve feet square. It had been cordoned off with a rope tied around stakes at its four corners. Two officers were posted along alternate sides, which hardly seemed necessary, given that the blazing lights were concentrated on this specific area. If anyone had decided to step inside for a closer look, *everyone* would have noticed it.

"Let us see what we have then," Colin said as he stalked over to the roped area. He squinted up at the glaring lights a moment before stepping inside and painstakingly picking his way to where the body lay.

The phalanx of men drifting about the periphery began closing in on Colin until the inspector gruffly shooed them away with a barked, "This isn't a bloody sideshow!"

His troops dutifully faded back into the blackness, including the two who had been standing guard, leaving me and Varcoe alone on the outside. It was clear that neither of us wanted to be admonished by Colin for stepping inside unbidden, so we stood there agape, watching as he slowly crept toward the body. Once there, he knelt by the battered remains of Arthur Hutton. It was an awful sight and I had no desire to look any closer, though I could tell that Varcoe was almost beside himself with eagerness to cross the barrier.

"Ethan . . ." Colin muttered after a moment, and then turned and looked at the two of us. "You too, Emmett . . ." he added as the afterthought it was.

I stepped over the rope at the precise spot where Colin had entered, a function of habit rather than forethought, but Varcoe was not so well trained. He began to enter to my left, which immediately brought Colin to his feet. *"Not there!"* he protested. "I've not had a chance to look there yet." He forced a thin smile and gestured to where I stood. "If you wouldn't mind."

The incandescent lighting revealed the depth of Varcoe's minding, as he flushed a noticeable pink. Nevertheless, he kept silent as he quickly fell in behind me. The two of us stole forward, me following Colin's footprints and Varcoe following mine, until we finally reached the body of Arthur Hutton. It was indeed a horrible sight, made worse by the fact that unlike Edmond Connicle, this body was fully recognizable.

Hutton had been severely beaten, his face misshapen by swelling, abrasions, and discolorations across the cheeks, eyes, and nose. His left eye was swollen completely shut, with something red and viscous drooling out the far corner and down into his hairline. He was on his back, legs akimbo, and it was obvious that he had been neither attacked nor killed here but likely pushed from the back of a moving wagon or carriage, as there were no signs of a struggle. The only thing the killer had stopped to do here was set Hutton on fire. The stench of kerosene on his clothing stung the eyes, but even so, his body hadn't caught well. By the time the killer disappeared the struggling flames had likely vanquished themselves, leaving the remains of Arthur Hutton only partially blistered from the midsection down.

"Who found him?" Colin asked as he glanced over at the inspector.

"One of my men. Mrs. Hutton sent word just after eleven when his horse returned home without him. She said he'd gone into town, but with things the way they are . . ." He shook his head and stared down at the body. "I sent a dozen men out here to look around." He scoffed and looked away before adding, "Bloody hell."

"Commendable instincts," Colin said. "Your men may well have interrupted the killer, which would explain why this body was not fully burned, as was clearly intended."

"I was wondering the same thing."

Colin's eyes flew to Varcoe and I could see a whisper of distress flicker through them at the notion of him and Varcoe being in sync. "Yes," Colin allowed rather weakly. "And did any of your men mention hearing or seeing anything while rooting about out here?"

Varcoe straightened up quite suddenly, his color flushing as he turned and hollered, *"Lanchester, get over here!"*

The surly young constable who'd been at the Connicle house the first day came jogging toward us. I remembered him as being rigid and self-righteous and told myself it was only because he looked no more than a minute past his mid-twenties.

"Yes, sir," he said smartly, coming to a halt outside the demarcated area.

"When you and the others were searching the woods, did anyone hear or see anything unusual?"

"Unusual?" he repeated, as though the word had multiple meanings.

"Yes!" Varcoe waved at him impatiently. "Like a horse bolting, or a carriage receding, or a man screaming bloody damned murder!"

Whether he meant to or not, young Constable Lanchester took a half step backwards. "No, sir."

"That's right." Varcoe allowed the sheerest of grins to alight on his lips. "You'd have told me if anyone noticed anything, right?"

"Yes, sir."

"Fine." Varcoe waved him off as he turned back to Colin. "My men are highly trained."

"Of course," Colin mumbled blandly as he knelt back over the body, leaning low across Arthur Hutton's savaged face. "Do you have a pen?" Colin mumbled over his shoulder to me.

"Always."

He stuck his hand out without turning and I slipped it out of my pocket and into his palm. To my dismay he gently poked it about the cheeks and chin and then, quite suddenly, stabbed it into the mouth, using it to pry the tightened jaws apart. Two fingers went in next as he extracted a small cloth sack. "Fetishes," he announced, though I had already figured that out and assumed Varcoe had as well. He stood up and handed the pen back to me, which I clutched between two fingers before depositing it into my handkerchief. I would throw them both out later. "Have your men dig beneath the body once it's been removed and see if there are more buried beneath as with Edmond Connicle."

"Of course," Varcoe answered curtly. "I was going to do that."

"Yes." Colin flashed a distracted smile. "And have them notice how they're buried. Carefully? Or clumsily like the last time."

"Yes, yes!" Varcoe snapped, as though, once again, he had been planning that all along.

Colin kicked at the dirt and grass on the far side of the body a minute before abruptly stepping over the periphery rope and stalking back the way we had arrived. I gave Varcoe a quick shrug as I hurried after Colin, afraid that I might lose him in the absolute blackness beyond the blazing lights. The rigidity of his movements told me he was distracted and displeased, so I was relieved that Varcoe was too busy barking orders to follow me. Orders that had been supplied by Colin.

I drew alongside him just as he began to diverge from the rutted trail we'd entered upon and follow a perpendicular path that headed slightly away from where the body was. "Have you spotted something?" I asked.

"It's as black as the devil's ass," he complained. "I can't even see my own blasted nose."

I tagged along quietly while he continued on his apparently rudderless trajectory, each step taking us farther from the murder scene. If there was any sense to his course I couldn't see it, so when he suddenly drew up short I plowed ahead several steps before realizing that he was no longer beside me. "What is it?" I asked as I scurried back to him.

"This bollocky case isn't making any ruddy sense!" he snapped. "We are practically handed the Connicles' scullery maid as the perpetrator until you found that pinky ring near Albert's body. That was enticing. It seemed to propose an alternate possibility." He turned and glared at me. "You should have seen Arthur Hutton's face when his wife said it was his." Colin brought his fists to his eyebrows and swiped at them. "And now he's *dead?!* What the hell? *What the bloody hell?!*"

"We're fact-finding," I reminded him. "You're always telling me the beginning of a case is about nothing more than assembling the facts."

Even through the mantle of darkness I could see the incensed look distort his face. "Three men have been murdered in as many nights." He turned and plunged away through the scrubby brush. "If this is the beginning of the case we're in a load of shite."

I knew better than to push the point, so I followed along behind him and waited for his next outburst.

"There has *got* to be some detrimental connection between Edmond Connicle and Arthur Hutton," he seethed. "Maybe it has to do with that damn scullery maid. *I don't know*. But we *must* figure it out."

"And Albert?" I blurted without thinking.

"You're not helping, Ethan!" Colin growled. I cringed as Inspector Varcoe hollered Colin's name. "Come on," he muttered crossly as he started back toward the crime scene, "before I change my mind about working with this bugger."

CHAPTER 19

Inspector Varcoe's coach rumbled and rattled along the cobblestones as we headed for the morgue. Colin had gone silent, but I continuously caught the inspector shifting his gaze to him and knew it would only be a matter of time before Varcoe felt compelled to say something. That he was bewildered was as irrefutable as the fact that Colin was frustrated. I wanted to caution Varcoe to keep quiet, but even as I had the thought he spoke up. "What are you making of all this?" he asked, trying to sound offhanded as he glanced back outside and pretended to be watching the black woods jostling past.

"You have to release the Connicles' scullery maid," Colin answered in a calm, even tone.

"Alexa," I supplied for the both of them.

"What?" Varcoe craned around and gawked at us. "What does releasing that woman have to do with anything?"

"There could be value in having her followed," Colin pointed out, keeping his own gaze fixed outside the carriage. "Find out if she makes contact with anyone outside of the house. Either the woman is peripherally involved or else someone desperately wants us to believe that she is. Perhaps she knows who that might be."

"Of course," Varcoe dismissed as though, yet again, he had already had that very thought.

Both men fell silent and remained so until we arrived at the morgue. It wasn't actually until the three of us pushed our way through the double doors into the outer room, ripe with its stink of death, that our moody silence was abruptly broken.

"I will not have those two...*persons*..." Denton Ross erupted, saying the word as though it were a euphemism for vermin, "...in *my* morgue when I have been rousted down here in the middle of the night. I was told this was an emergency," he sneered. "Need I remind you that I deal with the dead? *The dead!* There *are* no emergencies when it comes to the dead because they're already bloody damned well dead!" He stood there pink of face, his soft belly and flaccid chest heaving with the effort of his twaddle.

"Mr. Ross." The good inspector spoke in a clipped and searing tone. "You are an employee of the Commonwealth and will do whatever you are told by the Yard no matter what the bloody fig time of day it is. Are we clear?"

Denton Ross jerked his head, clearly taken aback by the unexpected détente between Varcoe and us. It is impossible to say what sort of response Ross thought he would get, but it was certainly not the one he received.

"Now you were told to have that African's body ready to be viewed," Varcoe went on, the only one of us who seemed perfectly content to bluster through this apparent new world order. "Have you done it?"

Denton flicked a glance among the three of us, his distaste as evident as the stench assaulting my nose. "This way," he answered in a tone as flat as my enthusiasm to proceed.

We followed him through the inner doors and found not one, but two covered bodies reclining on nearby tables.

"Who the hell else you got here?" Varcoe griped.

"Edmond Connicle." Denton stood halfway between the two bodies with his arms crossed, apparently trying to demonstrate his displeasure, though none of us cared a whit. "Your lackey said you wanted to see him again."

"And your report?" Varcoe barked.

"Next to the body."

"Good." Varcoe turned to Colin with a look of satisfaction. "There you are, Pendragon. Have at it."

Colin stood stock-still a moment, the incongruity of the situation not lost on him, before finally stepping forward and peeling back the sheet on the closer of the two bodies. The heavily bruised and abraded remains of Albert were slowly revealed. It was our first time seeing the injuries sustained across the entirety of his face, as well as his chest and legs. Seeing them made it clear that had he fallen from a tree he must surely have hit every branch and slid along the whole of the trunk on his way down.

"Tell me about these wounds," Colin said as he bent low over Albert's chest. "Were they occluded with dirt and debris?"

"It's in the report," Denton replied.

"Don't be a ruddy nob!" Varcoe roared before Colin could consider doing so himself. "Answer the blasted question or I'll have your ass for obstruction."

Denton's lips curled and his brow shriveled in on itself, making it look as though he were about to throw a tantrum. There might have been humor in his annoyance had the scene at hand not been so disturbing. "Yes . . ." he hissed.

"Sorry for troubling you," Colin mused.

"Will the two of you *please* stop pissing about and get on with it!" Varcoe snapped. "It's three bloody thirty in the morning. I'd like to get five minutes of sleep before this rancid night is over."

"Cause of death?" Colin asked.

"He fell from a tree." The answer was delivered as though to an imbecile.

"*What?!*" Varcoe bellowed as Colin stabbed a hand into the air, silencing him without a word.

"And these bruises and abrasions?" Colin asked with the patience of a sainted man, though I knew it was only a matter of minutes before that tolerance wore out.

"He *fell* from a *tree!*"

"Broken bones?"

"A cracked rib . . . maybe two . . . I don't remember."

"No cranial fracture?"

"I think I know the difference between a cracked rib and a cracked skull."

Colin glanced toward him. "Very well. And what do you make of these marks on his right wrist?"

"A minor abrasion," he dismissed. "No telling what he and that slag of his got up to."

Colin ignored him as he headed toward the other body. "Does it not strike you as odd that it's the same arm with the dislocated shoulder?"

"For chrissakes, Denton." Varcoe stalked over to Albert's body. "Have you even looked at his buggered shoulder?"

"It's a perfectly common injury that—"

"*Don't you dare!*" Varcoe blasted over him. "If I get so much as a ruddy *inkling* that you're impeding this investigation I will hang you by your bits off the Tower Bridge."

Denton's face pursed. "These things are hard to say for certain—"

"*Constable . . . !*" Varcoe hollered at the young bobby we'd left in the outer room. "Find this man's bollocks and tie them up."

"Inspector . . ." Colin interrupted from his position bent low over Edmond Connicle's charred remains. "You'll want to see this."

Before the inspector could cross to the farther table Denton Ross was already there. He was careful not to approach Colin directly but rather sidled up across from him in an effort, I presumed, to stay out of his line of ire.

"What is it?" Varcoe asked as he reached Colin's side.

"Have you stitched this man's lips closed?" Colin flicked his eyes to Denton, his tone neither accusatory nor disapproving.

"Why the hell would I bother when he's so badly burnt?"

"Because there are remnants of a stitch here." Colin pointed his little finger toward the center of the lips. "May I borrow a tweezers?"

"My tools?" Denton stared in disbelief. "It's not enough that you—"

"*Now,* Mr. Ross!" Varcoe fumed.

Denton released an aggravated breath as he fetched a pair of tweezers that he dropped unceremoniously onto the table. Without a word Colin snatched them up and began tugging at the tiny, single stitch binding the center of Edmond Connicle's lips together. It took only a moment before it finally gave way with a slight jerk. "It's a bit of wire," Colin said as he held it up and turned it about in the flickering light. "Whoever did this intended for Mr. Connicle's mouth to remain shut in spite of the immolation. Curious . . ." he muttered as he passed the tweezers and scrap of wire to Inspector Varcoe.

We were all so enamored staring at Varcoe's trophy that none of us realized what Colin was up to until we heard the crack of the mortised jaw. I struggled to keep my head from spinning as Colin quickly poked two fingers inside and then leaned over and took a careful look. He heaved an audible sigh as he stood back up, leveling his gaze on me. "Take a look, Ethan."

I would have been perfectly content not to take another step closer than my current proximity several feet away, but I knew Colin had made that statement with some purpose in mind. I gave as resolute a nod as I could muster and moved around beside him, the creosote smell of the burnt carcass stinging my nostrils. He flashed me an unseemly grin that I presumed was meant to assuage me, but it did little good. I have no stomach for this sort of thing and was certain everyone in the room knew it.

"The charred ring that was on the left hand . . ." I heard Colin saying to someone behind me as I girded myself to peer inside the gaping mouth. "Were you ever able to confirm with someone at the Connicle house that it belonged to Edmond Connicle?"

"Well, of course I did," Denton Ross sneered back. "The housekeeper—"

"Miss Potter?" Colin interrupted him.

"Porter," I corrected without a second's thought.

"She positively identified it," Denton went on. "I released it to her for her mistress, if you must know."

I tried to ignore the acerbic tone of Denton's voice as I sucked in a slim breath, determined not to swamp my senses with the fetid air, and finally leaned over. It took a moment for my eyes to focus inside the black gap and for my brain to process what was being relayed, but as soon as that happened everything clicked. Beyond the whisper of a hesitation I knew that this body, these curled, blackened remains, most certainly did not belong to Edmond Connicle.

CHAPTER 20

It was edging toward five, still predawn, and I was grateful to finally be back in bed. My body felt so heavy it was as if my blood had been displaced by molten lead, and my mind was little better, having been poisoned by the carnage I had just seen—*three* ruined corpses. Colin and I had come home and scrubbed at our hands and faces at the kitchen sink, the smells of putrefaction and chemicals refusing to give way easily. My harried mind became terrified that I would never lose the stench that clung to me. I ticked a glance at Colin to see if he feared the same and could tell by the steady crease of his forehead that his thoughts were traveling far afield. No matter what faced us next, I only wished for enough time to properly parse this night away.

"This case mystifies me," he said with a burdened sigh a short while later as we climbed into bed. "It seems so arbitrary. Haphazard. And yet there is clearly some purpose here. These are not the random killings of a madman. They are specific and purposeful, and yet . . ." His voice drifted off and I understood precisely what he meant. There seemed little logic to these killings, but there was always logic. Even a case as indiscriminate as the Ripper killings had been born out of both calculation and purpose.

"You'll figure it out," I said, uncertain whether I was trying to convince him or me.

He reached over and pulled me to him. "You always have such faith in me."

"What?" I lifted my head to peer at him through the darkness. "Is that self-doubt I hear?"

He chuckled and bussed my forehead. "You know," he said with a yawn, "one of us has to go out and tell Mrs. Connicle that's not her husband's body."

"Those teeth . . ." I curled my nose and set my head back on his chest. "I've never seen anything like them. They were worn down to nothing more than nubs."

"That they were." Colin exhaled. "I used to see people like that in Bombay, their teeth filed nearly away from working reeds or bamboo into pulp by pulling it through their teeth over and over until they produced just the right texture and thickness to weave baskets or mats or the soles of sandals. As soon as I saw that single wire stitch I knew something was wrong. We were never meant to look in that cadaver's mouth. Denton Ross's carelessness nearly cost us a crucial bit of information."

"Varcoe was threatening a magisterial hearing against him."

"As well he should. In the meantime we shall see if Varcoe can figure out whose body that really is." Colin heaved another sigh. "Though I doubt we'll ever know. In India he would be a member of the shudra caste or perhaps even an untouchable. There will be no record." He lifted my chin and looked at me, his eyes catching the moonlight from the window next to the bed. "Will you go see Mrs. Connicle tomorrow?"

"Of course." And now it was my turn to sigh.

"Thank you, my love," he said with a kiss. "You are so much better at that sort of thing than I am."

"I wish I thought that a compliment," I muttered. "It's just that Mrs. Connicle is so confounding. One moment as fragile as gossamer and the next, as when she was insisting she'd spotted her husband at Covington, almost feral."

"Well, now you understand why."

"All the same. I can see why she was placed in Needham Hills those years back. She's unsound . . . brittle . . . and that can be devastating."

"And you know too much about such things." He gently stroked the side of my face. "Let it be. We shall have further revelations tomorrow." He kissed me again and settled back, and before I would have thought it possible the world drifted away from me to be replaced by a singular female voice filled with vitriol and rage as it seethed up out of the murky blackness.

"The devil's spawn!" *she howled, her face shiny with perspiration as though she had just run up a flight of stairs. But it was her eyes, coal black and vacantly ferocious, as though she were registering everything and nothing.* "You're the devil's bloody spawn!" *she cried, and this time she spat on me.*

"Leave the boy alone, Amelia." *It was my father, his tone as calm and forgiving as always. I hated him for that. For not fearing her like I did.*

"He's tainted!" *she snapped back.* "You can't see it like I can."

"He's just a boy, Amelia. *Our* boy. Let him be."

She stared at my father and I wondered what she saw when she looked at him, as there seemed to be no recognition rustling behind her eyes. Even so, after a moment she wrenched my arm and shoved me away from her, as you would to something foul and unclean. My shoulder twisted under the force of her repulse, but I would not let myself cry out, not even if she jerked it from its socket again.

"Go on, Ethan . . ." *my father admonished, and I was certain he regretted having me too.* "Your mother is tired. Go to your room and fasten the bolt." *I knew what that meant, and when I heard the baby start to cry I did not need to be told again.*

The latch on my door clicked into place with the familiarity of a task done a thousand times, and as I was just short of ten, it felt every bit of my lifetime. The instant it was firmly seated I hurried across my room and slid under the bed as though the floor were slick with ice. I did not allow myself to stop skidding until my feet hit the corner my bed was wedged against, its solidity both welcoming and reassuring. And then I waited.

It didn't take long. It never took long. First came the rattling of the doorknob, and then, as if her inability to gain entry proved that I could not be there, she began to wander around and call my name. "Ethan...." The ferocity of her voice waxed and waned with her proximity to my door. "Ethan! ..."

"Leave him be...." my father pleaded, his tone unexpectedly worn.

I cowered in that corner beneath my bed and feared this would be the night he finally tired of protecting me and simply opened the door. But when I heard him coax her into their bedroom—telling her to bring the baby, that they would be fine, just the three of them—I was profoundly relieved.

Without even realizing it, I discovered I was crying. I had no notion of it until I tasted salty wetness at the corners of my mouth. My brain scolded me for my cowardice, insisting that I should go to them, but my body would not move. Even after I heard the soft click of their door latching, the baby's cries muffled by the distance, I still did not move.

And after some unaccountable time, for I had no notion of whether it was seconds, minutes, or hours, I heard four pops and smelled that smell. Burnt powder. Gunpowder.

I scrabbled out from beneath the bed as though I had been forcibly ejected. I could hear myself screeching and crying and felt the wetness at the front of my trousers as I fumbled with the lock on my door, my hands shaking so badly that it took several tries before I could get the bolt to slide back. The instant it did I flung the door so hard that it slammed against the wall and came hurtling back toward me, but I was already too far down the hallway and didn't even notice when it crashed back into place.

I was soiled and slick with tears when I reached my parents' bedroom door, bellowing for them with a madness that defied sanity. No answer came. I knew there wouldn't be. Without even thinking I reached for the doorknob and was surprised when it twisted freely. As the door yawed wide under the pressure of my hand, I found my family on the floor near the foot of the bed, my father wrapped around the baby and my mother tucked in tight behind him. It looked like they were sleeping nestled against one another except for the gaping bullet wounds and the revolver still clenched in the claw of my mother's nearer hand. And as I felt my mind curdle and my stomach heave its revolt, I knew I should have been there with them. That's what had been meant to be.

My eyes tore open and I found myself crushed in Colin's arms. "It's all right. . . ." he was saying. "You're all right."

The first tendrils of sunlight were just beginning to filter in through our bedroom windows. "Oh god," I slurred.

"It's okay," he said again as he kissed my eyes and then my forehead.

"I'm sorry—"

"Don't," he said at once.

I could find no other words to say and my mouth was so dry I thought surely I would choke on my tongue anyway.

He softened his grip and looked at me. "I have an idea. Why don't we take the day off. We'll have Mrs. Behmoth pack us a picnic and go out to Twickenham and get into some mischief in the woods." He snickered wickedly.

I managed a hoarse chuckle. "I'd sooner have this case behind us."

He continued to stare at me, studying me, before a gentle smile slowly overtook his face. "Then that is what we shall do."

CHAPTER 21

The Hutton children were a combination of sadness and fortitude. Anna told us she was eleven, and yet she had the deportment and dignity of someone years older. Her hair was long and dusky blond, and she was a sweet-faced girl who nonetheless did not have the striking natural beauty of her mother. What Anna did have was an unflinching maternal disposition toward her brother, who, she told us with great pride, had just turned six.

William looked almost to have been born of different parents, with his shaggy brown hair and broad, round face. But what merited the most notice was the fact that he seemed to be constantly in motion, his arms flapping or fidgeting even as his body rocked back and forth as though he were in a rocking chair rather than on the settee loosely enveloped in one of his big sister's arms. His eyes were equally frenetic, constantly darting about the room and never once alighting on a single person other than his sister and, even then, only for the briefest moment. He made sounds but did not speak, and I had the overwhelming sense that he was somehow trapped inside his mind and body without the slightest idea of how to break free.

Anna had joined us as soon as we had been ushered into the library near the rear of the house. She had fearlessly introduced herself to Colin, Inspector Varcoe, Sergeant Evans, and me and ordered tea for all of us as though she herself were the mistress of the manor. That she could be so poised under such circumstances was surely a sign of her remarkable fortitude.

It was as our tea was being delivered that her brother came romping in, his face and fists clenched even as his arms flapped rigidly in front of him. He was making a distressed sort of whining sound as he careened toward his sister, which seemed to wholly delight her as she squealed and threw her arms wide for him to crash into her. She was covering his face with kisses when the same young, redheaded woman we had met several days ago—Janelle, I recalled her name being—came bustling into the room with an exasperated expression clouding her face. "Now don'tcha be teachin' him that it's all right ta run from me." She huffed as she struggled to catch her breath. "Ya spoil him, ya do." As before, I was struck by her soft Scottish burr.

"Of course I do," Anna replied with a note of harshness. "You come right up here and sit by me, Willy," she said as she pulled him up onto the seat next to her. "You're being unkind. This is a terrible day. He needs to be with me." The young woman blanched as she stepped back without another word, hovering near the doorway by Sergeant Evans. Anna turned her eyes back to Colin, her face set with determination. "If there is anything I can do to help . . ."

He gave her a warm smile. "Your generous hospitality at such a time as this is assistance enough." I was relieved by his answer until I saw his brow furrow. "Though I would be interested to know when you last saw your father yesterday," he could not help but add.

"It was after William and I finished supper last night," she said at once. "He always likes to see me before he and Mum take their evening meal. Me and Willy," she corrected, squeezing her brother's shoulder even as he continued to rock incessantly beside her.

I was beginning to think we had made a mistake in coming here, that Mrs. Hutton would be unable to speak with us, when the young nurse at the door abruptly scuttled back into the room and hissed, "Your mum's comin', miss. I should take the boy out."

"No!" she snapped. "He's happy. I want him to stay."

There was no smile on the boy's face and his constant motion appeared to be more manic than gleeful, so I wondered what made her decide he felt thusly. Still, it was clear he had sought his sister's solace with good reason.

Not a moment later Mrs. Hutton swept into the room in a cloud of black crinoline and satin. Her startling beauty was fully in evidence with her sapphire eyes heightening the perfection of her strong cheekbones and delicately chiseled nose. Yet it was the rigidity of her posture and the thin set of her lips that most struck me as she turned to her son's nurse. "Take William upstairs at once," she ordered.

"But Mum," Anna started to protest. "He's fine with me."

Charlotte Hutton did not respond to her daughter's contention. She did not need to, as Janelle quickly moved in to seize the boy. It was the first moment that William seemed to fully connect with what was about to happen. He emitted a frantic howl and began flailing his arms about haphazardly as he sank back against his sister. Anna leaned over and whispered something in his ear, but it had no effect. Either he wasn't listening or it simply did not register. Whichever the case, a moment later his nurse had him clutched against her chest as she quickly swept him from the room, the sounds of his sorrowful wailing audible long after he had disappeared from view.

"William is not well," Mrs. Hutton said in a tight, clipped tone. "If you meant to wheedle information from him I am afraid you will find it quite futile."

"Mum!" Anna sucked in a sharp breath.

"You may go," Mrs. Hutton said to her daughter as she moved into the room and took a seat near the fireplace. "I hope these men have more pressing things to discuss than can be addressed with a child." Anna's face dropped, registering a look somewhere between betrayal and dismay, but she said nothing as she obediently left the room. "So tell me, Mr. Pendragon." Mrs. Hutton turned and set her glare on him. "Are you and the Yard so stymied in your investigation that you now seek the counsel of girls and simpletons? Your combined ineptitude has left me a widow. How many people have to die before the lot of you put an end to this horror?" She turned toward the fireplace, the light of its flames dancing across her face as though they had been placed there just to amplify her fury and the tears starting to collect at the corners of her eyes.

"Scotland Yard has committed every available resource to this case," Inspector Varcoe cut in, biting back his humiliation. "We are already implementing a twenty-four-hour patrol around the whole of this area until this thing is settled."

"This thing?!" She spun on him with the rage of an injured animal. "You would call my husband's murder a *thing*, Inspector?" She swiped at her eyes as though they betrayed her righteous ire.

Varcoe's face went crimson as Colin got up and moved to the far end of the fireplace, pulling Mrs. Hutton's gaze along with him. "Please do not lose yourself to the semantics of a poorly chosen word. We are here, all of us, to ensure that your husband's killer is brought to justice swiftly and appropriately. But to do that we must beg your indulgence at this most inopportune time. It is critical that you permit us to ask you some difficult questions. I will not fail you, Mrs. Hutton. I give you my word."

"He speaks for the Yard as well," Varcoe hastened to add.

Mrs. Hutton's eyes had gone stern again, and did not waver from Colin as she asked, "And how has your word served Mrs. Connicle?"

"That is entirely different," Varcoe fussed obtusely. "At this point we're not even certain her husband is dead."

Mrs. Hutton's face went slack as she turned on him. *"What?!"*

"This is a complex and ongoing investigation," Colin interrupted with chagrin. "There is much we don't yet know—"

She bolted up and stalked to Colin, squaring off with him as though to do battle. "Are you even certain that Arthur is dead?! Or have you gotten this household into an uproar over nothing as well?"

Colin's face went hard, and I prayed his better nature would lead his reply. "I am afraid there's no question of it," he answered smoothly.

She stared at him a moment longer, seeming to take his measure before abruptly moving away. "And what is it you are so eager to ask me?"

Colin struggled to produce the slightest of smiles, which Mrs. Hutton appeared to take no notice of. "Are you aware of anyone who had a recent falling-out with your husband?"

"My husband could be an abrasive man, Mr. Pendragon. There was little secret in that. He did not care if anyone liked him or not."

"I see . . ." Colin mumbled as he began pacing in front of the fireplace. "And did your husband have any business with Edmond Connicle or his firm?"

"Arthur invested a great deal of money with Columbia Financial. But Wynn Tessler handles our finances, not Mr. Connicle. And all Arthur did was complain that Mr. Tessler was a scourge anyway."

"Unhappy with your returns?"

"I really wouldn't know," she said, her tone like ice.

Colin allowed an irritated sigh to escape his lips even as he flashed a fleeting grin. "Was your husband preoccupied of late? Distracted perhaps . . . ?"

"You spoke with him yesterday," she answered brusquely. "Did you find him so?"

"I would very much prefer to hear what you think," Colin said, the strain in his voice threatening to rupture at any moment.

"My husband neither confided in me nor sought my opinion. If he was preoccupied or distracted I would not know it. Now have I not suffered enough for one day? Must I continue to be hounded by your inanities?" She glowered at Colin, her eyes piercing him as though daring him to press ahead, which, thankfully, he did not.

CHAPTER 22

I studied Mrs. Connicle's face, thin and sallow, her eyes shot through with threads of red, and regretted having allowed myself to be coaxed here. It was an odd confluence of emotion that coursed through me as I listened to her. Everything from curiosity to pity to unrelenting dread. There was no mystery in my discomfort around her. Around her mental frailty. I recognized its insidious grip. Even so, it did little to lessen the impact of sitting across from her.

"Dr. Renholme insists I not agitate myself," she was saying. "He has kept me swimming in laudanum for days now. It has left me quite addled, I'm afraid." She cast her gaze down to her trembling hands, seeming to fade even further away. "Things that I should know I cannot seem to pull forward. I cannot find them in the haze."

"Please don't," I tried to soothe, and was mortified when my voice caught. "You mustn't trouble yourself," I added as soon as I could draw a full breath. "Whether you can provide a single detail or not will have no bearing on how hard Mr. Pendragon works to determine if that was your husband yesterday at Covington."

"It was," she said with surety, her voice thick and sluggish. "You must believe me, Mr. Pruitt."

"I most certainly do," I answered at once. "Now that we know the body discovered on your property is not that of your husband, Mr. Pendragon and the Yard are redoubling their efforts to find him."

"Yes . . . yes . . ." she muttered as she wiped a handkerchief across her upper lip in a gesture that seemed at once as nervous as it was agitated.

I cleared my throat and tried to recall all the things Colin had instructed me to ask her about. He'd been quite undone by Mrs. Hutton's vitriol, suffering equal parts guilt and effrontery, and had been less than articulate as he sent me on this undertaking. "Has your husband ever gone off without telling you before? Perhaps on some quick bit of business that took longer than he meant?"

"Never. Edmond has always been the most considerate of men, patient and kind. I have never had a quarrel with him, Mr. Pruitt. If you are imagining such a thing I can assure you that you are wrong."

"I meant no offense." I felt myself flush slightly as I struggled to hold her determined gaze. "You understand that we need to rule out every possibility?"

"I understand," she said, though I caught a whisper of flintiness in her voice, "but my husband is missing and that means that something is terribly wrong. You and Mr. Pendragon must implement a search for him at once." She pushed herself forward on the settee as her delicate brow coursed into a frown. "Where is Mr. Pendragon? I have pledged good money for his services and yet haven't any idea whether he has given the slightest thought to what might be happening to Edmond." Her hands fidgeted in her lap as if they must surely ache.

"Please be assured, Mrs. Connicle, that at this very moment Mr. Pendragon is at Scotland Yard rereviewing the evidence they have collected from your gardener's shed as well as seeing to the release of your woman, Alexa. Your husband's well-being is very much at the forefront of his mind."

"Oh . . ." She sagged back in her seat. "Poor Alexa. What she has been through." She turned her eyes to me and I could see a well of pain in them. "I do not doubt her loyalty for a moment and you must make sure she knows she is expected back in this house."

"I will." I took a slow breath and tried to calm my ratcheting heartbeat as I tried to formulate the ground I had to travel. "Does your husband suffer from any illness that might—" But the words caught in my throat as Mrs. Connicle's face went ashen and the light in her eyes dimmed to a dull steel gray.

"He does not," she bit harshly. "Surely, sir, you are confusing him with me."

I nearly choked. "I beg your pardon. I didn't mean—"

She waved me off and began to weep, dabbing at her eyes with a handkerchief pulled from her sleeve as she struggled to contain her composure. "You must not judge my husband by my failings. Even as we sit here in our comforts, Mr. Pruitt, his life is almost certainly at risk. I shall never forgive myself if the taint of my infirmity should cause you to neglect to save my husband. Mr. Pendragon gave me his pledge," she gasped. "Now he must fulfill it without delay."

I nodded, afraid to say another word, for I dared not ask this brittle woman any more questions. As for myself, I could not bear another second here.

CHAPTER 23

The moment I entered the study I felt an unmistakable air of tension. Colin and Hubert Aston were seated across from each other by the fireplace, both stoic, both ramrod straight, and both displaying mild annoyance with one another. A notably inauspicious beginning, given that the Astons' oldest boy had informed me that Colin had arrived not ten minutes earlier.

"Gentlemen." I smiled gamely as I was shown in. "I apologize for being late," I blathered on, though we had not set a specific time, given Colin's preference to catch people at will. A behavior that is tolerated, if seldom appreciated.

"So it is to be the both of you again, eh?" Mr. Aston sniffed as he turned to me but did not bother to stand up. "I am afraid I have nothing to add to what has already been said. And I will have you know that you quite unnerved my wife the last time you were here. You might consider that should you mull a further return visit."

"It is certainly not our intention to cause Mrs. Aston distress," Colin answered with an embarrassing lack of conviction. "However, I would like to remind you that three men have been murdered—"

"I do *not* need to be reminded of any such thing!" Mr. Aston groused. "Do not presume to condescend, Mr. Pendragon. I shall not abide it."

"Condescend?" Colin repeated with the height of feigned surprise as he stood up and moved to the fireplace. "We have only come to ask a few simple questions and seem to have brought down a world of offense."

"Simple questions, are they?" Mr. Aston scoffed. "Damned personal ones."

"Nothing is too personal when people are losing their lives. Now I have asked you about the potential of Arthur Hutton's extramarital activities because it could be relevant to this case, given what you have already told us about Edmond Connicle's trysts. Surely you can understand that."

I cringed at Colin's tone, though curiously, Mr. Aston seemed not to care. He flicked his eyes at me, a hint of some perception brewing there, and then slid his gaze back to Colin. "How old are you, Mr. Pendragon?"

Colin leaned against the fireplace mantel as he studied Mr. Aston a moment. "Thirty-eight," he said at length.

"Thirty-eight . . ." Mr. Aston repeated airily, clearly pleased with the answer. "And yet no wife and no children." His gaze hardened. "How can someone like you understand what men like Edmond, Arthur, and me contend with? You come here looking for salacious details to infer all manner of indecencies that I, quite frankly, find insulting."

"I what?" Colin's brow crashed down. "If you believe my questions to be disapproving then you had best cleanse your conscience with your vicar. Be assured I don't give a ruddy piss whom any of you shag. I am looking for a connection, Mr. Aston."

"But you are doing so in the most sordid way!" he blasted back. "Has it occurred to you that our households all frequent Covington Market? Perhaps *there* is where your connections lies." His voice dripped acid. "And both Arthur and I are clients of Columbia Financial. Edmond's firm. Has that ever struck you? Not to mention that nearly everyone who lives out here is administered to by Dr. Renholme. Have none of those possibilities stirred within your tawdry mind?"

Colin's gaze was hard and unflinching. "And if I told you we have reason to believe that Edmond Connicle might still be alive? What other hypotheses might you have?"

Hubert Aston stopped and looked truly struck for the first time. "Alive?!" He scowled. "Are you referring to the ravings of Edmond's unhinged wife?"

"So you've heard her assertions?"

"Domestics gossip." He shook his head like a disapproving parent. "Really, Mr. Pendragon. Are you so naïve? It would seem a wonder the newspapers level such praise upon you." He brushed at his jacket's lapels and ran two fingers along the length of his overgrown mustache. "I don't see it."

"And if the evidence were conclusive?"

Mr. Aston chuckled, but there was no humor in it. "Then I should wonder about Arthur's supposed demise," he said as he stood up. "Not to mention the ineptitude of you and the Yard. Good day, gentlemen."

Colin tipped him a curt nod and charged for the door before abruptly swinging around as he reached the study's threshold. "Is your bookkeeper at Columbia Financial named Teller?—"

"Tessler," I corrected as I joined him.

"Wynn Tessler is a partner in the firm. He can hardly be classified a bookkeeper. I work with Noah Tolliver. Really, Mr. Pendragon, this has almost been amusing."

Colin flashed a fox's smile as he turned and barreled off.

I mustered what I could of a grin in the face of Mr. Aston's unpleasant gaze before hurrying after Colin. I caught up with him some distance down the graveled drive just as he dove a hand into his front pocket and extracted a coin. "Whatever do you suppose had him so tossed about?" I asked as I fell in step beside Colin.

"Hmmm . . . ?" came the distracted reply as the coin began

gliding deftly between the fingers of his right hand. "Mr. Aston? It would seem he feels distinctly reproached by us. Which is wearisome, given how little I care about what he does with himself short of committing murder."

"Yes, but what do you make of it?"

"Make of it?" He tossed me a wry look. "He is a haughty tosser who imagines himself above the likes of anyone not worth an elephant's weight in sterling. I should be delighted to reorder his thinking."

"He defends infidelity as though it were a birthright."

"Men like him believe it is. But you're missing the point."

"Which is . . . ?"

"How glibly he recriminates both Edmond Connicle's firm and the local doctor. He either means to steer us or is truly a reprehensible man. I haven't decided which yet."

"He is certainly dismissive of Mrs. Connicle."

Colin grimaced. "I'm afraid that's something we are bound to find prevalent amongst those who know her."

"Of course." I heaved a sigh.

"What I'm interested in," he said as we reached the street and he swung out an arm to hail a coach, "is this man at Columbia Financial we keep hearing about."

"Wynn Tessler?"

A hansom cab pulled over as Colin slid the coin he'd been flipping back into his pocket. He shouted an address up to the driver and we climbed aboard. "Charlotte Hutton says her husband complained about Mr. Tessler's handling of their money. And now we know that Hubert Aston, though he does not work with Mr. Tessler, is well enough acquainted to refer to him by his first name. I find that provocative."

"Seems a bit thin to me." I shrugged.

"Well, of course it's bloody thin," he shot back. "Do you have a better idea? Shall we go off after the country doctor? Or perhaps you'd prefer we just leave Alexa with Varcoe and let him settle on the voodoo bollocks."

"Don't be a twit," I admonished. "What happened at the Yard this morning? Did Varcoe finally release Alexa?"

"He did. That woman is ruddy well outraged at what's happened to her and I can hardly blame her. The evidence Varcoe has against her is absurd and yet he's treating her as though she were caught in flagrante. How did I forget what an arse he is?" Colin turned and glared at me. "Why didn't you remind me?"

I shook my head. "I will remind you that you need his help on this case. He has given you access to more information than you normally ever get."

He heaved a sigh. "You have more of a point than you know."

"Do I?"

"Varcoe showed me the photographs of the blood splatters in the Connicles' shed. Looking at them again, one after the other like that, it made me see something I had not noticed before. The patterns could not possibly have come from a single source, someone having been butchered with a knife while standing in the center of the space. Not unless the victim had spun completely around as he fell, which is preposterous. I'm convinced that scene was meant to do nothing more than throw the Yard off course. Make them believe that Edmond Connicle had died there in some ridiculous ritual. No." He glanced out at the passing streets as we crossed the Thames into the city proper. "Wherever Edmond Connicle is, he means to be thought dead."

"You think he's a willing part of it?!"

"It seems an awfully elaborate scheme to kidnap a man."

I exhaled my surprise. "What did Varcoe say?"

"About what?"

"Everything you just told me."

He gave a slight shrug. "I may have forgotten to mention it to him."

I laughed. "So that's how it works?"

"You don't think I've lost my mind completely, do you?"

"I should have known." I glanced around as great, long shadows from the increasingly condensed buildings began to block the light of the sun along the road. "Where are we going?"

"To meet Wynn Tessler."

"Is he expecting us?"

A rogue's smile slid onto Colin's face. "Now where would be the fun in that?"

CHAPTER 24

———❖———

We were waiting in a grand outer office with rich oak wainscoting climbing halfway up the walls and maroon velvet-flocked wallpaper with a subtle French pattern covering the rest. The parquet floor was a darker oak and had several plush area rugs placed about that looked like they came from someone's château in the Loire Valley of France. The furniture was substantial and covered in tufted leather the color of port. Each piece was so massive that even Colin, with his broad shoulders and powerful arms, looked about to be swallowed whole by the wing-backed chair he was trying to fill. But the single item that spoke most to the level of Columbia Financial's success was that the whole building had been converted to electric lighting.

"Mr. Tessler will see you now." A thin, stoic young man beckoned us to follow him. His deportment was so flawless that it seemed the firm must surely belong to him. At least until he brought us to a set of double doors, where he knocked once before swinging them open to reveal a huge office with room enough for several couches, a small bar beneath one of the windows, and an enormous desk behind which sat a barrel-chested man of middle years with dark features. "Mr. Tessler," our young escort said with the practiced ease of one who had done this a thousand times, "I have Mr. Colin Pendragon and Mr. Ethan Pruitt of Scotland Yard."

Colin cringed as Mr. Tessler came over to us and shook our hands with a ready smile. Mr. Tessler stood about three inches taller than Colin and possessed a swarthy handsomeness crowned by a raven-black nest of hair. "Gentlemen." His voice was as solid and resonant as his handshake was meant to impress. "Welcome to Columbia Financial Services."

"I'll bring some tea," the young man announced.

"You mustn't," Colin said at once. "We won't stay but a few minutes." The lad nodded and let himself out, pulling the doors shut. "We do appreciate your willingness to meet us without notice," Colin said as we followed Mr. Tessler to the couches. They were arranged in an open-sided square to create a sort of conversation area but in actuality reminded me of the seating at the Earl of Arnifour's opium den.

"I would be remiss not to," Mr. Tessler replied easily. "I assume this has something to do with Edmond Connicle's terrible death?"

"He was a founding partner, was he not?" Colin asked, ignoring the question.

"Indeed he was. Frankly, without Edmond there wouldn't be a Columbia Financial. He was the majority stakeholder in the beginning. It was only after we began making some real money about a dozen years ago that he finally became just another overpaid senior partner." He gave a light chuckle that quickly died in his throat. "It's all so horrid. Especially given his wife's delicate nature." Mr. Tessler shook his head. "Edmond made me the executor of his estate after she was hospitalized some years back. She spent several months at Needham Hills after suffering a terrible bout of hysteria. It took quite a toll on her."

"Yes. I have experienced the residue from that place myself," Colin said, and I was relieved when he did not elaborate. "What would you think if I told you she believes she spotted her husband near Covington Market yesterday?"

Mr. Tessler blanched as he stared back at Colin. "That would be dreadful news. Poor Annabelle."

"And what if I told you that I now suspect she may be right?"

Mr. Tessler's brow furrowed as he flicked his eyes from Colin to me in the space of an instant. It was as though he were checking to see whether Colin might be playing some awful joke on him. "Mr. Pendragon . . . ?" was all he said.

"Is it possible Edmond Connicle is off on some business?"

Mr. Tessler shook his head. "No. I would know that. Our business rarely takes us out of the city."

"Can you think of any reason he might want to disappear in such a way?"

"Such a way?"

"To be perceived of as dead," Colin said flatly, as though speaking about the weather.

"No. Never." Mr. Tessler continued to shift his eyes from Colin to me. "Are you jesting?"

"I do not jest when it comes to murder," Colin said as he stood up and wandered over to the large windows along one side of the office. "Was he having any trouble here at the office? Funds gone unaccounted for? A soured business deal? An angry client? A young lady come to call too often?"

Mr. Tessler looked noticeably uncomfortable, though by which suggestion I could not be sure. "Edmond was a considered and thoughtful man, which is what made him such an outstanding leader at this company. His ethics were beyond reproach. Everyone admired him. What you are suggesting is just"—he seemed quite beside himself as he searched for the right word—"impossible."

Colin nodded as he turned from the window. "Impossible . . ." he repeated, coming back over to stand behind me. "Such a curious word. Rather like a challenge. Tell me, Mr. Tessler, did he have any business dealings with Arthur Hutton?"

"Oh my." He drew in a breath and shook his head. "Another terrible tragedy. But Arthur was my client. I took care of him and Charlotte personally. Are you thinking there could be some correlation between what's happened to the two of them?"

Colin forced a hollow smile. "Beyond the wisp of a doubt."

"But what about that African? You cannot possibly think his death related to Edmond and Arthur?"

"You would be amazed at some of the things I think." He flashed a tight smile. "Did Edmond Connicle have *anything* to do with the Hutton accounts?"

"Never."

"Then what do you make of her assertion that her husband had grown displeased with the way their money was being managed?"

Mr. Tessler allowed the semblance of a smile to cross his lips. "Arthur made some foolish choices and he was not a man to own up to it very easily. I have no idea what he told his wife, but you know how women are about business. They haven't the first notion of any of it."

"And yet most manage a household quite handily," Colin shot back with an easy grin. "I do believe we've taken enough of your time." He nodded and headed for the door. "If you will permit me one last request . . . ?"

"Whatever I can do to help," Mr. Tessler answered smoothly.

"I should very much like to get a look at the Connicles' financial ledgers tomorrow morning, and perhaps those of the Huttons as well."

"I'm afraid I won't be here in the morning." He flung open the doors and walked us back through the waiting area. "I'm going out to pay my respects to Mrs. Hutton. You're free to come in the afternoon, but you'll not find anything of interest. You can be assured of that."

"Very well then." Colin smiled amiably. "We shall be here tomorrow afternoon."

"As you wish." Mr. Tessler shrugged, pulling the door to the suite open and offering his hand. And though his grip remained absurdly firm, it was the first time I noticed he did not meet my gaze.

CHAPTER 25

Dinner had been dispensed with, Mrs. Behmoth's preeminent corned beef and cabbage, and Colin was already throwing his dumbbells about. He was pacing in front of the fireplace, his arms straining against the weights, which seemed quite lost on him, given the otherworldly look clouding his eyes. He had said little during dinner, though there was much I was curious to ask. I settled into my chair and pretended to read the newspaper for a few minutes, Colin's pacing and huffing as steady as the clock on the mantel, before finally giving up my ruse.

"Do you suppose Varcoe is ever going to find out who the body we thought was Edmond Connicle really is?"

The dumbbells pistoned toward the ceiling, one after the other. "I shouldn't think so. Just ask yourself how many people could disappear in this city without causing a ripple?"

I nodded. He was right. Nobody knew that better than I.

"Someone, very likely Edmond Connicle himself, has been playing the Yard *and us* for fools all this time. Leading us like lemmings." Colin set the dumbbells down but did not stop his pacing. "I don't like being made a fool."

"How do you mean?"

"The body we thought was Edmond Connicle was burned

beyond recognition for what we now know are obvious reasons, while the fetishes beneath it had been conspicuously buried to ensure they would be found. Yet when it came to the murder of Arthur Hutton the fetishes were shoved in his mouth because now we were *looking* for them, while his body was barely burnt. It didn't need to be." He dropped into the seat beside me. "Somebody is working very hard to point us right where they intend for us to look."

"At the Connicles' scullery maid, Alexa."

"Precisely."

"And you think that might be Edmond Connicle?"

"Almost certainly. But to what end? And who else might be working with him? He cannot be doing all of this alone."

"Is Varcoe doing enough to try and find him?"

Colin stood up and stalked back to the fireplace, poking at the embers arbitrarily. "He's got a small task force trolling the East End and the wharfs, and he's sending a few more to stake out the Covington Market area, but I doubt that'll yield anything. Edmond Connicle couldn't be daft enough to show up there twice." He shoved the poker back into place and turned to face me. "Which is why we're going to have a look at his financial ledgers tomorrow. See if we can figure out what he might be up to. Beyond that . . ." He shook his head wearily. "I'm going to bed." He headed down the hall toward the back of the flat.

I heaved a sigh myself and decided bringing an end to this day might be just the thing when a sudden pounding drifted up from the door below.

"*I'm not home!*" Colin hollered.

I chuckled as I heard Mrs. Behmoth make her way to the door. I was fairly certain she would find young Paul on our front steps looking for another crown or two after his daylong siege shadowing Sunny Guitnu, but when I peeked over the balustrade onto the foyer below I found myself staring down at Inspector Varcoe's snow-white head.

"Where's Pendragon?" he barked at Mrs. Behmoth.

"And a ruddy good evenin' ta you too," she sallied right back.

Varcoe's eyes shot up and landed on me. "You'll want to hear this, Pruitt. You're both going to want to hear this." The thick foreboding in his voice made me immediately nod and wave him up. This confounding case, I realized, was about to get worse.

"I suppose you'll be wantin' tea!" Mrs. Behmoth groused as she shut the door and trundled back to the kitchen.

I did not bother to answer her but headed back to rally Colin even as I heard the inspector bounding up the stairs behind me. He would just have to make himself comfortable while I did so. I opened the door to our room just in time to find Colin flinging his undergarments into a pile near our armoire. "We've company," I said.

"The only company I want"—he looked back at me with half-lidded eyes—"is you."

"Would you settle for Emmett Varcoe?"

"Not when I'm starkers." He hurried across the room and began pulling his clothes back on. "Did he say what it's about?"

"He says he has something to tell us. Something we'll both want to hear."

"Interesting." Colin draped his tie around his neck and shrugged his coat on, not bothering with shoes as he pecked my cheek and yanked the door open. "Then let us see what our partner has to say for himself," he said as he padded off for the study.

"Pendragon!" the inspector bellowed the moment he saw Colin. Despite his being disheveled and in stocking feet, it earned him nary a flea's hesitation from Varcoe. "You are not going to believe who has just appeared from out of nowhere!"

"Edmond Connicle?" Colin responded without inflection.

Varcoe's jaw unhinged as he stared at Colin. "How could you know that? Are you keeping information from me?"

"Don't get yourself in an uproar. Whom else could you be here at such an hour to announce? It's fundamental. Now wherever did you find him?"

"Just past Tower Bridge by the Thames. A couple of my men came upon him being beaten nearly to death by some bloke whom they let get away. He's in hospital now. He hadn't regained consciousness when I left there to head over here. I've got him three armed guards posted outside his room." Varcoe's eyebrows furrowed as he bolted back to his feet. "This bloody case is going to be the end of me."

"Then we haven't a moment to lose." Colin snickered as he rushed back down the hall for his shoes. "And we'll need to make a stop in Holland Park on the way."

There was little I could do but give Varcoe a shrug. The fact that his normal pallor had shifted to something closer to cherry was not lost on me.

CHAPTER 26

Edmond Connicle's face, neck, and shoulders were horribly swollen and discolored in angry shades of purple, blue, magenta, and black. If the rest of his body was equally assaulted I feared he might not live through the night. Miss Porter had already been by to positively identify him, which was good, given that I could easily have been convinced that he was one of a thousand other brown-haired men, and even Varcoe wasn't going to make the same mistake twice.

Edmond was slender and of modest proportions, but other than the color and fullness of his hair I could draw no conclusions. His eyes were mere slits, pinched shut and oozing from within the confines of eye sockets so inflamed that they rose well above his brow. His nose seemed to stretch from one cheek to the next and I could tell that it was broken just above the bridge. I suspected his right cheekbone had also been fractured, given the peculiar angle at which it disappeared under his hairline, but we would not know until the swelling had at least partially receded. The worst of it, however, was his labored breathing, rattling from deep within his chest. Edmond Connicle, a man thought to have been already dead, was now perilously close.

"Was he conscious when your men found him?" Colin asked Varcoe as he leaned in close.

"He was muttering some at first, but nothing anyone could make out."

"And what of the man who did this? Could they describe him?"

Varcoe gave a foul expression as he shook his head. "Average height. Solid build. Not much else. They said it was too dark and he ran off down the quay as soon as my men saw what was going on. They had no idea the victim was Mr. Connicle until they got him down here and went through his pockets. That's when they sent for me," he added with a note of pride.

"Does Mrs. Connicle know?" I asked, anxious for her to know that she was right even as much as I did not want her to see her husband's present state.

"Nah. Just that Porter woman. I'm hoping they keep that balmy wife of his sedated until he recovers."

"That seems a bit harsh, given that she was the first to insist her husband was still alive," I scolded.

He shrugged dismissively and folded his arms across his chest. "Then you and Pendragon can tend to her when she gets here." He pulled some papers out of his pocket and handed them over to Colin. "They found these in his pockets. They're receipts."

Colin thumbed through them quickly before passing them over to me. "They're all dated in the future. . . ."

I glanced down and found four hotel receipts covering a week's stay each. One for a hotel in Paris, one from Lyon, one from Lausanne, and one from Geneva. And true to Colin's word, all of them were dated with consecutively running future dates, starting with the hotel in Paris and ending with the one in Lausanne. "How can that be?" I looked at the both of them. "Receipts for dates that haven't even happened yet?"

Varcoe curled his lips and shook his head. "We found 'em; you figure the damn things out. Now I'm going to finish up with my men. I won't be but a minute. If Connicle here wakes up you'd better not ask him one single question until I get back."

He glared at us from the doorway. "And I'm not bloody well kidding."

"He is infuriating," Colin exhaled the moment the door slid shut.

"Never mind that. Just get what you need from him and solve this case. That's all that matters."

"Always so optimistic," he grumbled.

"I try."

"It can be annoying, you know."

I chose to ignore him and return to keener matters. "What did you tell Paul when we stopped in Holland Park at the Guitnus'?"

"I told him to see if he can ferret out any information on this attack. Edmond Connicle didn't disappear into the East End only to suffer some random beating. This was premeditated. Which means that someone down there knows something."

"But he's just a boy! You can't send him snooping about with that rabble. Besides, who'll keep an eye on Sunny Guitnu? Make sure she doesn't run off with that Cillian lad?"

Colin waved me off. "She's not going anywhere. And do you really think that boy is going to abandon his mother?" He shook his head. "They'll be fine for one night. He can head out there again tomorrow morning. Tonight our clever lad should see what he can drum up. He said he lives near Saint Paul's. That means he'll be familiar with the area and the locals."

"Colin, he's too young. I'll go. You know I spent a fair many years amongst that sort of crowd and—"

He held up a single hand. "Stop."

Whatever else he was about to say was abruptly interrupted when the door swung wide and Annabelle Connicle came bursting in with Miss Porter, Wynn Tessler, and Dr. Renholme on her heels.

"It's true!" She swooned as she raced to the bed. "Edmond. *Edmond!*" She collapsed at the side of the bed, her hands clinging to his nearer arm as though receiving sustenance from it. "What have they done to you?" Her voice broke and she began to sob as Miss Porter, ashen and shaking, knelt beside her.

"It really is true. . . ." Mr. Tessler muttered as he sidled next to us. "I couldn't believe Miss Porter's words when she came back to the house. I simply had to come and see for myself."

"You can be sure there will be no further errors or presumptions on this case," Colin answered peevishly. I touched his elbow in an effort to encourage him to withhold his annoyance, but he only took a half step away from me. "How is it that you happened to be at the Connicle house when Miss Porter returned with her news?"

"What?" He shifted his eyes from Mrs. Connicle's prostrate form, Miss Porter crumpled on one side of her and Dr. Renholme on the other, and looked at Colin. "I was having her sign some documents," he said absently. "I . . ." He glanced down at his briefcase and shook his head, his eyes filled with confusion. "I guess there'll be no need now. . . ."

Colin released a labored sigh and turned his back to the women and Dr. Renholme. "I'm afraid his condition is very grave. You might just keep what you have prepared."

"Oh." He sagged slightly, his expression a mirror of the astonishment we were all feeling. "Of course."

"Where was he found, Mr. Pendragon?" Mrs. Connicle startled us as she turned from her husband.

Colin's lips drew tight and I could see his discomfort at the unsettling answer. "Along the Thames near Tower Bridge."

"Tower Bridge?" she repeated, clearly trying to fathom what he might have been doing in such a place, just as we were.

"A couple men from the Yard were on their rounds when they spotted your husband having been set upon. They haven't made an arrest yet, but we remain ever hopeful." He gave a tight grin that I was certain could not have soothed her. "It's fair to say that Inspector Varcoe's men surely saved your husband's life."

"Oh, thank god," she gasped.

"Are they looking for anyone?" Mr. Tessler's face came alive with his question. "Do they have a suspect?"

Colin shook his head as he glanced at Mrs. Connicle, seeing that she had turned her attentions back to her husband. "They do not," he answered quietly. "But they can be resourceful. And Mr. Pruitt and I are well into this now."

"Of course," Mr. Tessler said, but his voice was tainted with doubt.

"We will be on our way then," Colin said with what bravado he could muster. "Mrs. Connicle..." He stepped toward her, but she remained rigidly turned away, so he gave a quick and perfunctory shake of Mr. Tessler's hand.

"Please let me know as soon as you learn anything," Mr. Tessler said. "I shall stay with Mrs. Connicle awhile."

Colin gave an aggrieved sort of smile and nodded his head, and before I could properly bid farewell myself he pivoted backwards and barreled out of the room.

CHAPTER 27

The sonorous thundering slithered into my dream and spurred my body to jolt even before my brain could register the source of the disturbance. Colin's legs were intertwined with mine so that when I jerked awake he was forced to do the same, though with a hair's-breadth delay. As I struggled to achieve full consciousness the thundering quickly morphed into something more akin to pounding. I sat up and rubbed at my eyes with the heels of my hands and then blinked at the waxing light of the gray dawn streaming in through the windows.

"Get yer lazy arses up!" Mrs. Behmoth bellowed from the other side of the door. "It's near quarter past seven and ya got yerselves a visitor. Not that the scruffy little moppet is a proper visitor."

"All right then . . ." Colin called back as he climbed from the bed and stretched languorously. "Give the lad some tea and we'll be right out." He padded over to the armoire and began yanking out undergarments for us. "And be nice to him," he added, though no response was forthcoming.

I sat up and yawned like someone who had suffered a grievous lack of sleep, which was precisely the truth of it. We'd only gotten back to our flat just before two. Sleepless nights were becoming a habit on this case.

Colin dunked his head under the faucet, sending an explosion of water up and over the sink. "There," he said after a moment as he turned around with a self-satisfied smile, his wet hair pointing in a hundred different directions like an ill-tended wheat field. "Well, come on," he coaxed. "Our young liege may have something important to report. I must admit I'm heartened by his early arrival."

"Yes, yes," I muttered without a whisper of enthusiasm as I forced myself to stand up. "It's all terribly heartening."

Colin stared at me a second, an eyebrow arched toward the ceiling, and then promptly burst out laughing. "What a sight you are," he said with a dimpled grin as he pulled on his underthings. "Rouse yourself, love. I'm eager to hear what young Paul has to say but won't let him begin until you get there." He slid on a pair of pants and freshly pressed shirt, all the while continuing to chuckle as he forced his feet into his shoes and pulled a comb through his hair. "Five minutes then?" he said as he pulled on his coat. He gave me a quick peck and was out the door.

Though I had the best of intentions, it took me nearly fifteen minutes before I was ready to join the two of them. What I found truly heartening when I finally shuffled into the room was that the fireplace was already roaring and Mrs. Behmoth had brought up tea and fresh currant scones.

"At last," Colin enthused as I crossed to my chair. "The dead have arisen to greet the new day." The little pisser seemed to find that quite funny. Colin snickered as well while he quickly poured my tea with just a touch of milk. "Paul's been quite beside himself with news. You've kept him waiting an absolute lifetime for a boy of twelve."

"Horrors!" I groused.

"I found the man wot beat the other bloke last night," Paul burst out in a single breath. "'Ow's at fer somethin' ta tell ya?!"

"It'll be quite something if it proves to be true." Colin nodded, taking his cup and wandering over to the fireplace. "And how did you find this man?"

"I got me places."

"I'm sure you do." Colin eyed him with a smirk. "But if you expect me to pay you for your cunning, you had best start convincing me that you've done something worth paying for."

Paul scowled as he snatched up a scone and took a bite. "There's a bunch a pubs east a Tower 'Ill that I do a bit a business at now and then," he said, a waterfall of crumbs dusting his lap with every word. "I went ta all of 'em and asked a few mates if anybody 'eard 'bout a beatin' near the bridge." He laughed. "Course they did. 'Alf them bastards knew it 'ad 'appened, but none a them knew shite about it." His smile widened. "So I went east a there to the docks out at Wappin'."

"You walked all the way from Tower Bridge to the Wapping docks in the middle of the wretched night by yourself?" I blurted, certain he was making up stories for an extra coin.

"And why not?" He pointed his thin, hairless chin at me defiantly. "Mr. P. said I'd get an extra crown er two if I found somethin' out."

"Something verifiable," Colin corrected.

Paul stared at him blankly. "Wot?"

"True," I cut in impatiently. "It has to be *true*."

"This is true like the Queen 'erself spoke it."

"No doubt." Colin smiled as he shot a look my direction that I decided was meant to keep me quiet. "And what exactly did you hear at the docks?"

"Two men told me they 'eard a scuffle and saw a fight broken up by a pair a bobbies. Said the bloke that went down was ruddy well dead as alive 'cause the bugger that did it 'ad a length a pipe in 'is 'and. I asked who it was that done it and they said 'e were a foreigner. 'At's wot they said. Said 'e run off toward Stepney." His prideful smile widened as he snatched up another scone. "So 'at's where I went."

My stomach curdled at the thought of this boy running about the Wapping docks and Stepney Green in the middle of the night. But just as quickly I realized the soundness in Colin's decision to send Paul in the first place. These were *his* streets. He could scamper out of harm's way like a mouse because no one gave a second look at a mischievous imp. My own youth spent on those same streets bore out the truth in that.

"I 'ad ta go to a bunch a places, but I found the knave. A short bloke with 'uge shoulders and a scrabbler's chest like Mr. P. 'as. It'd take three a me ta be as wide as 'im. 'E were talkin' and throwin' money round and braggin' 'bout a job 'e got and 'ow much money 'e's makin'. 'E talked funny. Not like you two, but like 'e's got somethin' stuck in 'is throat that 'e can't 'ack up."

"Probably Prussian or Slavic . . ." Colin muttered. "Dark hair? Beard?"

"Yep. Like a monkey, 'e were so ruddy 'airy."

"And what makes you so certain he's the same chap those men at the docks spotted?"

Paul's face blossomed with a beatific grin. "I 'ad one a me girls with me. She pumped 'im for a sovereign an' a right lump a information."

"One of your girls . . . ?" Colin repeated, his voice betraying his surprise.

"'Ell yeah. I'm one a them enterpeders."

"Entrepreneurs," I said with a roll of my eyes.

"You are *not* running whores." Colin glowered. "No self-respecting slag is working for a cheeky little twelve-year-old."

Paul's smile wilted as he snatched up another scone. "So I ain't exactly runnin' 'em, but I look out for 'em. And when I ask 'em ta do somethin' for me, they do it. Like talkin' to yer bastard wot ain't from round 'ere."

"Fine, fine." Colin returned to his chair and shoved his teacup onto the table. "So what did this girl of yours find out?"

Paul glanced over at Colin as he took a bite. "'Ow much ya payin' me for all this?" he asked in a shower of crumbs. "I gotta cut 'er in, ya know."

"Enough to buy yourself three decent meals a day for a week. Now what the hell did she tell you?"

"'E were braggin' 'bout the devil 'e works for. Sends 'im stacks a cash with notes tellin' 'im wot 'is next job is. Last night 'e were told ta take a man down. Just like that." Paul beamed like the boy he was with no understanding of what it means to murder. "But 'e said a couple a bobbies interrupted 'im and 'e 'ad ta get outta there. 'E said 'is boss were gonna be mad 'bout that."

"And this boss . . ." Colin started to say before a pounding erupted at our door downstairs. He stood up and hurried over to the landing even as I heard Mrs. Behmoth heading down the hallway toward the door. Colin turned back to Paul and me. "Did he say anything specific about this boss of his?"

"Nah. 'E weren't really there ta *talk* ta me girl, ya know." He sniffed as though he were the most worldly of men. "But she did say 'e weren't worth the shillin's 'e gave 'er." Paul brayed a laugh as Colin stepped back into the room, followed closely behind by Inspector Varcoe and two of his men. *"Hey!"* Paul bolted off the settee and ran behind my chair, making me wonder what exactly he'd done to be so guilty.

"Did she get a name?" Colin asked as he waved Paul over and filled his hands with coins.

"No," the boy mumbled, his eyes glued to his scruffy boots, refusing to even look in the direction of Varcoe and his men. "But gimme another night. I'll find what yer after."

"You've done more than enough," Colin said as he walked Paul out onto the landing. "This man is not to be trifled with. Best you leave him to us."

Paul gazed at Colin, his face a mask of incomprehension. "Wot?"

"I've got it. You go keep an eye on the Guitnu house again, okay? Stay out of trouble."

"Wot trouble?" He glanced at Varcoe and then back at Colin. "I ain't in no trouble."

Colin patted the boy's shoulder. "See that you keep it that way." He gave him a wink and a smile as Paul charged down the stairs, followed by the immediate slamming of the door. "An outstanding lad," Colin announced as he came back into the study.

"Employing children now, Pendragon?" Varcoe scoffed, parking himself on the settee the boy had just vacated. His two bobbies remained just inside the room, serving no better purpose than bookends for the inspector. "Surely the whole of Scotland Yard can do better for you than that?"

"Don't get me started on what the Yard can do." Colin gave a warm smile that seemed to allow his words to glide past the inspector. "But I would assume you're here for some keener reason."

"Ach . . ." Varcoe muttered under his breath as he swiped a hand through his mane of white hair. "This blasted case is going to undo me."

"Now, now." Colin reached forward and poured himself more tea. "I don't think you'll ever be unseated. Tea?" He held up the cup Paul had failed to use and Varcoe grabbed it gruffly. "If your men would like some I'll have Mrs. Behmoth bring up more cups."

"They're working," Varcoe muttered, waving them off without a thought. "There's been another killing. Actually three more."

I choked on the sip of tea I'd been taking even as Colin bolted to his feet. "What? Who?"

"Not who." Again Varcoe ran a hand through his hair before grabbing for a scone. "It's the Astons' dogs. Three giant beasts of one sort or another."

"Irish wolfhounds," Colin said as he paced over to the windows.

The inspector flicked a disinterested gaze at Colin before taking a bite of the scone. "All three had their throats cut," Varcoe relayed mechanically, "but I'm betting they were drugged first. You don't just walk up to three brutes like that and hash their necks. Denton Ross is doing the autopsy now. There's certain to be tainted meat in their stomachs."

"Of course," Colin mumbled as he stopped and fixed his gaze at some distant place outside. Even so, I could tell his thoughts were a world away. "But why? There's no sense in it. What makes you think they're connected to the other murders?"

"Each of the dogs had a small fabric sack stuffed in its mouth with those blasted witchcraft items. So you tell me."

"Voodoo," Colin corrected while nudging a coin from his pocket and deftly coaxing it between his fingers. "It's a religion. It has nothing to do with demonic claptrap."

"I don't really give a bloody fig." Varcoe set his tea down and watched Colin pace across the front of the windows. "All I know is that African witch has got to be hooked up in this somehow."

Colin stopped and scowled at him. "I thought you've had her under surveillance since you released her?"

"Well, of course we do!" he snapped. "But just because she never left the Connicle house last night doesn't mean she isn't ruddy well up to her bodice in it."

"And what do you suppose is her motive?"

"*I don't bloody well know!*" He jumped from his chair and stepped directly in Colin's path, his face careening toward fuchsia. "You're supposed to be assisting me here, Pendragon, but so far you're about as helpful as the pox."

"Are you severing our trysts, Emmett?"

"What?!"

Colin waved him off and resumed his pacing. "Has Edmond Connicle regained consciousness?"

"No. The ruddy doctor just keeps shaking his head. Pompous bastard. They had to commit his wife, you know. She's on the floor below him now, sedated and lashed to the bed. Sixpence short of a shilling, if you ask me."

Colin stopped and glared at Varcoe before shifting his eyes to me. "I'd suggest we start with a visit to the Astons," he said, his voice tight.

"We've already been out there. You'll learn nothing more until we get the report back from the autopsy."

"I doubt we'll learn anything from that, either," he clipped, shooting me another look, which brought me to my feet.

"We'll go see for ourselves." I gave Varcoe a conspiratorial smile as though I agreed with him. "We'll meet you afterwards."

Varcoe's mouth curled as his forehead creased with displeasure. "If you must. Meet me at the morgue then. We'll see what Denton Ross has learned. Maybe then you'll have a clue about what the hell we should do next." He glowered at Colin, but Colin was paying him no mind, and after what was clearly an unsatisfying minute Varcoe turned and bolted from the room, his men dutifully on his heels.

"I cannot bear him much longer," Colin erupted the moment the door slammed downstairs. "You should have gotten him out of here a hell of a lot sooner, because I was on the verge of doing it myself. Through the window. But unfortunately, as much as I am loath to admit it, *that bloody buggery bastard has been helpful on this case!*"

I forced a steady breath. "Do you feel better now?"

He didn't answer, but when he slipped the coin back into his pocket I took it as a positive sign. "As soon as we're finished at the Aston house we'll stop by the Connicles' and have another word with Alexa. Someone is trying far too hard to frame her and I cannot believe she doesn't have some inkling of who it might be."

"She's an African. Plenty of people would consider that reason enough."

He waved me off curtly and started pacing by the fireplace again. "Why would someone murder three beautiful Irish wolfhounds? What could be the motive in that? How could their lives have anything to do with the other murders?"

"A warning to Hubert Aston perhaps?"

Colin came to a halt as a grin slowly blossomed on his face. "Outstanding thought. Or perhaps it's meant to throw suspicion from himself. Mr. Aston may be in this up to his bushy black mustache."

"And then we'll have to head to the morgue?"

"Whatever for?"

"To meet Varcoe. To find out the autopsy results from the dogs."

Colin screwed up his face as he dropped to the floor and quickly ticked off a series of push-ups. "There's nothing to be learned from the dogs' stomachs. They were killed and they were killed for a reason." He jumped up and gave me a dark grin. "And I'm thinking Hubert Aston knows that reason."

CHAPTER 28

Hubert Aston's face was a vivid red, though I couldn't be sure whether it was the result of his outrage or if he had been crying and was using his fury to cover that fact. Whichever the case, there was no denying that he was fuming. He had planted himself in front of his fireplace and had not spoken below a bellow since Colin and I arrived and, as was true on our last visit, his wife was apparently unwilling to make an appearance. "... *absolutely appalling*..." he was saying, "... *the whole damnable lot of you. You should all be censured by Parliament.*"

If the slaughter of his dogs had been meant as a warning, then I could see that he was well warned. If it turned out that he was actually a *part* of these murders, then he was doing a remarkable job of covering it.

"I am not here to give you excuses," Colin was saying with unexpected restraint. "Nothing I can say will ever make the murders of your three magnificent hounds tolerable. Children... animals... their innate innocence can never be made right when such things happen. Not ever. And I will not insult you by proposing to do so. But I need you to tell me if there is someone you suspect of having been able to do such a thing? Someone looking to impart an unmistakable message to you perhaps?"

Mr. Aston's expression remained livid as he repeatedly slid his fingers along his thick, black, heavily waxed mustache. The ritual, however, seemed to be having little impact on his mood. His voice dropped a decibel when he spoke again, his tone remaining brittle and tight. "There is no such person. You are flailing like a landed fish. It is inexcusable."

Colin cracked a wry smile even as he tossed me a look brimming with irritation. "Someone has murdered the men of your neighboring estates. So how is it that your dogs were killed in a like manner and yet you have no notion why? Surely the poor canines cannot be guilty of whatever has precipitated this rampage."

"What are you insinuating?" he snapped.

"I find your ire around the slaughter of your dogs disproportionate to what you displayed when confronted with the murders of the men who were your neighbors. Have you lost your sense of propriety or does all this bluster mean to deceive?"

"How dare you . . ."

Colin waved him off perfunctorily. "Are you aware that Edmond Connicle was found alive last night?"

"What?!" His face bore his shock as he dropped down onto the nearest sofa. "Then it's true. Annabelle really saw him?"

"It would seem so."

"But how could such a mistake have been made?!" he snarled, his brow furrowing as he seemed to regain his composure again.

"The body found on the Connicle property was similar enough to draw the initial conclusion, given the catastrophic damage it had sustained. There was little reason to think it might be someone else."

"I can't believe it. . . ." He shook his head and gazed off, though he seemed to be focused on nothing.

"Indeed." Colin sat down for the first time since our arrival, looking quite pleased with himself.

"Where is he now? Have you spoken with him?" Mr. Aston fired the questions off rapidly and I wondered if it was out of concern or something else.

"That's the thing." Colin heaved a sigh. "Mr. Connicle was the victim of a brutal attack. He has yet to regain consciousness."

Mr. Aston's brow knit as he swung his eyes back to Colin. "I take it his injuries are severe?"

"Regrettably so."

Mr. Aston shook his head repeatedly, banked embers reigniting behind his eyes. "And there it is. You don't even know who's been killed and who has not. You and that band of miscreants at the Yard are incompetents." He stood up again and glowered down on Colin. "You, Mr. Pendragon, are a disgrace. Good day." He turned from us with the assurance of a man above reproach and stalked out of the dayroom.

A houseman returned at once to usher us out, and given Colin's evident annoyance, I was relieved when the front door latched firmly behind us without another word spoken. I was about to say something glib to cajole him out of his mood when he abruptly turned for the side of the house where the hounds' bodies had been found. There was a lone bobby pacing around a demarcated area of some ten feet by ten feet looking as serious as if he were protecting the Queen's jewels.

"Constable," Colin mumbled as he stepped over the low rope cordoning off the small patch of grass.

"Mr. Pendragon. . . ." He halted with deferential attention. "Mr. Pruitt . . ."

"Has anyone trampled over this area other than you fine Yarders?" Colin asked as he knelt to study the lush emerald grass bent and dappled by a thick, viscous ooze of magenta black in three distinct places. The innate brutality of what had happened sent a prickle up my spine.

"No one, sir," Varcoe's man answered. "That's why I'm here."

"So it is . . . so it is . . ." Colin replied absently as he circled the three spots from his crouched position. "You're doing fine work," he added before stepping out the other side. In that instant I knew he was on to something.

I stayed next to the sergeant, engaging him in idle conversation as Colin slowly moved in an angle toward the edge of the yard where a great number of honeysuckle bushes created a hedgerow in front of the woods behind. After he kicked around the base of the bushes for a few minutes he called for me, earning me nothing more than a disinterested nod from the sergeant.

By the time I joined Colin he was crouched right up against one of the honeysuckles, its sweet floral scent hanging thickly in the air. "Look here." He pointed to the ground as he stood up. "What do you notice?"

I looked at the black dirt beneath the huge bush and noticed little more than some dropped leaves and snapped twigs. "The start of fall?"

He rolled his eyes. "Get down and look closer. And use your blasted nose."

"My nose . . . ?" I repeated as I squatted down, realizing almost at once what he was referring to. "Oh." I leaned forward until my face was mere inches from the loamy earth and immediately detected the acrid stench of burnt almonds in amongst the honeysuckle's sweet fragrance. "Cyanide," I said as I stood up, the greasy stain in the dirt and the tiny flecks of meat tossed about retaining the smell of the drug used to bring the dogs down. "However did you find that?"

"I followed the dog prints backwards," he said as he started back toward the front of the house. "And you can see by the leaves and bits of broken branches at the bottom of that bush that the three hounds were battering about it, causing all manner of damage. They were vying for the tainted meat that would drop them over there." He nodded toward the roped section of the yard.

"Then you're right about the cutting of their throats. It was as much a ritual as the fetish sacks stuffed in their mouths."

"Somebody seems determined to make the Connicles' scullery maid culpable."

"But why?"

He flicked a measured gaze at me. "Perhaps she's right. Perhaps it is for no other reason than because everyone is so eager to believe it so. I think it's time we find out."

CHAPTER 29

The Connicle estate looked frozen in place beneath the iron-gray sky pressing down upon it. Drapes and sheers were drawn across its every window as though the inhabitants were hiding from the world behind its considerable walls. Not a soul could be seen as we approached the house, though the breeze rustling the tops of the surrounding trees kept the scene from looking truly suspended. To my surprise, the gardener's shed where this case had begun five days before had been razed. Its absence left a square, discolored gash in the otherwise pristine lawn, serving every bit as much of a reminder of what had happened as the shed itself.

Colin was walking with such determination that we were able to cover the ground between the Astons' and Connicles' in just less than fifteen minutes. His face was grim and I knew better than to pepper him with questions. At this point I hardly knew what to ask anyway.

Miss Porter greeted us at the door and told us what we already knew: that Mrs. Connicle was not at home. She seemed startled when Colin told her we were there to speak with Alexa. And as Miss Porter ushered us inside there was a resignation to her manner that made me wonder if she hadn't been deliberating herself whether the Connicles' scullery maid might indeed be somehow involved.

Miss Porter brought us back to the kitchen, where Mrs. Hollings was working over a pot of something musky smelling. "The gentlemen have come to speak with Alexa," she announced lightly as she gestured us to chairs at what was clearly the staff's table.

"She's in the back cuttin' veg for me stew," Mrs. Hollings answered without looking up. When Miss Porter did not move, Mrs. Hollings glanced over and caught sight of the three of us. "Oh," she muttered awkwardly. "I'll go fetch 'er." She covered the pot, extinguishing the flame beneath it, and disappeared without another word.

Miss Porter snatched the teapot from the stove and poured us both a cup. She had no sooner set them in front of us when Alexa entered. Her face was flush from the work she had been doing, but her hair was neatly tucked beneath a white scarf and her black uniform was immaculate. She still managed to walk with an unfaltering dignity and pride that I could not help marveling at, given the loss of her husband and all she had endured since.

"I shall leave you be," Miss Porter said as she crossed back to the door we had entered through. "Please let me know if you require anything else." She offered the remnants of a smile and then disappeared out the door.

Colin turned his gaze to the West African woman and gave her a gentle grin. "Thank you for seeing us again, Alexa. Please . . ." He gestured her to a chair across from us. She held her ground a moment, her lips pursed and her eyes wary, before finally deciding to sit down with a guarded sigh. "I know you have been treated with disregard by Scotland Yard from the onset of this investigation—"

"Ya know dat, do ya?" She cut him off as she wiped her hands along the hem of her apron as though to clean the very soot of this case from them. "And jest wot you guon do 'bout dat?"

"I am going to solve these crimes and prove what I have believed from the start. That you have nothing to do with any of it."

I was surprised by his words and struggled not to show it. He had never told me that he'd released her of any complicity whatsoever.

"Ya know dat too, huh?" she said with an expression far more mocking than mollified. "Is dat why ya let me sit in jail? 'Cause ya t'ink me innocent?"

"There was nothing I could do to stop that lot at Scotland Yard. At least now they know you aren't the killer."

She let out a hollow laugh. "Naw. Now dey jest t'ink me da leader. I got dem followin' me like a pack a ruttin' dogs every time I show me face."

"I *will* clear your name," he answered more harshly than I'm certain he intended. "But you have to help me. You *must* have an idea why someone would be trying so hard to frame you for these murders?"

She leaned back in her chair with a derisive laugh. "It's like I tol' ya when ya sprung me from dat jail. Ain't ya looked at me? The color a me skin? The nap a me hair? How ya go askin' me a question like dat?"

"Oh, come now!" he snapped. "You cannot expect me to believe that you're being framed for murder for such rubbish."

"Den you a fool."

Colin exhaled brusquely and shifted his eyes to me, and I could see that he was dangling on the precipice of irritation. "It has to be something more," I said into the protracted silence. "Someone has gone to a great deal of trouble to make you look guilty. Why?" I pressed. "Why you?"

She shook her head. " 'Cause it easy. People wants ta believe. Yer Yard is happy ta find it so."

And even as she said it I knew she was right. Hadn't I been caught myself when Colin had just proclaimed her wholly innocent? Even knowing she couldn't have committed the murders herself, I was still content to believe she was likely somehow involved. My own willingness to continue to see her potential culpability was as infective as Varcoe's insistence that all the clues pointed to her. It *was* easy to believe, comforting even.

"Is there anyone you're aware of who has a particular distaste for you or your beliefs?" Colin picked right up as though she had not said a word.

Once again she let out an arid, cracking chortle devoid of any humor. "When yer different there's lots a distaste." She waved him off. "Why am I botherin' ta tell you?"

"I understand more than you know," Colin shot back. "I spent the first dozen years of my life in Bombay. The Indians looked at my fair skin, blond hair, and blue eyes and saw me as an object of curiosity or ridicule. In school it was largely ridicule. Some boys I learned to fear greatly. So let me ask you again, is there anyone you know of who holds you in particular disdain?"

She stared at him a moment, her eyes studying him cautiously, and I suspected she was trying to gauge the validity of a confession I knew Colin had been loath to make. "Den ya know da shorter list is who liked us. Jest da people in dis house. None more den da mister."

"Mr. Connicle?" Colin asked as he slipped a coin from his pocket and began easing it between his fingers. "And how did you come to work for the Connicles?"

"I was sellin' meat pies on da corner by his office. Tryin' ta keep me and mine fed. After twelve years da couple wot brought us here from Dahomey had died. Dey left us jest enough ta rent a small room fer a couple months. Bless 'em fer dat. Da rest went ta dey dogs. Dey loved dem dogs." She made the statement without a modicum of resentment, though I had to turn my head to keep her from seeing the shamed flush of my cheeks.

"Mr. Connicle had one a me pies and liked it," she went on with a grin. "Pretty soon he's eatin' 'em about ever' day. Even gets other men he works wit' ta eat 'em too. I was makin' a livin' offa dem!" She chuckled with the first good humor I had heard from her. "Den one day he asks if I wanna come work for he and his missus. Jest like dat. Wants me ta work in dey kitchen. I tells him me husband hasta work too and the mister says he can work dey prope'ty. Brought us home dat very day."

"And how were you received here?"

"Had ta prove meself to Mrs. Hollin's before she'd let me in her kitchen. After dat it were me job ta take orders from her and dat's wot I do." She let out a sigh. "Miss Porter don't have much ta do wit' me. She nice enough. I ain't said a hunnert words ta her. She takes care a da missus. Dey driver . . ." She shrugged. "He were nice enough ta me husband. He don't talk ta me. He don't have ta . . ." Her voice trailed off and she went still.

Colin waited a couple seconds, the coin flipping rapidly between his fingers, before he suddenly burst out with, "And Mrs. Connicle?"

Alexa took her time. "Da missus ain't well. I see it when she look at me. Mostly I stay outta her way."

"Is she uneasy around you?"

"She uneasy around life. Dat's jest da way God made her. She do what she can. Even when dat Yard bloke was sayin' I done somethin' to her mister she never looked at me bad. After me own husband died . . ." She shook her head and stared across at Colin. "She a good woman. She ain't had it easy."

"Are you referring to her illness?"

She screwed up her face and waved Colin off. "She ain't ill. She delicate, like a flower wot buds too early. Some a us are animals or bugs, some are trees or grass, and t'anks God some are flowers. We gotta take care a dem dat be flowers."

"That's all very good and well," Colin grumbled as he slipped the whirling coin back into his pocket, "but the one who needs taking care of right now is you. Every clue in these murders is pointing in your direction. Somebody is trying to frame you and I really need you to do more than spout trite sayings. I cannot protect you if you will not help me."

"Protect me?!" Alexa crossed her arms over her chest and glowered at him. "I ain't askin' you ta protect me. I don't need ya. I managed me whole life wit'out da likes a you and I plan on goin' right on about me business jest da same way. You wanna help someone, help da missus. I don't need shite from you."

"Pride is a fool's game."

She grinned. "I bet ya know somethin' 'bout dat." She stood up and adjusted her apron so it was sitting just right. "I get along fine wit' everyone in dis house. It's true. Been so for a while. Da mister . . ." She shook her head and sagged slightly. "I wouldn't be here if it weren't fer him. I ain't never wished him no ill. I'd be a fool ta a done dat."

"I never said you did." Colin got up and stabbed his fists onto his waist. "What I want to know is who wishes *you* ill?!"

For the first time she looked as though his words might finally have had an impact. And then she quite simply shrugged her shoulders and said, "Nobody and ever'body."

Colin pulled in a deep breath and let it out again before asking, "Could you be just a touch more specific?"

"I got vegetables ta cut. We done?"

His face went rigid and his eyes narrowed, yet he did not utter a word. It was quite extraordinary. I don't know whether it was because he truly did understand how she felt, but as they stared at each other for what seemed the longest time I knew something had passed between them.

"Ya know what I t'ink?" Her eyes sparkled as she managed a wistful smile, her gaze riveted on Colin. "I t'ink whoever done dees t'ings done 'em so you an' dem Yarders be followin' dere trail a crumbs jest like dey mean ya to." She gave a sardonic smile. "Dat's what I t'ink."

Colin remained resolutely mute as she nodded her chin at the two of us and took her leave.

CHAPTER 30

My head was pounding its irritation as I shut the folder and leaned back in the cushionless straight-backed chair. The chair, it seemed, had been aptly selected by the cheerless dark-haired young man who had shown me to this dour room with its lone window and clutter of filing cabinets and bookshelves piled up to the ceiling. It discouraged any but the most rudimentary comfort, which, given that this was the room where audits took place, made perfect sense.

"More tea, Mr. Pruitt?" Wynn Tessler gamely asked as he swept the folder I'd just finished reviewing into a box at his feet.

"Please." I gave him what I could conjure of a smile despite the steady pulsing at my temples. I had been staring at an assortment of calculations and figures for well over two hours and, as usual, they had been taunting my comprehension almost from the start. There was no surprise that Colin had left me here alone to start poring through the Connicle and Hutton accounts while he made an ostensibly quick detour to check on Edmond Connicle. For if I had an aversion to accounting it was practically toxic to Colin.

"I am afraid you have exhausted the Connicle ledgers," Mr. Tessler announced as though that were some sort of tragedy. "I do have most of the Hutton documents gathered should you wish to proceed."

"Of course." I nodded dimly, knowing I had no alternative. Colin had promised to meet me here to do his share of this drudgery, but as I flipped open the cover of my watch I knew he had found some pretext to forgo his assistance. If his excuse proved feeble I had already vowed to myself to make him share my current misery one way or another.

Wynn Tessler leaned over and flipped open another box as though we couldn't possibly be having more fun in our lives at this moment. He cheerfully dug out several thick folders and shoved them across the table at me. Each was labeled *HUTTON: WEST HAMPTON*, and each held enough papers to condemn many more hours of my life. My head immediately intensified its throbbing.

"Let me get us that tea," Mr. Tessler chirped as he stood up and called to someone down the hall.

His voice clawed at my temples as I sat forward and flipped open the top folder, once again assaulted by myriad accounts at all the same establishments: Bank of England, Royal Bank of Scotland, C. Hoare & Company, and Pictet & Cie. It appeared that Columbia Financial was consistent in their advice. As I sorted through the first layer of investments and accounts, I was struck by the disparity of holdings between the Connicles and Huttons. While either could have bought and sold me many times over, it quickly became clear that the Hutton family lived within far stricter means. Someone, Mr. Hutton himself I presumed, had made poor choices around a mining concern in South Africa, which had cost his family dearly.

"Here we are then," Mr. Tessler said as the same grim young man who always seemed to do his bidding entered with a tray of tea and scones. "Thank you, Sebastian. You can take the Connicle ledgers back with you." The young man set the tray on the desk, taking care not to disturb any of the documents I had spread out before me. He tossed Mr. Tessler a curt nod and swept up the two Connicle boxes as though they held no weight whatsoever, then took his leave. "Come, Mr. Pruitt." My host smiled.

"Leave those things for a moment and rest your eyes. You'll be cursed with spectacles like the rest of us if you keep at it too long." He laughed.

"I'm sure that day will come," I answered as I gladly set the file aside and picked up the teacup.

"I know it's all dreadfully dry, but it is a living."

"I should think it a great deal of pressure, investing someone else's money. Most clients' tolerance for failure must be minuscule. For instance, these mining investments the Huttons have in Africa; it appears far more money is going into them than coming out."

Mr. Tessler flinched and pursed his lips. "You're an astute man, Mr. Pruitt. More so than many of those we do business for. As you can imagine, while it is our goal to direct all financial holdings for our clients, we can only accomplish that which they will allow us to do. Arthur Hutton chose to heed the siren's call of purportedly easy money." Mr. Tessler sipped his tea as his eyes flicked up to mine. "Let me assure you, Mr. Pruitt, there is no such thing. So despite my personal protestations, Arthur quite literally poured a vast sum of money down mine shafts that were alleged to be filled with diamonds and such." He shook his head. "Now his widow must suffer the consequences of his imprudence."

"How unfortunate," I muttered, picking up a scone and nibbling on it in hopes it might ease the pressure in my head. "A particular shame, given the regrettable state of health of their son."

"And in that"—he stared at me with a grim expression—"you have the very heart of Arthur's decision. He worried terribly over William's care. The lad already requires constant supervision. Once he reaches Anna's age he's bound to be quite out of hand. He will need to be placed in a permanent facility and I'm afraid such places are only as good as one's ability to pay. It's tragic."

"Indeed," I answered flatly, swallowing the truth of how very much I knew of such places. "Do many of your clients fail to heed your advice?"

He gave an amused sort of snort as he refilled our cups.

"More than I would care to admit. Most can be reasoned with, but it does rather boggle the mind when someone pays our fees yet refuses to take advantage of the very advice he is paying for."

"Human nature, I suppose."

"Pardon?"

I looked over at Mr. Tessler and set a smile on my face. "The ability to believe that one is smarter than everyone else. It is certainly what has kept Mr. Pendragon and me in business." I took a hearty pull of tea and returned to the Huttons' folder even as a thought began to swirl around the periphery of my brain. "Did Mr. Hutton ever travel to those African mines?"

"Arthur . . . ?" Mr. Tessler let out a chuckle. "I don't think Arthur set foot outside of England the whole of his life. He certainly never traveled to Africa."

"Extraordinary that he would deem to invest such sums in ventures he had no personal knowledge of."

"How old-fashioned of you, Mr. Pruitt. Don't you know the world is shrinking all the time? What with telegraphs and that Scotsman Mr. Bell and his telephone, there is little one cannot find out about in much more than a day. I should think the day may come when travel itself will become irrelevant."

"How breathtakingly mundane we would all become were travel to ever become irrelevant," Colin piped up from the doorway, Mr. Tessler's assistant at his side. Colin looked tired, and there was an unaccountable dimness in his sapphire eyes. As he scuffled into the room, his usual ramrod bearing appearing almost leaden, I sensed that something was wrong. He nodded to Sebastian, who instantly evaporated back down the hall, and came into the room. "Are we going somewhere?" he asked offhandedly.

Mr. Tessler gestured at me with his chin. "Your Mr. Pruitt has been asking questions about the investments of Arthur Hutton. It would seem he believes I should have more influence than I do."

"Ah." Colin smiled thinly. "That must be the bane of your profession." He moved up beside me but made no effort to glance at the folder I held open. "I'm afraid I have some very bad news," he said after a moment, and I knew what he was going to say. "Edmond Connicle has died. He has succumbed to the sepsis of his wounds. His wife..." Colin shook his head and released a wearied breath. "She is inconsolable."

"Poor Annabelle," Mr. Tessler mumbled. "She has lost Edmond not once, but twice."

"She has." Colin dragged his eyes over to Mr. Tessler. "Do you have any idea why Mr. Connicle would have taken such sudden leave of his estate as he did? Or what he might have been doing at Tower Hill last night?"

"Edmond kept his own counsel, Mr. Pendragon. He did not confide in me. I served no function for his estate, nor did he for mine. Perhaps those are better questions asked of his wife."

"Mrs. Connicle is in no state for such enquiries. Is there someone here who worked alongside him? Someone who would have been privy to his business dealings?"

"Edmond stopped working on individual accounts years ago. He wasn't like the rest of us, you know; he never *had* to work. For him it was more a hobby. Or maybe a diversion. When we started to become truly successful it was like a game well played for him. So no, I am afraid there is no one here who holds the key to the things Edmond did."

"Are you telling me that Mr. Connicle maintained his own accounts?"

Mr. Tessler chuckled. "He kept a watchful eye on them, but no, one of our senior analysts took care of his bookkeeping."

"And who might that be?" Colin pressed.

"Noah Tolliver," Mr. Tessler answered, folding his hands on the table like a grade-school boy. The name instantly stirred in my brain and, as I glanced over at Colin, I could see that his brow had furrowed as well. "He would be the executor of the estate now. Edmond brought him into the firm. I believe they met at Cambridge."

"Tolliver...?" Colin repeated.

And as soon as he did, I knew where I had heard it before. "Isn't that Mr. Aston's accountant?" I spoke up.

"He is," Mr. Tessler answered amiably, seeming impressed that I would know such a thing.

"Then we should like to speak with him," Colin said.

Mr. Tessler sat back with a sigh. "Noah is on leave just now. The poor man suffered a terrible riding accident a few months back and has been convalescing at his country home ever since."

"How unfortunate," Colin muttered perfunctorily. "Nevertheless, I should still require a word with him."

"Of course." Mr. Tessler stood up and called out into the hallway for Sebastian again. When no response was forthcoming, Mr. Tessler excused himself and left the room.

"Poor Edmond," I said. "Did he ever regain consciousness?"

"He did." Colin shook his head with a grimace. "But he was incoherent. Mumbling drivel. I couldn't make sense of any of it no matter how hard I tried." He glanced away from me. "The doctor banished me from the room for getting in his way. A bloody lot of good *that* did."

"Colin . . ." I muttered, trying not to scold though horrified at the thought that he might have been a hindrance to Edmond Connicle's survival.

"What?!" he snapped back, and I knew the same thought was already with him. "Have you had any luck here?"

I poked at the papers laid out before me. "Precious little." I gave him a hurried recounting until Mr. Tessler returned with a sheet of paper clutched in one hand.

"Here you are then, Mr. Pendragon," he said as he handed it over. "Mr. Tolliver is out in Stratford. If you really wish to see him I'm sure I can have Sebastian arrange something for you."

"I would be most obliged. The sooner the better."

"Consider it done. We'll get word to you shortly."

"And should we require further access to these files?"

"You need only ask."

"Very well then." Colin shook Mr. Tessler's hand with an easy smile, but even so, I could see nettlesome doubt lingering behind his eyes.

CHAPTER 31

On the way back to our flat we stopped in Holland Park by the Guitnus' home to arrange for our young spy Paul to meet us later in the evening at the same pub where he'd spotted the foreign man tossing about copious coins and crowing about his benefactor. Whether this would prove a reliable lead was based more on hope than evidence, but it was something, and for the moment that had to be enough. We considered stopping in and speaking with Mr. Guitnu to offer a veiled sort of update on our progress, but Paul informed us that while the wife and all three daughters were at home, Mr. Guitnu himself had left some time ago. The information earned Paul a half crown and a sigh of relief from Colin. Neither of us was in any mood to address Mr. Guitnu's thefts with him until after we heard back from his daughter's Lothario, Cillian, whose answer was due tomorrow evening. I only hoped that he and Sunny would choose to do the right thing.

"Mr. Guitnu is going to have a fit when he learns we've implicated his own daughter and her beau," I muttered as I settled back in the cab for the remainder of the short journey to our Kensington flat.

"Mr. Guitnu is going to have a fit when he learns his daughter *has* a beau," Colin pointed out.

The cabbie had us home in a matter of minutes and that was when we discovered that our luck had run out. Had I been paying attention I would have realized what was awaiting us at the sight of the carriages pulled up outside our door, but I was not paying attention, and when I heard Colin mumble a curse under his breath I only imagined that he was still fretting about what had transpired in Edmond Connicle's room at the time of his death. So when we crested the top of our stairs and entered the study, I was quite stunned to find Inspector Varcoe pacing in front of the windows, anger evident on his already-reddened face, and Prakhasa Guitnu at his ease on the settee, sipping tea.

"Where in the bloody hell have you two been?!" Varcoe blasted before either of us had even fully entered the room.

"Betting the horses at Ascot." Colin flashed a tight smile as he made his way to Mr. Guitnu. "A pleasure to see you again, Mr. Guitnu. I apologize that we have been remiss in keeping in touch with you. Be assured that your case is never far from our thoughts."

"I know how busy you must be," Mr. Guitnu responded without artifice. "This poor man has been muttering under his breath since I arrived."

"You're damn right I have." Varcoe stalked over to us as we sat down across from Mr. Guitnu in our usual chairs. "You were supposed to have met me at the blasted morgue hours ago. I demand to know where you've been."

"Did you learn anything at the morgue?" Colin sidestepped easily as he poured us tea and refreshed the cup in front of Mr. Guitnu.

The inspector's face soured. "I am *not* about to discuss an ongoing investigation in front of a stranger."

"Inspector Emmett Varcoe . . . Prakhasa Guitnu . . ." Colin took a quick sip of his tea. "I'm betting Mr. Ross found meat in the poor dogs' innards. Something greasy like pork or lamb. And in six or seven weeks, when it no longer matters, Denton Ross will finally confirm that the meat was poisoned. Cyanide, I believe."

"*Pendragon!*" Varcoe bellowed loudly enough to bring Mr. Guitnu to his feet.

"I should not be here." Mr. Guitnu fluttered anxiously.

"You have every right to be here," Colin consoled as he nevertheless jumped up and escorted Mr. Guitnu to the stairs. "You are a wage-paying client while the good inspector does nothing but take." He chuckled. "Please know, Mr. Guitnu, that we have made significant progress in your case, and while I would like nothing more than to discuss it with you, as you can see, we are ensconced in a pressing matter for the Yard. Did you have the lock to your safe changed as I recommended?"

"Yes, yes . . ."

"And there have been no additional thefts of your valuables these past several days?"

Mr. Guitnu nodded eagerly. "There have not." He tilted his head and studied Colin a moment. "Significant progress?" he repeated.

"Significant progress," Colin restated with a Cheshire's grin. "If I may beg your further indulgence for just another two days then we shall come around and set your matter to rest once and for all."

"Of course." Mr. Guitnu nodded fervently. "I thank you most kindly." He headed down the stairs with an unmistakable lightness to his step.

"Now, Inspector." Colin came back and resettled himself in his seat. "Am I right about the dogs or not?"

"Lamb," Varcoe conceded with a grunt. "They had lamb in their bellies. And while it'll be some time before we know what it might have been laced with, Mr. Ross is suggesting they were most certainly drugged, given how cleanly their throats were sliced. So how the hell did you know that? And what makes you say cyanide?" Varcoe grumbled.

"Tea, Emmett?" Colin held out a cup, which the inspector gruffly snatched, his brusqueness reminiscent of his usual self, before our détente. "It's as you said," Colin carried on smoothly.

"Three wolfhounds. What's the first thing any man would do who meant to harm them? He would drug them." Colin slid his cup back onto the table and sauntered over to the fireplace. "And we happened to find a spot of grease near one of the bushes in the yard."

"A spot of grease?" Varcoe frowned.

"From meat. Undoubtedly from the lamb your Mr. Ross found in the dogs' stomachs. And there was the unmistakable residue of almonds about. Almost surely from the use of cyanide. But none of that matters. I presume you've been told that Edmond Connicle has died?"

"Well, of course I have," Varcoe puffed, glaring at Colin. "And I know you were there when it happened, Pendragon. Buggering up the doctor's efforts to save him."

"What?" Colin turned on him with a grim expression. "He was trying to speak. I was attempting to comfort him."

Varcoe looked at me and let out an amused snort. "You were trying to get some answers. I'd have done the same damn thing." A scowl set upon his face. "So what did he say?"

Colin shook his head and stared into the fireplace. "I couldn't make any of it out."

Varcoe's scowl deepened. "You better not be keeping anything from me—"

"Do I look like I'm doing that?" Colin turned on him, rage flaring in his eyes. "I'm just as frustrated by this blasted case as you are. None of it makes any sense." He stomped over to the windows and glared down onto the street for a moment. "It seems to me we have all done little more than follow the crumbs that have been left for us, and I, for one, am done with it. You want to know what you can do? Set the full weight and breadth of the Yard onto the Connicles' scullery maid, Alexa. Let's see if maybe there is some rival group unhappy with the way she practices her faith."

"Rival group?"

"The voodoo religion, Inspector. You've said yourself that it has permeated every aspect of these murders. Perhaps we've just not looked far enough afield yet."

Varcoe's brow caved in on itself as he studied Colin. "Are you saying that I might have been right about this voodoo piffle all along?"

Colin stared back at him from the windows but did not answer.

"And what will you and Pruitt be doing?" Varcoe asked warily, clearly loath to believe Colin's concession.

"Ethan and I will stay home tonight." Colin moved back over to the mantel and picked up a coin and began carelessly flipping it through his fingers. "I think I shall buff a few of my antique knives."

"You will remember that we are partners on this case," Varcoe warned.

"Nevertheless"—Colin flashed a roguish grin—"I'll not have you gawking at me while I partake of my hobbies."

"I mean to know everything you're up to," Varcoe growled, "and every thought that passes your mind!"

"You may find that a bit awkward at times."

Varcoe's face went as pink as a sunset as he stood up. "We are in this case together and if I get an inkling that you're withholding something from me I shall bring the full weight and breadth of the Yard down on your arse. I'll not be trifled with."

" 'Til tomorrow then," Colin said as he slapped the coin back onto the mantel.

The inspector did not look entirely placated, but he said nothing further before he took his leave, barreling down the steps like a battalion on the move.

"When did he get so suspicious of me?" Colin muttered as soon as the door slammed shut. "Is he getting smarter or am I getting predictable?"

"Perhaps a bit of both." I chuckled.

Colin scowled. "Well, I shan't be predictable tonight and neither will you. We have quarry to hunt. The Connicle case has taken a turn and I shall not be played a moment longer. Let us have dinner and don our garb for the evening. For tonight we shall change the rules of this ugly game."

CHAPTER 32

M̲y back was aching as I shuffled toward the next table, the one our young scout Paul had nodded toward the moment I'd entered this, our third, tavern stop of the evening. The cuff of my pants were dragging on the floor, occasionally sliding under my well-worn shoes, ensuring that I moved at nothing more than the ponderous pace of a beggar. And so I was. Garbed in a set of worn, ill-fitting, dirty clothing forever resigned to the cellar by Mrs. Behmoth but kept for just such occasions, I was limping from table to table with the street's detritus smudged on my face, seeking whatever handouts I could get. Thus far I had already received what added up to seven shillings for my evening's work. Perhaps there was hope for humanity after all.

Colin, who had arrived some fifteen minutes before me, was slouched in a corner by himself, his head hanging low under a drooping hat, a bottle of whiskey nearly empty in front of him. Paul had gotten booted from the pub shortly after my arrival for running a con with a deck of cards in a back booth. That he was also underage seemed irrelevant to the owner. Paul's sin had been distracting the patrons from ordering more liquor. Which was why I was quickly making my way to the table of the man Paul had pointed out. I knew it was only a matter of time before I too was tossed to the street.

"Ya seem like a fine gentleman," I muttered to the swarthy man, getting my first good look at him. "Could ya spare a bloke a bit a change?"

He glanced up at me with coal-black eyes, his broad face pocked and weathered, though I determined his age to be about the same as mine. He had a scruffy, misshapen beard, and as his lips parted in more of a leer than a smile they exposed yellowed teeth and a few vacant spaces. "Piss off, ya filthy shite."

"Prussian?" I asked, eager to engage him in any way I could, given that he clearly wasn't about to show me a slip of kindness.

He took a sip of his ale and stared at me over the rim of his tankard, revealing a deep-set malevolence bristling behind his eyes that made me falter slightly. "Makes no matter now, do it? 'Cause I'll sooner cut yer throat as give ya a squat farthin'." He slipped a large butcher's blade halfway out of a coat pocket and gave a mirthless snicker that came out low and cruel.

I shuffled back a step, anxious to move out of range should he decide to lash out with the knife, but not before catching sight of the coppery residue on the dark silver blade. Given the vibrancy of the color, I could see it had been recently used and that he'd not bothered to wipe it clean. It proved he wanted me, and anyone else he showed it to, to know it. "Sorry," I mumbled, continuing to back away until there was a table between us. With my heart hammering in my chest I endeavored to commence my charade of entreaty, keeping watch on the man as he returned to his stein, having secreted the blade back into his coat. Men like him were thick down here. They placed little value on life amongst those who responded far more rapidly to fear than kindness. For down here a life well lived meant little more than beating the odds.

Having collected a smattering more of pence, I finally made it back to where Colin was seated in the corner. His hat was pulled so low he looked as likely to be asleep as not and was listing ever so slightly to one side, his shoulders hunched and his chin appearing to be headed for the tabletop. "It didn't look like your charms had much of an impact on him," he said in a low, husky voice.

"He's foul. Flashed a butcher's knife at me with a residue of fresh blood still on the blade."

"Blood?" Colin made a motion of waving me off as I shook my handful of change at him. "Are you sure?"

"Are you really asking me that?"

He abruptly lurched to his feet and stared over my shoulder. "He's moving. Don't lose him. I'll head out the back and come around." I started to turn away when I felt Colin seize my arm. "Be careful, Ethan," he hissed under his breath. "I'll not have you hurt."

"The same to you," I said as he pulled away. I glanced back just as the man disappeared out the front door, the tails of his black coat snapping with a finality that sent my heart leaping up to my throat. Without hesitating I straightened up and hiked my pants so I could move properly, rushing to the front of the tavern and earning myself several stern glances from the more generous of the patrons. I slapped my bounty of change onto the end of the bar and stepped out into the night.

The streets were a frenzy of activity. Night had brought out the nocturnal creatures, those who counted on the darkness to earn a living. Prostitutes meandered about in pairs or trios until it became necessary to go their separate ways. Swindlers hovered in the mouths of alleys, beckoning one and all to take their chances in a game of dice or trying to guess under which of three shells a half crown had been concealed. Most catered to the throngs of factory men and dockworkers looking for any reason to delay returning home to their disgruntled wives and copious children forever reminding them of how woefully inadequate they were. Their night's revelries would be conducted through a haze of alcohol and opium, sometimes one or the other, very often both. Life appears better through their shroud, though the morning's light is ever the harsher for it. Even still I can remember that.

The noise and laughter added to the bedlam of humanity lunging past, making my heart race faster as I frantically scanned the crowds, cursing myself when I could not find the Prussian man. I spotted Colin at the mouth of the alley several doors down to my left staring straight at me. In spite of the distance between us, I was certain he could see that I had already failed. He tilted his head toward the street and shifted his eyes sideways, and as I followed his gaze I caught sight of the man, his long, black coat flapping about him like the broken wings of a crow as he barreled up the far side of the street with his shoulders hunched and his head down.

I hurried across the road and fell in some distance behind him, determined to neither lose him nor be noticed should he glance back over his shoulder. But he never did. He seemed intent to move with focused ease and dexterity, winding through the throngs with the practiced ease of a sea creature who had swum these waters a thousand times before.

I attempted to settle into a rhythm behind him, mimicking his pace, but it was nearly impossible, as he frequently shot out into the street and continued down the other side where Colin was keeping pace, before just as abruptly blasting back over to where I held steady. Each of his diagonal forays forced me to slow my step as he nimbly traversed the horses, carts, and carriages clogging the thoroughfare. Twice, when he suddenly burst out from behind an idled carriage, I'd had to turn on the person trying to press past me and beg for a handout to keep him from seeing my face. Had Colin and I not both been working to keep him within our sights he would have been impossible to follow. And I was certain that was what he intended.

He cut around another corner, and when I realized we were back in Fairclough Street I understood that he had doubled back in a great, circuitous arc. My spirits soared as I realized that he was not only a shrewd man, but also that he was very much up to something. I wanted to signal Colin, to let him know that he had been right, but he was nowhere near me, and then, in the draw of a single breath, the Prussian man was gone.

My stomach dropped and my heart seized so that in spite of the cacophony going on around me I was no longer registering a sound. It was as though my ears had suddenly ceased to process the slightest noise, leaving me to frantically search the surrounding masses of people even as my eyes felt like they were moving through a glaze of aspic. *You've lost him,* my brain screeched, *not once, but twice.* I spun around even as I continued to move forward, searching for Colin to see if he would again prove my salvation, and that's when a flicker of movement caught the periphery of my left eye. Black, quick like a scurrying mouse, the bottom flap of the man's jacket.

An alley had just slid past me and it was the light from the moon that had caught the tiny movement of the Prussian making his way down it. I immediately turned back and threw myself behind a group of garbage barrels at the mouth of the alley. My breath came rapidly as I struggled to rein in my fluttering heart and at some point my hearing also returned, as I found myself concentrated on the steady clicking of the man's shoes echoing down the alleyway. I had no idea where Colin was, but I told myself it didn't matter; I had found the man again and I was not going to lose him.

I crept farther down the alley with the stealth of a cat, keeping on my toes to stop my boots from making any sound. The man glanced back over his shoulder once, but I knew the darkness of my clothing would offer me what protection the alley's shadows could not. As it was, I could hardly see the Prussian and had to remain vigilantly attuned to the sound of his footfalls, grateful for the echoing confines of the space. Yet, as I struggled to remain silently on my toes, I knew those echoes would just as likely undo me.

The man's pace slowed and then halted, and as I too came to a stop I was suddenly gripped by the realization that he might have recognized me from the pub and led me here on purpose. That perhaps I hadn't been nearly as artful a tail as I had thought. If I'd been good at it once, that had been twenty years past and many pounds lighter. And then I heard a voice; "... time ..." it said. It was a man, but not with the accent of my quarry.

I knelt down on the cobbles and quickly untied my boots, carefully sliding them off my feet. The stones were cold and damp as I started to move forward in my stockings, but the effect was perfect. I only hoped I would not stumble upon anything predatory or sharp.

". . . money"—it was the Prussian man this time—"and I vill never be late." I heard him give a low, lecherous cackle, but the other man did not join in.

As my eyes tried to adjust to the great slashes of shadows and refracted moonlight in the depths of the alley, I saw another man step out from the far side of what I'd thought was the alley's end but could now see was an intersecting passage. The second man was much taller than the Prussian, looking at least my height. He was wearing a thick, black cloak that swept nearly to the ground, leaving little to be gleaned about his body beyond its stature. He wore a black hat with an oversized brim, not unlike the one Colin had been hiding beneath in the tavern, and for an instant I wondered if Colin was pulling off some sort of elaborate charade. But though Colin's shoulders were as broad as this man's, he could claim nothing of his height.

The Prussian moved forward with an unmistakable cockiness and I imagined an oily smirk on his face as he did so. It was evident he was pleased with himself, just as I could tell by the stiff bearing of the tall man that he was the person in charge. "Our friend died in hospital this afternoon," he said in a menacing tone.

"Tol' ya." The other man chuckled.

"It was no thanks to you," came the muffled reply, and as I stole forward to try to get a better look I saw that the taller man had a black scarf wrapped around the lower half of his face as if hiding from the cold in spite of the night's mildness.

"I put 'im dere."

"If he hadn't succumbed I would've put *you* there!" the tall man growled. "Did you take care of the last package tonight?"

The Prussian chuckled darkly, sending an icy shiver up my spine. "It's done. Dey von't find de little scruff."

"No?" The tall man's voice remained icy calm.

"Dey never look under dere own noses. Am I wrong?"

"You had best not be," the tall man answered, the note of threat unmistakable.

"You pay me," came the indifferent response. "You vill be happy."

"Yes." The taller man plunged a hand into a pocket of his cloak and pulled out something that glinted silver by the slender beams of the moonlight.

I realized before the Prussian that it wasn't crowns the taller man had extracted, so he was caught completely unawares when the first crack from the revolver flashed in a spit of fire. A second shot ripped out almost before the first had found its mark, dropping the Prussian to his knees before he crashed over onto his face.

The tall man looked ready to take a third shot when the sound of someone running toward us from the side alleyway caught his attention. He shoved the gun back into his pocket and came rushing in my direction. For an instant I thought I should tackle him as he tried to flee past me, but my saner mind—or greater fear—screamed that it would only get me shot as well. And then he was hurtling past, leaving me cowering against the wall in my stocking feet.

"Ethan!"

I heard the voice before I realized it was Colin. *"Here,"* I called toward the crux of the two passageways, where he suddenly appeared.

"Thank god." He heaved a sigh. "Thank god. What happened? I couldn't see a bloody thing."

"That man . . ." I pointed toward the mouth of the alley just as the tall man skidded around the corner and out onto the thronging street. "He shot the Prussian man. He's over there—"

"Help him." Colin jumped up and bolted for the mouth of the alley. "Get him to talk." And then he too was gone.

I sucked in a quavering breath, aware of the cold, musty smell of the alley as I listened for a second to the scratch and scamper of tiny feet: rats. It was enough to make me push myself off the wall. The man was gurgling, drowning in his own blood, and I knew I had to do something. I fumbled over to the black hulk of his crumpled body and knelt by his head. "Can you hear me?" I heard myself ask.

The only response I got was the continuing scamper of those tiny feet steadily, bravely moving closer. I leaned forward and muttered, "I'm going to turn you over," to the back of his head. He didn't respond, but then I hadn't expected him to. I meant only to warn him, to get him to gird himself if he was capable of such a thing.

I grabbed his shoulders and my left hand slid against something viscous and thick. Without thinking I lifted my hand to my nose and smelled the metallic scent of blood. I gripped him firmly and rolled him toward me, and he screamed. It was a wet, bubbling sort of shriek that assured me he had a chest wound even as it sent the alley's vermin scampering away.

His back rested on my thighs, his chest rising and falling in an uneven cadence as I glanced over him in the filtered remnants of moonlight that made it to the alley floor. There was a seeping wound in his lower abdomen, but I was most afraid of the gurgling rasp in his upper chest. His breath was coming out in frothy bubbles, made worse by the fact that his nose had been smashed flat when he fell. Even with his mouth unhinged and gaping I could tell he was running out of air.

"I'm going to get help!" I shouted at him. His eyes were closed and he made no motion that he'd understood what I had said. "Can you tell me who that man was?" His chest continued to expand and contract in its uneven rhythm as I dug a hand into my coat pocket and pulled out a handkerchief. If I could stop the bubbles' leaking from his chest I thought I might be able to get him to speak to me, to tell me who had done this to him, who had ended his life. "I'm sorry . . ." I muttered as I pressed the handkerchief with an unsteady hand down onto the wound at the top of his chest. His eyes instantly flew open and I faltered, releasing the pressure I had just begun to apply and causing him to gurgle another trail of dark foam from his mouth.

"I'm so sorry," I said again, my hand hovering over the wound as my eyes held fast to his, reflecting the arcing moon that was just now cresting over the buildings four stories above our heads. "What was his name?" I asked again. His body shook and his breath rattled from somewhere deep, but he only stared at me.

My own heart was pounding as I lowered my hand to his chest again, cautiously applying pressure to keep the wound from its steady seeping. This time he did not react as I pressed. His eyes kept their skyward gaze while his jaw listed in an effort to draw more breath. As his chest began to relax under my fingers I knew I had to find something to staunch the bleeding from his belly. There would be no saving this man, but at least I could give him some comfort and, if fortune would allow, perhaps I could get him to speak.

I reached my other hand down onto his abdomen, the side of my face hovering just above the lower half of his. My hand sank into a sticky morass almost at once, but I hardly noticed as some primal part of my brain finally registered something else, something far more fundamental: His breathing had stopped.

I don't know precisely when it happened. All I know for sure is that by the time I sat fully upright again it was to find his eyes still staring at the rising moon, but this time they were not seeing anymore.

CHAPTER 33

It was Colin's name that finally got me released from the bobbies I had flagged into the alley. I had used it frequently and insistently, repeatedly answering questions about where he lived (in a flat off Kensington on Gloucester Road), who his father was (the Queen's former emissary to India, Sir Atherton Pendragon), and where Colin had grown up (Bombay, India) before one of the men grudgingly professed to recognizing me. And so it was that they finally believed the story I had resolutely been telling them about the death of the Prussian man and deigned to let me return home.

The night had turned damp and cold, and while it did not start raining before I reached our flat just after two, I had known it was only a matter of time. I was exhausted and befouled by grime and coagulated blood on my sleeves, shirtfront, and pants as I quietly pushed through our front door. I set the latch behind me and stood there a moment in the darkness, leaning against the door, my head dully pounding as I closed my eyes and released a breath that made me feel as though I might collapse to the floor.

"Wot in bloody *'ell* . . ." Mrs. Behmoth's voice cut through me like a blade. "Get yer scrubby arse off a me door. Ya smell like a ruddy sewer and look like ya just crawled outta one. Get them filthy things off before ya take another step. I'll get ya a sack to put that rot in 'cause I ain't touchin' it. It oughta be burned."

The thought of arguing felt far more draining than simply following her orders, so I peeled off my coat and shirt and then pried my shoes from my feet. By the time I stripped my greasy socks off, made all the worse from my having padded around the alley in them, Mrs. Behmoth had returned with an old potato sack, holding it out in front of herself with an appalled look as I dropped my things inside. Only when I was standing in nothing but my undershorts did she finally draw the bag shut and sniff at me.

"Ya *still* smell like the bloomin' gutter. Get upstairs with 'im. 'E's been in the bath since 'e got 'ome a while ago. If ya got any sense you'll get in there with 'im." She curled her nose at me. "I can't believe you stayed out after 'e got 'isself shot."

"Shot? What?!" I was sure I had misheard her.

She held the sack away from her body as she turned away. "Ah . . . it weren't nothin'. Ya know 'ow 'e is." She turned back and looked me up and down. "Glad ta see ya ain't shot. All that blood on ya 'ad me wonderin'." She shook her head and then turned and pounded back toward the kitchen. "But yer too damned skinny. Ya got legs like a chicken."

The sound of the swinging door finally jarred me from my shock and sent me rushing up the stairs. I knew Colin couldn't be seriously injured, given Mrs. Behmoth's glibness, yet I nevertheless bolted right into the bathroom without so much as a tap on the door. "Mrs. Behmoth says you've been shot," I blurted.

He was stretched out in the tub, his left thigh red and swollen in a four-inch arc across it. "Where the hell have you been?!" he snapped as he sat up, wincing with the effort.

"In the alley where you left me. The Prussian man died in my arms. I had to report it to the police. I couldn't just leave him. And what happened to you?"

"I got nicked chasing that bastard in the black cloak and hat. I didn't know where you were. I was bleeding. . . ." His voice trailed off and I could tell he was piqued by his own reaction.

"And where are your clothes? Why are you standing there practically naked?"

"Mrs. Behmoth wouldn't let me into the house unless I took them off. I was covered in blood and—"

"Get in here!" he groused, the invitation, such as it was, not lost on me.

I tossed my undershorts near the door and climbed in with the greatest delicacy, eliciting several grimaces from Colin just the same as I settled in behind him. Only after he was leaning back against me did he allow a small sigh to escape. "Tell me what happened," I prodded.

"I'm being played for a fool."

"What? By whom?" I asked rather listlessly as the warm bath soothed my muscles and tugged at my mind, coaxing me to relax. I knew I should be more concerned by his words, that I should care deeply, but I could just as easily have fallen asleep with him tucked in my arms as hear the rest of his conjecture.

"I cannot shake the thought that this, all of this, has happened just the way it was intended to. That we have been following a carefully constructed plan whose outcome, even now, is charging toward its inevitable, calculated conclusion."

"You got all of this from being nicked?" I stifled a yawn.

He half-twisted to try to glare back at me. "Nicked, is it?! Easy for you to say since no one was shooting at *you*."

"I didn't mean—"

"And that had *nothing* to do with it anyway!" he groused as he settled back against me once more. "That bastard I followed had everything planned perfectly. From the route he took after he shot that Prussian to the placement of his horse about a half-dozen blocks away outside the back of a rowdy pub. Every bit of it was spot-on."

"I don't understand. What exactly happened?"

He heaved a sigh that made his body feel diminished within my grasp. "When I was chasing that bastard in the cloak, I realized he was taking the most heavily trafficked streets. Scores of people collided with me, not to mention carriages, carts, horses, and other detritus I had to watch out for. Every corner he took was purposeful, and all the while, with his hat tugged down and his scarf stretched across his face, it was impossible to take even the most benign accounting of him. He moved with such assurance. With his shoulders hunched forward and that blasted cloak billowing out behind him. I know he was prepared—" Colin's right hand abruptly bolted up out of the water and waved angrily through the air. "No . . . he was *expecting* to be followed and had left nothing to chance."

"You can't be sure of that," I started to protest.

"Oh, I can!" he growled. "I saw him duck down an alley and thought I had my chance to catch him." He tsked with disgust. "I waited five or ten seconds before I rounded the alley's lip and began creeping back, all the while hoping I had not lost him." He paused a moment and I let him, knowing he would make his point when he was ready. "I could hear the noise from the pub as I moved closer to the back of the alley, only one light over its back door offering any illumination. I figured he'd gone inside, just as he had intended me to believe, so I straightened up and stepped out of the shadows, and in that same instant he came careening out from behind an archway on horseback. I'd like to say I was brave, but I stumbled back like a drunken fool as he flew toward me, and before I could even get out of his way he'd fired his gun and grazed my leg. And when I fell to the ground . . . I heard him call back, '*Always a step behind, Mr. Pendragon.*'"

Colin's shoulders had gone rigid beneath my hands, allowing me to feel both the fury and the frustration of his tale. "Thank god his shot went wild," I muttered, disregarding the uneasy fact of Colin's name having been used.

"It accomplished exactly what he meant it to," Colin stated flatly. "It gave him his escape and ended any illusion that I'm getting close to a resolution on this wretched case. He knew who I was . . . that I would be there . . . and yet I cannot give you so much as an inference as to who he might be."

"We *are* getting closer . . ." I started to say, but the words sounded hollow even to me and before I could try to repair my tepid bolstering there came a banging on the bathroom door. "What is it?" I barked.

"It's yer inspector!" Mrs. Behmoth's voice barked right back. "Says 'e needs ta speak ta ya right now, so I suggest ya get yerselves decent or I'll let 'im in there. Makes no difference ta me." The sound of her heavy footsteps plodding away confirmed that she would not wait for any further reply.

"What the hell does he want?" I growled as Colin pulled himself upright and climbed out of the tub.

"Let us find out before Mrs. Behmoth drags him in here and permanently mucks up all the access to information we have recently extracted from him. Besides, I should hardly think this case can get much worse." A chill ratcheted up my spine at his words. I have often found that one is quite mistaken to presume the worst has taken place, for as would prove with this very night, it is almost never the way.

We were dressed and before Inspector Varcoe within a matter of minutes and found that he had made himself quite at home in front of the fireplace, having pulled one of the chairs right up to it. He was hunched over the cup of tea Mrs. Behmoth had already brought up as Colin limped uneasily to his chair and plopped down, the inspector's eyes glued on him the whole way. "What in hell happened to you?" Varcoe asked with little show of concern.

"I was slow getting out of the way of an errant bullet this evening."

"You what?!" Varcoe twisted around so quickly that some of his tea sloshed over onto his lap. "*Dammit!...*" he grunted as he jumped up, brushing at the wet spot. "What the devil are you talking about? What bullet? Who the bloody hell shot at you?" He shoved his cup onto the mantel and yanked his chair back over by us. "We're supposed to be partners!" he hollered. "I'll not have you gallivanting to God knows where getting yourself shot at and trying to solve this ruddy case on your own! *I won't have it!*" His voice had risen in decibels in juxtaposition to the deepening of his color to a ruby plum. "I'll have answers or you will never again have the cooperation of Scotland Yard!"

"Now, Emmett," Colin soothed. "You are upsetting yourself

needlessly. May I remind you that it is the middle of the night. Our first stop tomorrow was to be to your Yard. We would have fetched you tonight except we received a hurried bit of information and had to act upon it immediately lest it might evaporate before we could round you up."

"What bit of information?" he continued to grouse.

With a controlled exhalation of breath, Colin told Varcoe where we had been and most of what had transpired. Though he left certain details unspoken, Varcoe didn't seem to notice and, by the time Colin finished, both the inspector's demeanor and complexion had returned to something closer to normal. He turned to me. "You stayed with the victim while the constables investigated?"

"I stayed for a time and told them Colin and I would make a full report to you in the morning," I said, stretching the truth just a notch or two.

"And you have no idea who the man in the cloak was?" Varcoe pressed, flicking his eyes between Colin and me as though we meant to deceive him.

Colin met his gaze easily. "Nothing would please me more than to give you a name or even a hunch that we could all follow up on."

"*Bollocks!*" Varcoe snatched up his tea again. "The papers are roasting the Yard over these murders. I'll never get out of this one."

"Now, now . . ." Colin started to say.

"Piss off," Varcoe seethed. "Your bloody career isn't on the line."

"My career is *always* on the line."

"Horseshite," he grumbled as he pounded over to the windows, gazing down at the street. "Those newspaper nobs love you. And all the while me and my men work every damned day to keep this city safe without a piss pot of respect. Why the hell is that?" He turned on the two of us and I could see the tide of anger rising behind his eyes again.

"Because the Yard is at the forefront of everything that happens in this city. I, on the other hand, only work a case here and there. It is indeed an unfair comparison." Colin cast me a furtive glance before turning back to the inspector. "What is it, Emmett? What's brought you here so late?"

The inspector stared out the window again, the delicate teacup clutched in his meaty palm, and as I watched, his shoulders slowly caved in as though an unseen weight had been placed there. "It's the little Hutton boy," Varcoe said, his voice husky and dry. "He's gone missing."

"When?"

Varcoe continued to stare out the window, though his eyes had drifted up toward the skyline. "The boy's nurse came to the Yard about an hour ago. She said she put him down at his usual time, but when she went to check on him a few hours later . . ." Varcoe shrugged his shoulders. "Sergeant Evans is out there now. I came for the two of you." He took a quick sip of tea and straightened up before he turned and came back over to us. "I'll be downstairs in the coach. Don't keep me waiting." He set his tea on the mantel and disappeared down the stairs without a glance.

"Tonight . . ." I said the moment the door shut downstairs. "I heard the man in the cloak ask the other man if he had taken care of the last package *tonight*. I didn't know what he was talking about. Do you suppose he meant William Hutton?"

Colin yanked our coats from the hall tree and tossed mine to me. "It could be," he said as he shrugged into his.

"He's just a boy," I could not stop myself saying. "Why would they hurt a boy?"

"Why would they kill three dogs?" came the very answer I had not wanted to hear. Colin's face was set and hard. "They are leading us like lemmings!" he snarled. "We must not follow anymore."

He turned on his heels and barreled down the stairs, leaving me with my heart severed at the very thought of poor William Hutton. I wanted to ask Colin what he intended to do, but he'd already seized the door and stepped out into the night. And then, with the stealth of a whisper, the thought seized me that perhaps we had all already been led over the cliff.

CHAPTER 34

Mrs. Hutton held herself with dignity, and yet I could sense a great simmering anger just beneath her faultless exterior. Her behavior was in stark contrast to that of her missing son's nurse, who had been so bereft that Mrs. Hutton had banished her from the drawing room almost the moment we had arrived. I knew Mrs. Hutton was trying to remain optimistic about her boy's safety, so I hoped Colin and Inspector Varcoe would tread warily.

"It is not my habit to check on William once he has been put down for the night," she informed the inspector in a straightforward yet clipped tone. "As you know, he has a nurse whose room is attached to his. That is what she does."

"You mustn't take offense. I'm only trying to establish what has happened," he mumbled, his face quickly flushing a warm pink.

"What has happened"—she bit at the words as though chewing a piece of bitter fruit—"is that my boy has been taken. Have we not discussed it enough already? Is it not time for you and your men to do something?!"

"My men are upstairs now," Varcoe answered, pointing out the obvious, which only served to bring her to her feet.

"I am well aware that your men are pawing about my son's

room, Inspector, but I trust you will understand that it brings me little solace. I would presume them to be the same men who continue to allow my husband's murderer to roam free."

"I understand—"

"*You understand nothing,*" she hissed before he could finish his ill-conceived thought. "And you, Mr. Pendragon?" She snapped her eyes to him. "What have you to say for yourself?"

He held her gaze resolutely as he began to speak. "I will not hazard any further offenses by presuming what you are being forced to endure," he said, earning an immediate scowl from Inspector Varcoe. "I do believe it could be greatly helpful, however, if you would answer just a few more questions."

She pinched the corners of her eyes just above the bridge of her nose in an apparent effort to assuage some nettling pressure as she sat back down. "All right then," she said after a moment, her tone as sharp and hard as the blade I'd had flashed at me by the Prussian hours ago. "Say your piece."

I could see Colin struggling to achieve some measure of ease and knew it was not readily managed. "You must permit me to enter some uncomfortable territory—"

"It is the middle of the night and my son is missing, Mr. Pendragon. Please do not persist in patronizing me, for I will not sit here much longer."

Colin cleared his throat awkwardly. "Perhaps you could tell me how William has been adjusting to the loss of his father?"

She looked at Colin with pique. "William is six and he is not sound. He has little understanding that his father is gone."

"Has he been asking for him?"

"What *is* your point?"

"It is conceivable that he may have wandered off on his own. Perhaps in search of his father."

"William never goes anywhere without his nurse. Not ever." Her tone was harsh and unequivocal.

"He has never strayed off by himself? Or even tried?"

"His nurse is paid handsomely to watch him at all times, and if she is unavailable his sister keeps him close at hand. So no, Mr.

Pendragon, he has had neither the opportunity nor the where-withal to do such a thing."

"No?" Colin's eyebrows arched up and I wanted to signal him to stop this line of questioning. It was clear she would not tolerate much more.

As if to prove me right she narrowed her eyes while continuing to glare at him. "You met him. If you failed to notice the aberration of his behavior then I am truly a woman without hope."

My breath caught in my throat and time seemed to stretch like soft taffy as not one of us moved. Mrs. Hutton's words hung in the air between us, pointed, accusatory, demanding their due, but before I could collect myself to offer any sort of defense, Colin was already speaking. "I apologize if I have given you cause for concern regarding my abilities," he said with perfect restraint. "Perhaps you would share with us what the doctors have told you about your son."

"That he will never progress beyond the age of a child." She spat the words out as though they burned her mouth. "He will never read or write or speak worth a damn. The kind of life, Mr. Pendragon, that will be best lived sealed away in an asylum. So I will ask you again, what does any of this have to do with *finding* him?!"

He ignored her question as he leaned forward. "Do you have any reason to believe your son's disappearance could be connected to the death of your husband?"

She glared at Colin with an expression I could not decipher. The room had become chilled, as the fireplace had been allowed to die down, and I wondered that no servant had come to stoke it.

"William is as incapable of misdeed as he is of cohesive thought." Her words were brutal and I could tell she was well done with us. "How could there be any such connection between that broken boy and the man his father was? Your suggestion is absurd. But then I suppose I should expect nothing less, given what little use you and your inspector have been."

"Now, madam . . ." Varcoe started to say in an artificially conciliatory way as he rose to his feet.

"Do not trouble yourself, Inspector," she shot back as she squared off at us. "I have withstood your bumbling to the point of extinction. I will do so no more. It is clear you cannot protect me and my daughter, so we shall not spend another night here even if you ring this wretched place with a thousand regiments." She turned and swept to the door. "You and your men can finish what you will, but I'll no longer be at your disposal. Anna and I are going to my sister's in Paris as soon as I can make arrangements." And with that she was gone.

"*Shite!*" Varcoe howled. "Won't that just be ruddy perfect when Parliament finds out that our highest-taxed citizens are fleeing the city because they don't feel safe. I'll be lucky to investigate the bloody sewers once that gets out." He started for the door only to stop when he realized that neither of us was following him. "Well, are you coming?"

"We'll be along," Colin said calmly. "I just can't move as quickly tonight." He shrugged as he pointed to his left thigh.

Varcoe scowled. "I'll not have you squirming out of this case because of some bollocky injury you never should have received in the first place. If you'd fetched me first—"

"Yes, yes." Colin waved him off. "I got what I deserved."

Varcoe snarled his agreement as he turned and stalked from the room.

"This case is a muddle," Colin said as he stood up with nary a wince. "What do you make of it all?"

"Me?" I gazed back at him, my thoughts a jumble of discordant confusion. "I have no idea. That poor woman."

"Yes. . . ." He shook his head as we began to make our way to the door. "She has been through an enormous amount, I grant you that, but there is something that does not sit well with me. I almost prefer the hysterics of Mrs. Connicle."

"You cannot compare how a person handles their grief," I scolded.

He glanced back at me but said nothing, which proved to be the wisest choice, for when he turned back young Anna Hutton was standing in the doorway wrapped in a nightdress with a full-length pale yellow robe clutched tightly around her. "I don't mean to intrude," she said in a soft voice. Her face was ashen and drawn, and I wondered if anyone had given suitable attention to this poor girl.

"Not in the least," Colin responded smoothly, waving her into the room as though it were his place to do so. "We've been talking about your brother. As you can imagine, we are most anxious to find him as quickly as possible."

"I haven't a good feeling," she admitted as she perched on the edge of the sofa, her eyes sinking to the floor as her fingers fidgeted with her robe. "It's not like William to wander away. He never goes anywhere without his nurse, unless he's with me." She managed a burdened sort of smile. "I've not seen him since he was put to bed."

"Did you hear anything?" Colin asked as he knelt by her. "A cry or shout you thought he might have made in his sleep?"

"Nothing." She stared directly at Colin. "Which frightens me even more, because William does not like people he's not seen before. He wouldn't walk out with just anyone." Her eyes began to brim with tears as she dropped her gaze and girded herself to ask the question I knew had brought her down here in the first place. "Do you think he's been hurt?"

Colin drew in a breath and shot a look at me, his discomfort evident in his eyes. I thought he meant for me to say something, but he spoke up almost at once. "Do you know of any reason why someone would want to hurt your little brother?"

"No, sir." She shook her head as tears began to course down her cheeks. "He's just a boy. A good boy. He's never hurt anyone. He wouldn't know how." She rubbed the heel of her hand across her eyes before Colin could fish the handkerchief out of his pocket. "It's not been easy for him," she went on. "He hardly made a sound as a baby and my parents fretted that he would never learn to walk." She looked up and there was great pride in her laden eyes. "I taught him how to do that. About a year ago. I knew he could do it. I knew he could learn. That's when Father found the nurse. She's been teaching him so much more ever since."

"He's very fortunate to have you for a sister." Colin smiled and wiped her tears from one cheek. "You mustn't cry, Anna. Until a thing is settled there is always hope."

She gave him a crooked sort of smile. "Yes. Of course you're right." She looked at him for a moment and then, in a voice so fragile it was no more than the ghost of a whisper, asked, "Do you think someone will try to hurt me and Mum?"

Colin immediately drew her into a hug. "Mr. Pruitt and I . . ." He swept his arms wide. ". . . Indeed, the whole of Scotland Yard have you and your mother in our sights. There are men from the Yard here now and so they shall remain until we have brought an end to this case. You mustn't be afraid, Anna."

She managed a fragile smile.

"Now back to bed with you." He stood up. "The brightest minds in this city are looking for your brother. You must hold that to your heart."

"Thank you," she said quietly, and then scampered back across the foyer and up the stairs.

I turned to Colin and was startled to find him staring at me, his eyes as dark as the night sky, filled with immeasurable guilt and sorrow. And I suddenly recalled what the Prussian had bragged to his killer, how no one would ever find the *little scruff*. And in that instant, I knew what Colin was already certain of.

CHAPTER 35

Noah Tolliver had ceased to be a man of any real function months before we came to see him.

A carriage had whisked us the seven and a half miles out to Stratford to see Wynn Tessler's senior bookkeeper, the man who had once handled the Connicle fortune, but it had been for naught. It was evident that Mr. Tessler was unaware of the depth of Mr. Tolliver's condition, having told us only that the man had suffered a riding accident some months before and was at his country home recuperating. The truth of his condition was far more devastating.

His wife, a spare woman of middle years with the stature and movements of a hummingbird, showed us to a bedroom where he lay prone. She told us he had no feeling below the sternum and could only just move two fingers on his left hand. There was a gash in the front of his throat where a metal tube poked out, and I knew this to be an experimental procedure to assist him in breathing or for the administration of chloroform as necessary. He was not conscious during our brief visit, though whether this was due to chloroform I did not ask. It would have made little difference, as his wife eventually confided that he could neither talk nor recognize anyone. The blow to his head, she had been informed by a score of doctors, was debilitating and permanent.

Given our hostess's frayed condition, we declined tea, leaving as quickly as was forgivable, having thankfully kept the carriage waiting. I felt quite undone by our visit and was aware that Colin had grown quiet. Neither of our collective moods was aided by a quick stop at Scotland Yard, where we learned that the only clue they'd yet found regarding William Hutton's disappearance was traces of chloroform on his pillow. It was little to go on, though it proved the boy had not gone wandering off on his own.

And so it was that we finally returned home, our spirits as low as the dense, gray clouds that hung overhead. I worried about the scowl embedded on Colin's face as the carriage came to a stop at our flat. "Would you like to go back to the Hutton estate after dinner?" I asked, thinking he might feel better to have a second look around.

"No," he scoffed. "I've had quite enough for one day." He let a sigh escape his lips as he took my hand. "And I don't think I could face Anna again without some news about her poor brother." Neither of us made any move to get out of the carriage. "I don't really want to go back and start rooting about, you know? I'm afraid for what you overheard in that alley." He shook his head, but not before I saw the heaviness in his eyes.

"You will settle this," I said with the surety I felt as I squeezed his hand. "You mustn't ever lose hope."

He turned and gazed idly out the window. "I wish I had your faith."

"I have enough for the both of us."

"'Ey . . ." the driver's voice bristled from outside, and I pulled free of Colin's hand. "If you two blokes don't get outta there I'm gonna 'ave ta charge for yer time."

Colin climbed out without a word and trudged into our flat.

I paid the driver and hurried after Colin, finding him partway up the stairs with his gaze drooping morosely. "Do you smell that?" I said to his back as I shut the door.

He stopped and peered back at me. "What?"

"Earl Grey. Mrs. Behmoth is brewing tea. Do you suppose we have a visitor?"

He glanced up the stairs with a frown and then looked back at me. "But there was no carriage . . ." he started to say, but then his eyes lit with fire. "I'll bet it's Sundha Guitnu's beau. What was his name?"

"Cillian." I chuckled. "How is it you remember her name but not his?" Colin did not bother to answer, nor did he need to. Instead he turned and bolted the rest of the way up.

By the time I reached the landing it was to find both Cillian and Sunny seated before the fireplace on the settee, Colin poking the flames and commending them for having arrived precisely as agreed. For myself, I would have preferred a bit of time alone, but it was heartening to see the effect these two were having on Colin's mood.

Not a moment later Mrs. Behmoth brought up a tray of tea and ginger biscuits and placed it on the table between us. Colin shooed her away as he settled into his chair and began the preparations himself. He fussed over each cup, putting in just enough milk after inquiring as to the lumps of sugar required. Sunny and Cillian gave rote answers, neither delivered with more than a kernel of enthusiasm, which made me suspicious of what decision they had arrived at concerning her father's jewels.

"Biscuit?" Colin held out the plate with an enthusiastic smile. They shook their heads, further confirming my misgivings, though Colin seemed quite oblivious as he happily popped one into his mouth.

"It feels like an occasion to have you both here together," I piped up in hopes of relieving a bit of their tension, but as their eyes shifted to each other I decided I had only made it worse.

"You have both been very kind to us," Cillian muttered as he reached for a pack on the floor by his feet. "Very fair. And we have talked at length about what you said, Mr. Pendragon. About what we should do." He turned his eyes to Sunny, who instantly dropped her gaze, making me ever more uneasy as to what she and Cillian were about to say, especially given that he'd begun rooting around in his pack.

"What have you there?" Colin asked. Cillian abruptly slid the entire thing over to him and Colin leaned forward to peer inside. "Exquisite," he marveled as he reached inside and pulled out a single diamond bracelet, turning it around just inches from one eye. He immediately stuck his other hand in and came out with a strand of ivory pearls and two gold necklaces studded with sapphires. "Extraordinary."

"My father takes great pride in what he creates," Sundha said in a near whisper.

"Yes." Colin fingered the sapphires on the second necklace as he handed the other two items over to me. "That is evident."

"He makes pieces for all the finest families," she pressed on, though with no less timidity. "Even for the royal house."

"But of course." Colin chuckled. "Our modest Queen has always had an eye for the best baubles." He plunged his hand back into the bag and came out with a small cloth pouch from which he poured a veritable stream of loose diamonds, rubies, sapphires, and emeralds onto the tea tray between us. "Oh my," he tsked. "No wonder your father noticed something amiss. It would appear you have been most indiscreet."

"It's all there!" Cillian snapped defiantly. "Every last bit of it. We didn't sell anything. Not one stone."

Colin gave a patient smile as he gathered the loose gems and returned them to the pouch. "I shall have to take your word for it, as I don't have a precise accounting for what was taken. I suspect even Mr. Guitnu would be hard-pressed to make an accurate report."

"That's all of it," Sunny reiterated.

"And just how were you able to take it?" Colin asked as he returned the items to the pack.

"I watched my mother open the safe one afternoon. That's how I got the idea."

Colin stood up with his tea and wandered back to the fireplace, setting the cup on the mantel in exchange for a small knife whose blade he began to absently buff with a cloth. "And from there it was only a matter of secreting the things to Cillian until you decided you had enough, is that it?" He shook his head again.

"You needn't be so disapproving!" Cillian snarled as he stood up.

Sunny gripped his nearer sleeve and coaxed him back down with a look that was as adoring as it was controlled. I knew if she stayed with this boy she would spend her lifetime gripping him by that sleeve.

"I meant no offense," Colin muttered offhandedly, his attentions seemingly on rejuvenating the blade of his little knife. "What I really wonder is why you've brought all these things to us?" He looked at the two of them, one eyebrow arched skyward, as he finally set the blade down.

The two of them stared mutely back at him, their faces awash with trepidation and distress. As I watched them, I noted their hesitation to even look at one another and knew it hinted at something that suddenly struck me with the certainty of a coming storm. And when I glanced back over at Colin and spied the thinnest shadow of a smirk on his lips, I realized that he knew as well.

"I listened to what you said the other night," Cillian spoke up, his voice thin and tight. "I told Sunny everything. About being shunned . . . the color of our babies . . . not having much money." He slid his eyes toward Sunny, but she still did not look back. "We talked about all of it. . . ." His voice trailed off, though he had not yet managed to utter the very thing he had come to say.

It seemed a full minute passed, Colin idling before the fireplace and me nervously sipping at my tea, before Cillian finally sucked in a breath and said, "We want you to give everything back."

"Me?" Colin said simply.

"And you must speak to my father," Sunny added in a rush as she folded a hand into one of Cillian's. "You are a man. He might listen to you."

"Speak to him?" Colin's brow folded in tandem with my own. "About what?"

"Us," Cillian answered. "You must tell him that we are to be married. You must tell him we are in love."

Colin opened his mouth and then immediately shut it, turning his gaze to me with a confusion that would otherwise have made me laugh. "I should think," I spoke up, "if there is a conversation to be had with Mr. Guitnu, that you should be the one to have it, Cillian. It is the suitor's duty. It is the custom—" But as soon as I said that word I understood how wrong I was.

"The custom . . ." Cillian instantly pounced on the flaw of my words, ". . . is for Sunny's parents to decree who she will marry. A match bound by greed and obligation, not love." He looked over at Colin. "You know that, Mr. Pendragon. You lived in India. I haven't a chance."

Colin flopped into his seat with a heavy sigh. "The two of you have already made such a muck of this situation. If you ever had any chance I doubt one would remain in spite of your returning these things."

"You must try, Mr. Pendragon," Sunny pleaded, her voice shaking with desperation. "I love Cillian. I cannot turn away from him to marry another. It would be a lie of my soul and I could not bear that."

"You told me you understood," Cillian charged ahead. "The other day you said you thought you would lose your mind if you couldn't be with the woman you fell in love with when you were twenty-four."

"I don't think that's exactly what I said—"

"It *is* what you said," Cillian insisted. "Is she here?" He screwed up his face. "Is she the woman downstairs?"

"No. No!" Colin shook his head and rubbed his brow. "The person I . . . It's complicated, Cillian. And your life will be too. Not just now but every day going forward."

"Are you divorced?!" Cillian's face went white.

"No!" Colin leapt up and paced back to the fireplace. "But we live forever on the edge." He snatched up the poker and stabbed at one of the sputtering logs, splitting it in a shower of sparks. "Look . . ." He turned around, the poker still wielded in his hand. "I'll take these things back to your father, Sundha, and I will do my best to convince him about the two of you, but you must prepare yourself for the very real possibility that I will fail."

"He cannot stop us." Cillian glowered.

"But he can," Colin answered. "In this he can."

The two of them stared back at Colin with defiance, their hands clutched together so tightly that their fingers were coloring with the effort. Even so, I knew it would never be enough to keep them from being severed.

CHAPTER 36

The message, delivered mid-morning by Mrs. Connicle's young, awkward part-time maid, Letty Hollings, was unexpected and distressing. It felt ever more so given that the dawn had revealed itself to be another of brooding, steely clouds that had yawed wide to let loose a torrent of rain before we'd even had our breakfast. By the time Miss Hollings arrived, Colin had already stripped and cleaned two guns, re-buffed the blade on the small knife he'd been fretting over since the start of this case, flung his weights about, and finally retreated to the bathroom to ice his still tender left thigh. I, however, was hard-pressed to think of any reason to pull myself from the newspaper or the blazing fire he had built.

So I was alone in the study when Mrs. Behmoth, after ascertaining my availability by hollering up at me, sent Letty upstairs. I tossed the newspaper aside and went to the landing, intent on scowling at Mrs. Behmoth, until I caught sight of the young woman. Her face was pale and worn, and even from the top of the stairs I could see that her eyes were swollen and rimmed in red.

I kept quiet as I ushered her to the fireplace to warm up, wanting her to settle in while I rousted Colin, but she was far too agitated. Instead, in a single barrage, she told me that Randolph was downstairs waiting for her and that Miss Porter had only given her leave to be gone long enough to inform us of what had occurred. And then she had burst into tears.

"They've taken me mistress ta Needham 'Ills and moved 'er in," she said through a bray of sobs and sniffling. "They're closin' down the 'ouse and lettin' the staff go."

"What? Who took her there?"

"'Er doctor. 'E sent a man round with a note ta tell us."

"A note?"

"Ya." She swiped at her nose with her sleeve. "It were from that man what works for Mr. Connicle. 'E says they 'ave ta shut the 'ouse and sell it." She covered her face with her hands and wept, her whole body shaking.

I moved to her to offer what comfort I could, but she stepped away from me and I knew she was uncomfortable being alone with me. No matter that I was desperate to get more information, I knew none would be forthcoming. Not only had she become quite inconsolable, but also no one in the household would have taken her into their confidence. So with little other recourse I walked her back downstairs and delivered her to Randolph's care. I noticed the dazed expression coloring his face and knew what Colin was going to say about all of this. Which was why, not twenty minutes after they left, Colin and I were on our way to see Mrs. Connicle at Needham Hills.

The place sits like a long-forgotten dowager in Waltham Forest on the northeast side of the city between Leyton and Walthamstow. It was once the Wentworth estate, the noble home of the preeminent carriage-manufacturing family of two centuries before. Which is why it had a carriage house larger than most London homes, capable of housing more than three dozen coaches with room to spare. The stables were equally enormous, providing shelter for enough horses to convey nearly all of those carriages simultaneously. Yet all of it was overshadowed by the main home, a fortress-like façade of dark native stone that seemed to be reaching toward the sky at its two front corner turrets. The bevy of arched windows were all crenellated as if to keep invaders out, and the whole of the structure rose a height of four stories and covered a width of some five times greater than that. One would not be faulted for thinking it could hold a small village. Indeed, the early Wentworth families had been quite large, with staffs well in excess of a hundred. However, the modern age had been unkind to both the Wentworth business and family.

First an issue had developed with the axle assembly on several of their finest coaches almost fifty years ago. There had been rumors of sabotage, but nothing had borne out of it other than the mortal blow to their reputation. The eldest brother had committed suicide, leaving only a sister and sickly brother behind. The brother succumbed to his disease within that same year, leaving the sister to try to repair the damage done. She shuttered the business five years later, in 1853.

The sister never married but stayed within the confines of the house, if a home that size can be said to have confines, until her death eighteen years later. As she had left no heirs, the estate transferred to the county, where, due to the crenellations fronting the windows of the main house, it was determined to be an ideal place to house those of unsound mind.

I could not stop the shiver that slithered down my spine as we turned down the macadam path that led to Needham Hills. True to its name, there were small knolls that rolled off on both sides of the heavily wooded road. The main structure, the original house, could be seen peeking through the trees as we drew closer until, as though an invisible hand had been placed against the brooding woods, the trees abruptly fell back to reveal the cold, stone building looming under the steely gray sky.

I had not been back to this place in fourteen years. Not since I had shaken the clutch of opium. Rail-thin, hallucinatory, terrified, and running out of options, I had allowed my unexpected benefactor to convince me to sign my care over to him. He was a beautiful man who looked at me with wounded eyes the color of azure, and I wondered why he cared. I could not remember him paying me any heed during our mutual years at the Easling and Temple Senior Academy, and yet there he had suddenly been, affecting my heart and mind, and making me consider that there might be worth to me after all. So I had placed my shattered life in his hands. And he had brought me here.

As the carriage drew closer Colin's hand settled over mine as if he had read my thoughts, and I rather suppose he did. He twined his fingers with mine and squeezed, but neither of us spoke. There was nothing to say.

I had remained at Needham Hills for three months, enduring tortures designed to rid me of the weaknesses that had purportedly drawn me to opium. I had been confined naked in a small, makeshift room of the former stable for the first two weeks and pelted with buckets of icy water at all hours until I fully lost track of time and feared for the last threads of my sanity. Any infraction on my part was rewarded by a bucketful of frigid water: if I did not rise when a keeper entered, if I did not eat the sparse food brought me, if I dared refuse any question fired through the slot in the door. There was no bed or bedding of any sort, no furniture, and no visitors. I had nothing but my own rage and hatred.

One afternoon, when I was sure I had been abandoned by anything that was good, they threw a pair of muslin pants and a shirt at me. I had slowly dressed, the movements feeling stiff and unfamiliar, and they had taken me to the main building. How I had scowled at the afternoon sun that felt so harsh and foreign to my eyes.

I'd been delivered to a tiny room with two chairs and a table in what had once been the servants' quarters and told to wait without moving. And that is exactly what I had done, having become the well-trained creature they had made me. Several minutes later Colin had been shown in. I still remember the sight of him as clearly as if it had been an hour ago. He wore a navy-blue suit with a pale blue shirt beneath, his gold watch fob glittering from a pocket in his checked vest. His tawny hair had been combed yet still somehow managed to look tousled, and when his eyes met mine I found the same notch of pain that I had seen there before, and in that instant I had burst out in sobs. He reached me so quickly that I jumped at his touch, but even so, he pulled me to him while I wept like a madman. We stayed that way until the attendant knocked at the door again.

Colin bade me be brave as he left that tiny room, the grief in his eyes as tactile as the solidity of his arms. So I stayed.

They took me to a room in the main house after that. It was sparsely furnished with a cot, a chair, and a small, round table tucked up by the partially covered window, obstructed by its crenellation. I remained in the muslin uniform that had been provided me, and while I cannot say that the subsequent ten weeks were easier, at least the water dousing ceased. I was properly fed thereafter, but the best thing of all was that I was given pen and paper.

I spent countless hours at that tiny table pouring out my heartbreak, torment, and fear. Colin was allowed to visit me weekly, then every other day for the last two weeks. And he never failed to come. We talked as long as they allowed us to, and when I was alone I purged my demons onto that paper. Colin wanted to read it, but in the end I couldn't let him. I burned it instead.

"You all right?" Colin asked as the coach pulled alongside the stern, imposing façade of the main building.

I gave him a thin smile. "It's not me you need to worry about, but Mrs. Connicle."

"Yes," he answered vaguely as he hopped out of the carriage.

We located the medical superintendent's office only to find that he was out. His secretary was on the verge of refusing us entry when Colin threatened to bring the whole of Scotland Yard into her office within the hour if we were not granted an immediate interview with Mrs. Connicle. The poor woman in her late middle years went ghostly white, but she acquiesced. She had an attendant escort us to the fourth floor, where a series of small rooms were lined up like tiny soldiers, one after the other.

He slid open the slot on a door about three-quarters of the way down the second hallway and announced us.

"I will be back in fifteen minutes," he warned as he unbolted the door and heaved it open.

Colin waved him off without the slightest care as we stepped in, the door closing and locking behind us. The room was small, though larger than the one I had been held in. There were two chairs, a table, and a half dresser, and the bed was an actual bed, not a cot. Two small arched windows looked out onto the front drive, allowing a modicum of light, but that was impeded by the severely gabled roofline that angled harshly down from about the halfway point to the tops of the windows.

"Mr. Pendragon." Mrs. Connicle's voice was thick and leaden, and she did not rise from the edge of the bed where she was sitting. "Mr. Pruitt. How shameful that you should see me like this. I fear you are viewing the very end of me." She spoke not with malice or sorrow, but with a resignation that seemed wholly embraced. I could tell she was under the thrall of some drug. Her hair was down and had been cut exceedingly short, barely reaching the bottom of her ears, and she was dressed in the white muslin clothing that was still obviously the uniform of the facility. I don't think I will ever forget the rough feel of it on my skin.

"Mrs. Connicle," Colin said softly as we both sat in the chairs by the little table. "You must tell us how you've come to be here."

"It is the death of my husband that sees me confined to this place," she answered wistfully. "I have lost him twice and I could bear neither."

"But I should think you'd be best served in your home," Colin pressed gently. "Surrounded by those who care for you. How is it that you are *here*?"

She turned her gaze to him, and though her eyes were swollen and red, she did not cry. "I am ordered here on my husband's behalf," she said. "I am under the care of Dr. Renholme and Mr. Tolliver now." She sagged as her eyes dropped to the floor.

"Mr. Tolliver?!" Colin repeated with astonishment. "Noah Tolliver?"

"Yes," she exhaled. "He and the doctor will see to me now."

Colin's scowl said what he did not need to. With Noah Tolliver incapable of such a thing, who had given the order to confine this shattered woman to this horrid place, and why had it been done?

CHAPTER 37

———◆———

"You *will* calm down, Mr. Pendragon, or I will *not* continue this conversation." Wynn Tessler glowered, his eyes rife with warning as his lips pinched themselves into fine, thin lines.

"Forgive my agitation, Mr. Tessler, but you can imagine my shock at learning that *you* are the person who has sentenced Mrs. Connicle to live in that godforsaken place."

"It is a place of comfort and health," he protested.

"Only if you are a bedbug," Colin shot back as he pushed himself out of his chair and began pacing the length of Mr. Tessler's office.

"If I may . . ." I spoke with all the serenity I could muster, eager to diffuse the conversation before Mr. Tessler could decide to eject us from his office. "There is no denying that Mrs. Connicle is a brittle and sensitive woman, but in a time of distress such as this, don't you think she might not be better served at home with the people who have tended to her for so long?"

"Those people"—Mr. Tessler stared at me as though I had lost my mind—"are servants. They know nothing of caring for a woman who has succumbed to hysteria. And may I remind you that one of them is already under suspicion for complicity in this whole affair. I consulted with her doctor and did what needed to be done. Edmond would thank me for it."

"She has suffered the loss of her husband twice," I reminded. "To see her initial hopes dashed with such cruel certainty—does she not deserve our deepest sympathy and understanding?"

"Of course she has my sympathy," he punched back defensively. "But she is not served by such sentiments, is she? Pity will not see to her care and well-being, will it?"

"So you drop her into the midst of the feebleminded and insane?" Colin growled, and I felt my heart sink at his description of the place I once had to stay. "Is there any wonder she struggles for a will to survive?"

"Need I remind you that Edmond sent his wife there *himself* some years back. Surely you do not mean to chastise him?"

"Oh, but I would if he were here," Colin said as he came around behind me. "Which begs the question, Mr. Tessler, under whose authority did you have Mrs. Connicle remanded there?"

"My own," he answered, his posture stiffening and his face clouding with offense. "Because of Mr. Tolliver's current incapacitation I am the estate's temporary executor."

"*Current* incapacitation?!" Colin thundered over my left shoulder. "The man's incapacitation is clearly catastrophic and permanent."

Mr. Tessler went still. "Do you mean to suggest that you are a prescient medical professional as well as an investigator? Because I have not been told such a thing about Mr. Tolliver from anyone."

"Have you *seen* him, Mr. Tessler? Have you tried to *speak* with him?"

Wynn Tessler stared back at Colin with obvious confusion, and for a moment I thought perhaps he had not caught the scorn in Colin's question. But a minute later he gave a terse chuckle and stood up, taking his time to tug at the sleeves of his crisp white shirt and adjust the emerald-cut diamond cuff links pinching them together. Only after he had completed that bit of smartening did he finally cast his gaze at Colin with the well-worn patience of a shrewd negotiator. "Gentlemen," he said with ease. "I hope I have accorded you every assistance required. I have certainly done my utmost to try. But you must forgive me in my refusal to engage in your invectives. I am headed to Zurich on business in two days and there is much I must do to prepare. If there is anything further I can do . . . ." He crossed behind us to the door and cast it open with a flourish. "Well, you have only to ask."

Colin was out the door in an instant, leaving me to rally myself back to my feet and offer the necessary pleasantries before I could make my own escape.

That Colin was livid was unquestionable, so I was not surprised to find him on the street cursing every carriage that passed by as though it were a personal affront. Before he could throw himself bodily in front of the next one with the intent of ejecting some poor sod from his cab, I caught the eye of an approaching driver by discreetly waving a pair of crowns. The man deposited his current fare at our feet with a hurried excuse and we were on our way in a heartbeat.

I stayed quiet for a time, knowing Colin was best left to his brooding, but as we drew nearer to our flat in Kensington I could keep my peace no longer. "I hardly know what to think of Mr. Tessler—"

"The man is a bollocky, buggery bastard," Colin said, his face taut with fury. "Mrs. Connicle may warrant some treatment, but to commit her as he has done?! To discard her future as though it were piffle?! He is lower than a snake's balls." Colin turned his gaze back outside as we rounded the corner from Queen's Gate onto Gloucester.

I considered correcting his reptile physiology before deciding instead to mutter, "He *has* been helpful. . . ."

"As it suits him," Colin grunted as he sat forward and stared toward our flat. "And now Varcoe has come for yet another ruddy visit." I turned and caught sight of Varcoe's coach parked at our curb, one of his blue-suited bobbies milling about with evident boredom. "Perhaps I'll have Varcoe look into that accident of Mr. Tolliver's!" he groused as our cab pulled to the side of the road. "I'm beginning to find that whole affair unsettling." And before the driver could bring us to a full stop, Colin hopped out and strode to our door with such swiftness that the bobby only managed to come to attention after Colin had snapped past him.

"I suppose you'll be wantin' tea?" Mrs. Behmoth asked when I finally stepped inside after settling with the driver.

Heated words were already drifting down from overhead, and while I could not tell what was being said, there was no doubt of their disgruntled nature. "Yes," I said as I headed upstairs. "I'd say we will need a distraction."

By the time I reached the landing I knew I was right. Colin had planted himself in front of the fireplace and was swinging the poker around as though it were an extension of his arm. "I am *not* going over this again," he was raging as he turned and stabbed at a burning log, which I suspected was a surrogate for the inspector himself.

"You *will* go over it again!" Varcoe howled from his position behind the settee, legs spread and hands on his hips as though he were about to draw his gun. "And you will go over it as many times as I *want* you to."

Sergeant Evans was hovering just inside the room by the coatrack, his well-lined, round face peering at me with discomfort. He respected Colin with some consistency, unlike Varcoe, whose affections were as transient as a young girl's. "What are you two on about?" I asked with an overzealous smile.

Varcoe turned on me, launching a feral leer that warned me I was more at the center of this dispute than I knew. "Let's ask Pruitt again since he was there."

"I was where?" I asked with the innocence of ignorance.

"In a deserted alley in the East End with a known felon." A disingenuous grin bloomed across Varcoe's face. "A dead felon," he added.

"You should be thanking us," Colin put in gruffly. "Not grilling us."

"Don't get cheeky with me, Pendragon!" Varcoe snarled. "We're supposed to be partners on this case and all you've done is shuffle around me like the whole of Scotland Yard is at your disposal."

Colin gritted his teeth and sucked in a slow breath as he

turned and hung the fireplace poker back in its place. "You're right," he abruptly conceded as Mrs. Behmoth's thudding footfalls could be heard coming up the stairs. "I have been exclusionary and foolish." He threw himself into his chair with a feigned look of contrition that appeared to placate Varcoe at once.

Mrs. Behmoth set the tray of tea paraphernalia down with a sneer and I knew she wasn't fooled, either.

"Sit down, Inspector," Colin said. "Sergeant . . . We've some tea and Mrs. Behmoth's fine ginger biscuits." Colin gave her a smile that earned him a roll of her eyes as she headed back out. "I will catch you up on our endeavors and perhaps you will do the same for us. I leave that to you." He snatched the teapot and poured us all some tea as Varcoe settled onto the settee, followed by Sergeant Evans wearing an expression of barely concealed amusement. "So that sorry bloke turned out to be a felon?" Colin mused as he handed out our cups.

Varcoe snorted. "He had a litany of arrests going back almost twenty years. Some of them here, most of them in Budapest, Prague, and Munich. Not your stellar citizen. We can't even find a next of kin to notify of his death. Doesn't seem like anybody gives a ruddy shite."

"Pity . . ." Colin threw in without much effort, though I could see he was paying close attention. "What was his name?"

"Name?" Varcoe looked over at Evans.

The sergeant checked his notes. "Eckhard Heillert," he answered. "Prussian. Accused of his first murder at seventeen."

Colin slid a glance to me and I knew I was meant to remember that name. "How is it that our dear city draws such types?"

"Never mind that." Varcoe set his cup down and grabbed several biscuits. "What have you been up to? What brought a rogue like that into your line a sight?"

"It came to our attention that he'd been throwing money about," Colin offered lightly. "Living in East End squalor but flashing the sterling of someone who's gotten himself into some fine game, say murder for hire, for instance." He gave a dismissive shrug. "I thought it worth a look," he went on. "But all Ethan saw was the result of a deal gone sour."

"I suppose that's something Pruitt knows a bit about." Varcoe snickered. Colin's eyes narrowed, but it, as with so much else, was lost on the inspector. "Never mind all of that." He waved a hand through the air. "I want to know what you're up to on the Connicle case."

"Then you'd best mind your tongue where Ethan is concerned." Colin flashed a tight smile as he dug a crown out of his pocket and began coaxing it between his fingers.

Varcoe's eyes went hard as his face bloomed rose.

"Do you have any leads on who killed Mr. Heillert?" I asked, intent on returning the conversation to firmer footing.

"Nobody sees anything down there," Varcoe grumbled. "Like we were the bloody enemy. The problem is that nothing down there draws the least bit of attention. A man could rampage down the street with a bloody knife in his hand and no one would raise an eye. The Ripper has about proven that himself."

"Nevertheless"—Colin mustered a generous smile—"it would seem you put him out of business in spite of yourself. You must be pleased with that."

Varcoe pursed his lips and threw an ill-tempered glare at Colin. "How about we stick to Edmond Connicle."

"We have been searching for some correlation between the Connicles and Huttons beyond the proximity of their homes. We know that Edmond Connicle was a founding partner in—"

"Columbia Financial," Varcoe interrupted crossly. "And the Huttons were clients there too. Tell me you can do better than that."

"The man who was to have been the executor of the Connicle estate, Noah Tolliver, suffered a catastrophic riding accident several months back and has been rendered incapable both mentally and physically. As a result it appears control of their estate has reverted to Mr. Connicle's partner, Wynn Tessler."

"So what?"

"Mr. Tessler already controls the Hutton estate," Colin pointed out. "That would be the strongest correlation I have yet."

Varcoe's eyes went wide even as his brows caved in. "That's it?!" He looked at Sergeant Evans and gave a snort as he got to his feet. "Well, thank bleeding hell I ain't paying you." He saun-tered over to the fireplace before turning back to us, smiling as though he were landed gentry surveying his domain. "The Yard, on the other hand, has learned a great deal," he practically crowed. "We have found not one, but two other African groups who practice that voodoo twaddle here in the city, and one of them knows the Connicles' scullery maid by name."

"Alexa?" Colin said with obvious disinterest. "I should think it a small population. It would surprise me if they didn't all know of one another."

The smile dropped from Varcoe's face as he stabbed his fists onto his hips again. "Well, would it surprise you to learn that one of them accused her of malfeasance?"

One of Colin's eyebrows arced up. "It would surprise me if any of them knew what that word meant," he replied.

"She is despised in her own community!" Varcoe thundered back. "She is said to be haughty and feral."

"Feral, is it?" Colin repeated. "Did she bite someone?"

Sergeant Evans snorted into his tea, earning a momentary glare from Varcoe. "The poison they found in the stomachs of the Aston dogs was cyanide," he said as he circled around behind Colin's chair. "Something any scullery maid can get her hands on without even leaving the house. And Miss Hollings told us Alexa was afraid of the missing Hutton boy. Like his condition was some balmy sign of evil mumbo jumbo." He leaned over Colin. "We've also found something else you're going to be interested in, Pendragon." He chuckled as he ambled back over to the fire-place, a grin tickling the corners of his mouth. "My men discov-ered a crude ladder half-buried in the brush not far from the Huttons' house. It's crafted from wood rails exactly like those Alexa's husband was using to fix the Connicles' fence. We believe the ladder was used to spirit William Hutton from his room. And can you guess what was stuck to one of the corners of that ladder?"

"What?" Colin mumbled, any mirth gone from his eyes.

"A small scrap of black cotton like that used in a maid's skirts with enough chloroform on it to immobilize a man. Very sloppy.

Somebody who doesn't know a thing about chloroform. Probably never had a tooth properly extracted." His eyes flashed cruelly. "You know, like an African scullery maid. Denton Ross declared that given the cocked-up amount used on the boy, he would've stopped breathing within a matter of minutes. I've got my men out right now searching the woods on the property. We brought the dogs out a short while ago. So you see, Pendragon, there is much the Yard has been able to accomplish while you've had Pruitt here gallivanting about in back alleys for old times' sake."

Colin flashed a tight grin as he slid the crown he'd been shuffling back into his pocket. I worried what he might be about to say, but he surprised me, as he often does, by simply leaning back and stating, "It is indeed an impressive amount of information that you've been able to assemble. But I wonder to what end Alexa would have had all of these crimes committed?" he continued. "And what of her husband? What of *his* death?"

"Maybe he didn't like what his wife was up to. Maybe he threatened to turn her in." Varcoe shrugged blithely, and yet I could tell Colin had poked at the inspector's own misgiving.

"We have come upon murders with lesser motives," Colin admitted, his gaze drifting off. "Are Mrs. Hutton and her daughter still there watching your men and their hounds rooting about?"

"No. The two of them left this morning for Paris. And so much the better without them. She was threatening to single-handedly end my career," he griped. "And that after I told her the Yard was working around the clock on the case." His tone dropped and I could sense his displeasure. "I even admitted that we'd brought you in as a consultant, but she was not to be assuaged. I don't think she's much of a fan of either of us."

"She made that clear to me as well," Colin muttered, swiping a hand through his hair.

"She demanded we deliver her and the girl to Claridge's before sunset last night. Claridge's," he scoffed. "She refused to even go back to the house this morning. They left everything they hadn't taken with them yesterday and were off to Dover by nine. Went to stay with a sister, or cousin . . ." He waved a hand dismissively. "I don't remember. We've got the address. Not to mention that she's already contacted us once and she hasn't even been gone a damn day!"

"You can hardly blame her," I said, glancing over at Colin and finding him wholly preoccupied as he stared out the window.

"Evans and I are on our way over to have another go at that snarky scullery maid of the Connicles," Varcoe announced as he crossed to the doorway. "That woman is into this in some way. You can't tell me you don't agree."

Colin turned from the window and looked back at the inspector, his expression unreadable. "You certainly have some potent evidence against her," he allowed. "But what bothers me, what I cannot stop thinking about, is why?"

"Those people," Varcoe sniffed. "Life has no meaning for them. They kill their own like they kill the beasts for eating. You're looking for logic where there is none, Pendragon. You've been living too high for too long." A complacent smile curved Varcoe's lips. "We'll let you know if we need you anymore. Otherwise, stay out of the gutters, boys." He chuckled as he flicked a last mocking grin at me.

CHAPTER 38

———◆•◆———

Varcoe's warning meant nothing to Colin, as we were back to the same harsh East End neighborhood that very night. An incessant drizzle persisted in spitting from the thick iron-gray clouds brooding across the evening sky as the two of us split up and trolled through a goodly share of pubs and taverns seeking anyone familiar with the late felon Eckhard Heillert. For his part, Colin failed utterly. I, on the other hand, did manage to find one barkeep and two working ladies who recognized the name, though none of them could tell me much of consequence. The barkeep and one of the women remembered having seen Mr. Heillert freely spending a fair amount of money, but both insisted they knew nothing of how he'd earned it. The other woman recollected his bragging about doing a series of jobs for a gentleman but admitted she didn't care a whit about it as long as Mr. Heillert paid for her services. Which, after a second stout, she confessed she had adjusted upward and he had happily given. But beyond those meager scraps, we learned nothing.

I spent the better part of the next day completing my chronicle of our recent case involving the Arnifour family while Colin paced around our flat, tossed his weights around for a bit, took a walk, pretended to take a brief nap, and disassembled and cleaned four handguns and a rifle. When I began to fear he might be on the verge of tackling his knife collection he announced that it was time for us to visit Prakhasa Guitnu and return his bounty of jewels to him. So as tea time approached, we headed east to Holland Park.

We arrived to find the Guitnu family at home, including middle daughter Sunny, who looked positively ill at our appearance. Nevertheless, all three daughters were subjected to tea and the most delicious little coconut cakes for the first half hour of our visit before Mr. Guitnu finally released them, along with his wife, so we could turn to the crux of our visit. The doors to the great library had barely closed before Mr. Guitnu turned to us. "What have you learned? Do you bring me news?"

Colin picked up the valise he had brought and extracted the sack Cillian and Sunny had given us. "I believe you will find everything there," Colin said, his tone soft and, to my ears, filled with misgiving.

"What?!" Mr. Guitnu's eyes went bright as he pulled the sack open and fished a hand inside, extracting the same sapphire necklace I had so admired at our flat. "It is a miracle. You are a master, Mr. Pendragon." He beamed. Yet not a moment later his brow began to furrow as he quickly pawed through the items with a mixture of relief and mounting concern. "But how . . . ?" He looked at us.

"Ah . . ." Colin flashed a quick, thin smile as he sat back in his chair. "I shall give you a full accounting, but might I trouble you to answer a few unrelated questions first?"

Mr. Guitnu's smile was ready and warm. "You may ask me anything at all, Mr. Pendragon, as you have most certainly earned the right."

"Yes . . . well . . ." Colin flicked his eyes to me before plastering on his smile and looking back at Mr. Guitnu. "As one of this city's preeminent jewelry designers and fabricators, I was wondering if you were ever asked to craft anything for Edmond Connicle?"

"Oh!" His eyes lit up. "I made several pieces for his wife. Such a lovely slip of a woman. There was a small bracelet with tiny, round diamonds set in a delicate white gold strand, and I believe two pairs of diamond earrings, one pear cut and one round. I suppose she has a preference for diamonds, but I don't really know. I believe those were the only pieces I have made for her. Perhaps she does not like beautiful jewelry?" He gave a lilting laugh.

Colin chuckled. "I don't believe I have ever met a woman yet who does not appreciate fine jewelry."

Mr. Guitnu beamed. "Then you must let me make something for *your* wife, Mr. Pendragon."

Colin's grin shifted ever so slightly. "I shall certainly ponder that," he answered quickly. "And have you ever created anything for either Arthur Hutton or Hubert Aston?"

"Mr. Hutton commissioned me to make something for his wife only once, which I think is tragic, as she is a most beautiful woman with truly wondrous blue eyes. As you might suppose, he wanted a necklace of diamonds and sapphires and two pendant sapphire earrings ringed in tiny diamonds to match. The design of the necklace was exquisite if I may say, with a princess-cut sapphire surrounded by tiny diamond baguettes. The pattern repeated itself all the way around her neck." He shook his head with the memory. "But he never came to pick any of it up or settle his account. I heard there was some financial trouble, so I eventually sold the set to another gentleman. A gentleman with exquisite taste." He grinned.

"And Mr. Aston?" Colin persisted, though I could sense his mood waning.

"Yes, yes." Mr. Guitnu's smile tilted up at one side. "A fine man who has purchased many, many things from me, some for his wife"—his crooked grin became almost roguish—"some not." He winked.

"Is that so?" Colin's eyebrows popped up. "And how can you be sure?"

"Every woman has her preferences, Mr. Pendragon," he answered with whimsy, as though schooling ignorant children, which I suppose we were. "And beyond that, the colors of jewels may be right for one woman but wholly inappropriate for the next. Rather like clothing."

"Of course." Colin nodded solemnly, but I knew he had no idea what Mr. Guitnu meant. All Colin could be sure of was that Mrs. Behmoth had a preference for gray and black.

"Mr. Aston's wife is a broad-faced woman with alabaster skin and auburn hair," Mr. Guitnu continued. "She loves emeralds and diamonds, and they suit her well. And because she is an ample woman, she can wear large pieces with substantial stones. The last necklace I made for her had a magnificent eighteen-carat pear-shaped emerald set in gold with tiny marquise-cut diamonds around it. It was a masterpiece." He gave a sheepish smile. "There I am singing my own praises again. But it looked most spectacular on her."

"And the other jewelry he bought?" Colin prodded. "You said it was not all for his wife. Perhaps he bought pieces for his daughters?"

Mr. Guitnu gave a delighted laugh. "Oh no, Mr. Pendragon, not these pieces. When a man buys something for a daughter you can be sure it will be simple and chaste. Delicate-colored stones like peridot or tourmaline with straightforward cuts in unadorned settings. It is a father's curse to forever view his daughter this way. Woe to the man who should try to tell him otherwise." He chuckled merrily, sending a knot to my stomach as I thought about the real reason for our visit. "The other pieces Mr. Aston buys from time to time are much smaller and they are always set with rubies the color of blood. I remember one most particularly: a heart-shaped ruby just a carat and a half in white gold surrounded by tiny diamond chips. Another time he bought the earrings to go with it, and on a third occasion, the bracelet. These pieces are not for daughters and would never be worn by an ample woman with a penchant for emeralds and gold. Do you see, Mr. Pendragon?"

"Indeed I do." Colin released an easy smile. "Your information has been most helpful."

"I do not mean to speak out of turn about Mr. Aston—"

"Perish the thought." Colin's cobalt eyes brimmed with feigned innocence.

"Then please." Mr. Guitnu sat back in his chair and picked up his teacup again. "Tell me how you came to find my jewels. I will have the truth so I can punish the man who would dishonor me so."

"Well, Mr. Guitnu." Colin stood up and wandered over to a wall of books adjacent to where we were sitting, absently running his fingers along their spines. "I'm afraid it is a complex and uneasy answer you seek."

Mr. Guitnu's brow instantly furrowed as he stared at Colin. "Someone is robbing me. What can be complex about that?"

"What if I tell you the perpetrator does not work in your household?" Colin asked while casually studying a row of books.

"That would be wonderful," Mr. Guitnu enthused as he glanced back at me with relief. "I should like to think my staff worthy of my trust. You have already brought me peace." But his brow quickly furrowed again. "Then how did someone from outside gain repeated access to my safe?"

Colin heaved a sigh as he slid back into the chair next to me and set his eyes firmly on Mr. Guitnu. "I am not making myself clear," he said. "One of your daughters was involved. But before you say anything, Mr. Guitnu, before you determine what to think, I will ask you to hear me out. Will you do that?"

Mr. Guitnu's face went still as he placed his cup back on the table and gave the slightest nod of his head. It was not much, but it was something.

"One of your daughters has fallen in love with a young man and he with her. They did not mean for it to happen, but it has just the same. It is often the way." He gave a hesitant smile that Mr. Guitnu did not meet. "A person wants to follow the rules, to be like everyone else, and then he meets someone who makes his heart beat faster, his stomach roil, and his head spin. And no matter how hard he tries he cannot stop thinking of them. You are only truly happy when you are together. Nothing feels more *right*. So even though you tell yourself it cannot be, it *will* not be, you have already fallen well into the mire and no longer really even want to get out. No matter the consequences."

The three of us sat there quietly, my heart thundering so loudly in my ears I thought surely they would hear it. My breathing came shallow and tight as I waited for Mr. Guitnu to say something and, when I stole a quick glance at Colin, I saw the same dread in him.

"It was never your daughter's intent to defy your will," I spoke up, hoping to allay Mr. Guitnu's resistance. "You must have understood the potential risk when you brought your family here and exposed your daughters to our more liberal customs of courting." I thought it a logical argument, but it earned me a scowl from Colin.

"That is the fact then," he said as he took a deep breath. "And because of it your daughter made a terrible decision," he continued. "On her own, without giving you so much as an opportunity to speak your own mind, she determined that you would disapprove of her love for this young man and forbid them from marrying. So she sought to take some of your pieces to allow the two of them to start their life together. It was a regrettable decision. She admits that, which is why she has given me the jewels and asked that I return them to you. She seeks your blessing, not your money. That is what she now realizes holds the only true value for her."

Colin sat back and I felt the release of a sigh more than heard it. I peeked over at Mr. Guitnu and found that his gaze had drifted above Colin's head to one of the windows, his face remaining stoic and composed. I wondered if I dared hope that his love for his daughter might outweigh his traditions. That he might meet poor Cillian before deciding.

"Which of my daughters has disgraced me in this way?" he said in a thin, tight voice.

"She meant no disgrace," I corrected at once.

"I have listened as you asked," he said, "and will pay for your services. Now I shall have her name."

"Sundha," Colin answered.

I suppose I expected to see Mr. Guitnu flinch or sag, but he did nothing of the kind. He simply rose to his feet, pressed the fee into my hands with a nod, and showed us to the door. Even after we had crossed the threshold he said nothing further, merely closing the door without a second look.

We walked back to the street, my spirits sagging even as I hurried to keep up with Colin. He seemed oddly stirred and stepped right into the street, where he hailed a passing cab. "West Hampstead," he called up to the driver.

"What are we going out there for?" I asked as I climbed in beside Colin.

"We are going to pay another visit to Hubert Aston and see if we cannot coax some keener information from him, given what Mr. Guitnu has just shared with us."

"Ah." I leaned back as the carriage lurched forward, trying to imagine how that haughty man was likely to respond to such a tactic. "I cannot say I have a good feeling about this."

Colin waved me off. "You worry too much."

I ignored him as I returned to my thoughts of Sunny and Cillian. "Do you think Mr. Guitnu will meet with Cillian? At least give the boy a hearing?"

Colin looked at me as though I had sprouted a pair of horns from my forehead. "No. He was only kind enough to hear us out because he is a gentleman." Colin looked back out the carriage window as the teeming city began to give way to the verdant expanse of West Hampstead. "Once he has satisfied himself that Sundha's chastity is intact he will have her betrothed. It is simply the way of it, Ethan. It cannot end any other way."

"Then I am sorry for them."

He heaved a sigh and took my hand. "They're young. Let us hope they are equally resilient."

"Yes . . . well . . . I'm just glad I wasn't born to such customs."

He laughed as we pulled into the Astons' drive. "There'd be little difference, as you've already made folly of the customs you *were* born under." He chuckled. "Come now," he said as we pulled under the Astons' portico. "Pay the driver and let us get on with this. I can hardly contain myself."

I don't know what I thought was going to happen. Certainly Hubert Aston had been less than cordial on our last visit. Yet I suppose I had at least expected gentility. Never mind our feigned apologies for arriving unannounced, Mr. Aston was out of sorts from the moment he barreled into the library we'd been dispatched to. The first thing he did was dismiss his houseman by telling him there was no need for tea as we would not be staying, and then he spun on Colin with a deep-set scowl and snarled, "Why are you here?" before the door had even fully closed.

Colin smiled as he sat back on the settee, his pleasure unmistakable. "The murders of the two men who live on the properties that border your own, Mr. Aston, have been most confounding. Even now I continue to search for every possible connection that may have bound those men. And that fails to speak to the killings of the Connicles' groundsman, Albert, or your noble Irish wolfhounds. The only thing that seems to tie them is the fetishes, though that excludes Albert since his death was meant to appear an accident."

"Have you a point, Mr. Pendragon?"

"There is always a point." He flashed a calculated smirk before continuing. "You mentioned at one of our very earliest meetings that you believed Edmond Connicle to be engaged in an affair. You made the point that such liaisons are quite commonplace amongst your gentrified brethren."

Mr. Aston's face colored with anger, not embarrassment, as his eyes pinched and his mouth drooped down. "What is this about?" he demanded. "Your inference is neither appreciated nor will it be tolerated."

"I mean to imply nothing," Colin replied casually. "I simply want to know with whom Edmond Connicle was involved, and whether Arthur Hutton was similarly disposed?"

Hubert Aston stood up with all the authority and indignation of a church prelate. "As I told you before, Mr. Pendragon, I am not a gossiping washerwoman and will not sully the names of two decent and respectable men."

"Nevertheless . . ." Colin stared up at Mr. Aston as though at a disobedient pupil. "I am afraid I must insist."

Mr. Aston was so startled by Colin's response that he stood there a moment before collecting himself and snapping, "I beg your pardon?"

"There is a woman, Mr. Aston," Colin spoke as offhandedly as if he were describing the room, "who is young and petite, with fine, delicate bones and a decided preference for rubies. My guess is that she has dark hair, perhaps even black, and pale skin that immaculately sets off the necklace, earrings, and bracelet you gave her."

"How *dare* you!" he sputtered.

Colin stood up, refastened his jacket, and tugged his sleeves crisply into place. "I'll have that name."

The man huffed his indignation, stomping back toward an upright console festooned with crystal decanters containing a myriad of colored liquids, most of which I could not have deciphered. Mr. Aston, however, seemed to know precisely what he was after, as he snatched up a particular carafe and poured himself a finger of something amber. He downed it without a thought, not bothering to offer us a similar repast.

"I find your methods appalling!" he growled as he slammed the glass back down. "Blackmail is a devil's game, but this, Mr. Pendragon, is so very sordid." He glared at Colin with an undeniable loathing, his enormous mustache amplifying the disapproving droop of his lips. I thought surely Colin would defend himself or at least hurl some flip retort, but he did nothing, his face remaining as steady as his posture. "Edmond had been seeing Charlotte Hutton for years," Mr. Aston seethed, the words seeming to catch in his throat. "Are you satisfied?"

"It's a start." If Colin was as surprised as I was his voice and manner failed to show it. "And how did that come about?"

Mr. Aston's eyes went cold. "How does such a thing *ever* come about? Edmond found himself tied to an hysteric and Charlotte Hutton was bound to a fool of a man who had squandered her family's fortune before their daughter was even five."

"And Arthur Hutton?"

"What of him?" Mr. Aston scoffed. "He was a pompous prig whose death held little significance to anyone other than you and your ruddy Scotland Yard."

Colin's eyes narrowed. "What of his relationship with his wife?"

"How the bloody hell would I know anything of that?" he exploded. "I had no use for him. She's well rid of him if you ask me." He poured another drink and downed it. "I liked and admired Edmond Connicle, Mr. Pendragon. While that may mean nothing to men of your ilk, it carries a great deal of weight to a gentleman."

"Men like Mr. Hutton?"

"That man was a pox! I'm certain he's the reason their boy turned out so wretchedly."

Colin's eyes narrowed, but when a thin smile gradually formed on his lips I knew he was pleased with what we had learned. "Were you aware that Mrs. Hutton and her daughter have left for Paris?"

His eyebrows creased. "Isn't her boy still missing?"

"She claims to no longer feel safe in London." Colin gave a small shrug. "Understandable, I suppose." He tilted his head and peered at Mr. Aston. "Do you feel safe? After the slaughter of your dogs, do you worry about your safety? Or perhaps that of your family?"

"Why should I be worried? I've done nothing."

"Of course." Colin nodded at once. "I suppose then we cannot say the same for your dogs—"

"What the hell is that supposed to mean?"

"Forgive me," Colin replied smoothly. "I thought you meant to suggest that Edmond Connicle and Arthur Hutton were up to something. Something that should have caused them worry?"

He gritted his teeth and looked on the verge of assaulting Colin. "How eagerly you seek to impugn my words. Yet another of your contemptible games. Now if you are finished extorting from me, I have business to attend to."

Colin flipped open his pocket watch and glanced at it. "Yes. It is time for us to be off. We are expected next door at the Hutton property, where I am afraid things continue to be grim." He glared over at Mr. Aston. "Good that you are free of worry." He stood up and smiled. "Give our regards to your wife."

"Sod off," he said, clearly having caught Colin's meaning.

There was no further conversation after that. There was no need for it. Mr. Aston did not bid us anything, silently escorting us to the door and sending it crashing shut behind us the moment we had cleared his threshold. It earned a laugh from Colin, though I failed to find the humor in it. And while our visit had given us some modicum of information, I failed to see that it had drawn us any nearer to a conclusion in the case. All it had done for me was stir suspicions around Mr. Aston, though I could not settle on what his connection to any of it might be. I wanted to grill Colin for his thoughts, but his pace had picked up considerably as we cut diagonally across the Astons' property and I suspected he was trying to process everything himself.

The last tendrils of daylight hung along the horizon as we crossed the unfinished fence that separated the Connicles' land from the Astons'. I kept right alongside Colin as we circled north of the Connicle house, keeping along the irregular fence until we entered onto the Huttons' acreage. We continued to crash through the underbrush by little more than the light of the rising half-moon until we drew closer to the Huttons' home.

The sound of barking dogs drifted toward us before we'd even crested the last hillock. As soon as we reached the top of the slope we could see the stanchions of electric lights grouped in a semicircle and flooding a great wash of luminescence onto a swath of otherwise unremarkable earth. There looked to be dozens of bobbies milling about, with a core group clustered near the center of the focused lights. It didn't take long to spot Inspector Varcoe at the apex of it all, or the multitude of clustered piles of dirt scattered about as though someone had been trying to unearth a gopher.

"*Pendragon!...*" Varcoe hollered the moment we entered the periphery of the light. "My boy couldn't have gotten to you that fast."

"Your boy?" Colin said as we walked to where Varcoe was standing near a great commotion of flung dirt and tousled leaves.

"I sent Constable Lanchester to tell you what we'd found." He stepped back and nodded his chin toward a small, soiled body tossed at the bottom of a shallow pit. The hair was muddied and the face heavily smudged, but even I could attest to the fact that it was William Hutton.

"Oh . . ." Colin exhaled as he knelt down by the body. He prodded the boy's mouth open and plunged a finger inside, coming up with nothing. He looked at me. "Asphyxiation, don't you think?"

I stooped down next to him and looked at William's cherubic face, his eyes staring past me sightlessly. There were tiny red splotches marring the whites of his eyes, and when I leaned over to brush some of the dirt from a cheek there was a trace of a congealed bruise there, suggesting a hand clamped tightly against the front of his mouth. I was certain Denton Ross would find similar hemorrhaging around William's nose and chin.

"Stop touching him!" Varcoe barked, and I suppose he'd felt compelled to do so for the sake of his men.

"Right." I stood up and nodded to Colin. "I don't think he was ever meant to survive his kidnapping."

"You don't know that!" Varcoe groused. "And what are you doing here if my man didn't fetch you?"

"We've been at the Astons'," Colin muttered wanly.

"What the hell were you doing there?"

"Trying to collect information, Emmett," Colin said, taking a step back and seeming to collect himself again. "Why do you think we're here? We knew you and your men were digging about. We came to tell you what we've learned."

Inspector Varcoe opened his mouth and then shut it again, his brows knitting together as he seemed to be considering whether to believe Colin or not. "Yes . . . well . . . perhaps . . ." he finally conceded.

We slowly moved away from the heartbreaking scene, seeking the anonymity of the surrounding darkness, where Colin quickly revealed many of the details of our conversation with Mr. Aston.

Colin did not, however, share the information about the affair between Edmond Connicle and Charlotte Hutton, though he was quite forthright about Mr. Aston's animosity toward Mr. Hutton. In truth, I was hardly listening to what they were saying, as I could not stop thinking about that boy, cursed from the moment of his birth. Why would someone take his life? There could be no meaning in it. And yet, as I began to catch the rising pitch of Colin's voice, I was certain I had missed something.

CHAPTER 39

Fifteen hours later, buried under a pile of paperwork in the Foreign Services Ministry office, I was still dense with my ignorance, which had turned my mood quite sour.

The new day had arrived in a barrage of pelting rain that had evidenced no impact on Colin's disposition whatsoever. I had tried quizzing him the night before about his sudden raft of enthusiasm, but he would not be provoked into a discussion, professing to nothing more than a sense we were moving in the right direction. A sense: The very turn of phrase annoyed me. Yet he refused to be dissuaded, even after I accused him of condoning clairvoyance. It wasn't really his lack of disclosure that was nettling me, however, but rather the fact that he had relegated me to this place under the eagle-eyed scrutiny of the foreign minister's disapproving secretary, Adelaide Crouch.

"Please don't wrinkle the corners of the manifests," she sniffed at me with unfettered irritation. She didn't like me. Never had. She only had eyes for Colin, endlessly cooing and cloying at him and treating me as though I were a rival for his attentions. The poor thing had no idea.

I tossed her a grin even as I considered, just for an instant, tearing the manifests apart lengthwise. "I am doing my best to treat them with every due respect."

"Well, see that you do. I'll have to refile all of those," she scolded before pouring herself more tea. Tea I had been refused lest I should spill any on her inestimable paperwork.

I refrained from saying anything further as I returned my attentions to the manifests, lists really, of passengers who had recently been ferried from Dover to Calais. Colin wanted to know which ship Mrs. Hutton and her daughter, Anna, had taken and I was having a devilish time finding it.

"Are you certain this is all of them?" I asked as I reached the end of the final list for the second time. "I'm not seeing what I'm looking for."

"Of course it is. Are you suggesting I don't know how to do my job?"

"Not in the least." I held up my hands in surrender. "I thought perhaps Minister Fitzherbert had moved them or"—I couldn't even think of an or—"something. . . ."

"Well, he didn't and that's all of them."

"Right." I fought to keep from glowering at her. "Might I trouble you then for the day before and after this one?"

She afforded me no such similar courtesy, her brows caving in on themselves to make sure I realized how bothered she was by my request. All the same, she leaned behind her desk and quickly sorted through the same box that had produced the paperwork I was currently scouring through and yanked out a dozen sheets from varying places within. She stood up and tossed them at me on her way over to a filing cabinet in the near corner of the room.

"Mr. Pendragon is lucky I think so highly of him," she noted while pawing through one of the drawers. "I don't do this sort of thing for just anyone."

"Indeed." I gave her a grand smile, but only because I was certain it would annoy her. "I know he'll be most grateful for your generous cooperation."

"Pity he couldn't stop by himself," she said as she swept past me again, pitching a slender folder onto the table alongside the others she had already given me.

There were so many things I wanted to say back, but I knew my most irksome response would be to simply ask for more manifests. So that's what I did. I asked for every passenger list of each ship that had left Dover over that three-day period, and the bruising glare she threw me confirmed that I had hit my mark. Still, she did as bidden, yet as an inch-thick stack of papers piled up in front of me I realized I had only done *myself* a disservice.

Suppressing the sigh tugging at my chest and ignoring the smirk that had settled on Miss Crouch's face, I set to work, checking Boulogne, Saint-Malo, Barfleur, and Cherbourg, before casting my search broader to include Le Havre and Marseille, lest Mrs. Hutton had decided to sail to the south of France before heading back up to Paris. I could find no mention of her and her daughter. It made me wonder if perhaps an overworked purser had made an error in the spelling of their names, so I began my search anew, concentrating on boarding parties. Families were the most prevalent, couples with scads of children usually accompanied by a governess or two, and there were plenty of men on their own, no doubt attending to the businesses that kept those large families fed. What I could not find was more than a handful of women traveling with a single child, and none of them to any port in France.

"You're sure this is everything . . . ?" I foolishly blurted again.

"Really, Mr. Pruitt." Miss Crouch gave me a stare whose meaning could not be mistaken. "You vex me with the same question as though I were daft. Do you think the minister would keep me employed if I were as inept as you seem to suppose?"

I reminded myself that I needed this caustic woman and so bit my tongue. "My apologies." I dug up a smile. "I certainly meant no such disrespect. I'm only frustrated in that I cannot find the information Mr. Pendragon would have me gather."

She did not bother smiling back. "I fail to see how that is my fault."

"And in that you are correct." I held my grin in spite of its determination to fester. There was nothing else for me to say, so I quickly flipped through the remaining pages regarding ships bound for Spain, Portugal, North Africa, Belgium, the Netherlands, Prussia, Denmark, Sweden, and even Russia, taking a few random notes for no other reason than to make it appear that her efforts had not been in vain. With unbridled relief I shut the last folder and stood up. "I must thank you again for your cooperation, Miss Crouch. Mr. Pendragon will be most grateful, as always."

The hint of a smile cracked one corner of her mouth as she looked back at me. "Very well then. Please tell him I look forward to seeing him next time."

"Indeed I will." I gathered up my notes and gladly took my leave, pleased to be done with this meaningless exercise. I saw no point in knowing which ship Charlotte Hutton and her daughter had traveled on. For all we knew they had been ferried across on a friend's vessel anyway and so there would be no manifest.

I yanked the collar of my coat up against the day's chill as I pushed through the door back onto King Charles Street. Rain was accumulating again in the dense, gray clouds looming overhead, so I set my pace accordingly while keeping an eye out for a passing cab. Colin had instructed me to meet him at Wynn Tessler's office when I finished, which was too far to walk to if the sky didn't cooperate.

I was pulling my gloves on and moving with great purpose, having already made it to the corner of Whitehall, when I heard someone shout my name. It was a voice I would have sworn I didn't know, but when I turned back I found our young accomplice Paul running toward me with a great, loopy grin on his face. "Yer a crafty one," he snorted as he reached my side. "I took me eye off that ruddy door a bloody second and ain't that just when you come blastin' out."

"Yes . . . well . . . I am rather in a hurry. You will forgive me if I don't stop to chat." The boy brayed laughter, and if I hadn't already been worn away by Miss Crouch it might have occurred to me that we weren't simply meeting on happenstance. As it was, I had to struggle to tamp down my rising annoyance. "Really . . ." I started to say before he did me the courtesy of interrupting my unaccountable oblivion.

"I'm 'ere on account a Mr. P.," Paul said with a crooked sort of smile. "'E asked me ta come fetch ya when you came outta that place."

"Mr. P.?! Fetch me where?" I asked more gruffly than I had intended.

"'E said you'd trade me this for a whole crown if I'd bring ya." He held out his hand to show me half a crown.

I sucked in a breath and snatched up the piece before dropping a crown in its place. There was no question that he was playing me, but I hardly cared. The sky was lowering and the wind picking up, and I wanted to know where it was Colin needed me to go.

"Wait right 'ere." The scoundrel grinned at me. Before I could agree or disagree he spun about on his heel and roared out into the street with thumb and forefinger embedded in his lips, letting loose a ferocious whistle that brought several horses and carriages up short, one of which was a cab. "Over 'ere," he commanded, grabbing the horse's reins even as the driver cursed at the boy to let go. "Bugger off!" Paul hollered up at the man. "Matter a state, ya bloody wanker." He waved me over as he coaxed the horse to the curb. "Come on then. We can't keep Mr. P. waitin'."

I wanted to correct Paul, tell the rascal he had no right referring to Colin in such an informal way, but the cab abruptly lurched into motion and Paul dipped out of sight. It took me a moment to realize where he had gone until I craned around and caught sight of the top of his cap just within view out the back window. He was seated on the rear bumper as though he had purloined a ride. I banged on the glass to gesture him inside, but he only waved me off. And so we rode that way from Westminster to the corner of Threadneedle and Prince streets, the home of the Bank of England.

"'E said you was ta meet 'im at Lord somebody's office," Paul announced as I paid the driver and the cab pulled away.

"Somersby," I informed Paul. "He would be the governor of the bank."

"'At's 'im." Paul nodded with a grand smile. "Let me know if

ya need me 'elp again. I like you two. Ya don't try ta stiff a guy."
He tipped his cap with a flourish and started off.

"Paul . . ." I called to him. He spun back around with the
same smile. "Thanks," I said as I flipped his half crown back at
him. He continued to beam as he caught it easily before turning
and running off with a *whoop!* How was it, I scolded myself as I
entered the massive Romanesque building, that I didn't even
know his last name?

I made my way up to the third floor and was not surprised
when I heard Colin before I saw him. A fuss was being made, as
it always was, for Sir Atherton Pendragon's son. Lord Somersby
and Sir Atherton went all the way back to Eton together, and
while Colin and I had little reason to pay Lord Somersby many
visits at the bank, we had dined with him and his wife numerous
times at Sir Atherton's town house just off Belgravia Square.

"Mr. Pruitt . . . !" Lord Somersby's broad, lined face lit up as I
stepped across his office threshold behind the junior of the two
young men who attended him. "Now we are all here as we
should be." His rich baritone voice rumbled out a chuckle. "Do
get Mr. Pruitt some tea, Newcastle, and more of the nibbles if
you please."

"Of course, sir." The young man nodded and hustled off as
though he were the finest of household staff.

"Sit down, Ethan." His Lordship gestured me to a seat next to
Colin on a large, overstuffed sofa. "We shan't stand on ceremony
here," Lord Somersby said as he plopped down across from us.
"Not with what this one has asked of me." He arched his eyebrows toward Colin as he snatched up a shortbread cookie and
pushed the plate my way. "He thinks he can get me to do anything simply because I wouldn't be here were it not for his father." He chuckled.

"Now, Rufus," Colin said patiently as he sipped at his tea,
"you dishonor me. You know I mean to manipulate you on my
own merits."

Lord Somersby gave a delighted laugh as the young man he'd
called Newcastle returned with a china cup for me and another
sizeable plate of tarts and shortbreads for the group of us. And

then, as stealthily as the very best valet, he withdrew from the room. "There you go, my boy," Lord Somersby said, pouring me some tea. He remained as solicitous of me as ever, though what he and his wife made of my companionship with Colin had never been discussed. I felt it a profound implication of their affections for Colin that they asked no questions.

"And how is Martha?" Colin asked of Lord Somersby's wife.

"Oh . . ." He gave an affectionate snort as he snapped up another shortbread. "She's always on me to slow down. But I tell you, if I stayed at home for more than a day she would have me carted off. She cannot abide having me underfoot. Don't ever let her tell you otherwise."

We laughed just as Lord Somersby's senior aide, a man I had met before named Chiswell, came bustling into the office with a stack of ledgers and files nearly the height of his lanky torso. He scuttled over to a large table at the far corner of the room and began laying everything out in neat piles. I was too far away to determine the crux of his categorization, but the moment he seemed content with what he had done he stood back and turned toward the three of us.

"Will there be anything else, Your Lordship?" he asked.

"No, thank you, Chiswell." Lord Somersby got to his feet and with his teacup clutched firmly in his hand headed over to the table. "I'd say you and Newcastle have earned yourselves a repast. Close the door behind you, but do be back in thirty minutes."

"Yes, sir," he answered brightly, though what he made of all the documents he'd brought up intrigued me. The bank's business was conducted with the utmost discretion and propriety, and yet Mr. Chiswell had to know that all these ledgers and folders contained far more than the meager information relevant to what Colin and I owned.

"Do you know what you're after?" Lord Somersby asked as the three of us sat around the large table.

"If I did," Colin sighed as he flipped open the nearest ledger, "I certainly wouldn't be wasting your time having all of this fetched."

I looked at the spine of the ledger Colin was holding and read: *Edmond Connicle Family Trust 1893–1895*. My heart sank as I realized he meant for us to crawl through the bank's books to see if there might be any discrepancy based on what we had seen in the accounts at Wynn Tessler's firm. I could not help the wearied sigh that escaped my lips as I dragged another ledger toward me, only to be surprised to find that this one read: *Arthur Hutton Accounts 1890–1895*. What caught me most unawares, however, was that the ledger Lord Somersby was absently flipping through was labeled: *Wynn Tessler/Columbia Financial Services July–December 1894*.

"Something amiss?" Lord Somersby asked as he glanced over at me.

"I must confess," I said as I looked from him to Colin, "that I never expected to be looking through these."

"Oh"—Lord Somersby waved me off with a flick of his hand—"you aren't. This isn't happening. Wouldn't be proper. Wouldn't be proper at all."

"Of course," I said at once, taking note of Colin's single raised eyebrow as he peered at me from over the edge of the book he was studying.

And so the three of us remained, flipping through one ledger after another until well after Mr. Chiswell had knocked on the door and called out the return of him and Mr. Newcastle, which had earned him a rather gruff *"Not now"* from Lord Somersby. I continued to thumb through the Hutton accounts, noting a trail of poor decisions, ineffective investments, soaring medical costs for their unfortunate son, and, ultimately, initial paperwork to sell their West Hampton home. It was a sorrowful fall of fortunes that could only have aggravated the loss to Mrs. Hutton of her husband and son. It made me realize that I might not have found her name on any of the ship manifests because I'd been concentrating only on the first-class passengers when, in fact, she and Anna might have been forced to travel more frugally.

Colin tossed the ledger he'd been studying aside and snatched up one of the files. "What are these?"

"The most recent transactions," Lord Somersby replied.

"They haven't been entered into the ledgers yet. Such a tedious task. Our poor bookkeepers remain eternally two or three weeks behind."

Colin shuffled through several of the folders, scribbling a few notes, before settling on a pile of papers in one particular file. Lord Somersby snatched up a folder as well, leaving me the only one who continued to flip through the book I had been handed. Given the state of the Huttons' affairs, there didn't seem much reason to check the latest accountings. The Hutton accounts were emaciated, with the only sizeable withdrawal having been made for the single night's stay Mrs. Hutton and Anna had made at Claridge's before heading to Paris. There were no further entries.

"Here's something a bit peculiar," Colin spoke up as he reached out and grabbed one of the ledgers he'd just laid aside.

"Hmm?" Lord Somersby glanced over from above the rim of his reading glasses.

"Mr. Connicle has been making steady and substantial transfers on a biweekly basis for just over a year. One week before his supposed murder, the amount quintupled. It did the same again three days ago."

"Let me see . . ." Lord Somersby said as he leaned over and peered at the ledger Colin was holding. "Automatic transfers. Most clients use those for retirement savings, but that wouldn't have been a concern for Mr. Connicle." He chuckled.

"How would the amount have gotten increased?"

"A written request."

"But he truly was dead when this one was completed three days ago."

Lord Somersby scowled. "If his wife or a business partner was listed on the account they could have requested the alteration. I'd have to check the initial account records, which I'm afraid we keep off-site."

"And what of this account the funds have been transferred to? A curious number: *47-381936225*. It strikes me as oddly familiar, but I'll be damned if I know why."

"Well, I don't know why it would," Lord Somersby sniffed.

"They're usually random, though we do let our bigger investors choose their own numbers as long as they're at least eight digits and have a hyphen separating two or more of the numbers. Security, you know. They like to ascribe them to their best dog's KC number or their mistress's birth date," he snorted before quickly sobering. "Don't you *dare* tell Martha I said that."

Colin cracked a wry smile. "Perish the thought."

"I, however, may really have found something," Lord Somersby announced as he pushed himself to his feet, taking the file folder he'd been holding with him. "There are several unusual codes here. I shall have Mr. Chiswell check them out." He pushed through the door, shutting it carefully behind himself.

"I'm not having much luck," I sighed as I dropped the folder I'd been pawing through onto the table.

"Well . . ." Colin leveled a sigh himself. "About the only thing I can tell you is that Edmond Connicle was an exceedingly savvy and wealthy man. His widow will live an opulent life if we can get her out of that bloody awful place."

"Do you see the trust for Mrs. Connicle's care that Mr. Tessler spoke of?"

"It's here." He shook his head. "A tidy sum that will allow for whatever needs she may have within the confines of that horrid asylum. Nothing for her household or staff. They're to be released and the whole of the estate liquidated."

The door to the office swung wide again and Lord Somersby returned with the same file still clenched in his hands. "Mr. Chiswell is doing a touch of research," he announced as he came back to the table and sat down, "but there are some curious anomalies here that you'll likely wish to pursue."

Colin closed the file he'd been studying and leaned in toward Lord Somersby. "What have you found?"

"It would seem," His Lordship began, scowling at the pages through the window of his spectacles perched at the edge of his nose, "that your Mr. Tessler has been rather busy of late moving quite a sum of money through his accounts. A far larger sum, I might add, than what he himself is capable of covering on his own."

"What?!" I could not stop myself. "How is he moving money through his accounts that isn't his? Where is it coming from . . . ?"

"Where is it going to?" Colin asked with a good deal more perception.

Lord Somersby peeled the glasses off his nose and leaned back in his chair. "All exceptional questions, lads, but questions I cannot answer until Mr. Chiswell returns. But what of the two of you?" He glanced between us with something of a twinkle behind his eyes. "Am I to be the only one who finds anything of interest in our clandestine little venture?"

"You've outdone me," I said with a shrug. "Mr. Hutton had no head for money and I'm afraid he's left his poor widow in rather a sorry state."

"Well, I can report more than that." Colin sat up and spread the contents of the folder he'd been sorting through across the table in front of him. "The Connicle fortune is vast and, as we have seen in the accounting books at Columbia Financial, a very knotty bit of business indeed."

"Knotty?" Lord Somersby rubbed at the bridge of his nose. "I should think you won't find anything unusual in that. The more money these chaps have the more ways they find to secrete it from our dear monarch's Inland Revenue. Your own father has something of a knack for that himself," he added with a wink.

"I only wish my esteemed father had the assets to make such machinations worthwhile. I should think Ethan and I would be lounging somewhere high above the Amalfi coast right now were that the case."

Lord Somersby laughed. "I'll not feel sorry for you, boy. It's enough that you've inherited your father's favor at court. Neither of you will ever want for what you need."

"And yet it's so seldom about need." Colin snickered as another knock rattled the door.

"Oh. . . ." His Lordship chuckled as he ambled over. "Such sentiment does chill my Tory heart." He opened the door just enough to wedge himself into the gap. I heard a rash of clipped whispering before Lord Somersby waved his visitor off with a *tsk* and a *tut,* stepping back and sending the door gliding shut without another word. "Chiswell is as fretful as a nursemaid. You would think I was his charge rather than his employer."

"All forgivable," Colin said as he craned to get a look at the sheaf of papers Lord Somersby returned with, "if he has brought us something of use."

"I should think you will find it so." Lord Somersby smiled as he began to systematically lay the pages onto the table. "Do you know what you're looking at?" he asked with a sly grin.

I looked down at the raft of papers hand scribed with figures, calculations, and the names of several banking institutions but could otherwise make no sense of it. As I glanced over at Colin I could almost guess what he was going to say.

"It's banker's folly with no greater purpose than to mystify the rest of us."

"Perhaps . . ." Lord Somersby nodded with a laugh. "But this bit of folly has something intriguing to tell us. It states that Mr. Tessler's personal accounts are guaranteed by the full faith and credit of Columbia Financial Services. Which explains how he has been able to move such vast sums through them over the past dozen days."

I turned to Colin with amazement and found a deep knit in his brow. It was evident he was already whirling through some permutation I had not yet come to, so I looked back at Lord Somersby and asked, "Are you saying that no matter how much money Mr. Tessler withdraws from his accounts, even if he keeps no more than a farthing in the lot of them together, his debts will be covered through the assets of Columbia Financial?"

Lord Somersby clouted my nearer shoulder. "There you are, Ethan. Every bit as bright as your companion."

"Are you quite certain?" Colin asked.

Lord Somersby sniffed as he turned a stolid glare at him. "You did not just ask me that."

"Now, Rufus." Colin offered a patient smile. "You know I don't mean anything by it. These are delicate matters. Lives have been taken. An innocent boy of six among them. I cannot be bandying about such accusations without absolute certainty."

"You cannot bandy a word of this to anyone, dear boy, because you have not seen these records. I would never allow such a thing."

"Of course, of course," he answered too readily, and I suspected he was already trying to wheedle some way around that conundrum. "And where is all this money being moved to?"

Lord Somersby adjusted his reading glasses again as he flipped through several more pages. "It looks like a portion of it has been funneled over to Banque de Candolle Mallet and Cie in Geneva." He lifted his gaze without raising his chin. "You'll not get so much as a 'piss off' from those people. They're a private firm and those Swiss don't give a fig about playing by anyone else's rules."

"And the rest of it?"

He dropped his eyes back to the loose-leaf papers. "The vast majority of funds have been wired off to Deutsche Bank in Berlin. I'd say some million-plus pounds' worth."

My jaw unhinged. Even the Queen herself would be hard-pressed to quantify her liquid worth at so high a figure.

"Are you telling me that Columbia Financial has that depth of reserves?" Colin prodded as he yanked the papers out of Lord Somersby's hands.

His Lordship flipped through several other pages repeatedly before looking back at Colin with a bit of a shrug. "Hard to say. Some of the money is most certainly coming directly from Columbia Financial, but there is another amount, a greater amount, that appears to be funneling through from somewhere else. I'm afraid Mr. Chiswell would need to do a great deal more research to discern the source of those funds. And even so, if they were being fed through shell corporations, foreign accounts, or both together. . . ." He removed his spectacles and flipped them onto the table. "Well"—he rubbed at the bridge of his nose again—"we might never really know for certain."

Colin bolted up so suddenly that he sent two ledgers and a sheaf of papers skittering onto the floor. "I've been a fool," he announced with utter conviction, clutching one particular page in his hand.

"We all have our moments," Lord Somersby snorted.

"What are you talking about?" I asked as I too stood up.

Colin jotted something down from the paper he held and then dropped it back onto the table. "We've not a moment to lose," he announced, snatching his jacket from the back of a chair and quickly shrugging into it. "We've a train to catch and shall need to fetch the inspector straightaway."

"Varcoe?!" I said with astonishment.

"I cannot thank you enough, Rufus." Colin hurried back and hugged Lord Somersby.

"You know Martha and I can refuse you nothing," he said as he followed us to the door. "Shall I have Mr. Chiswell continue to do a spot of research?"

"That would be too much to ask."

"You didn't ask." He smiled. "Just remember, you cannot use a word of this unless it is ordered by the courts. You have seen nothing from me."

"Everything will be good and proper when the need comes," Colin assured him. "We are in thick with the Yard on this one."

"I find that oddly discomforting," Lord Somersby mused. "Good luck to you then."

Colin whisked the door open and bounded through as I turned back to Lord Somersby and shook his hand with my customary bemused grin. "I'm not sure if it's luck we need, as I haven't a notion as to what he's suddenly off about."

To my surprise, Colin heard me and tossed back over his shoulder, "Come now, Ethan, did you learn nothing from Sundha Guitnu's Irish bloke? What was his name?"

"Cillian," I answered, offering little more than a shrug to Lord Somersby as I followed Colin out. Mr. Chiswell and Mr. Newcastle glared at me as I made my way past them, most certainly aware that we'd been up to mischief in their employer's office. But I hardly cared, for I was rushing off to catch a train to an unknown destination for I knew not what, with Inspector Varcoe along for the ride.

CHAPTER 40

—◆◆◆—

Dover was at least ten degrees colder than the city had been and there was a harsh wind blowing in off the Channel. The water was whitecapped and roiling and all I kept thinking was how grateful I was to not have to climb aboard a ship and venture out upon it.

"Just looking at it makes you green." Colin chuckled beside me.

"You're not funny," I grumbled back, even though I knew he was right. It wasn't just the swell and swoon of that great body of water that had my stomach unsettled, however; it was also our conversation on the train. Both what he had shared with Varcoe and what he had chosen not to share.

Before we'd been able to leave Scotland Yard for Charing Cross Railway Station with Varcoe and Sergeant Evans in tow, we'd been stalled for almost an hour while Colin gave just enough information to pique the inspector's interest. Even then Varcoe had insisted on sending out a handful of telegrams before finally conceding that it was time to head for the coast. That one of the telegrams was to Wynn Tessler's aide to confirm Mr. Tessler's travel arrangements to Zurich had been understandable. The remainder seemed like a waste of precious time, though I was glad to see Varcoe and Sergeant Evans head off for the telegraph office the moment we arrived. I wanted some time to sort things out with Colin.

"What's the name of the ferry he's booked on?" Colin idly asked as we gazed out upon the thronging docks where two ferries and a huge ship were moored.

"The *Prince Edward*. After our next monarch, I would presume."

Colin gave me a small shrug. "Not at the rate his mother is going. He'll be lucky to serve a day." He started for the nearest pier. "So let us find that vessel and locate Mr. Tessler. I should very much like to get to the heart of this case. Too many people have been killed and some of them clearly innocents."

"Some of them?" I parroted as I hurried to keep up.

"Well, of course," he tossed over his shoulder as he barreled toward the ferry at the farthest berth, where the name *Prince Edward* was emblazoned across its side in royal blue. "Little William Hutton; the Astons' dogs; Alexa's husband, Albert. I should think all of them have the angels on their side. The rest of them . . ." He let his voice trail off.

"You mean Edmond Connicle and Arthur Hutton then. You think their murders were respective of something they were doing?"

"Perhaps . . ." he muttered as he charged up the ferry's gangplank. "We should have our answer soon enough."

"How can you be so sure?"

He paused as he stepped onto the deck. "It's what I do," he answered brashly.

"Colin . . ."

"Because Wynn Tessler is about to be in for the most staggering surprise," Colin said with sly enthusiasm. "He'll not take it well. Mark my words." And with that he turned and headed off as though he knew right where he was going.

"What about Eckhard Heillert?" I persisted.

"Who?" he blurted as he charged up a metal stairway to the next level.

"The Prussian man shot and killed in that alley."

Colin halted just before he reached the top of the stairs. "A convicted felon. Nothing more than a killer for hire. Now stop pestering. I've told you everything I'm certain of. The rest will have to unfold as it will. All I can do now is present what I'm convinced is true and hope Inspector Varcoe will be able to prove it once he arrives."

"Doesn't it feel strange to be beholden to the Yard?"

"It doesn't sit right at all," Colin mumbled as we started up the stairs again. "But this once, they could prove our salvation."

We made a hard right at the top and headed straight for the bridge, the very idea of being rescued by Emmett Varcoe and his Yarders feeling as vexing as the Channel itself. "Please keep your eyes open for their return," Colin spoke up as he shoved his way through the door and onto the bridge. "Gentlemen!" he called out brightly.

"You ain't allowed up here, sir." A man in a scrubby pair of overalls stepped toward us. "It's off-limits to passengers."

"Colin Pendragon," he answered with a smile and his hand. "And this is Ethan Pruitt. Where might we find the captain?"

"Mr. Pendragon . . . Mr. Pruitt . . ." A gray-haired man came forward with a like-colored triangular beard and a white cap on his head. He had small gold epaulets of some design on the shoulders of his jacket that I couldn't make out. "Captain Trenton Dorchester at your service. It is a pleasure to have such distinguished guests on our crossing this afternoon."

"I'm afraid we'll not be along for the journey"—Colin offered a quick nod—"and may in fact be responsible for delaying it some. We have an urgent matter to discuss with a man who *is* to be a passenger and would very much appreciate your summoning him here and allowing us a private quarter to attend to our business. I promise you we will not hold up your crossing any longer than will be absolutely necessary."

The captain's brow sank minutely. "Perhaps you would prefer to remove him from the ship and interrogate him in the embarkation station?"

"Interrogate . . . ?" Colin gave a generous smile as he glanced at the other two officers on the bridge before looking back at

Captain Dorchester. "I only mean to have a simple discussion with the man and would much prefer *not* to take him ashore. I trust you understand." He flicked his gaze over to me and I nodded as though I had any real inkling as to what he was up to.

The captain pulled out his pocket watch and gave it a cursory glance before allowing a small sigh to escape. "You realize, Mr. Pendragon, that I am held to a strict schedule by our home office. Delays cost money that I am held accountable for."

"Then we had best snap to it." Colin clapped his hands and extended an eager grin. "I'll not be the cause of your incurring any sort of levy."

I could see at once that it was not the answer Captain Dorchester had been hoping for. Nevertheless, after only the barest hesitation he spurred his men into action and within a handful of minutes we were ensconced in a small meeting room just off the rear of the bridge. It held one long, unusually tall table with clips scattered at its four edges and nary a chair to be seen. Cubbyholes ran along the far wall and each was stuffed with a rolled document. This, I realized, had to be the map room.

Our page blasted over the loudspeaker while we settled ourselves. Colin ordered me to plant myself by the porthole with a view down onto the dock. It was imperative, he repeated yet again, that I keep an eye out for Varcoe and Sergeant Evans.

We did not wait more than a minute before Wynn Tessler was shown in, and though I could tell he was trying to restrain it, I could see the shock behind his eyes. "Mr. Pendragon . . . Mr. Pruitt . . . how unexpected," he said quite smoothly, his voice tight and controlled as a gracious smile shifted his lips.

Colin stepped forward and shook his hand, bringing him farther into the small room with what I recognized as singular purpose. "You must forgive our rousting you just as you're about to leave on vacation—"

"Business," he corrected at once. "I have business in Zurich."

"Ah yes, so you said." Colin tossed a perfunctory grin.

Mr. Tessler glanced at his pocket watch and frowned at Colin. "What is this about? The ferry is set to leave in a few minutes and I cannot afford to be delayed."

"Of course," Colin responded without conviction as he took up a position on the far side of the table, leaning against it rakishly. "Our visit is about several things, really. Some of which have very much to do with you. Things I suspect you will be most grateful to learn."

"And what might those be?" he sallied back, his tone tinged with wariness.

"I'm afraid you will find the first of the news most distressing. Scotland Yard has found the remains of William Hutton."

"Oh no . . ." Mr. Tessler's shoulders drooped with practiced care as he shook his head. "That poor boy. What a sorrowful end to a tragic life."

"Tragic, was it?"

Mr. Tessler's brow quivered minutely as he looked back at Colin, a seed of something unsettled behind his eyes. "The boy was never right. You don't know how hard that was for the Huttons. The endless worry and concern . . ."

"There certainly was great cost attendant with the boy's care. The last time we spoke with Mrs. Hutton she mentioned her husband was trying to find a permanent place for the lad. Certainly a prohibitively expensive proposition."

"Really, Mr. Pendragon." Wynn Tessler scowled with distaste. "Your sentiment is crude. Were you a father you might understand that such concerns pale when talking about the care and well-being of your child."

The whisper of a smile brushed across Colin's lips and I suspected Wynn Tessler was heading right where he intended him to. "I am certain you are right about that. But I have since come to realize that the Huttons had no such sums of money to afford that sort of care. In fact, I have learned they were on the verge of losing their home."

"I should think I understand the nature of their finances a good deal better than you," Mr. Tessler shot back. "Mrs. Hutton does not have the means they once did, but she is hardly destitute."

"I should think not," Colin agreed as he idly tugged at his chin. "And yet, do you know what I find most disconcerting?

Scotland Yard has been unable to find Mrs. Hutton in the last fifteen hours to give her the tragic news about her son. They sent a telegram round to the address she left in Paris and it has been returned undeliverable. It seems there is no such address. They even dispatched a gendarme to knock on other doors in the neighborhood, but no one has seen a woman and daughter fitting the descriptions of Mrs. Hutton and Anna. Now what do you make of that?"

Had I not been watching Mr. Tessler I might have missed the slight bristling of his brow that vaulted so quickly across his face. He cleared his voice as a feigned expression of indifference settled over him. "I make very little of it, Mr. Pendragon, other than the fact that you and your Yard have made a blunder in capturing her whereabouts. You may get the correct address from my office. We most certainly have it."

"And so we did." Colin nodded. "But your office proved to have the same incorrect information." He turned to me and I caught a spark of exhilaration coiled behind his gaze. "So Mr. Pruitt went down to the Foreign Services Ministry to check the passenger manifests of the ships that left our fair shores for Calais the day after Mrs. Hutton and Anna spent their night at Claridge's. And do you know what he found?" Colin's face was a veil of innocence. "Nothing."

I took another quick look out the porthole for Inspector Varcoe or Sergeant Evans before I turned my attentions to Mr. Tessler. "Not only was there no Charlotte or Anna Hutton on *any* ship that left that day," I said, "but as you might imagine, there were very few women traveling alone, and even fewer traveling with a young girl. Not one of them headed to France."

For the first time a thin flush rose to Mr. Tessler's cheeks and his eyebrows knit perceptibly as he flicked his eyes between me and Colin. It was almost as if I could see Mr. Tessler's brain working: weighing, sifting, considering our words. Even so, I could discern little from his eyes in spite of the distrust that appeared to have settled there. "That isn't so," he finally said, making it sound more like a challenge than a statement.

"In fact," I added, still leaning against the porthole, my arms folded across my chest, "of the women traveling alone with a single girl, one was bound for Copenhagen, one for Leith, and one for Warnemünde."

"You must think me a fool." Mr. Tessler suddenly laughed. "Charging aboard this ship to tell me things I have no way of verifying. And what does any of it have to do with me?" A corner of his mouth drew up in an expression so cocksure I found myself doubting Colin's conjecture. But when I turned my eyes back to him I found that he'd stepped away from the table and was leaning against the wall with utter tranquility. If I was harboring doubts, he most assuredly was not.

"If I tell you I think you a fool," Colin began languidly, "it will not be for the reason you suppose. For there is more, Mr. Tessler. I suspect it will not come as a surprise to you that sums of money have been funneling through your personal accounts to Banque de Candolle Mallet and Cie in Geneva over the past two weeks. Sums that are guaranteed by your Columbia Financial."

"That's all perfectly legitimate. . . ." he started to protest as Colin held up a single hand.

"Yes. I suppose it is. But what if I told you that far greater sums were also being moved out of your personal accounts to Deutsche Bank? Sums backed not only by Columbia Financial, but also by the Connicle estate. An estate you now solely control, given Mr. Tolliver's terrible accident months ago."

"What?!" And now there was no subterfuge to his reaction. No hooded façade meant to belie some hidden truth. "That's impossible."

"Is it?" Colin remained just as he was, looking content and calm as though we were discussing banalities. "You gave her access to your accounts, didn't you? That was the plan. That she would use a bit of money to go first and set herself up, and you would join her a few days later. The two of you bilking both the Connicle fortune and Columbia Financial into an untraceable account in Geneva. And then what? You disappear together somewhere on the Continent? I dread to imagine what your plans were for Anna, given how mercilessly you dispatched the others who stood in your way."

"Yours is an astounding imagination, Mr. Pendragon"— Wynn Tessler's voice rumbled with strain—"but I have nothing to say to such drivel."

"You will," Colin replied simply. "For I have an inspector from Scotland Yard on his way over this very minute and he will be bringing a great many documents that I am sure you will find of interest."

"I don't know how that could be," he answered with bluster, pulling out his pocket watch again and checking it. "We are about to set off and I should hardly think any grandstanding by you or some rogue from the Yard will interfere with that."

"Then you will be pleased to learn that the captain has agreed to allow us a spot more time here. Which could impugn your schedule, given that your continuing train ticket is actually to Paris, not Zurich. And that could quickly become an impossible connection for you to make."

Mr. Tessler stiffened. Even beneath his cloak I could see his shoulders rise and his spine stiffen as though he had been prodded in the kidneys by something hot or sharp. "If you must know," he abruptly snapped, "I have a meeting in Paris tonight and will be heading for Zurich tomorrow!"

Colin flashed a patient smile. "I don't believe I asked. And none of it makes any difference anyway, because whether you realize it or not, your business in Zurich has ceased. The rogue from Scotland Yard, as you so astutely refer to him, will be bringing copies of your accounts from the Bank of England. You will see that Columbia Financial and the Connicles have been quite gutted, just as you and Charlotte Hutton planned. But you will also see that the final move in this rogue's game, Mr. Tessler, has been played against *you*. For not only are your personal accounts thoroughly pilfered, but I'd wager you'll not find Mrs. Hutton awaiting you in Paris. She has disappeared to Berlin and already siphoned off all but a pocketful of change. I'm afraid that is all you're likely to find when you check your account in

Geneva. But then I cannot prove that bit to you. You know how clandestine those Swiss are."

"They're here," I said from my vantage point at the porthole as I watched Varcoe and Sergeant Evans come racing up the gangplank. "Inspector Varcoe has a handful of papers with him," I added for Mr. Tessler's benefit, and so he did. For once it felt good to be working with the Yard. I glanced back and recoiled when I saw the gun. How foolish we had been.

"You will both ease your coats to the floor," Mr. Tessler seethed as he pointed the revolver at Colin's head while moving closer to him. We did as he demanded and I lamented that Colin had not chosen to secrete one of his own guns. Mr. Tessler kicked our coats aside and quickly patted Colin's waist and forearms before doing the same to me. With his gun hovering at my temple he snarled in my ear, "I'll not have those two on this ship. You get what they've brought and bring it in here. *And get them off this ferry!*" he blasted at me, my knees buckling as his breath lashed the side of my face. "I'll see the two of them on the docks or when I shoot Mr. Pendragon this time it won't be in the thigh."

Colin's face was grim and taut, though he remained by the far wall as though watching a scene that did not involve him. I could not claim the same level of detachment, as my heart had leapt into my throat and felt like it might cut off my air supply if I could not swallow it back down. It skittered like a jackrabbit in my ears and left my legs so feeble that I had to reach for the wall behind me to steady myself. "Don't do anything foolish," I heard myself mumble.

"Then get to it!" Mr. Tessler snapped.

As I fled the room, carefully closing the door behind myself, I realized I wasn't really certain whether my statement had been for Mr. Tessler or Colin. I didn't trust either of them, which left me even more afraid for Colin's life.

"You gentlemen about done?" the captain asked, startling me as I came around the corner and back onto the bridge.

"I need to get the documents from the inspector," I prattled, my voice catching precariously at the back of my throat.

The captain's shoulders sagged as he pawed for his pocket

watch, but I kept moving and so gave no quarter to his time constraints. "I'll not give you much longer!" he shouted after me, to which I did not bother to reply.

I found Inspector Varcoe and Sergeant Evans on the main deck near the stairs to the bridge. Varcoe was already red faced and agitated, and when I told them they would have to wait on the dock where Wynn Tessler could see them he grew even redder. "The hell I will," he fired back. "How do I know you and Pendragon aren't just up to your usual bollocks? Trying to usurp the good name and hard work of the Yard?"

Without an instant's hesitation I grabbed his lapels and dragged him inches from my face. "The man has a gun pointed at Colin's head, Emmett. Do I look like I'm buggering around?!"

His color drained and he shook himself from my grip, yanking his coat back down. "Yes . . ." he muttered, ". . . of course. We've got to be careful. You take the documents and Evans and I will determine what to do."

"You will get your ruddy asses off this ship and stand on that dock where Mr. Tessler can see you," I demanded without a shred of patience as I pulled the sheaf of papers from his hand. "I already watched this man shoot and kill that Prussian in the alley without a second thought. And he shot and grazed Colin that very same night, so you will *not* do something stupid. Now get the hell out of here." I headed back for the metal staircase but not before turning back to ensure that they were following my directions.

I rushed back to the bridge and managed to avoid the captain before rapping on the door of the map room and calling out my name. As I let myself in I found that Mr. Tessler had moved to the porthole I'd been standing at earlier, his gun still trained on Colin, who was just as I had left him. Once again I carefully shut the door before stepping forward and laying the myriad papers across the map table.

"Where's your inspector and his man?" Mr. Tessler barked.

"They sh-sh-should be there," I stammered. "I gave them specific instructions just as you said." Without thinking I stepped toward the porthole to search across the docks until I felt the gun swing around toward me. My eyes locked on the cavernous hole at the end of the round, jet-black cylinder that promised to be the last thing I would ever see.

"Don't . . ." I heard Colin say, but it sounded ridiculous and irrational.

"Where are they?!" Mr. Tessler growled.

I desperately searched the area at the bottom of the gangplank before I finally spotted the two of them stepping back onto the dock, Evans in front and Varcoe right behind with his blaze of white hair. "There. . . ." I pointed at the two of them, made conspicuous by Evans's uniform, just as I noticed that it wasn't Varcoe at all. It was a man very much like him in stature and coloring, but it was not he.

"Very well." Mr. Tessler took a step back, the gun still leveled at my face. "Tell the captain he may raise the gangplank and get under way," he instructed Colin.

Colin did exactly as he said, moving with a grim rigidity that only further unnerved me, and within a minute the gangplank had been stowed and the sound of the engines could be heard rumbling to life far beneath our feet.

"Now then." Mr. Tessler seemed to relax as he stepped away from the porthole, prodding me toward the table with his revolver. "Let us see what trifle you have brought."

Colin sidled across the table from us, his eyes locked on Wynn Tessler, making it impossible for me to catch his attention. I was terrified that he would try something heroic, so was not surprised to find my hands trembling as I laid out the loose documents. What made it worse was not knowing what Inspector Varcoe was up to. That fact scared me more than anything else.

"Describe what it all is!" Mr. Tessler snapped at me. "I'll not take my eyes off this weasel." He leered at Colin as he fixed the revolver closer to my head.

"You mustn't keep pointing your gun at Mr. Pruitt." Colin spoke with calm assurance. "Because if you shoot him, even by accident, I shall rip your bits out through your eye sockets."

I could not breathe. The air was thick and heavy, and I was certain the only sound that could be heard was the thunderous galloping of my heart. Neither Colin nor Mr. Tessler said anything further, so I began reading aloud the first telegram lying on the table in front of me.

"FROM THE BANK OF ENGLAND.
CONFIRMING INSOLVENCY OF ALL
ACCOUNTS BELONGING TO WYNN TESSLER.
STOP. COLUMBIA FINANCIAL SERVICES
NEARLY SO. STOP. STILL VERIFYING
ADDITIONAL ACCOUNTS FROM WHICH
BULK OF FUNDS ORIGINATED. STOP. ONE
THOUSAND POUNDS TRANSFERRED TO
BANQUE DE CANDOLLE, ETC., GENEVA.
STOP. REMAINING FUNDS TO DEUTSCHE
BANK OF BERLIN. STOP. LORD RUFUS
SOMERSBY. GOVERNOR, BANK OF
ENGLAND."

I looked up to find Wynn Tessler scowling at me, his lips taut and his brow furrowed with a hatred that made me fear the gun wavering near my head even more. "Read the next one," he demanded.

As I leaned forward to grab another telegram I slid slightly to my right, hoping the gun might stray more toward my shoulders than my head.

"FROM DEUTSCHE BANK. HEREWITH VERIFY
FUNDS MOVED FROM W. TESSLER
ACCOUNTS AT BANK OF ENGLAND. STOP.
2,958,010 SWISS FRANCS. STOP. ALL FUNDS
TRANSFERRED SUCCESSFULLY. STOP.
GERHARD VON HOFFMAN, SENIOR VICE
PRESIDENT, DEUTSCHE BANK."

"The next one . . ." Wynn Tessler's voice came out harsh and dangerous.

Again I leaned forward, and slid myself just the slightest bit to the right. "Deutsche Bank again," I said, clearing my throat as a wave of sweat breached my forehead. I glanced at Colin and found him glaring at Mr. Tessler, his eyes hooded and narrow, and once again I found my senses ratcheting toward panic.

"RECIPIENT ACCOUNT OF W. TESSLER FUNDS FROM BANK OF ENGLAND OPENED BY WOMAN. STOP. MARY ELLEN WITTEN. STOP. MAJORITY OF FUNDS ALREADY TRANSFERRED TO SEVERAL NEW CORPORATE ACCOUNTS. STOP. WILL REQUIRE ADDITIONAL TIME TO DETERMINE FINAL STATUS. STOP. GERHARD VON HOFFMAN, SENIOR VICE PRESIDENT, DEUTSCHE BANK."

"Next!" Mr. Tessler's feral growl came again.
"This is from the White Star Line," I muttered.

"CAN CORROBORATE DESCRIPTION OF PASSENGER FROM WEDNESDAY LAST AS MARY ELLEN WITTEN. STOP. EMBARKED IN DOVER, ENGLAND, WITH HER DAUGHTER, ELIZABETH. STOP. DISEMBARKED IN WARNEMUNDE, PRUSSIA. STOP. CHEERS. TERYTON MAYWEATHER, PURSER, OCEANIC, WHITE STAR LINE."

Wynn Tessler's breathing had become irregular and staccato. I could hear his jaw clenching and the sound of his teeth grinding with ferocity. *"That goddamn bitch!..."* he hollered. "I'll kill her. I will hunt her down and rip her into a thousand ruptured pieces with my bare hands. Thinks she can play me the fool!"

The timbre and intensity of his voice rose with every curse that passed his lips. His face had gone crimson and the hand holding the revolver had started to quake with the intensity of his rage.

I tried to think what I should do but found I could not move. He continued to rant, his words erupting like water through a fissure in a dam, yet I could not even decipher what he was saying anymore. It was all coalescing into a discordant sound that spoke of hatred and violence and the complete rupture of sanity. Time itself ceased, seeming to flatten and ooze sideways, leaving me unsure whether seconds or minutes had passed. And still, Wynn Tessler's voice accelerated in both volume and force, his whole body now shaking with the vastness of his outrage, and I knew he was going to shoot us.

Before I could even process that thought I felt Colin's fingers thread through mine and had to force myself not to cry out. I knew he meant for us to die together, side by side, hand in hand, and I desperately wanted to turn to him, as I could not bear the thought that Wynn Tessler's detestable face would be the last thing I should ever see on this earth. But before I could even *try* to shift my eyes, Colin tugged on my arm just as a loud bang erupted from across the room near the door.

He jerked me to him so suddenly that I lost my balance and careened like a rag doll into his powerful chest. He shook free of my hand and shoved down on my shoulders, sending me to the floor in a flail of unaccounted-for limbs. As I was falling, I caught a glimpse of shocking white hair and realized that the explosion had been the screech of the metal door as Emmett Varcoe had burst into the room with a thunderous *crash!* He was crouched low in the doorway, his black eyes darting about from within his perpetually ruddy face, and I was never so glad to see him.

My hands abruptly collided with the floor, and I barely kept my chin and nose from doing the same, as I struggled to see what was happening.

And then I heard the shots. Four of them in quick succession. Too quick. And before the sounds could begin to recede, just as the burnt smell of spent gunpowder started to assault my nostrils, Colin collapsed on top of me.

CHAPTER 41

———◦———

Twenty-seven years ago the murmurings inside of my mother's head became too much for her. As a result, with little warning, she took my father's small derringer and shot him in the head with it twice. She then reloaded the gun's two chambers and shot my eight-month-old sister, who was squalling in my now dead father's lap. The last thing my mother ever did was put that gun in her mouth and squeeze the trigger one last time. Four shots.

The only reason I survived was because I was a coward. I was locked in my room, trembling beneath my bed, when my mother pounded on my door and demanded I open it. Her voice had been brittle, and shrill, and heavy with anguish, and even at nine I'd understood that I must not answer. So I had kept silent, retreating into a tight ball at the farthest corner under my bed, not even moving after I heard my father's soothing voice urging her away. Urging her back to their room. Nor did I move after the first two shots were fired. I didn't even move for a time after the second two shots were fired. I have lived with that knowledge every day since.

Three days after that I stood in the churchyard before the coffins of my parents and infant sister with my maternal grand-parents hovering somewhere behind me. They were careful to hold their distance as the minister spoke haltingly and briefly, his discomfort plain to see. My grandparents had procured this unorthodox burial for their only daughter through a generous donation to the church, desperate to keep tongues from wagging. But the only time either of my grandparents had touched me that day was when my grandmother leaned forward and pinched my shoulder when I started to cry. I believe they were afraid of me. Afraid that I too carried the madness that had driven my mother. They saw no honor in my having survived. In truth, I was afraid of myself.

My grandparents did not invite me into their home. I was sent at once to Morrissey House, a group home for boys who were either indigent or troubled, though I was neither. I spent almost three years there before being transferred to the Easling and Temple Senior Academy for a proper education. I never saw my grandparents again. They did not write to me, nor I to them. When they died I did not attend their funerals. In fact, I have never attended the funeral of anyone since that day in the churchyard staring at those three rectangular boxes, two adult sized, the third unmistakably smaller. I saw no point in such attendance. For whom would I be attending? Not for the deceased, as they could not possibly care. Certainly not for me.

Which was why I felt so completely overcome standing in my white shirt and crisp black suit, head bowed against the ornate casket I did not want to see. I would have done most anything not to have come here, but there had been no choice. And just as I had feared, I felt like that nine-year-old boy all over again: terrified, tortured, and afraid to breathe. I waited for the pinch on my shoulder to staunch the flow of tears brimming in my eyes but instead felt Colin's hand snake into my own and squeeze it, firmly and discreetly, before pulling away.

It did not matter that Emmett Varcoe could drive Colin to distraction. That Varcoe was almost always more an impediment than an aid. In the final moments, when it had mattered the most, he had acted with unaccountable bravery and it had cost him his life.

Of the four shots fired in that small map room on the ferry, the one Inspector Varcoe had managed to squeeze off had embedded itself in the wall directly behind where Wynn Tessler had been standing. Two shots struck Inspector Varcoe, one in the chest and one in the shoulder. The fourth had come from a derringer Colin had hidden up one of his pants legs. It had entered Wynn Tessler's neck at an upward trajectory, passing through and exiting out his opposite cheek. It was not a fatal shot, but it had been enough to render him unconscious.

Five days later we were here in this cemetery, the formal service behind us. The ornate casket had been moved to this site to the melancholy dirge of a single bagpipe. We were surrounded by what looked like half the contingent of Scotland Yard as the coffin was carried into place. Emmett was a widower. I had known that. But it turned out he had grown children, two sons and three daughters, and all of them were there. I had never thought of him as a father, but then I don't recall ever asking. That realization made me profoundly sad.

There was a final cacophony of rifle fire from a dozen Yarders standing a short distance away and then it was over. I struggled to temper my grief and was grateful when Colin was drawn into conversation with Emmett's children. Memories were shared. I participated as best I could, but my mind remained fixated on that day, twenty-seven years before, when my life had come utterly apart at the sound of four gunshots.

It was only after Colin and I were on our way home that I could finally fold and stow those thoughts away again. It was almost a relief to have the case to focus on. "There is one thing I still don't understand," I said with perhaps too much bravado. "How did you figure out that Edmond Connicle had become so enthralled with Mrs. Hutton to participate in a plan to fake his own death?"

"Ah." Colin nodded, and I decided he was as grateful as I was to have something of substance to discuss. "It was that account Edmond Connicle had been moving steady sums of money into for the better part of a year. A week before his faked death the sums funneling into that account suddenly exploded. Do you remember how I said the number looked oddly familiar?"

"I remember."

He dug a scrap of paper out of his pocket and wrote the number down and handed it over to me. "Do you see a pattern there?"

I stared at it a minute. *47-381936225*. As hard as I searched for some reason amongst the arbitrary grouping I could find none. "No."

"It's a cipher. And a simple one at that. It's nothing more than a monoalphabetic substitution."

"A what?!"

One corner of his mouth curled up as he quickly wrote out the alphabet. Next, he placed a number beneath each letter from one to twenty-six. "It's child's play, really," he said, sounding exasperated with himself. "Look at the numbers after the dash. *C* is the third letter of the alphabet. *H* is the eighth. *A* is the first. *R* is the eighteenth. Eighteen is a one plus an eight, which equals nine."

And suddenly I could see the pattern he was referring to begin to emerge. "*L* is the twelfth," I piped up, "one plus two, which is three. *O* is the fifteenth, one plus five, equaling six. *T* is the twentieth, a two. There are two of those. And *E* is the fifth. *Charlotte.*" I looked at the first two digits. "And the forty-seven at the front?"

Colin's crooked grin went rigid. "*My.*"

I cringed. "It was Edmond Connicle's pledge to her. The only sort of commitment he could make, given that they were both married."

"Which is why Mrs. Hutton undoubtedly helped him hatch a plan against his wife to have her committed. Most assuredly with the promise that she would also get rid of her husband one way or another so they could then be together. And that was what Edmond Connicle intended. He meant to convince his wife to think him dead, even going so far as to put his ring on that poor murdered soul's finger, which would have taken some clever explaining when he finally showed up again. But in the meantime he was going to make sure his pitiable wife spied him here and there until her grip on sanity eventually became so tenuous that he could return from his supposed business abroad to seal her fate."

"Only he didn't know that Mrs. Hutton and Wynn Tessler were plotting against *him*."

"Precisely. Edmond Connicle had no idea that he was standing in the way of their far grimmer plot." Colin shook his head. "And all the while Wynn Tessler himself was but a pawn for Mrs. Hutton." He heaved a wearied sigh. "It wasn't until after we spoke to Sundha Guitnu's Irish boy—"

"Cillian . . . ?"

"Yes. He reminded me of the incredible depths some men are willing to go to for a woman. For better and for worse. And I as foolish as the rest of them. She led us like dullards, every one of us, just as she meant to."

I squeezed his hand but could think of nothing further to say as we rode along in silence for a while. We reached our neighborhood just as the sun poked out of a cloud bank, and I finally felt my spirits beginning to ease. "Wouldn't Emmett have loved the pomp at his funeral?" I said with a laugh.

"A lifetime of mediocrity crowned by a moment's glory in the line of duty." Colin gave a small chuckle. "He had the final laugh on us all."

"You're being disrespectful."

"I'm telling the truth. If Emmett were here he would agree."

I was about to say something, to defend the poor man, but then it occurred to me that perhaps, just perhaps, Colin was right.

"How unexpected . . ." he muttered as our carriage turned into Gloucester Road.

"What?"

"It appears we have a visitor," he said, craning to get a look at the small, black carriage parked at our curb. "No markings on the coach. Whoever could it be?" As the driver slowed, Colin leapt out and bolted up the steps to our front door, disappearing inside.

As I stepped in after him, I found Mrs. Behmoth planted just inside waiting for me. "Ya got a visitor," she said needlessly. "She don't look well. I took tea up and some biscuits, but ya let me know if ya need anythin' else."

"I'm sure we will." I nodded as I hurried up the stairs, my heart sinking at the thought of having to begin a new case so soon. I'd been hoping we might be able to nip out of town for a few days. Get a change of scenery. Clear our heads. I knew I was in need of it.

I heard Colin's voice before I was halfway up the stairs and recognized the lilting tone of the woman he was speaking with the moment she responded. When I reached the landing and came through the doorway it was to find Mrs. Guitnu perched on the settee across from where Colin was pouring tea for all of us. She was dressed in black and wore a small black hat with a half veil covering the upper part of her face. She was, I instantly feared, in mourning.

We exchanged greetings, though her manner remained stiff and formal, which seemed lost on Colin, who was as warm and friendly as if she were a lifelong friend. Only after we had all been served did Mrs. Guitnu finally turn to the purpose of her business. "You must forgive the impropriety of my visit," she said, her tone soft and melodious. "Unannounced and unescorted."

"Please." Colin waved her off with a smile. "You are in a house filled with impropriety." He flashed a smile, but I could see she had no idea what to make of his words.

She let a moment pass before she reached over and picked up a plain, cloth sack from the floor by her feet, setting it onto the table in front of us. "I need you to find my Sunny and deliver this to her. She had a terrible row with her father and is no longer part of our family. I cannot go to her, you understand. I cannot dishonor my husband." She looked up and I could see tears glittering in her eyes in spite of the mesh veil. "He is a good man. A kind man. He has always provided for his family with great generosity and care. It was his idea to move to England so our girls would have the opportunities they could never have in India. He has done well by all of us."

She took a deep breath and fell silent, taking a sip of her tea with the delicacy of one who might come tumbling apart at any moment. And, indeed, I thought she must truly feel that way. For while I might have been incorrect about her mourning, I had not been wrong.

"Sunny has disgraced our family with that boy," she went on. "And now she has disappeared with him. My husband had her room emptied the same day, furnishings, clothing; even the walls have been repainted. It is as if no one has ever lived there. It is how it must be." She set her tea down and removed a small lace handkerchief from her purse and dabbed at her eyes. "You must forgive me, but I am a foolish woman sometimes."

"You are no such thing," Colin said. "You are caught on a precipice from which there is no easy passage. And yet"—he leaned forward and opened up the sack—"it would seem you are doing what you can to bridge that chasm."

Mrs. Guitnu gave a laden smile. "She remains the flesh of my heart and I will not see her end in misery."

Colin nodded as he pawed through the sack. "Aren't these the very jewels your husband paid me to find?"

She stood up suddenly, her posture ramrod straight. "You mustn't concern yourself with my husband, Mr. Pendragon. I will attend to him. You must do this thing for me and give me your word that it will be done."

"I give it without hesitation," Colin answered as he walked her to the landing. "We know where the boy lives. Be assured your daughter will receive your parcel within a day."

She looked at us with a well of sorrow. "You are most kind."

"No." Colin shook his head. "It is you who are the bearer of extraordinary kindness. And of love. We are but messengers grateful to do your bidding."

A hint of relief flickered momentarily behind her eyes before she turned and fled down the stairs.

CHAPTER 42

Annabelle Connicle was ghostly pale and paper thin, but her eyes had the fire of life in them. It was enough to steal my breath and sting my eyes as I got my first look at her standing in the doorway of her sitting room, resplendent in a pale blue dress that hung far too loosely at the shoulders and waist. There was no denying the toll her stay at Needham Hills had cost her, yet this petite, frail woman had persevered beyond what I had imagined possible. It reminded me how those seemingly most fragile can oftentimes be the most resolute.

Miss Porter was at her mistress's arm offering support, wearing her own smile as rich as our surroundings. As Colin and I stood to greet the two of them I found myself diverting my gaze and pulling in a deep breath so that the lump swelling in my throat would not suddenly leap from my eyes. When I managed to steal a glance at Colin I was fortified by the great smile on his lips, his blue eyes alight with joy as he grasped Mrs. Connicle's hands as though *she* had just rescued *him*.

"It does my heart wonders to see you back at home," he enthused, plucking her arm from Miss Porter and helping her to a nearby chair.

"I have you to thank for that, Mr. Pendragon." She grinned.

"For without you and Mr. Pruitt I am certain I would never have left that regrettable place."

"'Ere, 'ere . . ." Mrs. Hollings cheered as she came bustling into the room with a tray filled with tea and biscuits. "These are me butter biscuits fresh from the oven and me 'omemade jams. Fit fer the Queen, they is, but jest right fer all a you," she announced as she set the tray in front of Miss Porter.

"You make me blush." Colin chuckled, though I doubted such a thing was even possible.

Mrs. Hollings snorted a laugh as she left the room and Miss Porter served the tea. She handed us each a cup and our own plate of biscuits before taking a portion for herself and discreetly retreating to a seat against the wall behind Mrs. Connicle. Whether it was a mandate of Mrs. Connicle's release or a consequence of her unease at her sudden freedom I could not say.

"I'm afraid you've missed Alexa," Mrs. Connicle said. "She's already been sent to market. I know she would want me to thank you."

"No thanks are necessary," Colin said as he stared at his tea. "I only regret that it took us so long to resolve. . . ."

Mrs. Connicle shook her head with a wearied sigh. "I'm just grateful that you resolved it at all. That is enough." A small smile gently blossomed across her face. "I'm sure you know I will be selling this drafty old house. It's far too much for me to care for and I haven't the means to do so anyway. I shall be well rid of it," she said in a tone void of self-pity. "I will find a suitable flat in the city and Miss Porter and Mrs. Hollings have both agreed to remain with me. There is simply nothing more I could want for. Isn't it marvelous?" She gave the first truly heartfelt smile I had ever seen her offer.

"Indeed." Colin beamed back, but I could tell his own look was tinged with remorse. "And what is to become of Randolph . . . and Alexa?"

"Randolph has decided to retire as soon as I'm situated and is going to live with his sister in Cornwall. I only regret that I cannot give him a stipend to take with him," she sighed, "but he has asked nothing further of me."

"He is a fine man," I added, remembering his having cautioned me to heed his mistress's words when she had insisted she'd seen her husband near Covington Market.

"As to Alexa . . ." Mrs. Connicle gave a wistful smile. "She is anxious to leave the city, so I gave her an exemplary recommendation to a family in Cardiff, where she will begin working within a fortnight. It will be a fresh start for her." She sipped at her tea and leveled her gaze on Colin. "You saved an innocent, Mr. Pendragon."

"I did what I could." He glanced away as he said it and I knew he was thinking about the innocent lives he had not been able to save. From the unknown homeless bloke whose charred body had briefly stood in for that of Edmond Connicle to little William Hutton, who had committed no crime but being born to a woman who did not want him.

"I try to understand it all. . . ." Mrs. Connicle started to speak, her voice thick with anguish, "but I cannot seem to assemble it in my mind. Will you tell me once more, Mr. Pendragon? Will you do me that final kindness?"

Colin's face paled and his shoulders stiffened, but before he could say anything Miss Porter spoke up. "You mustn't, madam," she said as she hopped out of her seat and came right up beside her employer. "You mustn't do that to yourself again. There is no value in it. It isn't healthy."

Mrs. Connicle reached out and patted the back of Miss Porter's hand. "You are right, of course. But if I don't hear it, I won't understand it and I shall never be able to let it rest." She turned back and settled her eyes on Colin. "Please, Mr. Pendragon."

Colin brushed a hand through his hair and flicked his eyes to me, and I could see how loath he was to be having this discussion again. He had not wanted to come here in the first place. I had insisted. I felt we owed her something more, but as we sat there I began to wonder if it hadn't been to assuage a ghost of my own.

"Well . . ." He cleared his throat awkwardly. "Your husband—"

"No . . ." she interrupted him at once, "I know about Edmond. I don't need to hear about him. Tell me about Albert. Why did he have to die?"

"The morning your husband disappeared Albert had been out checking the fence at the edge of your property. He told us he'd seen someone, a man on horseback who had tried to chase him down. I'm quite sure that man was the Prussian felon who'd been hired to perpetrate your husband's disappearance. Once he had been spotted by Albert, I'm afraid Albert became a liability."

"That poor man," she groaned.

"It is my belief," Colin spoke slowly and carefully, as though picking his way through a patch of brambles, "that this whole business began and ended with Charlotte Hutton. Locked in a marriage she could not abide to a reckless man who had squandered their money, she began to plot a way out for herself. Her escape comprised two crucial elements: the need for a vast sum of money to afford the existence she desired, and the necessity to rid herself of a husband she hated and a son who represented nothing more than a lifetime's encumbrance."

Miss Porter sucked in a startled breath even as tears began to roll down Mrs. Connicle's cheeks. "What I would have given to have a child," she muttered, dabbing at her eyes. "Please go on. . . ."

Colin drew a labored breath and continued. "About a year and a half ago Mrs. Hutton began her dalliance with your husband. At some point she was able to manipulate him into setting up a personal account in her name. Most likely with the pretense of proving his intentions toward her. But what your husband did not know is that Mrs. Hutton had also begun a liaison with Wynn Tessler. They not only conspired to have her husband and son murdered but also *your* husband once they managed to gain the access they wanted to his fortune. That moment came when your husband's financier, Noah Tolliver, suffered a debilitating riding accident. No accident, I can assure you.

"Control of your assets reverted to Mr. Tessler, who added Mrs. Hutton as a silent partner to all of his accounts, just as your husband had done, to prove his fealty to her. An egregious mistake.

"That's when Mr. Tessler enlisted that scourge from Prussia to do their bidding. First he took the life of the homeless man whose body stood in for your husband's. The use of the voodoo fetishes was intended to deceive the Yard, and it was a clever ploy, given our country's lamentable distrust of those foreign born. But it was all pointed and sloppy," he scoffed. "An imbecile could see it was so. Even the ruddy Yard came to realize it."

I cringed at his words, for both Inspector Varcoe's memory and for those at the Yard, like Sergeant Evans, who had helped us. But Mrs. Connicle seemed not to have noticed.

"We will never know for certain, but I don't believe your husband had knowledge of the killings Mrs. Hutton and Mr. Tessler had planned. Given his unfortunate end, I think he believed he could steal Mrs. Hutton away from her husband with minimal effort. The death of a nameless sot, and Alexa framed for the murder, must have seemed a worthy price to pay."

"Then *he* was the fool!" Miss Porter snapped, her lips little more than thin, white slits.

"Indeed." Colin nodded. "But his plan to drive you, Mrs. Connicle, to madness was incalculably cruel. He was already armed with his faked receipts when we discovered him in that East End alley. They'd confounded us when we found them on his body, but with those in hand, and his insistence that you had known of his trip all along, it would have permanently sealed your fissure from reality. He would have been free to woo Mrs. Hutton once she divorced her husband."

Mrs. Connicle swiped at her eyes with her handkerchief again as Miss Porter sat down next to her, clutching her arm like a protective sister. I was desperate for Colin to stop, but when Mrs. Connicle nodded at him again I knew she meant to hear it all.

"The moment your husband put his plan into motion, allowing you to spy him at Covington Market, Mr. Tessler had him dispatched. Enough damage had already been done for him to confine you to Needham Hills. And with you and your husband summarily dispatched, he was free to have at your fortune for him and Mrs. Hutton. But he was blind to the fact that Mrs. Hutton had already begun savaging your accounts. And his as well. For she had a plan of her own. One in which Mr. Tessler was played the biggest fool of all once he had seen to the murders of her husband and son." He sighed and rubbed his forehead. "The slaughter of the Aston dogs served no greater purpose than to mystify the Yard"—he rubbed his forehead again—"and me."

Mrs. Connicle's face was pale and drawn, but her eyes had gone hard as her voice came out flat and determined. "I shall never comprehend the mind of that woman."

"And that is what proves the soundness of your mind and the rupture of hers," Colin answered.

"And what of Mr. Tessler?"

"He shall pay for his complicity with his life. He not only murdered his Prussian conspirator but a distinguished inspector of Scotland Yard as well. The noose is already tied for him."

"Then there will be *some* justice," she said, and I saw Colin flinch at her remark.

"Scotland Yard is already working with the Federal Ministry of Justice in Berlin to locate Mrs. Hutton. She will be marked by a substantial trail of blood money. It won't be easily hidden. She *will* be brought to justice," he said, but I was unsure whether he was trying to convince Mrs. Connicle or himself.

"Justice can be a fragile mistress," Mrs. Connicle stated, "but Mrs. Hutton will face the consequences of her actions in the end."

Colin gritted his teeth and I knew that answer did not suit him. Not at all.

CHAPTER 43

A week passed with Colin fretting about the flat, alternately lifting a variety of weights as though fearful his muscles might suddenly atrophy and cleaning every gun, knife, and sword in his considerable collection. In an effort to ease his restlessness I arranged for us to take a trip out to the countryside so he could teach me how to shoot—again. While I do not confess to being enamored by the thought of wielding a gun, I was so grateful that Colin had brought one the day we'd confronted Wynn Tessler that I thought it time I learned to respect the device rather than just fear it.

Colin was ecstatic at my renewed interest, and I discovered that I was fairly adept with his little derringer as well as those guns that shot twenty-two-caliber rounds. Those of a higher count, however, intimidated me with both the level of their decibels and the severity of their recoil. More than once my forearm kicked up with such ferocity that a spent shell casing, metallic and hot, came flying out the top of the empty chamber to bounce off my forehead, leaving a pale pink scorch in its wake. Nevertheless, I vowed I would continue to practice.

Mostly we waited for news of Charlotte Hutton from Scotland Yard. Sergeant Evans appeared to be in line to replace Inspector Varcoe, which was a relief given that he had always been civil to us. He was also proving generous with the first bits of information beginning to come out of Berlin about Mrs. Hutton. They were still struggling to trace precisely how and where she had moved the siphoned funds from Deutsche Bank. Her trail was proving to be shrewd and circuitous, making it evident that she had learned much from Wynn Tessler.

"Maybe it's time for us to take a holiday," Colin announced one afternoon as he stoked the fire against the chilled drizzle outside. "What would you think of that?"

"A bit of heaven. What do you have in mind?" I asked, turning away from my notes on the Connicle case. I was certain I knew what he had in mind. He would want to go to Berlin. He wouldn't be able to stand the thought that Charlotte Hutton had outwitted him.

"Spain . . . France . . ." He shrugged as he picked up one of his large revolvers and began to disassemble it yet again. "Maybe Switzerland. It might be nice to get some of that Alpine air. . . ."

"Alpine air?!" I repeated, my brow curling as I stared at the side of his face, certain he was being facetious. "Since when do you give a whit about Alpine air?"

He glanced over at me as he pulled a telegram from his pocket and handed it over. "Since this came from Sergeant Evans while you were out earlier."

I unfolded and scanned it quickly:

NEWS OF CHARLOTTE HUTTON. BULK OF
FUNDS WIRED TO CREDIT SUISSE ON
WEDNESDAY NEARLY A FORTNIGHT AGO.
BANK ACKNOWLEDGES RECEIPT. NO
FURTHER INFORMATION FORTHCOMING.
WOULD TAKE AN ACT OF GOD. DOES YOUR
FATHER KNOW HIM? CHEERS, SERGEANT
EVANS.

I looked back at Colin. "You think she and Anna are headed for Geneva then?"

"There's a fair chance of it. She can drop the girl at a private school and be done with her. From there . . ." He let his voice trail off as he concentrated on boring out the barrel of the revolver with his little oiled brush.

"It's all so ghastly."

"And that's precisely why we should go." He looked up at me with a crooked smile. "You know, on holiday."

"Holiday." I laughed as a knock came to the door below. "Perhaps we have more information arriving even now," I said as Mrs. Behmoth's heavy footfalls crossed beneath us. Not a moment later Mrs. Behmoth gave a delighted squeal and I knew it could only mean one thing. She pounded up the stairs with unaccustomed speed, Sir Atherton Pendragon in tow.

"Look 'oo's come ta visit," she enthused as he glided into the room and gave me a hug and then dispensed one to Colin. "You'll stay fer supper or I'll throw yer arse out the winda right now."

"How could I possibly refuse such an offer as that?" He chuckled. "You will remember my delicate digestion—"

She waved him off. "It was me what 'elped give ya that. I know jest wot ta make fer ya." And with that she was gone.

"I'm not so sure we'll get any tea in the meantime." Colin stared after her.

"It's no matter." He sat down in Colin's usual chair by the fireplace. "I'm here to speak with you both and would just as soon do it while she is otherwise engaged."

Colin set the pieces of the revolver he'd been cleaning onto the table and took a seat on the settee as though he were suddenly the client.

"How have you lads been?" his father asked incongruously as he reached out and snatched up the sundry parts of the revolver and quickly reassembled it. He studied it closely a moment before setting it down and looking at the two of us.

Colin's brow furrowed. "What kind of question is that?"

"I'm just trying to be cordial. You will remember I spent a

lifetime as a diplomat." Neither of us said a word. "Well, all right then. I have received a telegram."

"A telegram . . . ?" Colin parroted.

His father stared across at him. "Yes. What *are* you on about? You're coiled up like an asp."

"It's nothing," he answered too quickly.

"It's a case," I corrected. "He solved it save for the fact that the woman at the very heart of it has managed to slip away. He's been treating himself unforgivably ever since."

"Ah." His father smiled. "I'm afraid that's a character flaw."

"Will you please just tell me about the bloody telegram?" Colin snapped.

His father looked back at him reproachfully. "And *that* is why you are *not* a diplomat, boy." He sat back in the chair as his eyes slid over to the fireplace. "I'm afraid it's bad business. News from a bishop who was working in Bombay when we were living there. Ambrose Fencourt. Do you remember him?"

Colin pursed his lips and seemed to ponder it a moment before shaking his head, which came as no surprise to me. He was far more likely to remember the man's face than his name.

"No matter. He's the bishop for East Sussex County now. He's a good man. A pious man. And he sent me a telegram today and asked if you would be able to help him."

"Help him with what?" Colin asked, and I could hear the wariness in his voice.

"There's a monastery in the small town of Dalwich called Whitmore Abbey. A group of monks living obedient lives of poverty reside there. They have almost no interaction with the outside world." He cleared his throat and shifted in the chair, his discomfort at the topic evident. "Early yesterday morning the abbot was discovered murdered in his chamber. He'd been stabbed dozens of times and his tongue was cut out. It's missing. They cannot find it."

Colin's posture stiffened as his eyes slid away from his father. "It sounds extraordinary, but I should think men like Ethan and me would be most unwelcome at a monastery."

"Well, you needn't post a notice on your forehead. Besides, I've already written him that you'll go. Tomorrow."

"I'll not be anyone but who I am."

"God help us"—Sir Atherton rolled his eyes—"if my son should deign to compromise."

Colin pursed his lips as his eyes pinched together. "All right," he said as he turned to me, the scowl darkening his eyes to cobalt by the light of the fire. "Then we shall start our holiday in Dalwich."

ACKNOWLEDGMENTS

If you enjoyed this read, and I most certainly hope that you did, then you must permit me one more moment of your time to thank and acknowledge the people who were so vital to me in bringing this story to your hands in whatever form it took.

I am incredibly thankful to Kathy Green, whose early support of me cannot be overstated. Her guidance is always appreciated, as are her ever thoughtful notes. She brought my work to Kensington, and it is to the staff there that I must give my next round of appreciation. First and foremost is John Scognamiglio, who is patient and intuitive and provides me with the most amazing support. I know Colin and Ethan are in good hands when I turn a draft over for his review, and I am forever grateful for that. Vida Engstrand is tireless in helping to get these books out to the wider world, and I hope she knows I am forever at her beck and call to do whatever bidding she desires. Kris Mills never ceases to please me with her eye-catching cover designs. I look forward to seeing them as much as anyone. And to freelance copy editor Barbara Wild I give my hearty thanks for her diligence and detail in copyediting the books.

If there are mistakes in the timing, vernacular, or history of these stories, it is NOT the fault of Barbara. I'm afraid those belong to me alone. I will admit to a bit of literary license here and there, though I try to behave within the period at hand. I hope you will permit me my freedoms now and again and not judge too harshly.

I have received unending support from my family and friends. In particular, as with the first two books, Diane Salzberg, Karen Clemens, and Melissa Gelineau provided critical assistance. Their careful notes during early drafts prod me to reach higher, and I cannot thank them enough for that. Likewise, I owe a heartfelt thanks to Carla Navas, who is a far better promoter of me than I am of myself. Ladies, you all honor me extraordinarily.

I must send my love to Tresa Hoffman and to the memory of her husband, Russell. A second set of parents for me at a time when I needed them the most. Thank you is far too tepid. And lastly, to the memory of their son, Russ. Always to Russ.

Please turn the page for an exciting sneak peek of
Gregory Harris's next Colin Pendragon Mystery

The Dalwich Desecration

coming soon from Kensington Publishing!

CHAPTER 1

———◆◆◆———

Silence hung over the monastery like a pall. Not only did no one speak to us as we followed Father Nolan Demetris down the barren hallway, the muffled rustling of his black cassock the only sound accompanying us other than the clicking of our own inapt boots, but no one tossed us so much as the slightest of looks. It was as though the three of us could neither be seen nor heard. As if our presence here were as ethereal as the deity the monks dedicated their lives to. And yet there was something oddly guarded about the way the monks scuttled past us, their eyes diverted down and away. Something awkward and rigid and almost pained in their movements. And while I was certain they did not wish us to be here, I also sensed an acceptance that seemed to border almost on relief. For one of their own had been murdered. The man at the very heart of their community. Their abbot.

We turned a corner on yet another stark hallway, and as we made our way down it, I realized the ceiling looming just over my head was contributing to my feeling of unease. Standing at precisely six feet, I could sense there were no more than a handful of inches from the crown of my head to the yellowed lath and plaster crowding down upon me. Neither Colin nor Father Demetris seemed to take the slightest note, however, given that

Colin was four inches shorter than me and Father Demetris one or two below that. When we finally stopped outside one of the countless doors studding this and every hallway we had been escorted through, I could see that I was going to have to duck to get inside.

Father Demetris seized the small ring of bronze keys he had grabbed upon our entry into the complex and slid the one with the notched head smoothly into the keyhole and, giving it a firm twist, handily sprang the lock. He released a muted sigh as he reached for the short, wrought-iron lever, pressing it with noticeable hesitation just before he pushed the door wide with a disquieting *screech*.

"This is the Father Abbot's cell," Father Demetris said from the doorway, staring into the black space a long moment before releasing yet another small sigh and plunging forward. "He lived here for ten years," he added as he struck a match and lit the two oil sconces on the wall and a single oil lamp on a small, square table shoved into the far corner of the tiny room.

"Did you call it a cell?" I blurted without thinking, Colin and I still hovering in the doorway as the space gradually revealed itself in the blooming light of the three flames.

It was indeed an apt description, for it could hardly have been called a room. It stretched back no more than twelve feet at the very most and looked only half again as wide. Other than the little table with its equally diminutive lamp and the homemade-looking wooden chair shoved up beneath it, there was only a single-sized bed—which was really nothing more than a wood-sided cot—a tall, round stand across from it upon which sat a white porcelain bowl, though its matching pitcher was conspicuously absent, and a square cutout bit of plain rug made of some sort of reed or fiber by the bedside. There were no windows, no adornments of any kind, and nothing to suggest any but the most rudimentary levels of comfort. I found it startling, though I suddenly could not fathom what else I should have expected.

Father Demetris smiled at the two of us, his brown eyes crinkling at the corners in such an easy way that I knew my question was one he had heard many times before. "The brothers of Whitmore Abbey live a life of religious asceticism in their devotion to God. They are Benedictine monks, you see, and have accepted the vows of stability, *conversatio morum*, and obedience."

"*Conversatio morum . . .*" Colin said as he slowly entered the minute space. "Latin, of course. Conversion of life?"

"Well done!" Father Demetris's smile widened. "It refers to the acceptance of the monastic life." He spread his hands wide and gestured around himself. "This life."

"Yes . . ." Colin muttered as he gently ran a hand across the table-top. "And I would presume obedience refers to the church . . . ?"

"Of course."

"And stability?" He stepped away from the table and knelt down beside the undersized bed. "How ever is that defined?"

"The commitment to remain in the same monastery for the rest of one's life. Even in death; a monk will be buried on-site." Father Demetris came back to the door, where I had remained, as Colin began to widen his study of the plank flooring in an ever-expanding arc. "Once a novitiate accepts the Benedictine vows he enters this community and, for the greater part, leaves the outside world behind. It is a profound and admirable dedication."

Colin stood up and glanced quickly around himself one last time. "It is certainly bleak."

The priest gave a soft chuckle as he stepped back out into the hallway. "It is not for everyone. And even a man of faith can have his doubts now and then." He sighed. "I suppose that's a part of the human condition."

"A condition, is it?" Colin muttered absently as he snuffed out the three lights before backing out of the tiny room, his gaze remaining intensely focused inside despite the immediate blackness.

"More of a curse, I should think," Father Demetris responded solemnly as he slid the skeleton key back into the lock and re-bolted the door, "when compared to the glory that awaits us." He started off down the hall again, and we quickly fell in line behind him.

I had a hundred questions rattling through my mind and

knew Colin would surely have twice as many more, but the two of us remained silent as we followed the priest through the somber space. Each hallway we traversed was punctuated by only the minimum amount of light from smoke-stained glass sconces interspersed too infrequently along the way. Their thick, oily scent permeated the tight space and stifled the air, putting me in mind of the opium clubs I had spent too much of my youth in. The thought made me cringe, and I wondered why they had never converted the monastery to gas. If nothing else, it was safer than these oil lamps that continuously needed their wicks trimmed and oil pots refilled.

"Here we are then," Father Demetris announced in his quiet, easy manner as we turned into a slightly brighter and wider hall-way with a ceiling that thankfully lifted several feet above my head. "We'll talk here in the Father Abbot's office."

He swung the door open onto the first vaguely acceptable space I had seen since our arrival. The room was a suitable size, big enough to hold a large desk of dark, almost black, wood that was ornately carved in a seemingly bacchanalian fashion with cherubic faces, a tendril of vines, and small bunches of grapes. A huge, overstuffed chair sat behind it, covered in a deep burgundy fabric with a nap that appeared to be velvet. Facing the desk were two plain, straight-backed chairs that I was certain would be as uncomfortable as the Father Abbot's looked inviting, and behind those was a plaster-fronted fireplace painted dark gray that held the faces of eleven men in relief—five on one side, six on the other—that I thought I should recognize but did not.

The best features of the office, however, were the two narrow, leaded-glass cathedral windows that rose up along the opposite wall from where we stood, letting in a veritable ocean of pris-matic light across the room. Given that we were already past midday, most of the sunshine was stretching across the wall of bookshelves rising up from behind the desk and along the door-way wall. Although the windows did not reach the full height of the room, some fifteen feet, they were large enough that I knew they could not have been brought in by way of the short, narrow hallways we had just traversed.

Father Demetris gestured us to the harsh-looking chairs as he settled himself behind the desk in what would have been the seat of the abbot, the man whose murder we had been sent to solve. "It doesn't seem right to be sitting here," Father Demetris said, and, indeed, he did look ill at ease. "Abbot Tufton is only the second man to lead this pious brotherhood since Whitmore Abbey was consecrated almost thirteen years ago. His predecessor served only eight months before he was called home to the Heavenly Father, so it has really been John Tufton who created the fine community you see here today."

"Where did Abbot Tufton serve before coming to Whitmore Abbey?" Colin asked.

"Mostly in Ireland. He spent time in several dioceses under several different bishops. He was highly regarded, even as a young man. He was allowed to spend time in the Papal State studying under His Holiness Pius the Ninth when he was just out of seminary. A remarkable feat for a young man." He gave a wistful smile. "He could have risen much higher in the church, but this was his calling. He was happy here. Bishop Fencourt considered Abbot Tufton his monastic blessing." Father Demetris chuckled as he said the words.

"How many monks live here?" Colin pressed forward.

"Thirty-three, not counting the abbot. It is a small order, but then the town of Dalwich cannot claim more than five thousand residents itself. I don't think the whole of Sussex County is even half a million."

"Still"—Colin gave a slight smile—"that's a fair amount of souls to save for such a small band of men."

Father Demetris shook his head with a patient grin. "Ah, I'm afraid you confuse these monks with missionaries, deacons, and vicars. The brothers of Whitmore Abbey do not conduct services for the public, nor do most of them have much contact with any laypeople beyond these walls. They are monks, Mr. Pendragon. They are here solely to dedicate themselves to prayer, divine contemplation, and devotion to God. They are a rare and august breed of acolyte, you see. Very few receive such a calling or are up to the challenge of accepting it if they do."

"Of course," Colin muttered with a note of irritation, and I knew he was annoyed at having made such a fundamental error. "Have all of the monks been here from the beginning?"

"A good many, but not all. The church built an additional dormitory about three years ago. It can house ten additional monks, but for now there are only three brothers living there. As I said before, this is not a life for everyone."

"Quite so." Colin flashed a tight grin. "And are those three monks the last to join the monastery?"

"Precisely. You see, once a brother moves into a cell, there is no reason for him to change. Life in a monastery is not about the earthly comforts but rather the promise of divinity thereafter."

"Indeed." Colin nodded. "That bit I noticed." He sat forward in his chair. "Now you must permit me to ask you about the murder of Abbot Tufton. If we are to accomplish anything, we shall need to understand exactly what transpired."

Father Demetris exhaled deeply as he shifted in the chair as if it could possibly be causing him pain. "Of course," he said with obvious reluctance. "But you will forgive me should I find myself overcome. I considered the Father Abbot a dear friend and find it difficult to consider how he must have suffered at the end."

"You mustn't give it a second thought," I answered at once. "We are regrettably familiar with the confluence of emotions attendant in situations such as this. You must put yourself at ease."

He nodded with the ghost of a smile. "You are most generous. I have known John Tufton almost forty years. We spent quite a bit of time together in seminary back in Dublin. He will be sorely missed."

"Your memories do him fine honor," I managed to say, even though I found the priest's sorrow keenly distressing. While I understood how he would miss his friend, I had thought he would be held fast by his surety of the afterlife. For if he was not, then what did that suggest for one of tentative faith like me?

"Please . . ." Colin prodded gently, and I suspected he could sense my mood. "When did you and Bishop Fencourt learn of the Father Abbot's murder?"

"We received a telegram the day before yesterday, not an hour after sunrise. Abbot Tufton failed to appear for morning prayers, so one of the brothers went to check on him." He shook his head and gazed out the windows, the pained look on his face in marked contrast to the sunshine filtering through. "They tell me it was a terrible scene."

"Who told you?" Colin pushed a bit more forcefully than I thought appropriate.

Father Demetris glanced at him. "Brother Morrison and Brother Silsbury, mostly. And, of course, poor Brother Hollings, the young monk who found him."

"Of course," Colin repeated perfunctorily. "And what exactly did Brother Hollings find?"

"The Father Abbot was collapsed across the floor of his cell with one arm stretched out as if he was reaching for something while the very life force drained out of him. A horror," he tutted as his eyes drifted back toward the leaded-glass windows.

Colin and I remained quiet, and after several minutes of transfixed rumination, Father Demetris continued. "There was no mistaking what had happened. The walls were splattered with blood. Brother Hollings said he didn't even enter the cell to check on John . . . Abbot Tufton . . . but turned and ran at once to fetch Brothers Morrison and Silsbury."

"Why them?" Colin asked.

"They're both senior members of the community, and Brother Silsbury also attends to the infirmary. While he is not a doctor, he is a man with some knowledge of health and healing."

"And what did they determine when they went back?"

Father Demetris sucked in a rasping breath as he closed his eyes a moment before answering. "Brother Silsbury noticed slash marks across the back of Abbot Tufton's nightshirt that were stained with blood. So he and Brother Morrison rolled John over and . . ." His voice broke, and he closed his eyes again, his lips silently reciting something before he looked at us and began again. "They tell me his face was covered with blood and that the front of his nightshirt was slashed almost to shreds.

There were wounds beneath . . ." He let his voice drift off as he shook his head and turned back toward some distant place out the window. "I understand it took some time before Brother Silsbury realized that the Father Abbot's tongue had been removed. I suppose it must have been the amount of blood across his face. I have not asked." He abruptly flicked his eyes back to Colin, his face a torment of grief. "I will leave that to you, Mr. Pendragon. I haven't the stomach for anything more."

"Nor is there need for you to," Colin answered at once. "Did Brother Silsbury make any determination as to *when* the attack may have occurred?"

He nodded slightly and wiped a quick hand across his brow, making his relief at leaving that topic physically evident. "Given that the Father Abbot was still in his nightshirt with no covering upon his feet, it is likely he had not yet risen when the murderer entered his cell. Since Abbot Tufton was known to arise at four each morning to begin his personal devotions, it has been presumed that someone must have set upon him deep in the heart of the night."

"What time of night do the brothers usually retire?"

"Most of them return to their cells shortly after supper. Some will pause to congregate for a brief time to discuss matters of the monastery or share evening prayers, but I should think every man has gone back to his cell by nine thirty at the latest. They are all up by four thirty, you see, as I am sure you are aware that idleness is the devil's tool."

"But of course," Colin said, flashing a grin. "No one understands that better than Mr. Pruitt and I, as we have both been witness to many of the sins of those idle hands. Do the men ever gather in small groups in their cells?"

Father Demetris chuckled, his brown eyes crinkling with a touch of amusement for the first time since we had sat down in this office. "You have seen the space allotted to the Father Abbot. I suppose it would surprise you to learn that it is larger than that of the average monk. Most of the brothers have nothing more than a mat on the floor for sleeping and a woolen blanket in winter for warmth. There is no room for congregating in cells. You must understand, Mr. Pendragon, that these monks have been called to a life of singular devotion to God. They have forsaken the comforts and social pleasantries of our modern age with the sole aim of drawing themselves closer to the divine."

"Then it would be uncharacteristic for one monk to go to another's cell under any circumstances?"

He nodded, his face drawn with seriousness again. "Only in the case of an emergency. But there was no such occurrence that night."

Colin pursed his lips and I wondered if he was already beginning to weigh some possibility. "We certainly appreciate your speaking with us today and escorting us around."

Father Demetris smiled at Colin. "When your esteemed father sent his telegram to Bishop Fencourt to say that you had agreed to come, I insisted that I should be the one to govern your introduction here. I know your father and the bishop go back many years. And, quite frankly"—he gave a swift sort of shrug— "this is not an easy community in which to insert oneself unless you are among its ranks. Even I cannot claim more than a diffident association with most of the brothers here. But John Tufton was my colleague *and* my friend. As I told you, we went back to seminary. And while I have no quarrel with death, no man should lose his life like John did."

"And so we shall ensure that his murderer is brought to justice," Colin spouted off without hesitation. "That the man responsible for this atrocity is made to pay for his crime."

Father Demetris allowed another sigh to escape as his face softened. "And so I hope you shall. But do remember, Mr. Pendragon, that vengeance belongs to the Lord. The man has already cursed his own soul for the whole of eternity. Whatever justice you bring will be but a nuisance in the scheme of the Divine Father."

Colin's spine stiffened as he struggled to maintain an air of ease. "Yes . . . yes . . . of course," he muttered with a note of dismissal that fortunately was lost on the priest. "Can you tell me if there has been any word back to the bishop about dissension here within the monastery? Disagreements or fractures of any sort that perhaps Abbot Tufton had sought the bishop's advice on?"

"As with any community, there can be the occasional harsh word or impassioned debate," the priest answered. "The monks here are but human. Nevertheless, I know of nothing that was causing the Father Abbot any undue concern. And nothing would have reached Bishop Fencourt that had not first come through me."

"And yet you do not dwell here?"

"Oh no . . ." Father Demetris shook his head patiently. "I live in the rectory in Chichester, where I attend to the bishop and the congregation of the cathedral. It is a magnificent structure that has served as the heart of God's word for nearly eight hundred years. You really must come and pay a visit before you leave Sussex County."

"We shall make every endeavor to do so," Colin said with an air of amusement, and I knew he was tickled at the preposterousness in our having received such an invitation. "How familiar are you with the daily workings of Whitmore Abbey? Do you visit here often?"

"Once or twice a year. But there are no mysteries to life here. As I've said before, these good monks lead a simple and pious existence."

"So I have seen." Colin nodded. "Do any of the townspeople of Dalwich have access to Whitmore Abbey or the other buildings of the monastery?"

Father Demetris frowned slightly as he studied Colin. "Well, I suppose they do. There are no locks on most of the doors. I only had the one placed on the Father Abbot's cell after his murder. It seemed the wisest thing to do until we could learn what had happened."

"A thoughtful choice," Colin agreed. "And you say there are no services for the people of Dalwich at Whitmore Abbey?"

"Quite so. Whitmore is intended only for the monks who live here. Dalwich has its own church, though it is nothing like what we enjoy in Chichester." He could not help but give a proud smile. "The monks here provide for themselves, and there is little need for interaction with anyone from Dalwich. Other than Abbot Tufton, I would say no more than two or three of the monks have ever even been there."

"I see . . . I see . . ." Colin rattled distractedly, his mind clearly leaping ahead. "And what about outside workers? Do you employ anyone from Dalwich to cook or do any sort of cleaning or tending to the grounds?"

"Never." Father Demetris shook his head decisively. "The brothers take care of themselves in all ways and in all things. Each monk is assigned daily tasks, whether they be preparing meals, scrubbing the common areas, or tending the fields along-side the refectory. Only the care of their clothing and cells is the responsibility of each individual. You have already seen the sparseness of their cells, and I can assure you that the extent of their clothing is little different. So their commitment to fussing about themselves is kept to the barest minimum, as it should be."

"Certainly." Colin nodded with the hint of a scowl. "You have been most clear on the subject of their life's simplicity, and I must apologize if I am being obtuse."

Father Demetris laughed. "Not at all. It is hard for most people to understand. I myself do not believe I have the fortitude to live the monastic life."

"You certainly come closer to it than I." Colin smirked, making me cringe until the priest let out another laugh.

"We would be a finite species if we all received the same spiritual calling," Father Demetris responded with a grin.

"Indeed." Colin matched his smile, clearly pleased with the priest's response. "I shall only pester you with one last question then. Have there been any recent changes to the order here at Whitmore Abbey?"

"Nothing at all since the Benedictine Confederation was established by the Holy Father some twelve years ago. It is this steadfastness of the church that is one of its most compelling attributes, you see, for God's way is neither random nor shifting. And so it has been from the moment of creation."

Colin flicked his eyes to me before nodding perfunctorily at the priest. "I do believe I envy you the stoutness of your convictions."

"Faith is a mighty sword," Father Demetris replied. "And available to all. May I ask in what denomination you were raised?"

"I was baptized a Protestant, but having been raised in Bombay, I must confess to having spent more time learning the precepts of Buddhism and Hinduism. Such fascinating and provocative tenets."

Father Demetris blanched slightly before leaning far back in his chair and allowing a cautious smile to alight upon his face. "Then let us pray . . ." he said with great sincerity, "that we can settle your mind and spirit during your time here."

Colin blinked twice, his expression momentarily vacant, and I could see that the priest had caught him well off guard. It amused me, though I feared what sort of retort he might give once he regained his bearings. He surprised me, however, by simply changing the subject. "Will the monks be willing to meet with us individually to answer our questions? No one has taken a vow of silence, have they?"

Father Demetris shook his head with a chuckle. "Benedictines do not take such vows, though you *will* find their words few and carefully chosen. Nevertheless, every monk here will be at your disposal as you require." He leaned forward and leveled a keen look upon Colin. "I would ask that you try to be sensitive to the routines the brothers follow in practicing their daily devotions. They are the foundation of life here, you see, and I am anxious for these men to return to some semblance of normalcy as quickly as possible. You would, of course, be welcome to join in their prayers anytime you wish," he added with an impish grin.

Colin's blue eyes sparked as though he might actually be considering it. "And so I may . . ."

"Splendid!" Father Demetris clapped his hands as he stood up. "Now let us get your things and I will show you to the cells we have set aside for your use while you are here."

"No, no." Colin quickly waved him off. "There is no need to disturb these good monks by having us constantly under foot.

Mr. Pruitt has already procured rooms for us at the inn in Dalwich. What is the name of it again?" he asked as he turned to me.

I stared back at him for a minute, wondering what it was he expected me to say, considering I had done no such thing. "I rather forget . . ." I settled on muttering.

"It has to be the Pig and Pint," Father Demetris filled in with a smile, "as that is the only place with rooms to let in Dalwich. They've good food at their pub, but I should doubt you'll find their hospitality up to the standards you're used to in London. Should you change your mind, there is always room for you here. The cells may be sparse, but they are piously clean and I can promise you beds rather than a mat on the floor," he added with a chuckle.

"We shall keep that in mind," Colin answered a touch too heartily as we went back out to the hall. "Might we be able to meet some of the monks this afternoon? Perhaps some of the more senior brothers?"

The priest fished a watch out of his cassock and flipped it open. "I'm afraid they will be in their afternoon prayers just now. I suppose I could ask one or two to step out if you really need, or perhaps you might return at suppertime? Their meals are simple but quite good. You'll not leave hungry. And it would give you a chance to not only acquaint yourself with the brothers but also to get a feel for how they live."

"An excellent suggestion." Colin offered a tight smile, and it seemed to me that he was somehow unaccountably relieved.

"Very well." Father Demetris ushered us around the corner and down a short hallway that led to a set of double doors. "Do remember that the monks retire early. They have nightly meditations in their cells, but all will be asleep by ten. Four thirty comes very quickly."

"Four thirty. . . ." Colin repeated with a shake of his head. "Now I know I should never fit in here."

Father Demetris laughed as we walked past a small door off a side entry. Though the door was closed, I could hear the low, sonorous cadence of male voices chanting some indecipherable litany from behind it. The sound was mystical, almost unworldly, and yet it also seemed to contain an edge of something darker, something vaguely foreboding. It struck me like the conundrum of religion itself in that while it seeks to embrace, so it also willfully divides, culling those it judges worthy from those it deems reprehensible. People like me and Colin.

"There is one last thing I should like to know straightaway," Colin spoke up as we reached the main entrance, where we had left our trunk and pair of valises.

"Whatever I can answer."

"Has the abbot been buried yet?"

Father Demetris shook his head with a grimace. "He has not. The brothers very much wanted to hold services, but Bishop Fencourt forbade it after your father said you would come. He thought you might want to see . . ." He left the rest of the statement unvoiced.

"Very good," Colin said at once. "Then we shall look at his remains first thing tomorrow morning to avoid any further delay."

The priest gave a tight nod. "I know that will be appreciated. I shall speak with Brother Silsbury and have him arrange a viewing for you."

"Thank you. You have been most kind."

"I could do no less for my fallen friend. God rest his soul." Father Demetris crossed himself. "And I do hope you will understand that I also must return to Chichester tomorrow afternoon. I have a service to prepare by Sunday, and Bishop Fencourt will expect me back."

"Of course. May we count on you to be available to return should we require any further assistance or wish to question you again?"

Father Demetris's eyes conveyed his shock. "Question me?! You make it sound as though I were a suspect." He laughed, but it came out awkward and unsure.

Colin flashed yet another tight grin that I knew would offer little reassurance. "While that is obviously unlikely, given the distance between Chichester and Dalwich, orders of murder *have* been known to be given from a continent away."

The priest's face crumpled. "I can only imagine," he said. "And yet I should hardly think you could suspect any man of God of such a thing as this."

"In fact I suspect everyone at this moment, Father. Even good Pope Leo himself." Colin gave a teasing smile, but as Father Demetris's face continued to register dismay, I knew Colin had made his point.